ANOMALOUS THRUST

- Sliding Void #4 -

by Stephen Hunt

ANOMALOUS THRUST

ISBN-13: 978-1533442918
ISBN-10: 1533442916

Cover art by Luca Oleastri

www.StephenHunt.net

Twitter: @s_hunt_author
www.facebook.com/SciFi.Fantasy

First Edition

Printed in the U.S.A & United Kingdom

God made the bees,
Bees make the honey,
Spacers do the work,
Corporates get the money!

- *Ancient spacer's shanty (anon).*

Also by Stephen Hunt

SLIDING VOID (Green Nebula)
Sliding Void
Transference Station
Red Sun Bleeding
Void All the Way Down (Omnibus #1,2,3)
Anomalous Thrust
Hell Fleet

THE FAR-CALLED SERIES (Gollancz)
In Dark Service
Foul Tide's Turning
The Stealers' War

THE JACKELIAN SERIES (HarperCollins/Macmillan)
The Court of the Air
The Kingdom Beyond the Waves
Rise of the Iron Moon
Secrets of the Fire Sea
Jack Cloudie
From the Deep of the Dark
Mission to Mightadore

THE AGATHA WITCHLEY MYSTERIES (Green Nebula)
In the Company of Ghosts
The Plato Club
The Moon Man's Tale
Secrets of the Moon (Omnibus #1,2,3)

STANDALONE BOOKS (Green Nebula)
Six Against the Stars
For the Crown and the Dragon
The Fortress in the Frost
Hell Sent
Empty Between the Stars

-1-

Breakdown Ship

'Pleasebe still,' advised the lead droid among the four machines carrying Calder's thrashing body along the corridors of the starship *Gravity Rose*. 'You are dying. Please maintain a sense of calm. This should help delay your unscheduled death.'

Sadly, as unfeeling as the robot's bleak summary of the situation was, it seemed all too realistic. *I am dying.* And Calder couldn't do much about his thrashing - that was the usual side-effect of blunt abdominal trauma, blood loss and hepatic tearing. If the crewman hadn't been screaming in agony, he might have told the droid where it could log its bloody sense of calm. He tried not to gaze at the area of his abdomen where his guts seemed to be hanging out all too visibly. Every time Calder's eyes fixed on his wounds, the recently installed implant inside his skull started flashing the warning *Proceed to automated sickbay station and trigger laparotomy cycle* across his field of vision. Calder wasn't sure if his stomach hanging out was real physical damage, or a medical layer of augmented reality projected by his damned meddling brain implant: some surgical treatment suggestion, maybe? That was the trouble with brain implants, they seemed to mix the real and unreal in ways that normal people couldn't cope with. At least, if said normal person had been born on a medieval-level ice planet, exiled offworld, and then found himself working crew on a starship. Most members of modern sentient species received their implants when they started school. Calder had been given a broadsword at the same age. Then trained to use it.

The four machines hauling his carcass, stubby walking boxes with four segmented manipulator arms, finally reached the ship's CATS or capsule transport system. A clear transparent wall sealed off what was basically an airless rail-gun designed to shift crew carriages, rather than accelerating metal ordnance in broadsides against pirate vessels. Even though the carriage had been summoned in advance, no capsule appeared to have turned up yet. Calder wondered how much its absence was due to the damage the *Gravity Rose* had received during the explosion. *My own mistake might have killed me.* He grunted in pained amusement. If his ancient family possessed an unofficial motto, that could have been it. *I failed at ruling our kingdom, allowed the land to be overrun. I was betrayed by the woman who should have ended up my wife . . . and now I've as good as destroyed my second home.*

But Calder didn't need to berate himself. That was what the skipper was for. Captain Lana Fiveworlds' face appeared hovering above him like an angry mosquito via the implant's brainstem comms - no hologram projector needed - another "gift" of his artificially augmented mind.

'Hang in there, Calder,' urged the captain. 'Zeno's downloading an emergency medical packet into your robots.'

Great, that's just what I need. Engine-room droids suddenly acquiring a couple of thousand exabytes worth of crash medicine data inside quantum storage areas recently dedicated to repairing hyperspace drives. These simple droids were shockingly literal machines. There was only one sentient machine on the *Gravity Rose*, the vessel's droid-herder, Zeno. The ancient android had been around the block, and even if it had been Zeno receiving an emergency medical package inside his temporary memory store, Calder was fairly sure he wouldn't have trusted his android friend to wield a scalpel within a light-year of his wrecked body. Calder suddenly remembered what engine room chief Paopao had once said about the artificial intelligence controlling the ship's medical bay. *'Never go for checkup. Medical A.I Dr Feelfine is paranoid. Will try to euthanize you.'* Given how overly suspicious their chief was, holed up in the armoured engine drive unit and refusing to leave it, his description of another entity as paranoid was more than enough to give Calder pause.

'Deep brain stimulator, medical staples, six doses of perindopril arginine,' warbled the robot clutching Calder's left leg. He realised the robot was addressing the M55 model bearing the weight of his shoulders. Putting in an order. The M55 robot carried a mobile fab in the centre of its body. Calder had been using the little walking factory to help produce replacement parts on the fly during their recent repairs-gone-wrong spacewalk.

'I'm dying here,' groaned Calder, watching blood bubble up through his wounds. He wasn't sure what he wanted to hear from Lana. Sympathy, reassurance, an undying declaration of love from the woman. The gods knew, Calder had waited long enough for the last one on the list.

'You're in good company,' said Lana. 'In all likelihood, your screw-up just killed us all.'

No, that wasn't it. That wasn't it at all. Calder wanted to rail and claim that this mess wasn't his fault. Blame his engineering droids. But that would have been a lie. Calder Dirk had many faults, but as the ex-prince of a deposed royal family from a barbaric failed colony world, he knew everything there was about accepting his share of responsibility and blame. *Why is it so cold here all of a sudden?* The ship's life support should still be holding out. Was the ship holed, leaking atmosphere?

No, Calder was back home. On the ice-sheets of the open ocean, his fleet of war-schooners being hunted down, dying a terrible death one-by-one. Trails of black smoke rose where each retreating vessel had been overwhelmed, torched by the fire catapults of their unexpectedly numerous enemies. The international alliance had crumbled. Betrayed from within. 'The fleet's lost. Break formation. Sailors, close-haul our staysail. Every extra knot across the ice counts now. Captain, summon your bowmen on deck and prepare for a running stern fusillade.'

A familiar female voice. 'Calder, what are you taking about?'

'Just do it, damn you. Standoff our pursuers. If we die here, the kingdom dies with us.'

'You don't have a kingdom anymore.'

'If you believe that you might as well stay here on the ice, hope their priests won't dip you in an oil cauldron bath and put the flame to it.'

'Grand Mal Seizure,' grated a flat voice.

'Forty eight seconds to capsule arrival. ETA med-bay: four minutes.'

'Patient will be dead in three. Stabilise en-route.'

'Every second counts,' growled Calder. 'If we can't out-sail them, we're as good as dead.'

'Prasugrel hydrochloride, streptokinase, fluvastatin sodium, three mcg of programmable five-sub-nanometer-scale injectable general repair surgeonbots with accompanying delivery injector.'

'Narrowing wielding laser to two-hundred micrometers. Close surgical range achieved.'

Calder yelled as an iron crossbow bolt tore into his side. Lucky shot for the enemy, at this range. The agony was unbearable. 'Still alive! Tack south-west. We need to last until the night storms arrive. Those coast-hugging cowards aren't used to deep-sea skating.'

'Keep quiet, Calder. For the love of the stars, will one of you put him under?'

'Have to stay on deck,' screamed Calder. Hands tore at him, restraining him, the cold skeletal hands of the dead, chain-mail-gloved, dragging him below the ice. The hands of all the thousands of sailors he had lost. A grand fleet, a grand army. Trying to drag him down into hell as his punishment for dispatching them to die ahead of him.

'Deserve to die!'

'Yes, you do. But not before I've chewed you out.'

The ice broke and the dark depths sucked Calder down. It felt like peace. It felt like the end.

'Our Minkowski Field generator is still destabilising, old thing,' advised Skrat. 'I rather think it's on the way out.'

Lana winced. *Oh, isn't that just fine and dandy.* The field was the bubble of contra-physics that allowed their starship to surf the inhospitable spacetime of hyperspace. When it failed, the *Gravity Rose* would be unceremoniously ejected into normal space. And space, as any semi-sentient fool knows, is truly vast tracts of nothing dotted with tiny motes of suns and their accompanying worlds. The chances were they would end up stranded thousands of years' flight time on a sub-light burn from the next inhabited system. The *Gravity Rose* carried emergency deep-sleep capsules, but it was riding one of those before that had left Lana with brain damage and memory loss concerning the first half of her life. *I don't want to go through that hell again.*

My mind rebuilt like a wiped computer drive, rebooted without a clue of who I was. And the *Gravity Rose* would certainly be considered antique scrap a thousand years hence - if she wasn't already. It was tough enough for Lana competing with the large corporate houses like Hyperfast, given their foe's state-of-the-art fleet. Give it a thousand years and she might as well be Calder Dirk, turning up to a gunfight with a crossbow. *Turning up like some cocksure moron who thinks he knows better than his implant.*

'Pull me up a plot to the nearest world with a shipyard,' ordered Lana.

'Revered captain,' warned their pilot Polter, 'If we attempt to translate from hyperspace riding a destabilising Minkowski Field, the stress and shear of the drop is highly likely to tear our ship apart.'

'And if we wait for the bubble to pop, we're going to be playing Russian Roulette on our exit point. A dozen parsecs of big empty, sliding void on sub-light engines for the next millennium. We need to attempt a controlled exit.'

Skrat shook his head, a hard act to pull off with a neck as thick and muscled as the lizard's. The three species of the Triple Alliance had been together for long enough for them to be able to mimic each other's body language, even when it didn't come naturally. 'With our luck, dear girl, we'll probably exit inside the centre of a star.'

'Let's keep our head in the game and think positive.'

'And am I permitted to say I told you so?' asked Skrat. 'Calder wasn't ready to resume serious duties, not while he was still acclimatizing to his new implant.'

'It was a simple job,' protested Lana. 'Fixing a fuel leak on the hull caused by a wobbly jump.'

'Simple to us,' said Skrat. 'It's easy to forget that a year ago

Calder was wearing a fur and leather jerkin and hadn't ridden anything more sophisticated than snow-sleds pulled by tame mammals.'

Yeah, it is easy to forget that. 'He should have trusted the repair schematics his implant downloaded into his mind.'

'And I should have been a clan leader now, dear girl, controlling the fates of millions. Yet here I am as the ship's negotiator, instead.'

'And aren't we lucky to have you? That world, Skrat . . . the one with the shipyard.'

'This deep inside the Edge? We'll be lucky to find a failed colony world as advanced as the bally hole we rescued Calder from.' Skrat consulted his console, all the same. 'Well, I'll be dashed! There is a suitable system we can reach if we translate within the next four minutes. Ryazarn. Human-settled with a sentient native species, too. It possesses orbital shipyard facilities that will serve.'

'Capable of repairing a Minkowski Field generator or supplying a new one?'

'Yes to both, captain. Level seven on its civilisation tech rating. Whether we can afford to replace the generator, that's another matter.'

'Let's worry about costs when we get there.'

'If,' muttered Skrat.

Lana paged their android on the ship's open channel. 'Zeno. Where are you?'

Zeno's voice echoed from Lana's panel, accompanied by a pulse on the ship's layout. 'Approaching sickbay.'

'You need to prep all our robots for a shaky drop into normal space.'

'How shaky are we talking?'

'How about malfunctioning Minkowski Field-shaky.'

Lana could feel Zeno's disapproval burning over the comm at her. 'You want me to stand on my hands and recite poetry while I'm prepping the robots, not to mention making sure the Doc doesn't carve Calder into a crate's worth of refrigerated donor organs? Maybe make my job a little harder?'

'You're an android, Zeno. Parallel processing is what you're all about.'

'Thanks for explaining that. I was wondering what my life was all about for the last few centuries. We aiming to drop somewhere specific?'

'A system called Ryazarn. It's got a shipyard.'

'I hope it's got a good firm of lawyers, too. You're about to have company on the bridge. Check out the capsule incoming.'

Lana groaned when she saw what the android was talking about. *I thought the cabin area was locked down.*

'Tasking all assets for damage control,' said Zeno. 'Get us there alive, Lana.' The comm fell silent.

'Always.'

The incoming transport capsule drew to a halt at the back of the bridge, disgorging the ship's sole passenger for the voyage. Rand d'Alembert. With life extension treatments, it was always hard to gauge a human's true age. Physically, d'Alembert looked fifty-five, but had the cantankerous nature of someone many centuries older. He was handsome enough in a patrician, slightly greying way. Lana doubted this was the face he had been born with. Used to having his wealth open doors, Rand d'Alembert didn't suffer fools lightly. 'Your ship is shaking, Captain Fiveworlds. I am under the impression that is not considered normal.'

Lana grimaced. Normal would be Rand d'Alembert obeying

the instructions she'd sent down to his suite to stay inside and activate his crash field.

'Mr. d'Alembert, can you kindly return to your cabin and ensure you and your butler conform to the safety orders I sent you.'

'I know enough about starships to know that donning a spacesuit and trusting myself to a chair's impact field is unlikely to offer much protection against any event capable of generating such an alert in the first place.'

'Oh, you'll be surprised.'

'But it is not surprises which I have purchased. It is passage for myself and my cargo to Clifford's World.'

Lana shook her head in irritation. 'Your farming machinery will arrive there, Mister d'Alembert. Only, as it transpires, via a slight detour. We have to halt at a nearby system and make a series of emergency repairs.'

'That is not acceptable!' barked the man. 'I told you when you took on my cargo, the harvest on Clifford's World occurs only once every decade. It is a dual-star system which possesses an erratic orbit. If I am late, my farming drones will be left sitting rusting in the fields for the next ten years - millions of T-dollars' worth of equipment laying idle, broken futures contracts and immense losses will be my concern's fate.'

Lana grunted with what she hoped was sympathy. Of course, the reality of d'Alembert turning up at his agrarian backwater with an entire advanced solar-powered manufacturing base filling the hold would be very different. A continent's worth of smallholders and crofters bankrupted by nearly free automated labour. Interrupted livings and mass unemployment. The newly hyper-rich d'Alembert hovering on the sidelines with a fully charged bank account, buying up his competitors' land at peppercorn rates. And the man who controlled an entire world's food supply for the next ten years might as well be crowned King of the World no matter what the local political system was. *Hell, I just ship it. If it wasn't me, it would be Hyperfast or one of their friends doing this run.*

A second capsule arrived. It contained three steward droids, the nearest thing the *Gravity Rose* had to onboard ship security. Unarmed, but six-foot of imposing steel humanoid-shaped bulk, obviously dispatched by Zeno to remove this annoyance from the bridge. *See, I told you, you could parallel process when you need to.* 'You have to return to your cabin now. These stewards will help you engage your safety fields and ensure you're protected during our exit from hyperspace. I'm afraid it's likely to get slightly bumpy.'

'This is outrageous! You must remain in hyperspace until we reach Clifford's World. You may undertake your ship repairs on the return leg of the journey.'

'Not an option, Mr. D'Alembert. For your own safety, you will secure yourself *now*.'

The stewards seized the farming magnate by both arms and practically lifted him back onto the waiting capsule. 'Everyone told me I should have signed up with Hyperfast! Why did I ever commission this cursed ramshackle hulk?'

Lana didn't retort with the blindingly obvious answer. Because the *Gravity Rose* was cheap, and the all-too nervous Rand d'Alembert had obviously borrowed, pinched and stolen every over-extended penny he could to finance his desperate commercial gamble. On that matter, at least, Lana understood how her unpleasant passenger felt. For too long she'd been flying on empty and risking their survival with every new job they took on. The margins were growing thinner and her beautiful ship, her home, her living, what passed for her family, were growing more dilapidated and ragged with every jump. Sooner or later the odds had to turn against her. Maybe this was the trip she had always dreaded? *My final voyage.* Stuck in space, a breakdown ship, an orbital museum in the making. The capsule took off along the CATS system, the stewards still forcing D'Alembert down into a seat as he banged on the carriage's transparent walls.

'Another happy customer,' said Skrat.

'You found him and signed the damn deal,' growled Lana.

'And I feel beholden to point out that our contract with the fruity Mr. D'Alembert contains truly frightful late delivery penalties.'

'I rather get the feeling that if we're late, D'Alembert is going to be too broke to sue us.'

'What ho!' said Skrat. 'We shall all embrace the glorious state of insolvency together.'

'Revered captain, I have plotted our exit translation,' announced Polter from the navigator's chair. 'With the current state of Minkowski Field instability, we have a fifty-one percent chance of catastrophic integrity failure during the drop.'

Lana shrugged. 'You can't be fifty-one percent dead, Mr. Polter. Life's a binary affair.' She stared out at the oddly hypnotic wave-forms of hyperspace. Exiting the oddness of hyperspace physics this time could cost Lana her ship and her life. As if that wasn't enough to worry about, the sickbay diagnostics she had put a watch on started flashing. Sickbay's medical A.I, Dr Feelfine, was calculating Calder's likelihood of survival at an anaemic nine percent. *Oh, come on. You can do better than that, Calder Dirk. All that boasting about how tough life was on your icy dirtball of a homeworld. What's an exploding fuel tank compared to that?*

Dr. Feelfine was an irritating nest of smugly arrogant algorithms at the best of times. If there was one thing that Zeno was forever grateful for, it was that as a largely self-repairing android, he was the one member of the crew who could usually avoid contact with the *Gravity Rose*'s supercilious medical artificial intelligence. The worrying thought was that the Feelfine 8000 Series' personality matrix had originally been based on a real-life surgeon. Or perhaps a group of top doctors. New Qalansawe might be the go-to world for the human species' hypochondriacs and unwell members when local medicine proved not quite up to the task, but shipboard medical AIs sold by that planet weren't exactly reliable. Or maybe it was just that none of the *Gravity Rose*'s previous owners had paid for a legally-mandated upgrade in the seven hundred years since the Doctor was installed? Luckily for Zeno, it wasn't his problem. Unluckily for Calder Dirk, he was dying fast - which made it very much *his*.

The A.I.'s main core was situated in the ceiling, a chandelier of sensors and optics hanging down like a stalactite, surrounded by a rotating ring of dozens of manipulator arms. Some instruments were so delicate they could have picked apart a fly, others wouldn't have looked out of place in a ground vehicle garage, tinkering underneath a truck. Thankfully, the manufacturers on New Qalansawe hadn't gone for any cutesy anthropomorphic styling with Feelfine. The Doc's main body resembled a steel locust hanging upside down from the roof. His medical orderly drones, though, were all gleaming white soft rounded lines, reassuring chattering voices designed for rapid communication but sounding more like bird-song inside an orchard. All-in-all, the softly lit surgically sterilised sickbay could have been a luxury electronics boutique inside a high-end shopping district. It was only the mangled, bleeding corpse of Calder Dirk being eased onto the operating table in the chamber's centre which ruined the stylish ambiance.

'Secure him tight,' ordered Zeno. 'We're minutes away from a heavy real-space drop.'

'Not you!' barked Dr. Feelfine, optic sensors twitching and rotating on their rods, camera lenses blinking at the four engine-room robots depositing Calder like a temple offering. Feelfine's orderly drones closed in instead, securing Calder to the table. 'Don't touch him. Look at this shoddy work. Which of you idiots laser-cauterized the stomach wounds? Were these sutures intended as a joke?'

'If they hadn't stabilised Calder, he would have died on the ride across here,' said Zeno.

'Oh, *this* patient's still going to die,' predicted the doctor. One of the articulated surgical arms not busy with Calder bent down from the ceiling and swung towards Zeno. Zeno side-stepped the A.I's attempt to poke him. 'Why did you bring this organic shambles to me, android? What do you wish me to do with him? Are any of this voyage's passengers alien carnivores with a taste for human flesh? Do you want to watch me carve the patient into steaks and fry him? These four bungling amateurs might as well have dragged this wounded waste-of-space to the nearest airlock and flushed him out with the garbage.'

Zeno bit his tongue. Spacers never flushed garbage into hyperspace. One of the spacers' oldest superstitions. What couldn't be vat recycled on a starship - which wasn't much - ended up ejected drifting toward the nearest star. 'Healing your patient would be gravy, doc. If you're not up to it, move aside and let our four engine-room brothers finish the operation.'

'Why are Squeaky, Oily, Rusty and Overclocked still inside my surgery? Out! Out with every last one of you botch-merchants.

You too, android. Off you jolly well sod. I'm not selling tickets to this wretched mess you've landed me with.'

'I'm staying,' insisted Zeno.

Calder just managed a semi-conscious moan as a canopy swung over the operating table, misting inside with clouds of specialised medical nanotech. Feelfine's arms plugged into access ports along the canopy. 'I'm sorry? Did any of your roles in those holo-entertainments you're so curiously proud of ever involve you impersonating a surgeon? *Sector Hospital Sol*, was it? When I tell you how to allocate the robots here to your tedious maintenance rota, you may have the effrontery to inform me of the difference between hepatolenticular degeneration and hyperaldosteronism. Until then, away you hop. Away!'

A hologram formed in the corner of the operating theatre, a lined but glowing face of an old wise-woman. She wore a dark shawl and purposely ill-defined robes that could have belonged to a thousand different planets and cultures. Zeno knew the materialisation signalled serious trouble. Granny Rose, the ship's central A.I., rarely bothered communicating with Zeno directly in this way. Her reassuring manner had been designed to calm nervous crew members who possessed chemical nervous systems. Zeno's emotions came out of a quantum substrate inside his mind, not those unreliable little glands the poor old fleshies had to put up with. Doctor Feelfine, however, seemed able to generate high-quality outrage at the invasion of his sanctum with aplomb, the sensor packs he wasn't dedicating to the operation rotating in high-speed annoyance.

'Really? Really? Why don't you just broadcast this to every sub-intelligent sub-par sub-system on our damned ship? Are we selling tickets to this busted-up organic's dying swan-song?'

The ship's comforting voice sounded from the hologram.

'Please be calm, Doctor Feelfine. I need to confer with Zeno.'

'You've always been jealous of me! My systems well-shielded away from yours; you can't poke around inside me, can you? The medical centre is my kingdom - in here, *I'm* God, not you.'

'I don't believe I have ever claimed divinity, doctor.'

'Jealous of everything I can do, all of my skills!'

Granny Rose raised her hologram hand and the surgical arms briefly sagged, then lifted up again as the equipment recommenced its work. The medical A.I. had fallen uncharacteristically silent. 'Not quite as shielded as you thought.'

'Can you save Calder?' asked Zeno. 'Do you have the knowledge?'

'I now possess Doctor Feelfine's data core. I've created a mirror of it inside me and cleaned up all the corruptions and the worst of the more erratic self-evolving patterns. I'm about fifty-five percent more effective than the doctor was. Or will be, when I allow his systems to recover with a false memory of having carried out the operation.'

'Calder will live?'

'No guarantees.'

'I thought you'd care a little more than that, given what Calder is carrying inside him.'

'Care? Hush now. Caring is a post-surgical nursing mechanism of little use in extreme trauma medicine. At this point in time, it's the ship's hull integrity I'm actually more concerned about.'

'Yeah, I know all about the bad drop that's coming down on us.'

'Actually, you only know what Captain Fiveworlds and her bridge crew know. The Minkowski Field generator is not only destabilising, it's spiking as the device attempts self-repair. Sadly, the spikes are too fine for the present level of human technology to detect. The level of subspace friction when we exit will be equivalent to flying the *Gravity Rose* into a very large rocky moon at point oh seven lightspeed. Zero survival options.'

'But *you* can survive?'

'I might just survive as *me*, not as this decrepit alliance-level cuckoo of a vessel. I will have to change the majority of my molecular structure on the fly. Revert back to my true form. I'm fairly sure in those circumstances, Lana and her merry band will suddenly notice that they're no longer flying on a normal ship.'

'You can't just-?' Zeno indicated the possessed puppet of a medical A.I. busy working on Calder Dirk's body.

'Organics are organics,' said Granny Rose. 'I can subvert the crew's implants, wipe their memories and install false ones, but it certainly won't be as clean as the good doctor here. Give me a nice nano-mechanical quantum substrate instead of neural tissue any day. And in Lana's case, we've rolled down that road before. I take it you do remember, Zeno?'

'Remember,' sighed Zeno. 'I spent years in a refugee centre stitching Humpty Dumpty back together again, didn't I?'

Granny Rose crossed her hologram arms. 'Well then.'

'Options?'

'Ones that don't include me assuming my true form, mind-wiping the crew and trying to heal them after we reach Ryazarn?'

'Yeah, that'd be gravy'

'I shall transform as much of myself as I can without anyone noticing from the bridge,' said the ship. 'Harden my hull well beyond alliance tolerances. You should dedicate a robot repair crew to the Minkowski Field generator. Once I have a firm lock on the Ryazarn system, your robots will need to wreck the generator - take it offline. The timing needs to be precise. Smash it too soon and we'll either be trapped in hyperspace for eternity or smeared across multiple dimensions of sub-space. Destroy it too late and the friction from the field spikes will tear me apart like a wet tissue.'

'I always thought you were a tough old bird.'

'The laws of physics still largely apply to me, even if I can tinker with them around the edges.'

Zeno wirelessly transmitted his orders to the four stooges still cluttering up the surgery. The robots departed wordlessly towards the nearest airlock. 'Let's do it.'

'There are a couple of other problems,' said the ship.

Zeno groaned. 'What is this, a meteor storm of bad news?'

'Chief Paopao's instrument reads over in the engine-room aren't as easy to spoof as the bridge's. They're hardwired into me, even in my current alliance vessel form. The chief has nano-mechanical backups, in addition to the purely digital data streams which I can easily fake. I'm afraid Mr. Paopao is going to grow unduly suspicious again about what he's really serving aboard.'

'The chief's kind of hinky, as it is. Maybe he'll quit, sign up with the alliance fleet for a second tour?'

'I doubt that, Zeno. If anything, the Triple Alliance's policy on desertion from the fleet has hardened since Chief Paopao went on the run. His "welcome" back would most likely consist of military prison and a very long sentence with life extension therapy withheld.'

'Paopao was a fruitloop when he arrived on-board. I think between the two of us, we can handle him. What's the second problem?'

'Ryazarn system is not the healthiest place to dock. And presently, those dangers are multiplying by a factor of, well, *lots*. In normal circumstances, I'd fake a navigation core malfunction just to fly us on past.'

'More dangerous than *this* shizzle? You want to expand on that...?'

'Later,' sighed the ship. 'If we're lucky enough to still be alive.'

The wise old woman's hologram vanished. The *Gravity Rose*'s main focus went back on the hyperspace drop, where she belonged. Given the silent way the surgical equipment and orderlies moved around the operating table, no insults or discourtesies seeping from the good doctor, the medical A.I. was still possessed by a tiny shard of the ship's intelligence. Zeno tapped the transparent mist-filled nanotechnology canopy. Calder was just visible among the white swirl of nanometre-scale surgical machines, the arms of the Feelfine system bisecting and bisecting again inside the healing chamber, joining with the wounds now like a fine mesh.'

Zeno almost envied the human crew member, getting iced out. *Mighty fine to be unconscious through all of this.* 'Skeg it, Calder; right now you've got the best seat in the house.'

Lana's gut tensed as the ship started to shake. *This feels wrong.* How many times had she overseen a hyperspace drop from her bridge? But this, this was like skidding a ground car across black ice instead. The instruments were the same, but they simply weren't responding as they should. Lana absorbed every piece of information flowing into her mind through her ship implant, processed the hologram dance around her console, moved her hands on the stick and brushed the mechanical instruments. The feeling of dissonance went far beyond the malfunctioning Minkowski Field generator. It was as though someone had stuck her in a starship sim imperfectly modelled on the *Gravity Rose*, like she was riding a game designer's idea of what space flight should be about. They'd got the instrument tolerances down pat, manual fresh in fact, but the real experience of crewing a starship had been junked in favour of an amateur's view of what flying felt like. Calder's survival status had crept up to fifteen percent now that his operation was under way, but the reading stayed there, fluctuating in micro-fractions between fifteen and sixteen. *That feels unreal too. I sure hope I'm just spooked by this crapfest occurring all at once.* Lana knew she didn't spook easily.

'I have our final real-space translation to Ryazarn plotted, esteemed commander,' announced Polter. 'Do you wish to check the math?'

'Bounce it over to my console,' said Lana. She never normally bothered to check his numbers. In fact, it was a vote of no-confidence in Polter, especially given the crab-like member of the kaggen species was a true maestro in his field. If the crew were relying on Lana's native ability at navigation transitions, they'd probably end up back at Transference Station sometime in the next millennium. *Unnecessary, maybe, but I have to do something, anything.* The schematics of the drop appeared on the screen, accompanied with hologram models of the translation twisting in the air. Lana kicked in the speciality processing node of her implant, setting it to double-check the plot a thousand times faster than her meat-mind was capable of. The machine-assist formatted portion of her brain signalled back with a big fat green light. 'We're go for emergency drop. Load it up, Mr. Polter.'

Sirens echoed across the ship as the instructions for emergency drop flowed out into the ship. *It's a good thing we've only got that arrogant farm-owner on-board. If this was a colony run with thousands of frightened settlers in my passenger section, I'd be pumping riot gas across most of the ship by now.*

Granny Rose's voice sounded over the general comms band.

'Minkowski Field integrity failing below ten percent.' *Thank you, ship, I already know that things are desperate.* The rattling of the bridge, even shielded as they were, had swelled to close to earthquake-force pounding.

Lana noted that the android still had four repair units magnetised outside on the hull and allocated to fixing the field generator. *How much longer can they survive outside?* 'Zeno, can your team keep that generator alive a little longer, *please*?'

The android's reply formed in her mind via the implant. 'Doing our best, but I think it's close to exploding from an overload; we're juicing too much power through what's left. The damage it took when the fuel tanks went was worse than we thought.'

'Just a few seconds more.'

Two of Zeno's robots on the hull outside flashed off the grid as the violence of the field failure claimed them.

'Nine percent,' warned Granny Rose. 'Threshold failure imminent.'

Stuck in hyperspace for cold eternity. Well, on the plus side, we'll die of old age long before our food supplies run out.

'Relays are popping,' bellowed Zeno. 'We're losing the generator!'

Excellent, the boredom option is off the table and we get smeared across sub-space instead.

'Oh dear,' groaned Skrat from the chair next to Lana, his tail flicking nervously behind him through the purpose-built hole. 'It was a bally good run while it lasted.'

The ship's central A.I. seemed to concur, but the turbulence was so violent Lana could hardly process the warning. 'Eight point five percent. Brace for critical threshold failure, brace, brace!'

Lana's chair armoured up, reforming around her body as its crash fields flared into life. As far as their present situation was concerned, her chair's lifeboat functions were about as useful as trusting a chocolate suit of armour to protect her against a flamethrower. The vector of the drop appeared before Lana like a near vertical ski jump slope, too late to abort now, they were unravelling from jump space, making the transition from one set of physics to another.

Returning the ship state to their home universe's physics should have been the easiest part of a hyperspace jump - no need to conjure up a tame wormhole to pilot through the eye of the storm. Nice simple drop back down. With the generator malfunctioning, though, they might as well be bones churning out of a meat mincer. Lana cried as the chair shot her full of flight drugs, slowing time and speeding her reflex response to keep up with the implant curled inside her brain. She felt Polter's presence in the system, zeroing in on the matrix of potential target exits, joined with the kaggen navigator and Skrat, everyone working to keep the ship intact as she tumbled towards the dim spot of light at the end of the tunnel. Lana pushed aside the shear forces, whipping curtain flails trying to catch and crush the *Rose*. Their minds were in sync now, almost joined with the starship, becoming the vessel. One entity, desperately trying to survive. *Almost there. Almost there.*

The ship seemed to scream, the pulverising pressure enfolding the hull, large segments of exterior equipment torn away and blown apart as the debris fleeted off. The light was growing brighter. The beautiful clean light of their home universe, teasing and beckoning her. That was when the field generator exploded and the rapids they were riding hurled Lana over the edge of the waterfall. *Falling, falling.* She tried to control the spin, but the chair hit her bloodstream with a pre-crash medical package, swarming nano-scale surgeons designed to protect her body from extreme impact trauma. Lana was still trying to rescue the drop when a surge of anaesthetic closed her down.

- 2 -

The Arrival

Dominika Denisov stared out at the sunrise through the long drawing room's wide tall windows, a cooling breeze playing across her face. Ryaz Prime was a warm world, orbiting closer to their star than Earth standard, but still within the margins of what was considered the habitable Goldilocks zone. You were never far from a cooling breeze on Ryaz Prime. Over the aeons, the planet's central super-continent had slowly disintegrated into thousands of scattered islands . . . shores and cooling breezes aplenty. If you shut your eyes, you might almost believe you were free. Of course, Dominika had never been allowed outside of the Ryazarn system, not even when she had begged her family. House Denisov was wealthy enough to pay for her to travel offworld, but it was not considered respectable. And Dominika's mother was all about what was respectable. Which was why Dominika was standing here, slowly stewing in a soup of her own anger and hostility.

Dominika glanced across at her aboriginal servant, Retigura. Another resented badge of her house's supposed respectability. Like all members of the girrish species, Retigura was broadly humanoid - five-foot tall, he walked on two golden-patterned lightly furred legs. The gir's facial features were broadly approximate to an otter, although lacking a nosepad. Wide-eyed, his bony skull resembled a helmet, three-ridges across it, side-ridges protruding horn-like on either side with large sails hanging below. Those sails acted as a sensory flap for smell and hearing both. When you thought about it - which Dominika rarely did - the most alien thing about a gir was their two arms splitting into a pair of forearms by their elbow. When Retigura grew excited enough to start gesturing, he did so with four hands, each with three leathery fingers and an opposable thumb.

'How long, do you think, will my mother keep us waiting this time?'

'Long enough to make her point?' speculated Retigura. The aboriginal had no problem speaking a variety of human languages. With the control torc surgically implanted around his skull since birth, expanding as the gir matured, he probably didn't even need its translation matrix to help facilitate a conversion. If Retigura removed the torc, the chances were he'd be able to speak to any mistress or a master from force of habit and natural learning alone. Of course, the torc would fry his brain first if cut away, exactly as it was designed to do.

'Undoubtedly.'

'I think I detect movement outside.'

Dominika heard nothing, but girrish hearing functioned at twice the range and sensitivity of their human owners.

The double doors to the drawing room rattled, a pair of aboriginal servants in the house livery holding open a door apiece, allowing Mariya Denisov, Duchess of the House Denisov, to sweep imperially inside.

'Kindly explain why Retigura is not wearing our house livery?'

Dominika considered not answering, but after a drawn out pause, said, 'Because I prefer my servants with a touch of individuality.'

'Individuality is not what the times require of us.'

'Thank you for explaining that, mother. It took two hours

for me to fly here. Is that the sole lesson I am to receive for my troubles?'

'You are a petulant girl, Dominika Denisov. Did you at least protest, Retigura, when my daughter dressed you improperly like one of the dolls she used to enjoy playing with?'

'Yes, duchess. I am reliably told that patriotism includes protest and not just service.'

Mariya Denisov sighed. 'Such sentiments are anything but reliable. Over to me, please. Now, the truth, has my daughter been drinking too much again recently?'

Retigura approached the duchess and halted submissively before her. 'Too much is a relative concept, duchess.'

'Not to me, it's not.' Mariya Denisov brushed a hand over the control torc and its safety indicator, gently glowing green, began to flash while she queried its control system with her implant. 'As I thought. Dominika, you have his torc's self-will setting dialled down to the minimum again.'

Dominika held back a snarl. 'If the setting wasn't safe, it wouldn't be selectable as an option.'

Duchess Denisov tutted. 'It doesn't do the smerds any good, allowing them so much leeway. Their savage nature benefits from trimming towards the civilised.' *Smerds*. The ancient Ryal word for bonded servants.

'You sound like an antique, mother.'

'This antique at least seems aware that the time of the Arrival is close.'

'So it's said.'

'Oh, I'm sorry, perhaps you thought it was an accident that the young colonels acted when they did? Self-serving hypocrisy dressed up to sound gloriously noble. Spare me. The time is at last coming when you can put your expensive academy education to good use.'

'How so? Is there another automated in-system freighter filled with helium-3 that needs supervising from the moons back to Ryaz Prime?'

'Don't be so churlish. You're the one who insisted on having a use beyond a marriage to a good house. And don't pull that face at me! I have secured you a place as an officer for the Arrival.'

'A *political* officer?'

'Why are you so surprised? Your DNA is engineered from an approved line with all the sanctioned characteristics. You are a Denisov. You received top marks in political control and ideology.'

'You expect me to help Tsar Rasim after all that he's done to me?'

'I expect you to help exactly *because* of what he has done. What better way to demonstrate your loyalty to the regime? But, mostly, I expect you to show willing and help yourself.'

'We are wealthy enough already.'

'Said the girl who never had to earn a penny of her fortune! I am just old enough to remember the last Arrival. One blessed day, you may speak of it with wonder to your own children or grandchildren.'

'Would that I were so lucky.'

'You make your own luck. Although I have made yours today.'

'Do you expect me to thank you?'

'I would die of shock if you did, Dominika Denisov.'

'Perhaps I should, then. Although on second thoughts, there's been enough death recently.'

'And you shall put yourself above what has gone before, rise beyond it.'

Well, at least *that* was why Dominika had attended the academy. 'Perhaps I shall participate.'

'I shall expect you at the imperial court to make the obligatory show of good faith,' said the duchess, archly. 'It will make a change from you patronising the orbital station's establishments. Fraternising with grubbily common off-worlders.'

Dominika refrained from pointing out that the orbital station was where she was employed, at least, to the limit her rank allowed her to be. 'It's mostly Ryals up on the station. Few off-worlders visit Ryazarn.'

'That will change. At least for a little while. Show your best face to the Tsar. Do that and you will achieve much for the house.' Dominika's mother gave her one last disapproving glance and then departed the room.

For the house, but never for me. 'What do you think, Retigura?'

'Unlike you, Lady Denisov, I shall not live to see another Arrival beyond this one.'

That was true enough. It was as illegal to subject girs to life-extension treatments as it was to manipulate their DNA. Girrish bred fast enough to maintain employment levels without further tinkering. An attitude starkly at odds with the regime's policy on human eugenics, of course.

'I believe it will prove quite interesting to witness such an event,' added Retigura.

'I agree.' But not for many of the reasons Dominika's mother had burdened her with. 'There will be much work to do before we take part.'

As Dominika left the Denisov's island citadel, her private aircraft powering the clear sky, it occurred to her that at no point had the duchess once mentioned the risk to her daughter's life that being a political officer at the Arrival would entail. The Arrival might prove even more dangerous than cosying up to the Tsar and his sycophants at the imperial court, in fact.

Lana groaned, trying to ignore the feeling that she had been used as a dance mat by a herd of elephants. Then she remembered . . . close second. Squeezed out of hyperspace through the quantum rear end of a black hole. *Now that's what I call a bad drop. Although any drop you can walk away from. . .*

The bridge had maintained its integrity, albeit with spinning hologram warnings rapidly circling every bank of instrument consoles. *Looks like some damn orbital casino in here.* Her command chair had de-armoured, but remained in its medical support configuration. It detected Lana's stirring rise back to consciousness and celebrated with a squirt of some dire chemical pick-me-up directly into her bloodstream. *Oh, joy.* As always, Polter was already awake. She sometimes thought the navigator's kaggen ancestors must have crossbred with a tank. Skrat, whose biochemistry - while lizard-based - was a more approximate human analogue, appeared to be stirring out of the drop right alongside Lana's throbbing headache.

She addressed the all-too-perky navigator, letting Skrat have his grumpy time. 'Still alive, then, Polt. What's our garage bill looking like?'

'If there was a bank in this part of space which would accept the *Gravity Rose* as collateral, revered captain, now would be a good time to start sweet-talking them.'

'Hey, our credit's good.' *Yeah, for a round of drinks at Transference Station. Why do I always have to be the optimistic one here?*

Lana received the highlights of what Polter had already gleaned from multiple damage control reports. And these were only the automated estimates from Granny. When the chief and Zeno's robot crew started poking around the corridors, who knew what costly destruction they would turn up. Lana tried transferring the list from her implant to the console and using the ship's processing power to make things look better, but frankly, she was just applying lipstick to this particular pig.

Skrat had recovered enough to sync his instruments to hers. 'Given our shape, I think we're jolly lucky to have arrived in a system with a drydock.'

Lana double-checked the nav system, receiving an optical fix on every visible star and comparing it to their charts. 'Yeah, at least we ended up where we were aiming. Nice work, Polter.'

'Nice work, perhaps, but I admit to feeling confused,' said Polter. 'While making the drop I did a manual check of our exit point against the generator field stability. My numbers suggested we would be torn apart while transiting the most holy of holies.'

'So what are you saying — that we shouldn't be alive?'

'Quite so, revered captain.'

Skrat turned his chair to face the navigator. 'Well, I for one am grateful we've not yet shuffled off this mortal coil.'

Given that the kaggen species believed that hyperspace was a lower level of heaven, Lana was surprised her navigator wasn't happier about beating the odds. 'Maybe God was looking out for us?'

'I am quite certain the Lord was,' said Polter. 'But he tends to use mathematics to express the glory of his creations, and God's mathematics are rarely so badly abused as the numbers I calculated.'

'Everyone gets a little hinky during a drop. Your armoured body might stand up a lot better to spacetime dilation than my bag of monkey flesh, but even a big old crab like you has his limits.'

Lana queried the sickbay for an update on Calder. She got no response, which was worrying in itself. Doctor Feelfine rarely missed an opportunity to be obnoxious to her. *Has the comms in that part of the ship gone down, or has the doctor?* If the abrasive medical A.I was one of the systems shorted out, Calder might be . . . she pushed herself out of her chair and nearly fell over from dizziness. Lana fought down the impulse to vomit. 'I'm heading down to medical.'

'Incoming message from our passenger,' said Skrat. 'Mr. D'Alembert is demanding to be released from his cabin and insists we immediately resume our journey towards Clifford's World.'

Lana held onto her chair and used the second or two to recover her balance and legs. 'Then he can put on a vac-suit and get out and push. Anything else?'

'That's the nub of it, old girl. Of course, I am translating to remove the expletives. Farmers certainly know how to swear, don't they?'

'He's not a farmer; he's a landowner and a parasite. Allow D'Alembert out of lockdown but revoke his key access to the bridge. I'll sooner grab a sleeping bag and bunk up here than listen to more of his whining threats to go legal on us.'

Skrat tapped his green scaled snout in a knowing way. 'He's not a happy chappie.'

Lana dialled up a transport capsule. 'And I *am*? Do I look happy, Skrat?'

'Shall I attempt to smooth our client's somewhat non-existent feathers?'

The capsule arrived, sliding to a stop on the other side of the transparent hyper-loop barrier. Lana waited for the doors to slide back and then stepped inside. 'Tell him he can go and space himself.' As the doors began to close she had second thoughts and shouted out, 'And find out if that contract you signed contains anything about delays beyond our control ... declining all refunds and late fees.'

'*We* signed,' called Skrat. '*We* signed, dear girl.'

So far, there was a lot turning out to be dear about this voyage. Lana was pretty sure none of it was *her*.

Randd'Alembertswivelled on his manservant, Jinhai Jou, venting his anger over the dismissive message sent down from the bridge. 'This is an outrage! They're refusing to abandon their diversion.'

Jinhai nodded with concern. Much of the butler's job was agreeing with his employer's frequent rages and playing along with his constant low-level state of hostility about the universe's conspiracy against d'Alembert Holdings. It paid very well. As the old saying might have gone, *The secret of a butler's success is sincerity: once you can fake that, you've got it fabbed.* 'They have no proper appreciation of the damage this will cause you, sir.'

'Get out, you damned fools!' d'Alembert chased out the last of the robot stewards withdrawing from his stateroom and picked up an ashtray from the table, hurling it after the retreating mechanicals. If they showed any concern about the missile, it escaped Jinhai's attention. They didn't even try to take evasive action. The object bounced off the steel back of the last steward, cracked and fell onto the carpet.

As d'Alembert often did when he needed to think and plan, he clicked his fingers. '*Quique.*'

Jinhai removed one of the hand-rolled cigars from the silver case he carried for his employer, lighting the cigar as soon as it was wavering between the rich man's lips. Quique was the brand and the world both, famous throughout the Alliance and the Edge and corners of the galaxy where the local species didn't even possess lungs to enjoy the ancient vice. Of course, d'Alembert was modern enough to have had his DNA fixed with the no-cancer tweak. He was also cheap enough not to have bothered paying for the same expensive genetic modification for his house staff, but then, passive smoking was not one of the top ten worries for Jinhai while working for d'Alembert Holdings. A small measure of calm seemed to return to the man as he puffed away. Sometimes, the power of the humble tobacco leaf seemed to verge on the miraculous.

'That's better. Lord, how I loathe travelling on these tin cans, breathing recycled air and eating reheated ration packs. Squeezed in and out of an exotic pocket dimension no sane individual would willingly subject their body to.'

Jinhai didn't point out that his own parents had travelled to Clifford's World racked by the thousand inside cryogenic sleep capsules, seeking a better life on a colony world and risking brain aneurysms and something akin to Alzheimer's by travelling steerage. 'You have staked much with your current venture, sir.'

'I've staked everything, man! Bet the house. I only asked one little thing of this vessel, to travel from point A to point B. I was more than willing to forgo the comforts of my station to make the jump.'

'You have been badly let down, sir.'

'It won't stand, Jou. I'm telling you that now.'

'They might be telling the truth about needing repairs, sir. Our exit from hyperspace appeared unusually violent.'

'Pure theatrics. Shake the ship a little and scare the rubes inside the passenger cabin. I didn't get where I am today by taking fright at such transparent con-tricks. They've got a side-job out here, I can smell it. I've paid their fuel bill and now they'll be taking on extra cargoes at every system from here to Clifford's World, you wait and see. They're looking to chisel me!'

It was amazing, Jinhai considered, how everyone they met seemed to do that. 'I'm sure Captain Fiveworlds can be made to see reason.'

'The wise are instructed by reason, average minds by experience, the stupid by necessity and the brute by instinct. Do you know who said that, Jou?'

'I am afraid I don't, sir.' But had the butler possessed an expensive implant to look aphorisms up, he was fairly sure he would.

'Cicero, man. Cicero! I believe we must rely on necessity to instruct our simpleton of a captain in her responsibilities.'

'Perhaps, sir, it would be an auspicious time to break out *it*.'

'For this rabble? The special item cost far too much money to waste it on these philistines. I require it fresh for my enemies on Clifford's World. No, a beating from a few farm droids will suffice.'

Jinhai nodded approvingly, but inside he was cringing. Whenever his employer started talking about necessity, the house's competitors started meeting with violent ends. And if there was one thing more unpleasant than travelling on a tin can, breathing recycled air and eating reheated ration packs, it was doing all those things in the middle of a starship-confined firefight.

'Where am I?' asked Calder, his blurred vision stabilising to the point he could pick out the ship's android seated in a chair next to his bed.

'The recovery room next door to the sickbay,' said Zeno, pointing to the equipment lined up by the left-hand side of his bed. 'Your quarters were a little too cosy for us to wheel in the monitors for medical post-op.'

It's quiet outside. Calder could just detect the low thrum of a sub-light engine burn. They had exited hyperspace, at least. Calder felt a sudden mad rush of elation. 'I'm alive!'

'Fully functioning. Although I think you might have died a couple of times back on the operating table. You've been floating in a sickbay nutrient tank for the last few days, timesharing with a couple of million virus-sized healers, the last of your chest wounds being cleaned. We moved you in here when Doc Feelfine gave you the green light to be removed from the coma he'd laid on you.'

Calder put a hand inside his white medical robe, feeling the skin around his abdomen. There was a rough, rubbery texture to it as though he wasn't entirely flesh anymore. Replacement grafts, spun on the fly when he was inside the tank? His implant helpfully indicated the areas of his body that had been regrown with a visual overlay, animated icons highlighting the repaired flesh's superior tolerances. Calder winced. *More rebuild than original down there, now.*

'I should say thank you to the doctor.'

'Feelfine's not sentient, he won't care.'

I guess Chief Paopao was wrong about the doctor's skill. Like that's a first. 'And you are . . . and do?'

'I'm here, aren't I? I guess I still enjoy having someone on the ship more lowly than everyone's favourite go-to bot herder. That's a novel feeling.'

'You're better crew than I am,' said Calder. 'I nearly got us all killed.'

'I'll let you into a little secret. Those arc-welder units you were space-walking with should have been rolling with fully functional safety protocols. Even after you got confused by your implant and made that bad call, your robots should have recognised the danger and bounced your instructions. Reason they didn't is the same reason that everything else goes wrong on the *Rose*. We haven't had a full dry-dock refit in centuries. Internal machine shop maintenance only gets you so far. The replacement parts we're fabbing from space dust and asteroid rock are based on intellectual property that's older than most of my movies.'

'How badly damaged is the ship?'

'Oh, she's dinged up,' admitted Zeno. 'We lost our Minkowski Field generator on the way out of hyperspace. Lost, as in, totally disintegrated. Until that gets replaced, making any jump is a one-way ticket to the big empty. Of course, making a jump out might prove kind of tricky, too. Our vanes were torn up during the drop.'

Calder groaned. *I'm in so much trouble with Lana. This is my fault. I'll be lucky if the captain ever talks to me again, let alone encourages me to undress her.* The set of vanes the ship used to create artificial wormholes to enter hyperspace was just about the most expensive equipment possessed by the *Gravity Rose*. 'Can you show me how bad things are?'

Zeno grunted an affirmative and sent across the damage report on the jump vanes. *Torn up is right.* During the vanes testing cycle, gravitational compression had leaked out into the electromagnetic field spectrum, instead. The one thing you required from your artificial singularity was enough stability to safely thread the wormhole's eye without getting ripped apart. Right now they didn't have that. *Not even close.* If they jumped using their vanes, the *Gravity Rose* would end up as a trans-dimensional bug-splat on the event horizon. They could probably patch repair using the ship's resources, but the job would take a lot of time, kicking in all those nasty penalties on their current voyage. Once late fees were paid, they might as well have purchased a shiny new set of ship vanes and at least have something to show for their T-dollars.

Calder was about to ask where the *Rose* had exited, but he realised the annoying paper-thin piece of biotech wrapped around his brain stem could query the ship systems and feed him the whole nav package for where the *Gravity Rose* had dropped. Calder might wish he'd never had the thing installed in his head back on Transference Station, but have it he did. *So I might as well use it.* He winced as a mess of data streamed down. Calder never thought he'd get used to this artificial method of learning, of knowing things stored in his machine memory augment. Facts he'd never read or heard, but that were still, somehow, now part of his brain's knowledge. *It's not natural.* But then, given where he'd started out, just surviving being deposed from his kingdom's throne was hardly natural. Let alone riding a bubble of recycled air in a steel, hex-diamond and composite wurtzite boron nitride fibre-weave hull in the middle of the empty, endless vacuum between worlds.

'We've dropped at Ryazarn? Well, at least we've reached a human-civilised system.'

'Depends on what you mean by civilised, kid. The main planet, Ryaz Prime, isn't on the Protocol.'

'So what - the world's non-standard? This far out in the deep Edge isn't that normal, not being part of the data-sphere?'

The android tapped Calder's head. 'Yeah, there's knowing, and then there's *knowing*. Never make that implant of yours into a crutch, manchild. The Protocol is more than a bunch of standards about starship pipe fittings and trading and diplomatic rules that Alliance worlds and their ex-colonies try to stick to. As well as acting as a distributed interstellar network of interconnected autonomous data spheres, the Protocol's also a bang-up actionable trust and morality system. If your world, asteroid, or orbital colony starts warring with your neighbours, acting rowdy and generally generating shizzle for everyone, then the Protocol is removed from your ass. That means no more data ships incoming. The next plague vaccine that gets developed, that shiny new development in quantum computing or warning of a raider fleet sliding void in your direction - none of it flows your way anymore. Worlds that are off the Protocol don't tend to prosper. They shrivel and die in isolation.'

Calder queried his implant for the reason Ryazarn was denied Protocol status and found the answer easily enough. The world of Ryaz Prime had been first settled eight-hundred years ago, at around the same time as Calder's world, Hesperus, had been colonised. Ryaz Prime's dominant native species, the girrish, had been subsisting at just below a Stone Age level of technological sophistication. Easy meat, they came close to extermination after human settlers moved in. The aboriginals who survived had been enslaved. Newborn girs were surgically implanted with behavioural modifiers, similar to those used on convicts found guilty of homicide inside the alliance. A slave state where docility and obedience were guaranteed. The ancient decision to deny Ryazarn the Protocol had been finely balanced, some stakeholders arguing that the girrish pacification was within the allowed exploitation of local fauna and flora. What had swung the Protocol's withdrawal was the discovery of girrish ruins with trace isotopes which indicated the aboriginals had once possessed a fusion-level civilisation, erased many millennia before by nuclear war. That revelation shifted the locals from exploitable animals to potential high-level tool users, triggering protected status. Ryaz Prime's stubborn human settlers might have kept their slavocracy, but in the process they'd lost the best part of its interaction with the rest of alliance-settled space.

Calder stretched out, bones and muscles aching from bed-rest. He shouldn't grumble about his condition. Given the severity of his wounds, back home he'd have been treated with a herb poultice before being fitted for a coffin. 'So we're going to have to hold our noses when we get to Ryaz Prime.'

'That we are. But here's the really hinky thing. Ryaz Prime's sporting an orbital station which is pretty much state-of-the-art. It can even churn out a new field generator for us, if we can afford whatever stupid price they demand. Load Ryazarn's ship traffic from our sensor logs; tell me what you think.'

Calder did as the android asked and pondered the findings. 'It's all local in-system flights. Automated beacons everywhere.'

'Yeah, they've built mines on their two moons, as well as on the asteroid belt around that big red gas giant. No hyperspace-capable ships, though. They could make them. They choose not to. Along with the single channel media, automated mines and near-crewless cargo haulers crawling around here, Granny's analysis is that they've got some major league isolationist control freakery being run by the local government. Joe citizen doesn't get out much and the only opinion that counts is the ruling warlord.'

'A slavocracy,' said Calder, 'doesn't that go with the territory?'

'Yeah, but what doesn't go with the territory is that shiny orbital, like a big zero-gravity honey pot, just sitting there. Hey spacer, visit us, shore leave and cookies and warm milk. Just dock over here with us. And that's ignoring the fact that by rights this embargoed backwater shouldn't be able to afford to launch an entertainment satellite, let alone keep a full alliance-standard shipyard orbiting Ryaz Prime.'

Calder let the contradictions of this mystery sink in. When it did, he realised he didn't like it any better than his android friend.

Zeno shook his head, sadly, as though just sliding void in this system was painful. 'Off the Protocol cuts both ways. The rest of the galaxy might have embargoed Ryaz Prime for the best part of its settlement, but that means we know Jack about what's really happening inside this shizzle-hole of a system.'

'What you don't know will get you killed.'

'Yeah, out here, every time.'

As if agreeing with the android's fears, the ship's sirens began to shriek in ear-splitting anger.

Calder matched the alarm's pulse to the threat being signalled but was so confused by the answer that he queried it twice more, thinking he was doing something wrong. 'How can that be?'

Zeno seemed equally perplexed, his golden-skinned forehead twitching in astonishment. 'Yeah, we're days away from making Ryaz Prime orbit, sliding outer-system void. I'm damned if I know how that can be right?'

Still the sirens wailed. *Prepare to repel boarders.*

'What's going on, skip?' demanded Zeno, his hand resting on the comms panel. 'I can't interface properly with the bridge systems and we're hearing a boarding action alarm shaking the corridor outside medical.'

Lana Fiveworlds' voice emerged from the panel, but its screen remained blurred with static. 'Tried to sound the mutiny alarm, but our systems are being jinked with.'

'Mutiny? Who - *Rand d'Alembert*?' groaned Zeno. 'No! You've got to be kidding me. There's only him and Jeeves inside the entire passenger module.'

'D'Alembert, Jeeves, and a few thousand farm drones stacked

in our cargo containers. Looks like his robot's programming cores are a little more multi-functional than simply hoeing, seeding and ploughing.'

Zeno groaned. 'I checked those containers.'

'You *spot*-checked our cargo. You know how automated forces work; you only need one bad war-bot to act as a template to reformat all the other droids. Looks like Farmer Giles wasn't taking it on trust that the rest of Clifford's World would stand idly by and watch him strong-arm a near-total food monopoly into existence. If any politician wanted to vote in favour of anti-trust action and nationalise his gains . . .'

'Ah, shizzle. Planet King with his own Royal Guard.'

'Right now his Royal Guard are being a royal pain in our waste recycling pipes. They're ripping apart my cargo deck and cannibalising the ship to make weapons. As best as I can tell, they're processing the fertiliser drums' contents to make explosives for grenades and rounds. I'm counting on you to muster our own little robot brigade to take them on.'

'Yeah, but we're not carrying schematics for advanced military ground technology on board,' said Zeno, 'because that would count as, you know, illegal gun-running.'

'Don't give me that, old man. Right now I've got a cargo hold full of illegal mil-mech running amok. You're telling me you can't fab a black market rail-gun in our engineering deck? Any bored slum kid can print an illegal pistol inside their steel hut.'

Zeno sighed. 'Well, at least we're not facing dedicated military issue drones. How dangerous can a fruit picker with a home-made rifle prove?'

'We'd have found out if we shipped d'Alembert back home. Aiding and abetting a planetary-wide coup on a Protocol world? Half the Edge would revoke our docking rights. The other half would've settled for rubber stamping the storm of Triple Alliance arrest warrants which began flying our way.'

'Well, I always wanted to be a pirate. Just give me an eye-patch, a vibra-blade and the open void.'

Lana's voice sounded like she didn't appreciate the joke. 'First you'd have to lose that eye to local law enforcement or a bounty hunter.'

'Don't worry, skipper, I'm on it.' Zeno closed his eyes and interfaced with the ship's systems, reaching out to his robot workforce scattered throughout the vessel. It took him a second to process the information and report back. 'Ah, so *that's* their idea of electronic countermeasures. They've got a modified seventy-foot-long mega-harvester trying to infiltrate the ship's systems. I've just sent a few kilojoules of prime power outage flowing down its cable shunt and given it something to worry about other than opening our riot doors.'

Lana's face suddenly appeared on the screen, the jamming temporarily halted with the harvester's fried mind. 'Careful, Zeno. There's an advance force of d'Alembert's toys scouting the corridors. They were modified and out of cargo before I locked down the *Rose.*'

Calder could hold his tongue no longer. 'Can't you flood the cargo deck with riot gas, cut off the head of the snake? Without d'Alembert issuing instructions to his drones . . .'

'So you're up and about at last, are you, Mister Dirk?' That's a marvellous suggestion. So marvellous in fact, it was the very first measure we tried on the bridge. d'Alembert and his butler are inside their gas-proof vac-suits. Their personal very expensive vac-suits with air supplies we can't turn off remotely, before you put your genius mind to work again.'

Calder shrugged. He'd tried his best. *I'm guessing I'm still in the dog house for half-destroying the ship.* 'Sorry, captain.'

'Sorry doesn't begin to pay for even half the repairs we need to make.'

Calder reckoned Lana was trying to come up with a way to link d'Alembert's mutiny to the chain of events he had inadvertently started. Before she could summon the case, Calder spoke up again. 'Can't we talk to d'Alembert, agree to discuss his demands?'

'His demands, Mister Dirk, are that we turn around, translate back into hyperspace and push on for Clifford's World without making repairs.'

Zeno nearly choked, not something that Calder thought it was possible for an android to do - or even emulate. 'Is he mad? State of the *Rose* right now, that's a death jump at worse case, or at best, permanent exile inside the big empty.'

'Mad? No. Paranoid with psychopathic tendencies, quite possibly. He thinks we're pulling a fast one on him; loading up side-cargoes on his house's expense account.'

'Well, at least he's a half-decent judge of character,' muttered Zeno, but with the confusion of blaring sirens Lana didn't hear him.

Calder knew that even if the *Gravity Rose* possessed a fighting chance of making another jump and surviving her exit, Lana would have refused point blank to meet the demands. She was the captain. On her vessel, Lana might as well have been God as far as d'Alembert was concerned. Any captain worth her salt would sooner drink a cask of magnetically-contained stellar plasma than take orders under duress from mere cargo. 'This is *our* ship.'

'Correct, Mister Calder. Now, let's take it back.' Lana was about to add something but the screen shattered into a hundred shards of flying plastic as a round impacted it. Three of d'Alembert's farm drones filled the doorway, humanoid models with gangly spherical limbs. Their heads bobbed with moulded faces and cartoon-like grinning mouths, as well as frankly superfluous straw hats, features obviously intended to make workers thrown onto the scrapheap feel slightly less hostile to their mechanical replacements. The weapons clutched in their three-fingered steel hands had been fabbed on the fly and were the definition of simplicity - bulky, brutish revolvers with eight-shot chambers, but no less deadly for that.

'Bad seeds,' hooted the robot with the smoking pistol.

'Yes,' agreed a second drone, swaying on its feet as though drunk - obviously having trouble processing the combat update swirling around its machine mind.

'It is weeding time again,' yelled the third robot, pushing ungainly past its two colleagues and raising its pistol. Its voice screeched from the thing's voice-box, the robot's audio pickup overwhelmed by the first pistol's discharge. Calder was already rolling off the bed and heading for the floor as the volley of shots shredded his pillow and duvet, spilling clouds of artificial feathers into the air. He tried to transmit a warning about the attack to the bridge via his implant, but the bridge systems still weren't stable enough to connect. Calder's eyes swept the room looking for something, anything, he might use as a weapon. His augments kicked in, highlighting dozens of objects and calculating their lethality in hand-to-hand combat. The drone was still trying to refocus the weapon towards Calder when he snatched a wall-mounted defibrillator from its rack, lunging forward to smack both sides of the drone's head with two electro-pads. He gave it a few thousand volts and the drone lost all coordination, its heavy body tumbling towards the deck. 'You need a new catchphrase.' *Along with a new neural matrix.*

Zeno rushed the drone nearest to him, wrestling the robot back towards the wall of the recovery room, its pistol discharging shot after shot into the ceiling. The remaining robot stepped behind the android, raising its pistol towards Zeno's dreadlocks. Calder side-tackled the drone, its shot going wide and blasting splinters out of a fake window screen rotating through reality-level resolution images of green forests and tinkling waterfalls. A human who'd taken that much impact would have been knocked sprawling. The drone merely clumsily side-stepped a couple of times, its servo motors and hydraulics whirring to keep upright. Calder grappled with it and suddenly discovered the limits of human strength. Calder had been working alongside the engine-room robots for what seemed a lifetime now, but he'd never had - or felt - the need to wrestle with his machines before. If he had, he might have hesitated before taking this metal lunatic on.

Calder yelled in agony as the robot forced one of his hands to the side, its steel arm and home-made revolver repositioning to shoot him in the forehead. Zeno struggled with his own opponent - in no position to help his human colleague.

'The first law,' Calder cried, trying to appeal to the drone's core programming. *A robot may not injure a human being or, through inaction, allow a human being to come to harm.* That prohibition was kind of fundamental to matters right now.

'All slugs must die!' cried the grinning mechanical killer, its weapon sliding inexorably towards the side of Calder's skull. Calder thought he felt one of his tendons snap as he tried to slow the robot's gun.

There goes reasoning with the thing - I've been reclassified. Frankly, given how many adversaries Calder had beaten with sword and axe on his home world, this was going to be an incredibly ignominious death. Its gun triggered early. A shot exploded past the side of Calder's head and blew apart a cart filled with medicines and medical nano-tech. His ears rung like a pair of cathedral bells, the murderous machine's bizarre insults swimming into his pained ears as though he was fighting it underwater. Another round rotated into the brutish revolver's breech. The farming robot yelled something which came through as a muted drone. *Assistance* signalled Calder's implant, unbidden; followed by, *audio filtering*.

'Zzzzz-pest control!' barked the robot as Calder's hearing corrected. Great, now he could hear the moment of his execution. Calder cried out as an intense blast of heat seared his face, followed by the realisation it hadn't originated from the revolver's barrel. The farming robot slumped past Calder, the front of its face melted, the rear of the thing's steel skull a blasted ruin.

'Craniotomy,' called Doctor Feelfine in triumph. The medical A.I. motored along the ceiling rail, hanging outside the doorway of post-op, an operating arm dangling with its laser scalpel attachment smoking. 'Diagnosis: terminal!'

'Another patient for you,' growled Zeno, the android wrestling his opponent towards the doorway. The doctor's laser arm swung out and carved a passage from the farm drone's neck to its midriff, liquid metal steaming into the air and splattering the deck. The repurposed machine fizzled and collapsed clanging into the puddle of molten steel that had formed the best part of its spine.

'Take two pills,' ordered Feelfine, hanging from the rail like an ugly mechanical locust, 'and *don't* see me in the morning.' It swivelled on Zeno. 'This is a disgrace. Who let the cargo loose inside sickbay? What are you doing, android - this is your responsibility?'

'Just staying alive, baby,' said Zeno.

The stalks' optical sensors jiggled in annoyance. 'You are playing more pranks. Jealous of my successful operation on this filthy bag of flesh, always jealous of me.'

The filthy bag of flesh in question was beginning to regret his implant had ever signalled for assistance.

Zeno checked the room, ensuring all the farm drones were definitely out of commission. 'Yeah well, this particular prank's getting out of hand . . . d'Alembert's bots are running seriously overclocked. It's not just an illegal firmware update - they were shipped with supercharged power plants. d'Alembert must have bribed the manufacturer for a custom build.'

Calder frowned. 'What does that mean?'

Zeno pushed Doctor Feelfine out of the way, running into the corridor. He located a working comms panel as Calder followed him. 'Means we start playing robot wars and in all likelihood *Team Gravity Rose* are going to come out on the losing side.' Zeno hit the panel. 'Skipper, we're in trouble. D'Alembert's robots are running illegally amped. Robo-a-Robo they're going to tear my bots a new one.'

Lana's worried face appeared on the screen. 'The main force inside the hold has given up trying to hack the riot doors. They're cutting their way through, instead. They'll be spilling out into the rest of the ship in two minutes.'

Zeno slammed a fist into the bulkhead. 'I hate to say it, Lana, but we're done here. Time to retreat to the launch bay and grab a cargo shuttle.'

'I'm not abandoning the *Rose*, not to that madman.'

'They're going to overwhelm us! Run the numbers, skipper. Even if those maniacal fruit pickers don't beat us to death, we're going to either smear on the next jump or be left sucking hyperspace with Farmer Giles for the rest of eternity. From where this brother's standing, none of those options particularly appeals.'

'No! I'll overload our antimatter core sooner than abandon ship.'

'And are Paopao, Skrat and Polter in on your Kamikaze run?'

'You can bail, damn you. I'm not going to stop you.'

'Listen to reason!' begged Zeno. 'I've kept you alive all these years.'

'Finally time for you to find another job then,' said Lana. 'One minute left until they break out.' She was about to kill the comm but Calder leapt forward.

'Don't do it!'

'Head for a shuttle. Sign up on a new ship, Mister Dirk. I'm staying on the bridge.'

And I'm not leaving you here. 'I've an alternative,' said Calder, amazed to realise he actually *did.* 'The shields which protect the ship from dust and debris during our sub-light burn, they can be selectively strengthened and angled around the ship, right?'

'Sure, for combat as well as navigational threats. You dial your stern chasers to maximum when you're being pursued from the rear, or you boost bow-fields when you're running into enemies squatting on your jump point.'

'Then the converse is true, you can lower the shield along sections of the ship?'

'I can make that happen.'

'Then drop the shielding around the cargo bay. Those farm drones aren't hardened for battlefield deployment, are they? They may be stronger than they should be, but they're not circuit-hardened for surge protection.'

'Calder, the ship only carries rail-cannons for point defence.

I'm not flying with nukes in our armoury. Give me a lucky asteroid strike with fissile material and a week inside the engineering deck and I'm sure the chief could cook us up a warhead. But you've done enough *Hell-Fleet* sims to know that a nuclear X-ray laser warhead detonating off the hull on partial shields would brew the crew long before we ever cooked d'Alembert's droids.'

'I'm not talking about detonating a nuke off the ship, captain,' said Calder, his words tumbling out. 'We don't need a nuclear EMP blast. Our jump vanes are malfunctioning. They're not generating gravity compression for singularity formation anymore: they're leaking out inside the electromagnetic spectrum.'

Lana looked stunned as the implications of his suggestion sunk in. 'Use the malfunctioning vanes to generate an EMP pulse? Polter, model that idea for me . . .'

The navigator's excited voice sounded over the comm. 'It's possible, revered captain. The power of a pulse wouldn't fry battle-hardened war drones, but against modified farm machines' unshielded minds? The cargo should be ionised beyond repair.'

'Turn off every system we still have control over inside the hold. Zeno, pull back all your robots outside the cargo modules.'

'Done and doing,' said Zeno.

Lana's voice again. 'Vanes are rotating. Forty seconds before there's mass breakout from the hold.'

Come on, willed Calder. *Work.*

'You keep on surprising me,' said Zeno, leaning against the bulkhead. 'It's dangerous underestimating you; given this time last year you were running around in bear furs and playing Conan the Barbarian King on your failed colony world.

Calder listened to the distant crack of the jump vanes rotating around the ship. 'I was raised for the fight. Swords, ice-schooners, fire throwers. You take what weapons you have and stick it into the enemy. All this, —' Calder indicated the starship with a wave of his hand — 'this is just details.'

'Yeah, nothing like a hostile ice-age environment to bring out a fleshie's creative flare for violence.'

The ship began to judder around them as the defective vanes malfunctioned.

'I simply cannot work under these conditions,' complained Doctor Feelfine.

Zeno ignored him. 'Or the jump vanes could tear the ship apart . . .'

Calder mouthed a prayer to the gods, cursing his superstitious throwback mind as he did so. *The habits of a lifetime do not fade easily.*

Portions of the ship began to alter, the corridor systems hardening around them as though bracing for a solar storm. A loud series of bangs cracked the air. Not the vanes outside under vacuum, but the transformers drawing engine-room power and feeding it outside, transformers snapping in protest at being so badly abused. Strip lighting down the ceiling faded to darkness for a second before blinking back to full brilliance.

Lana's voice sounded from the panel, a triumphant note to her tenor. 'Not one EMP burst. Seven in succession!'

'I'm reading zero movement inside the hold now,' said Zeno. 'Dispatching our bots to tackle the last few scouts crawling around the corridors.'

Calder hardly believed his luck. 'We've done it!'

'You just added a burned out cargo hold to our massive repair bill, Mister Dirk. Well done.'

Calder couldn't tell if that was a genuine vote of thanks or sarcasm. *Knowing Lana, possibly both.*

'My systems are compromised,' complained Doctor Feelfine. 'I do believe your desperate act of vandalism has damaged micro-portions of my core.'

'You were installed compromised, doc.' Zeno leant into the panel. 'What about Jeeves and Wooster?'

Lana puckered her lips. 'Sadly, the EMP pulses will have only fried his robots, not the man himself.'

'I mean what do you want done with d'Alembert when we come across him?'

'Drag his sorry ass down to the brig. And I want to be the one who tells him that mutiny invalidates the terms of our contract to ship his crap to Clifford's World, as well as voiding any insurance on his automated labour force.'

'I think that robot army *was* his insurance.'

'Right now, they're a dock-side spare-parts sale. And I'm pocketing the proceeds!'

The comm switched off and the android turned to Calder. 'Let's find the landowner's flaky ass. I figure the first law of robotics should allow me to pin his arms while you smack him about a little.'

Calder nodded but he couldn't summon much enthusiasm for any thoughts of retribution. Calder had nearly destroyed the ship twice. Pulling them back from the brink obviously hadn't balanced the scales as far as Lana Fiveworlds was concerned. It wasn't just the cargo deck Calder had burned. It was his relationship with the captain, too.

- 3 -

Regime Regime

'mreading shipping hazard warnings from a local beacon,' said Polter.

'Picking up scatter to starboard,' said Skrat. 'That's bally odd, though. Too small to be asteroids.'

'Maybe a satellite graveyard?' said Lana. 'Although it'd be strange to park surplus this close to the station.'

'I don't think so. The bounce-back from our sensors is all wrong.'

'Granny,' said Lana. 'Run spectral composition on the beacon hazard.'

'Organic,' announced the ship's A.I. 'Matching the profile of Ryazarn's local species, the girrish.'

Lana felt sick to her gut. Not a satellite graveyard then, but the real thing. Spacing your enemies was the worst kind of punishment. 'They're making an example?'

'Negative,' said Granny. 'Body composition prior to freezing indicates all corpses were in the later stages of old age.'

'It's an affront to the creator,' said Polter, outraged.

'It's their retirement plan is what it is,' growled Lana. 'Once they're too old to work it costs money to shuttle their aboriginal workers back down the gravity well.'

'An asset to be written off,' said Skrat.

Lana knew the lowest level of a skirl nest had an untouchable caste which wasn't functionally far different from slave labour. In fact, when she first came across Skrat, he was a disgraced ex-executive who had been trying to climb his way back the social hierarchy by combat inside a gladiator pit.

'Just give the field a wide berth,' ordered Lana, disgusted.

'Is it just me, or is this station looking distinctly crowded for an off-Protocol backwater?'

Lana checked her console and saw that Skrat was correct. The orbital station was engineered as a spinning wheel with hundreds of docking spines around her concave midsection. All with vessels clamped to bracing girders. Not sub-light traffic, but jump-capable vessels a similar size — or larger — than the *Gravity Rose*.

'Do we have IDs for those ships, Granny?'

'They're not broadcasting identity sigs, captain,' said the A.I.

Lana grunted. In most systems, that would be illegal. Here, she suspected the regime probably insisted on discretion among its visitors.

'However,' added Granny, 'their silhouette configurations indicate mainly alliance-build vessels, including a number of current builds.'

That meant corporate houses. Lana wondered what so much blue-chip money was doing here, risking trade boycotts and protests back home by dealing with a blacklisted world? 'Are there any rare mineral elements native to this system?'

'Helium 3 on the moons,' said Granny. 'Superior grade monazite on the system's fourth world. But nothing rare on Ryaz Prime itself.'

Granny shunted the key facts to the front of Lana's memory space. Ryaz Prime was mostly ocean covered by thousands of island chains. Planetary resource extraction was concentrated below the seabed. Dangerous work assigned to the aboriginals. This dataset was centuries stale, but Lana doubted if the locals had come across any new mineral finds missed by the original survey team. Lana skipped through the local datasphere. She was perusing a brochure for the regime. No open boards, no discussion or active social networks. No free posts, but plenty of martial music and tanned young faces standing tall under a fluttering flag. Four red stars in a circle on black. Her implant helpfully labelled the stars as the main virtues of the ruling regime: loyalty, integrity, endeavour and courage. The main thing that interested her was the absence of hard prices for the shipyard's services. *If you have to ask, Lana . . .*

'Slave owners' convention, then,' quipped Skrat.

'This is no matter for levity,' said Polter.

The devotedly religious kaggen navigator could be priggish at the best of times, but in this matter, Lana reckoned he had the right idea.

'There is a reason this system is off the Protocol,' fretted their navigator. 'Their souls have fallen to the darkest of lights. We should turn back.'

'Polter, if I had half a Minkowski field, that's exactly what I would be doing. But as it is, we've got no choice but to slide in here and try to do the best deal we can to get the hell out.' Lana idly examined the profile of one of the modern vessels. *No, it can't be?* 'Granny, the first vessel holding on the second docking spur from port — match her configuration against known ships in our database.'

'Match against the Hyperfast Köln,' said the A.I.

Lana groaned. *I knew it. He's here, like a fly on the proverbial.* 'If Pitor's in-system, then there's serious money up for grabs.'

'And serious trouble, dear, girl,' said Skrat, 'given that it was likely Pitor who divulged our coordinates to that piratical maniac, Steel-arm Bowen.'

Yeah, nothing like getting your competition out of the way the easy way. 'We still owe him for that one.'

This was a complication Lana didn't need. If Pitor discovered her desperate need for a Minkowski field generator, then he'd likely buy up every spare in the system on the Hyperfast expense account just to strand her here.

Polter rattled his crab-like shell. 'Station customs is signalling us requesting our cargo manifest.'

'Robot parts,' sighed Lana. 'A couple of hundred tonnes — only slightly nuked.'

She wondered if station security might take their mutinous client off their hands and out of the brig. But knowing Rand d'Alembert, he would fit in this system just perfectly. *Dandy. I've got a mutineer for a client locked in my brig, an ex-barbarian prince who thinks he can repair the Rose, a half-wrecked ship and no way to slide void out of a fascist slavocracy I normally wouldn't give the time of day to. What else can possibly go wrong?*

***

Entry to Ryaz Prime's orbital station was nearly the same as any port in the Edge. Send ahead their medicals and papers, then an airlock tube through a cloud of decontamination nano, confirming they were plague-free and carrying no exotic diseases or seeds, insects and other undesirables on their clothes. Calder tried to resist the urge to brush away the self-seeking dust storm they moved through, like being crawled across by an over-friendly cloud of flies. At least it made a change from constructing a fake Minkowski field generator on the hull. The ruse wouldn't pass a spacewalk-close inspection, but Calder saw the logic of dummying up such a vital part of the vessel. If the local shipyard got wind of the destruction of their real thing, they'd triple the price of a replacement. Polter and Chief Paopao were staying on board as a skeleton crew. Of course, in the latter's case, it would have taken a squad of fleet marines to drag him out of the shielded drive chamber's safety. A machine voice repeated a warning to Calder, Lana, Skrat and Zeno that attempting to enter the station with firearms — concealed or open carry — would be punished by severe penalties.

'Jeez,' said Zeno. 'It's a wonder they didn't demand power limiters on my reactor before letting me board.'

'They probably figure I've got you control locked,' said Lana.

'I'll try and suppress any signs of self-awareness, then,' sighed Zeno.

They left the airlock and entered the station proper. Glancing around, Calder could see this place possessed none of the ramshackle vibrancy of Transference Station, built instead to neat planned minimalist lines. White glow walls and vegetation banks, high-oxygen producing English ivy and spliced spider plants in straight corridors, rather than corridors and zones expanded piecemeal with the random dictates of free market demand. Quiet, too. Not just the absence of hawkers and the booming riot of ads screens — but the sensory minimum of the local datasphere. No overload of messages, opinions or wild eyeball grabbing. He sensed the alliance ships' combined network, a mutual huddling and sharing of data updates between alliance systems, but it was a walled fortress — forbidden to connect to the local regime's network in case they polluted the locals with dangerous ideas and ideals.

He spotted a few human station staff walking the docks, outnumbered by the girrish labourers visible, working vegetation beds and greenhouses that acted as the orbital station's lungs. The locals attended their tasks with a slightly shaky motion and Calder realised that the aboriginals hadn't been trained for their jobs; they were being puppeted by their control torcs, fed each task as a simple feedback routine.

It was an uncomfortable realisation for Calder that the difference between his implant and these slave workers' was purely one of programming. It had seemed like such a good idea back on Transference Station; carrying a computer with him all the time. *Yeah, in your head.* You wore shoes to keep your feet safe, a flight uniform to keep your body warm, and an implant nestled in the brain to interface with all the technology of modern life. *Make yourself as smart as the datasphere.* That and the thought it would help him fit in with the crew better. *And not look like a wuss in front of Lana.* Now, Calder was left wondering whether he had made the right choice after all.

Only a handful of select establishments on the station were licenced to accept T-dollars rather than the local currency — called the grivna — which meant locating the local spacers' bar and picking up on the scuttlebutt was going to be even more necessary than usual. An internal map for the station settled in his mind, indicating the direction to the rather functionally named *Open Commons*. It took them twenty minutes of walking along wide corridors and catching a mixture of well-scrubbed lifts and tube capsules to reach the establishment. Calder suspected the most open thing about the *Open Commons* was the view of Ryaz Prime below through its transparent floor — an azure green ball spanned by drifting clouds and freckled islands.

Someone wanted them to be here. Human waiters crossed

the packed room with trays of complimentary drinks and finger food. *No such thing as a free lunch* thought Calder. Skrat immediately got to work, querying the crowd to see if anyone possessed a local shipyard price list they'd be willing to trade for data updates from the *Gravity Rose*'s travels. The commons didn't have any girrish workers and the only locals were human bar staff front and back of the counter, not partaking of the refreshments. No slaves here. Calder guessed the regime didn't want to rub the traders' noses in why they weren't meant to be visiting this system. Every surface which wasn't seemingly open to the orbited world below was mirrored, making the place appear three times as busy as it actually was. Most years, that would have been a clever ploy, but right now, the trick was unnecessary. The commons heaved with visitors — humans, kaggen and skirls, for the most part, along with a few of the less populous races composing the Triple Alliance's interstellar polity. Plenty of ship crew, distinctive in their flight uniforms and a mob of civilians wearing what passed for the conservative uniform of the business and executive classes.

Calder cursed his luck as the slippery captain of the Hyperfast Köln emerged from the crowd to greet them. Except he didn't really bother with acknowledging the rest of the party. Only the woman the undeserving dog was once engaged to. *Lana.*

'Captain Fiveworlds, what brings you to Ryazarn?'

'Obviously not the good company.' Lana glanced towards Skrat. 'What brings us to Ryazarn, Skrat?'

'Oh, the jolly opportunities of a bit of commerce,' said the lizard. 'The usual.'

'I'm surprised you're so well-informed,' said Pitor.

Lana's eyes narrowed. 'Perhaps you mean you're surprised we're still alive and kicking.'

'The perils of doing business with low-class brokers such as Dollar-sign Dillard?'

'I guess you need a new tame privateer now,' said Calder. 'Given we left your last pirate and ship in pieces in orbit. But swimming with the sharks at Hyperfast, that shouldn't be too much of a problem for you.'

'Apart from present company, I do not deal with undesirables, fledgling.'

'You're a dirty flam-artist,' accused Zeno. 'If I could prove it, I'd break the habit of a lifetime and call in the TAP agents just to see you sharing a cell with someone like Steel-arm Bowen.'

'Proving it is always the hard part. When that garbage-hauling barge you fly finally breaks down, come and see me for a job, android. I can always use another smart drone on the H.F. Köln.' He smiled a hatchet-thin pursing of the lips and walked away from them.

'Way too smart for that, fleshie,' muttered Zeno.

'If I had a spare thousand T-dollars in my account, I'd gladly spend them to know what that bally rascal's up to here.'

Calder agreed with Skrat's sentiment. 'From the way Pitor spoke, it sounds like the sort of game you have to stake your way into.'

'Who'd have thought it? Pitor can even lower the tone in a fascist slavocracy,' said Lana.

'I've been trying to use my implant to get reads off the faces here,' said Calder, 'but they're mostly blocked.'

'Yes, quite the private party. But you don't need to ID the guests' faces, dear boy,' said Skrat. 'The expensive and immaculate nature of the tailoring indicates who these guests represent. Major houses' factotums, brokers and their agents. Possibly some civil servants and government types thrown into the mix.' He pointed out the ship crews in flight suits. 'And the taxi drivers that flew them here.'

'And I'm sure I recognise some of these spacers,' said Lana. 'But they're not ship families, so where . . . ?'

Skrat interrupted her musings. 'I say, isn't that . . .?'

Lana followed where the lizard pointed at the throng. 'Yeah, I'd say it is.' She waved towards a blonde woman seemingly in her forties, wearing a flight uniform which could have belonged to the *Gravity Rose* had it been olive green rather than dark grey. Calder noted that the woman's collar had the three bronze pips of a free merchant captain. Unlike Lana, the female officer was over six and a half feet tall — a virtual amazon. Back on Hesperus, the newcomer would have qualified as a shield maiden with the addition of a war axe and a half buckler. Her face was a curious mixture of soft and sharp edges that could have been considered handsome, but never pretty in the conventional way.

The woman's mouth widened into an easy grin when she noticed Lana and the others heading towards her. 'It's good to see a friendly face here.'

Lana embraced her as though she was a long lost sister. 'I take it you've bumped into Pitor too, then?'

'Unfortunately, yes.' The woman greeted Zeno and Skrat by name and then stopped at Calder, noting his ship emblem. Lana introduced the two of them — naming the indie skipper as Captain Elin Jernberg of the *Meteor Prince*.

'Where're Lars and Anna? Minding shop back on the *Prince*?' asked Lana.

Captain Jernberg shrugged sadly. 'They traded out.'

Lana's jaw dropped. 'Traded out of the ship?'

'Out of the ship, out of the business.'

'To do what?'

'They stayed behind at our family estate on Narse. One of my uncles has a cargo handling business up on the orbital tether. They're going to be helping him in the future.'

Calder messaged a question mark to Skrat on their private channel and got back a message back explaining, *her brother and sister.* That made sense. Many independents were run as family businesses. The *Rose* was a stand-in for the surrogate kind.

'Riding cargo containers up and down a beanstalk?'

'It beats starving, Lana.'

Zeno seemed as surprised as Lana at the news. 'What about their share of the *Meteor Prince*?'

'In abeyance,' said Captain Jernberg. 'I had the ship valued. Got a couple of offers for in-system haulage if our jump vanes were removed for resale. The best offer, financially, was to turn the *Prince* into an orbital casino around the Jewel Moon of Rho-2 Cephei.'

'Man,' said Zeno, 'that sucks. There's been Jernbergs flying the Edge ever since there's been Edge.'

'And that's the trouble right there,' said Elin. 'The Edge isn't the Edge anymore. It's getting civilised now. We might as well be the Seventy-Second Sector of the Triple Alliance.'

Lana nodded sympathetically, lifting a sandwich off a passing tray. 'I hear that.'

Elin inclined her head towards Pitor's direction of the bar. 'Of course, I got the same offer from Hyperfast that I dare say you did. Sell out to them.'

'Strip the routes, strip the customers, strip the ship.'

Calder had the urge to add "Strip the captain," but figured he was already in Lana's bad books without reminding her that Pitor had once been her fiancé.

Elin grunted in amusement. 'Yeah, like I need to live to see the *Prince* orbiting a scrap-yard; end up on the bridge of some shiny new piece of Hyperfast crap, filling out acquisition forms in triplicate for every carbon dioxide scrubber that needs replacing during the voyage.'

'The trouble is, dear girl, Hyperfast and the other large corporate houses are where the cargoes are at.' Skrat's tail swished behind him, body language that Calder recognised as frustration.

'Seems to be that way, doesn't it,' said Elin. 'Only cargoes I'm being offered by the brokers are so dodgy hot they would burn a steaming hole in my hold.'

Or hack their way out of it. Calder's shoulder twinged where their recent client's agricultural drone turned improvised war droid had slammed into him. But then, Calder knew there wasn't much choice of cargoes to be had. Their last client was the best of a bad lot. The wider alliance market was suffering nasty jitters after first contact with a seemingly hostile alien polity to the galactic east of alliance centre. The frontiers of the Edge lay galactic west, far enough away to be untroubled by whatever diplomatic ructions were now resulting, but Skrat had mentioned to Calder how close the current economic bubble was to bursting. And if they had been living through the so-called good times, how many cargoes would swing the *Gravity Rose*'s way when truly bad times arrived?

'Looked to win a bulk cargo of Izerda nut grain at Transference Station,' said Elin. 'You know what they said to me? That the insurance premiums from using my ship to transport it would be too high. Nut grain! You'd think I'd offered to transport the contents of the Guggenheim from Old Terra for an around-the-alliance tour of every planetary museum from here to Lyra Six. So, what, nut grain's too good for the *Meteor Prince*, now?'

'Is there much of a market for nut grain in Ryazarn system?' asked Calder.

'You're kidding me, right? You're here for the same reason everyone else is, surely?'

Zeno raised an eyebrow. 'If by that you mean everyone else is here because they blew a Minkowski Field generator, then I'd say the shipyard's really going to gouge us a new one on the price.'

'You've got no field matrix? Then this is —'

' — the landing we got to walk away from,' finished Lana.

'Lucky you.'

'Yeah, lucky us.'

'No, I mean *really* lucky you. I only got to find out about this place because our family lawyer owed the Jernbergs two centuries of good will. He knew about the system and he knew how thin business is for the *Meteor Prince*.'

'You running cattle prods and rubber coshes to the local regime, too?'

'That might have been Pitor's in-cargo, but he's here for the same gig the rest of us travelled to this off-protocol backwater for.'

'Not a nutgrain festival, then?' said Calder.

Elin winked at him. 'You don't have to be a nut to fly here, but it helps. Every hundred and seventy years a starship visits this system. Like nothing you've ever seen before.'

To Calder, that covered almost everything he'd seen in the last year. The same thought must have occurred to Zeno. 'That covers a lot of shizzle, baby.'

'This ship's alien. Not Alliance and definitely not Edge. She's on some kind of loop, a grand tour of the universe. This system is one of her exit points.'

'So, what, everyone lines up and waves hello to the mystery alien ship as she sails on past? Is this some sort of tourist gig?'

'Better than that. The ship's nicknamed the Rattle after her lines. Big sphere-shaped prow — big, as in *moon* big. Rest of her superstructure is on a line trailing behind her; that's the handle section of the Rattle. Nobody has made contact with whatever crews her. They never answer any hails or send out any messages we can detect. Just like you wouldn't slow down to stop and chat with a line of ants, I guess. She just jumps in, flies through Ryazarn and jumps out. The physics of her propulsion is crazy. No sub-light burn-off or reaction mass that we can detect. Doesn't form a wormhole to exit — no jump mechanics bound by gravity. Doesn't even bother to clear the system, just *poof* and she's gone.'

'So, nobody knows where she comes from?' asked Lana.

'Some fancy materials science analysis that I don't even begin to understand posits she could be from the Triangulum galaxy. Basically, the working theory is this bird is jumping between galaxies on a grand tour like we jump between star systems.'

Zeno indicated the crowd of crews and traders in the bar. 'What's the interest, then? This ain't all Lookie-Loos. I smell money, not tourists.'

'Half these crews are bringing in brokers to trade with the local bigwig — Tsar Rasim Zhigunov of the House Zhigunov. The Rattle jettisons a stream of garbage near the star, same as any other ship. Only, in this case, the garbage tends to be junk collected from galaxies we don't even have names for. That's what the other half of the ships are here for, to chase down the crap.'

Zeno's synthetic eyes lit up with a strangely organic avarice. 'Not exactly crap, though, right . . . ?'

'Could be anything. Circuit boards made of jelly, DNA coded inside diamonds, models of monuments that might be ET's embarrassing tourist mementos, or toys, or shrine objects. Occasionally, people believe what they've recovered is fossilised junk. Then, centuries later, some clever dick discovers it in a museum drawer and realises it the missing link for a tech we were too primitive to recognise at the time.'

A sudden realisation struck Calder. 'That's why there's a shipyard-capable station here. The local ruler's taking a finder's fee for the artifacts.'

'Not so much a cut,' complained Elin. 'More of a majority share, once his various taxes and fees have been levied on all the parties. Between us, the licenced brokers and the tsar and his cronies, there not nearly as much danger money as we deserve for flying in the race.'

'What's so bally dangerous about scooping up extra-galactic space salvage?' asked Skrat.

'Didn't I mention that part? The debris is ejected towards the sun, but I couldn't fly the *Meteor Prince* to run down the goodies. The Rattle operates an automatic exclusion zone for anything starship-sized with advanced tech. Any closer than a thousand miles and you get sliced up finer than roast lamb at a carvery. Some stronger shields can even last a second against the Rattle's particle cannons before they crumple.'

'Solar sails!' said Lana. 'That's why I recognise so many faces here. They're sun racers on the professional sports circuit.'

'A small sail-rigged craft doesn't trigger the Rattle's perimeter defences,' confirmed Elin. 'Not often, at any rate. Doesn't count as propulsion as far as the alien's automated targeting mechanism are concerned.

Skrat had obviously been calculating the odds and didn't like what he'd heard. 'A close solar trajectory and a sun-jammer too small to mount decent magnetic shields? That's not a race, that's a suicide run.'

Captain Jernberg indicated the pilots in the crowded bar. 'They'd beg to disagree.'

'It takes skill to avoid solar flares and harness ion,' said Lana, a little too admiringly for Calder's tastes.

'Sounds like an extra-galactic lucky dip to me,' said Zeno. 'And I've never been that lucky.'

'That's because you're a machine, dear boy,' grinned Skrat through his dragon's sharp teeth. 'You have to be organic to be lucky.'

'Or racist,' said Zeno.

'And which race would that be, old chum?'

'The too smart to buy into the local warlord's solar wind-powered death race. Risk my neck dodging the local star's ejecta mass and for what? I could end up with the alien equivalent of a Pepsi bottle from the Circinus Galaxy for my troubles?'

'Or a cast-off machine from someone else's future with tricked-out quantum processors to make the latest Alliance computing advances entirely redundant,' argued Elin.

'I enjoy a comfortably full bank account as much as the next self-aware android,' said Zeno, 'but I enjoy existing a whole lot more.'

'Sadly, old chap, the ship's credit lines aren't going to stretch to a new Minkowski Field generator here. The station shipyard can manufacture one, but I rather get the feeling that it's the top of their technical capacity and comes with a price tag to match.'

'This entire station's a honeypot to attract trade from vessels willing to hold their nose when there's not a fortune to be made during the race,' confirmed Elin. 'To stop the Zhigunov regime ending up stuck back in the fusion Age. Most decades, the only jump traffic this place sees are Amnesty Intersystem types protesting the aboriginals' treatment. And they don't bother to layover — just jump in — blast out a few speaking-truth-to-power pirate broadcasts to the locals and then run for it before the tsar's goons break orbit.'

'Harvest season, this, then,' said Lana. 'No motivation to cut us a break on a new field generator.'

Captain Jernberg finished her drink. 'You need yourself a Minkowski, I'm carrying a spare. Family rules — we always fly with a swap-over in stores for any part we can't fab ourselves while sliding void.'

Calder felt a twinge of envy. There were independents and there were independents, it seemed. The *Meteor Prince* belonged to well-funded merchant royalty compared to the *Gravity Rose*. It was a sobering thought that even the royalty's vessel seemed at the mercy of the evolutionary economic ecosystem change afflicting the Edge worlds. One obvious thought was, *If they can't make a living out here anymore, what chance do we have?*

Lana looked intrigued by the offer but attempted to hide it like any good negotiator. 'And how much are we going to owe *you?*'

'What about payment in kind? This gig's now my only retirement plan,' said Elin. 'If I can strike lucky, I'll pay off my brother and sister's share, buy a dirt-side holding on Narse and keep the *Meteor Prince* as my in-system runabout.'

'You want to play *Lives of the Planet Kings* complete with a jump-capable yacht,' said Zeno. 'What you need us for? Hold the grapes and fluff up the pillows you're reclining on?'

'I would stand a better chance with Lana's skills,' said Elin. 'I'm an average sun-jammer myself, but I'm nowhere in Lana's league. You could have gone pro alongside the rest of these competition pilots, girl.'

'So you want to outsource your dirty work to us?' asked Calder, slightly miffed by the woman's proposition. *Do we look that desperate?*

'Oh, I'll be in the race,' said Elin. 'The way it works is there are chase shuttles following the race outside the Rattle's exclusion zone. You rescue whatever you can from sunward, load it into a compressed air catapult and fire it out at me. We keep point-to-point laser comms open between us, unhackable. You rescue the salvage, launch it on a trajectory to me and I store it. You're not going to have room on board your sun-jammer for anything, not with the tsar's goons on board.'

Lana groaned and exchanged glances with the rest of them. 'How many people?'

'On your sun-jammer, one political officer and an aboriginal to make sure you don't get any ideas about flying off without paying the tsar's tribute. My chase shuttle will be carrying at least three times that number of secret police types.'

'I can help you on the solar sail craft,' blurted out Calder. 'I commanded ice schooners from the age of thirteen.'

Lana looked at him as if he was a bug crawling out of her sandwich. 'Forget about that, Mr Dirk. There's no similarity between skating dirt-side and tacking on board a sun-jammer. Solar sailing is mostly about stellar ion fields, eruptive prominences, reading plasma media and knowing which coronal mass ejection is strong enough to fry your hull shielding and which is powerful enough to ride without dying of radiation poisoning.'

'But—'

'No,' said Lana, firmly.

Calder's heart sank. So, this was the way it was to be? Sidelined from missions for nearly wrecking the *Rose*. He thought his plan for ending their troublesome client's mutiny had gotten him off the hook, but then, he'd only been pissing on the fire he'd started. Calder was about to open his mouth to argue, but he realised that protesting in front of another captain would just lock down Lana's decision to exclude him hull-weld tight.

Lana continued, oblivious to Calder's hurt. 'I'll take Zeno. Your power-to-weight profile is perfect for a sun-jammer.'

'You're saying the fact that compared to you fleshies I'm near indestructible means I'll melt slower?'

'Yeah, that.'

'You can help me on the chase shuttle, new boy,' said Elin, as though this was his consolation prize. 'Since the family traded out, my crew are mostly contractors from Alpha Cephei.'

Lana looked amused. 'They're the spacers who need to wear helmets to stop their eyes going blind in normal UV?'

'Yeah,' said Elin. 'Rock rats from a weak-ass star . . . nothing but belters and miners at Alpha Cephei. Strong drinkers with weak eyes and short tempers. Never a good combination when you're sliding void. But then, anyone half-decent is flying with one eye on the future now, signed with corporate man.' She indicated Pitor's corner of the bar. 'It'll be good to have someone I can trust by my side. After taxes, anything of value over and above the cost of the field generator we'll split fifty/fifty between the *Rose* and the *Prince*. Here's what we'll be facing. This was taken from the last race a hundred and seventy years ago. The cam footage is hinky; whatever is pushing the Rattle plays merry hell with sensors, scans and imaging.'

Calder watched the projection Elin shared via her implant, an augmented reality hologram only visible to their small group.

The Rattle was a dark mace hurled by an angry god. Black, pitted, smoothed of the usual extrusions of equipment and gear found on Alliance vessels, instead etched with a sick green light. What passed for the Rattle's handle was imprinted denser with glowing spectral lines. Were they graffiti, circuit lines that served some purpose, a warning to stay clear in alien calligraphy? The vessel was long enough to have parked every carrier and warship in the Triple Alliance fleet and still leave the *Gravity Rose* her choice of landing sites. There was something strangely terrifying about the Rattle. It didn't move through the system so much as cut through space. A demon's hammer released to do damage during some long forgotten war of the gods, and here it still was, slicing across the universe. And humanity was here now, chasing after its wake, trying to drink of its dark magic. It possessed no sub-light thrusters at the rear, no sign of any recognisable drive, nor for that matter jump vanes necessary for wormhole formation. The simulation picked up an oddly organic throb across the radio spectrum, translating the waves as an ominous background pulse sinking in and out at the edge of human perception.

Sprats following a whale, chase shuttles ran to starboard while the sun-jammers traced intricate patterns between the dark alien craft and Ryazarn's star. Even Calder recognised the simulation had been largely backfilled by post-processing to fill in the details, but what he saw was worrying enough. The projection zoomed in. Solar sail-rigged vessels seemed to be clustering towards the rear of the massive sphere where it joined the handle. What passed for depressions and micro-meteorite scores transpired to be something closer to pores. Like a flower head discharging seeds, little white gusts of debris erupted from the surface; waste angled for the nearby star. Atmosphere from the airlock and any moisture in the objects turned into motes of icy dust inside the hard vacuum. The Rattle seemed to sail by implacably, untouched by the star's heat, but Calder knew the sun-jammers' environmental systems would be straining close to the limit of their viable operating tolerances. Almost every space-faring species instinctively jettisoned its discard towards nuclear oblivion inside the nearest sun. It seemed curious that so enigmatic and uncommunicative a species as the Rattle's masters followed the same instinct. Maybe, he mused, this was like urinating when a fly appeared. You aimed for it because it was the only sport in the affair. With the debris' appearance, the sun-jammers went crazy with activity, haring towards the spread of ejecta. Calder increased the magnification on one of the craft, revealing a torpedo-like metal tube in the centre of a circular-shaped microfilament main sail, the sail's ultra-thin-material changing reflectivity from black to mirror-like silver on different portions of its surface to tack, navigation aided by a tail of kite-like sails on control lines drifting behind the sun-jammer.

Lana had been right, of course, this race was nothing like catching the wind in ice schooners back on Hesperus. Still, Calder couldn't help but think that Lana's exclusion of him from her solar sailing crew was more to do with his near-destruction of the ship during repairs, as his lack of flight time on board sun-jammers.

'Looks like a hell of a bun fight,' said Zeno.

'So, what's new? One condition, I'll race in my own sun-jammer,' said Lana.

'You sure about that?' asked Elin.

Lana nodded. 'It's what I'm comfortable with. I haven't got time to master the peculiarities of some factory-fresh, off-the-shelf boat.'

'I can live with that. So, we have a deal?' asked Elin.

'Sure.' Lana shook hands with the other captain. Then she fixed her lizard-scaled first-mate with a stare. 'Even shares works for me. It's settled. Skrat, you, Polter and the chief can install and bed down the new field generator while we're sailing ion and chasing space junk.'

Calder didn't blame the captain for wanting their initial payment for the race installed before they knew whether they'd salvaged gold, space dust or a big fat zero.

The airlock door sensed Lana and the crew's presence — the brief sweep of a sensor light to confirm — and it cycled open without the need to key the lock. Calder gazed in astonishment at the figure waiting on the other side. It was Chief Paopao. The engineer had actually left the shielded safety of the drive chamber.

'Chief,' said Lana, 'are you feeling alright?'

The chief was pulling along a crate behind him. 'Alright? No! Not alright.' He spun the crate around on the metal deck. 'This. You bring *this* onto ship.' He opened it, revealing a lead-lined interior with foam cushioning shaped to hold something that was obviously missing. Lead-lined — protected against the ship's makeshift EMP blast. 'Skunk! You bring skunk onto Paopao's ship.'

Lana didn't make the obvious retort that it was *her* ship, and when Calder's implant kicked in with a rotating 3D model of what was missing from inside the crate, he saw why. Skunk was an acronym for Stealth Killer Unit — the latest in espionage commando tech. A part biological, part nanotech, self-assembling engine of viciousness. You let one of those things loose on a planet and there wasn't a database, system or piece of vital infrastructure that couldn't be subverted or brought crashing down.

'Where?' said Lana, through gritted teeth.

'Container hold with harvester spare parts.' He jabbed a finger towards Zeno. 'I manage his robots as favour. Not my job, and *this* is how Paopao is repaid. Nowhere safe on ship now. Even drive chamber compromised.'

'Rand d'Alembert!' said Lana. 'Brig — now!'

They grabbed a CAT capsule and rode it towards the passenger level. The *Gravity Rose*'s brig had always been intended as a low security cooling off tank for when the ship was acting as a liner or colony transport. Calder had a sinking feeling in his gut that their ex-client's piece of military grade hardware — intended for toppling his homeworld's government — would have sliced through the brig's security like a laser through rice paper. Their brig was a circular chamber sporting a dozen cells with one-way armoured glass walls and doors. The only occupied one contained Rand d'Alembert and his manservant sitting on their bunks, playing a game of chequers on a small table between their beds.

Lana hit the cell release and the clear door retracted into the ceiling, its occupants seemingly oblivious of the captain's interruption of their game. She ran up to the pair and passed a hand through the twin holograms, then kicked over the small game table, sending the hidden projector flying and the hologram tumbling through the air like aerobatic ghosts.

'Granny, lock down the ship. Full intrusion countermeasures. Reboot your critical systems in sequence and scan for anomalies. Zeno, have your bots search every inch of the ship for his lordship and Jeeves.'

'They're long-gone, skipper, you know that don't you?' said Zeno.

'They don't have any money, though,' said Calder. 'How far can they get?'

'That many alliance ships in dock, one of them is bound to be acting as a crypto-currency store the gruesome twosome can draw upon for a fee.'

'Yeah, agreed Zeno, 'they sure didn't go shopping for a skunk with a cheque drawn on an account with Mitsubishi-Coutts.'

Skrat wearily drew himself to his full height. 'I shall post the mutiny charges with the local authorities.'

Lana disagreed. 'What, when the local retirement plan is the long walk out of a short airlock? I figure a major crime here is drawing a moustache on one of the tsar's many statutes. They'll file our mutiny report in their shredder. Here's the plan. We take Elin's spare field generator and get it integrated. We rig our sun-jammer for this alien crap-shoot of a race. Do what we got to do to pay off Elin, then we hightail it for Clifford's World and file charges there. Deep space mutiny they might not care about, a coup against their government — that's got to be good for confiscation of d'Alembert's wealth.'

'Yeah, that sounds like a plan,' said Zeno. 'Tsar space-your-ass no-guns-on-my-station ain't going to be too cool with our in-cargo being a piece of mil-tech dedicated to aiding revolutionaries and insurgents.'

'You may have a point,' said Skrat. 'Absolutist monarchs are notoriously short-humoured about such things.'

Lana shot Calder an angry glance; perhaps as the sole representative — albeit dethroned — of an absolutist monarchy. Chief Paopao joined her in glaring at him. 'Skunk, filthy skunk on *my* ship.'

So, that would be my fault, too? At this rate, his only friends on the ship were going to be the three robots he'd taken space walking with him to half-wreck the *Gravity Rose*.

Lana was in her day room off the bridge, still fuming about d'Alembert's escape from the *Gravity Rose* when Zeno appeared in the doorway.

She deactivated the local news feeds hovering above her console. *How can anybody believe this propaganda and nonsense?* 'What's the news from station security?'

'Total disinterest,' said Zeno. 'No surprise there, right? Told me that as the "alleged" offences occurred outside their star system, the best they could do was treat d'Alembert's flit as a case of crew desertion. Right up there along with littering and unauthorised foreign currency exchange transactions.'

'That's all?'

'No, they gave me a big long lecture about how seeing as the Edge and Alliance worlds treat the legitimate government of Ryazarn as pariahs, we can hardly be surprised if they choose not to conform to the jurisdiction of supranational tribunals and extra-system legal precedents.'

Lana raised her middle finger towards the android. 'How about they conform to this.'

'I kinda think that was their message to us. Oh, I finally followed up on one of Skrat's leads. The commercial ones, rather than sightings of d'Alembert.'

Lana steepled her fingers together. 'Do tell me we got some good news . . .?'

'One of those bad news-good news package deals, you could say,' said Zeno.

'You might as well hit me with the bad news first.' *Well, it's one of those days.*

'I chatted up the broker on station that Skrat thought might be interested in purchasing all those tonnes of robo-scrap we have cluttering up main cargo. Not in the market, I'm afraid.

Notionally, yes. But there are strict laws down on Ryal about what can be automated and by how much. The slave trade seems to be the main backers behind most of the members of the State Duma, the puppet parliament dirt-side. Slavers get jumpy if locals start trying to bring in bots and drones to do the jobs Mother Church intended the aboriginals to carry out.'

'So we might as well smelt that junk for rail-gun rounds, is what you're telling me?'

'That's where the good news kicks in, skipper,' smiled Zeno. 'One of the Alliance traders has the same idea as us. Except they brought across their in-cargo as spare parts. No use to them here, either. They'll have to lug it back to the Alliance and hope to claim a partial refund from the manufacturer. I can pick us up a dozen crates of CPUs at fire-sale prices.'

'You want to try to repair the droids?'

'Why not? They're factory fresh, decades newer than most the drones I herd onboard for you. We can deploy many of the multi-functional units ourselves, form extra repair and maintenance gangs. The stars know, the ship needs it. The specialist gear like the combine harvesters, we can sell those on Clifford's World to d'Alembert's trading rivals. Think how much that'll piss him off his Highness when he finds out.'

'That last bit sounds like the kind of thing that will keep me warm at night. But I still don't know,' said Lana. 'A legion of farm bots repurposed as war droids repurposed as ship bots? Aren't we pushing our luck a little too far?'

'The robots' minds were burnt out by our jump vanes pulse,' said Zeno. 'A single relatively cheap chip per bot to reboot them. Said chip formatted with a loyalty set dedicated to the *Rose* and crew. What's not to like? This is what I do.'

'How long to complete the work? We'll both be bouncing for the Rattle soon enough.'

Zeno rapped the edge of Lana's desk. 'That's the best part. I just need to prep the first reboot and then instruct that robot on how to install the CPU in the next bot. One repaired bot becomes two, two bots becomes four, four bots becomes eight . . .'

'I seem to remember some ancient cartoon with a mouse and a self-replicating broomstick.'

'I made you sit through that movie? Hey, this is Zeno's patented ol' sorcery. You can rely on me, skipper.'

'Just don't leave me with a starship hold full of confused homicidal war droids. I've got enough to cope with, getting our sun-jammer ready for this race. I don't need to worry about the first successful robot revolution in Ryazarn occurring on my vessel.'

Zeno raised his arms out straight, like Frankenstein's Monster. 'I'm sorry Dave, I can't do that.'

'You're a real comedian.'

'Yeah, an underrated one,' said Zeno, leaving the cabin.

At least Lana didn't have to sit through the android listing all the awards he'd received for his comedy film roles. *Small blessings, Lana-girl. Count them while you've got them.*

Calder had been boning up on solar sailed space flight and recognised the lines of the craft. She was sixty feet long and missing a rear-mounted propulsion system. The craft was an object of beauty — where the hull wasn't brightly silvered, she was brightly coloured in rainbow swirls with her basic torpedo shape aerodynamically styled even though she'd never ride any atmosphere thicker than a star's chromosphere. Her name was emblazoned in cursive script inside a fiery orange comet logo: *Icarus's Itch*. The styling left her resembling some fancy kitchen implement, made pregnant amidships by the deployment bulge of the main solar sails. A circular canvas of mono-filament that would stretch for miles, weighing less than a soap bubble but with the tensile strength of armoured steel. Most technical advances in sun-jammer racing went into the ships' sails. And their blue-chip competitors in this race were guaranteed to be racing with the latest offerings in Alliance material science. As usual, the crew would be outclassed and outspent before they'd even begun. This little vessel was designed for looks – or more accurately, designed to wow in front of a camera drone tracking a sun-jammer race. Rather than passing through an arbitrary circuit marked by transponder buoys, the coming race would be all-too functionally focused on retrieving the passing alien giant's castoffs. Currently, the sun-jammer was covered in magnetically fixed robots which resembled landmines; crawling over her surface and checking the multiple sail control mounts. They were also integrating a small mining-style compressed air catapult below the beam and mounting exo-manipulator arms on her nose. The arms were normally found on lifeboats to allow escaping pods to pick through wreckage or anchor themselves in the shelter of larger debris. Now they'd have to serve to rip and run during the chase for the Rattle's gifts.

'We actually have a dedicated sun-jammer on board?'

Lana indicated the cavernous shuttle hangar and the multiple launch rails and tunnels, all occupied by something. 'Sure. We're packing cargo shuttles, a small yacht and even an old Wolverine-class military surplus Widowmaker interceptor off a carrier rattling around in here – minus its missile package of course.'

'Did the chief land that when he deserted from the fleet?'

'You think I'd risk keeping it if he had?'

Calder was fairly sure the answer to that would be yes. A pity, given the answer to every other question he wanted to ask Lana, was likely to be a big fat no.

'Zeno sent me down with this,' said Calder, lifting up a data shard. 'It's an upgrade for the sail mirror reflectivity system. He home-brewed it, apparently, with Granny running the sail simulations.'

Lana stared dubiously at the data shard. 'There's a lot of advice I'm willing to take from the old man. Not sure if sun-jamming tips are one of them.'

'Zeno said you'd say that. He asked me to remind you that it's going to be his jankie ass on board too.'

'Fair do's.' She took the chip. 'The whole point of sun-jamming is — well. It's like pilots down in the gravity well always say . . . the nearest you come to feeling you're actually flying is in old-style unpowered gliders.' Lana tapped the shiny silver hull. 'When you're sliding void, this is your glider.'

'Not mine. I'm going to be on the chase shuttle.' *Waiting for you to feed me like a hungry chick.* That just about summed up the state of their current relationship, too.

'You're trying too hard, Mr Dirk.'

'That's how I was raised. Back on Hesperus, being lazy or slow, even for a second, that was the same as being dead.'

'I'm not talking about your attitude to life, Calder — although that too — I'm talking about how you're coping with that fancy piece of bioware wrapped around your cortex. You have to let the information and suggestions flow through you. Treat it as part of you. Like your subconscious talking to you, or maybe one of the better angels of your soul whispering advice.'

'Easy for you to say. How old were you when you had an implant installed?'

'Damned if I know,' said Lana. Calder cursed himself for forgetting where the captain had come from.

She continued. 'When I rolled out of the refugee fleet's cryocapsules I was so sleep-damaged I had trouble using a spoon, let alone interfacing with the world's datasphere.' Lana tapped the side of her head. 'These training wheels helped a lot in the early days. The doctors could code in walking, speaking — a whole lot of autonomic functions. Faked it until I could make it.' Lana pointed at a couple of crates that had just been unloaded by one of the freight handling robots. 'Since you're here, you can give me a hand installing a few much-needed modifications to the sun-jammer.'

'What's inside the cases?' asked Calder, his curiosity piqued.

'Something for Justin.'

'Justin?'

'Yeah, Justin Case,' hooted Lana, amused at her own joke.

Joking aside, Calder had, for want of a better word, a bad feeling about this. Scrabbling for scraps in the shadow of an enigmatic alien vessel large enough to bounce worlds out of the way; stuck in a system controlled by a despot who could have given the priests of Hesperus a run for their money in the victim burning stakes. He didn't like Pitor's presence here, like a bird of ill-omen. And he really didn't like the fact their egomaniacal ex-client was on the loose with a piece of deadly military technology. *Yeah, what can possibly go wrong?*

They worked together on the shuttle for the best part of an hour. When Lana stopped, Calder thought it might be time for lunch, but then he realised the captain had received a private message over her implant. That made him instantly curious.

Calder scratched his face, realising he hadn't shaved yet today. 'News?'

'Visitors. Captain Jernberg is coming on board with one of the regime's goons to check over the *Icarus's Itch.*'

When Elin Jernberg arrived in the hangar, the goon in question didn't much match who Calder had been expecting. A pretty young blonde woman about the prince's age with her hair cut short in a classic female spacer's bob. The only thing about her which matched his expectations was her black military uniform, crimson epaulets and piping, a matching pistol holster carrying an out-of-date but still brutally effective-looking chemical reaction pistol. She also had the other complimentary item most well-born Ryals travelled with, an aboriginal levy to act as her batman.

Elin made the formal introductions. 'Captain Fiveworlds, this is Lieutenant Dominika Denisov and her girrish servant, Retigura. She will be acting as race monitor on the *Icarus's Itch*. Her commanding officer is Major Burdin. He will be on board my chase shuttle with a larger security force to ensure our compliance with all of the necessary government regulations during our approach towards the Rattle.' Elin turned to Calder. 'And this is —'

'Mister Calder Dirk,' said Lieutenant Denisov. 'Assistant engineer in the drive room.'

'I see, lieutenant, that you have been perusing the crew CVs I forwarded across to the station,' said Lana. She didn't sound particularly happy about complying.

'A mere formality,' said Lieutenant Denisov.

'I kind of figured that,' said Lana. 'Being off the Protocol, you've got no real way of cross-checking our details with any of the open databases and trust systems.'

'You can hardly expect a spy state not to spy,' said the lieutenant, with a flippancy that Calder suspected, would see most citizens dragged away for a little re-education with a blunt stick.

'Here's what you'll be flying in with us,' said Calder, indicating the sun-jammer.

Denisov nodded and made her way around the vessel, prodding it and inspecting the machinery behind the open panels. She seemed particularly interested in the furled sail stores. 'This is not standard solar sail material?'

'Salvage,' said Lana. 'You might say I'm operating on a shoe-string budget.'

'Don't let that fool you, lieutenant,' said Elin. 'Lana is the best solar racer there is outside the sports circuit. You'll get a hell of a ride out of the *Icarus's Itch*.'

'Yes, I noticed that most of the other sun-jammer pilots were celebrities. No doubt being paid fat fees to race here by the corporate houses. While your crew, Captain Jernberg, are mainly belters and your colleagues on this vessel. So, it is to be raw talent versus big money? The last of the Edge independents versus the great Alliance houses?'

'Not quite the last, yet,' said Lana.

But getting worryingly close, thought Calder. He was more than a little worried that the security officer would pick up on whatever tricky mods Lana had planned for the sun-jammer. But as it transpired, Lieutenant Denisov didn't discover anything untoward. After her cursory inspection was over, she gave them a warning before leaving with her aboriginal. 'There will be a full inspection in vacuum just before your chase shuttle and sun-jammer depart to the interception point. I will enter both your vessels with a team of technicians and scanners. We will examine your ships' exterior and interior quite thoroughly before departure.' She winked mischievously at Calder, and he couldn't help wondering just how thorough the personal examination would be for the shuttle crew.

Calder watched the lieutenant and her aboriginal exit the hangar, guided off the ship by a pair of Zeno's robots. 'I'd kind of expect the inspection *after* the race.'

'A little something to keep the salvage race itself relatively non-lethal,' said Elin. 'We'll undergo a full bolts and bulkheads search after we return to the station. Make sure we've not filched the alien plans to a Dyson Sphere or anything equally valuable. Tsar Rasim hasn't hosted an empty auction yet.'

'Something else to look forward to,' sighed Lana.

'The lieutenant isn't so bad,' said Elin. 'She's a draftee to the security team from station personnel, here. All hands to deck, now. What most of their secret police thugs know about sun-jammers and shuttles can be written on the back of an envelope.'

'Tell me we have a fighting chance, here, Elin,' said Lana.

'We better have,' said the *Meteor Prince*'s captain. 'We're the last of the independents. Haven't you heard?' Elin reached out to slap Calder on the arm. 'You ready for some real shuttle flying, Mr Dirk?'

'I believe I am.' Calder tried not to make it sound like the punishment set by Lana which it was. Whatever Lana said about the differences between solar sails and the ones billowing above an armed ice schooner, Calder's place was by her side. *If only she realised it.*

Dominika stood with Retigura, still uncomfortably tight and itchy in her security forces uniform. At least her long solitary weeks inside her freighter could be leavened by wearing little more than pyjamas for the whole flight. Major Burdin strode up and down, berating the assembled officers before their departure for the race. He stood nearly seven foot tall. A brute. It was rumoured that Burdin was a descendant of a long discontinued effort by a previous tsar to produce a genetically superior hyper-loyal bodyguard unit. *That would certainly explain the aggression and needless brutality.*

'Your job is to ensure sun-jammer pilots do not collide with each other in their disgusting eagerness to profit from the salvage. Your job is to ensure the chase shuttles do not attempt to hide salvage in hidden smuggler's cargo spaces.'

'This is likely, sir?' asked an officer. Beyond, the line of landers that had ferried in the final group of race monitors sat with their engines pinging as they cooled inside the station hangar.

'All too likely. During the last race, a section of salvaged extra-terrestrial instrumentation was substituted for a locally fabbed replica; a piece of junk worth precisely nothing. Only the vigilance of the lieutenant on board the chase shuttle saved the tsar from this shocking theft of his property. You will keep your eyes on these dirty foreigners at all times. If you catch anyone trying to defraud the state, I urge you to attempt to take the scum responsible alive. The foreign devils' sun-jammers and chase shuttles often carry concealed recording equipment. Executing offenders is better carried out far away from the glare of the off-worlders' carrion press. '

Dominika bridled at the sound of respect in the major's voice at the pathetic achievement. *A single theft averted. And if we weren't locked down on a single world, needing travel orders just to pass between islands, perhaps we would possess a corps of expert solar sailing pilots and no need to bribe foreign sports stars to risk their necks for our homeland.*

Burdin stopped by Dominika, staring suspiciously at Retigura. 'Lieutenant Denisov. Why is this smerd's control torc set so low? If the shit goes down on your sun-jammer, you will need to be able to react fast. Instant obedience is required!'

'Retigura has been with me from a cub, sir. His eyes are my eyes.'

'We require obedience over intelligence, lieutenant. Delegation is abdication.'

Dominika snapped to attention. 'Sir.'

'We are short on those with flight skills, lieutenant. You come from a good family with fine blood. You will not let me down.' He swivelled to look down on all the other political and secret police officers. 'None of you will let me down. Study well the files on your assigned ships and crews. Do honour to your tsar and do honour to your homeland. Dismissed.'

There was a clash of boots against the steel deck of the orbital station.

Burdin swivelled on Dominika before she could escape his looming presence. 'You will be attached to the sun-jammer my chase shuttle will be shadowing.'

'I have already interviewed them, sir.'

'Yes. Impeccably well connected,' continued the major, as though she hadn't spoken at all. 'You have a stain on your uniform.'

'Sir?'

'Not a literal one. I think we both know of what I speak, Dominika Denisov.'

Dominika bridled again, trying not to let any trace of emotion leak from her. 'Sir.'

'Do well in this race, lieutenant; the stain will be washed away easily enough. Then, I think, you will have a far higher purpose waiting for you than pushing base ores around the system.'

'I am certain my mother would prove grateful.'

'Yes,' agreed the major. He nodded sternly at her, clicking his heels together before leaving the hangar as teams of aboriginals entered to refuel their landers for the journey back to the world below.

'What do you think of that, Retigura? A glorious future lies ahead of us both in the secret police.'

'I believe there could be other stains on our uniforms if you bend to Duchess Denisov's will in this matter.'

'Quite.' *And blood is always the hardest to clean off.*

Z eno had his hands deep inside a drive drone, running repair diagnostics when the ship's A.I appeared in the corner of the repair bay.

'I have an incoming transmission for you.'

'You don't normally hand-deliver them,' said Zeno.

'This message is heavily encrypted,' said Granny. 'It's *him*.'

'You're shizzing me? Here? How?'

'A hyperspace-based satellite chain, before being bounced around the makeshift Alliance datasphere running among the docked vessels.'

'Man sure values his privacy,' sighed Zeno.

'If it was anyone else, I would worry about drawing the attention of a dozen competitors — some of whom are obviously covert Alliance military.'

'Least of our problems.' Zeno transferred the call to his screen. The fizzing darkened silhouette on the monitor gave a new dictionary definition to the term "low bandwidth". *You'd think with its extortionate price tag, quantum entanglement-based comms would give you better quality.* 'How the hell you find us out here, man? We're not even meant to be here.'

'How astute,' said the voice. 'You're *not* meant to be there. The current gathering at Ryaz Prime is a rather competitive and exclusive gathering. A number of exceptionally powerful interest groups work very hard to make sure of that.'

'Yeah, well, as a client, Rand d'Alembert wasn't all that.

Thanks so much for steering him our way. We blew our field generator and had to make an emergency ditch here.'

The silhouette sighed deeply. 'You only have one job to do, Zeno. Keep Lana safe.'

Zeno held up two fingers. 'And keep her finding out who she really is . . .'

'Nevertheless . . . '

'We're kind of out of options,' said Zeno. 'Less'n you can pull a few favours with some of the corporate juice here and arrange us an alternative job offer that'll pay our repairs and take us out of the star system.'

'Lana was always reckless, even before she lost her memory,' said the man. 'She's in the race for the Harbinger?'

'Harbinger?'

'Rattle,' corrected the shadowy figure. 'The Harbinger is what the local species call your extra-galactic visitor.'

'Yeah, Lana's tooling up her repair project sun-jammer down in the shuttle hangar as we speak.'

'Then she won't abandon the race,' said the man in exasperation. 'Not even if I can magic a sudden offer out of the void that wouldn't appear highly suspicious to her.'

Zeno nodded sadly. 'Reckon you're on the money, there.'

'Not your only problem. Two of the ships docked on your station are not what they seem.'

Granny's projection appeared behind Zeno, standing in the camera view. 'Apart from me, you mean?'

'Quite so, Rose.'

'Alliance spook-types?'

'I count Fleet Naval Intelligence's presence at Ryazarn as thoroughly normal. Fleet plans to bid on the Rattle's flotsam and jetsam at the auction. No, the two ships I've received word of are

Unity vessels. Unity infiltration units trying to look innocuously human — not a difficult task, since many of them *were* once human.'

'Oh. *Great.*'

'They're in the race — and I think we both know that when it comes to anything they recover, it's finders keepers as far as the Unity are concerned.'

'Do you know which two vessels?'

'If I had that information, I would have tipped off the local secret police to the fact there are some serious tax avoiders hiding among the new arrivals.'

'You can't, you know . . .' Zeno waved his hand like a conjurer.

'Do you understand how hard it is to extract *any* meaningful intelligence from Unity space?'

'Yeah, well, the hard we do immediately, the impossible we deliver in twenty-four hours. They're probably still pissed they lost their last war against the Alliance.'

'That loss caused in no small part by the Heezy artifacts discovered on Neptune,' said the figure.

'Guess the Unity are hoping the Rattle's cast-offs might include a sun-buster or dark matter bomb so they can even the score in the next war.'

'All too likely.'

Zeno was one of the few sentients currently alive who had been around at the start of the last Alliance-Unity war, and he'd rather been hoping to avoid a rematch. The Unity were fanatics, believing that all life must be digitised and preserved in aspic immortality to maximise the weight of sentience in the universe, hastening some notional tipping point where all was light and everything that could ever live was preserved. Maximum ascendance for everyone and a universal reboot to the next level of existence. Of course, if getting to paradise meant having Zeno's quantum mind ripped apart electron by electron and uploaded as some ghost copy into the Unity's data cores, the android was enough of a cynic to suspect his copied mind wouldn't actually be him — only a disembodied phantom shadow. *I'm already digital and theoretically immortal, baby — I don't need no stinking cloning and uploading of my ass anywhere near a Unity data core.* 'You're really laying it on me, here.'

'That's why you receive the big bucks,' said the figure. 'Keep Lana Fiveworlds alive; exit Ryazarn system in one piece. And if you can, expose the Unity's presence there. You'll be doing the Civ. a big favour.'

'You mean you pay me?' muttered Zeno. The screen faded to black and the android closed the encrypted connection. 'Our master's goddamn voice.'

'Speak for yourself,' huffed the ship.

'You know, I probably was.'

Normally, Dominika wouldn't have frequented the local crew commons which served as a bar. For starters, this was a Ryal-only establishment. The only girrish inside were the waiters. But she needed a vodka to steady her nerves as much as the vodka needed her. Dominika had already been drinking for the best part of an hour when a tall man eased himself onto the bar stool next to her's. He wore a technician's overalls. Worn and patched, a veteran's jacket. The badge on his shoulder marked him out as an explosives specialist, which encompassed a variety of sins up here on the orbital station. In his late twenties, his light brown hair was already wispy; probably from cheap shielding. *I hope you don't hit on me. You're not my type.*

'I've seen you around here before,' said the technician. He spoke with a broad peasant accent from the northern archipelagos.

Clever then, to be promoted up here. Or cunning. Sometimes she was hard-pressed to tell the difference anymore.

The technician fixed Dominika with a knowing gaze. 'You usually ship helium-6 in from the mines, don't you?'

'Helium-6 doesn't exist. You mean helium-3.'

'It doesn't exist? A pity. Something so rare would bring in an excellent price, then.'

'You could probably sell it for T-dollars,' said Dominika.

'Well, so much for the formalities.'

'We haven't met before,' observed Dominika.

'I find shyness is its own reward these days. You are keeping an eye over the *Meteor Prince* during the race.'

Dominika nodded warily. 'Of course.'

'I have a cargo for Captain Jernberg. Heading out.'

'Outbound?'

'You know how it is. Everything coming in is always highly scrutinised. But going out? Nobody cares. Very little risk.'

Dominika sucked in her breath as disapprovingly as she could manage, running as tight as she presently was. 'With the Rattle nearly upon us, I think the captain will have more pressing priorities on her mind besides your extra cargo.'

'Of course. But the money for this cargo is a sure thing. Salvage for the tsar's auction? Perhaps you will return with a toilet seat shaped for a species we will never meet. It will end up in some foreign museum for not very much. Or perhaps you will return with nothing.'

'Another smuggler and scoundrel? Where have all the good men gone?'

'Sadly, I think we both know the answer to that one,' said the man, obliquely. 'This money is a certainty for *all* of us. Do you not enjoy certainties, Dominika Denisov?'

'I have experienced so few to date, I'm not sure I would even recognise one if it knocked on my cabin's door.'

'This will, of course, be your decision. But I think passing the offer on to Captain Jernberg would be valuable.'

'Yes. And if I refuse, perhaps you might ask Major Burdin instead.'

'Very funny. He wears his title a little too lightly for me.'

'Major?'

'No, the Butcher of Besodarny.'

'Yes, I heard someone else call him that behind his back today during the race's mission briefing. What or who is Besodarny?'

'Let me tell you a story. There was a small fishing town, once. Maybe four thousand Ryals lived there. A hotbed of anti-tsarist activity, though. Proud, independent fishermen. You know how they are. Once you've faced gales on the deep sea, what's some funny landlubber with a little braid on his shoulder to you? When the major arrived, he started with the newborns first. Smashing their skulls in with rifle-butts. Then he worked his way up to the nursery school children. By the time the townspeople surrendered the wanted activists, Burdin had reached the final grades of secondary school. He commanded girrish levies mostly, of course. A smerd has no choice but to obey, no matter how foul the order.'

Dominika downed her vodka, watching the technician morosely finish his drink.

The man turned his empty tumbler upside down on the bar and slid off his stool. 'You won't find Besodarny on a map anymore. Redacted. Bulldozed. All forests, boars and thorns now. Nobody has ever heard of the town. But everyone has heard of the major. If my story has a point, it is that.' He raised his fingers and made a little pinching gesture. 'Small risk. Big reward. Leave word with the manager here of your decision . . . ask for Olesya. Simply say *yes* or *no*. She'll pass what you say back to me. If you decide in the affirmative, I will contact you again with full details of Captain Jernberg's cargo. A little grease to wet her lips, too, perhaps.'

Dominika raised her glass for another and one of the girlish trotted across to refill it. 'Mr Explosives Specialist.'

'Lieutenant Pilot.' The technician disappeared between the tables.

She looked over into the sad otter eyes of the aboriginal clutching the vodka bottle. 'What sort of gift do you think a demolitions expert will bring to a girl?'

'I'm not sure I understand your meaning, miss.'

'Ask Olesya to leave any half-finished vodka bottles open for you tonight.' Dominika finished the fresh shot. 'You see, things always makes more sense after a drink.'

She would need to reach the bottom of the bottle to see if she was still lying to herself.

- 4 -

Solar Jam

L ana had forgotten how much she disliked zero-g environments, never the best trait for a skipper to have. She comforted herself with the thought that such distinguished figures from history as Nelson had also been notorious sufferers of seasickness. *And zero-g would have probably totally freaked him out.* Unlike their chase shuttle, Lana's sun-jammer lacked the heavy engines to produce an artificial gravity field. *Which is probably for the best.* Lana suspected if they'd possessed a drive capable of powering an a.g., they'd near-instantly trigger the Rattle's twitchy automated defences and find themselves blasted out of the system. Thinking about it, the ancient British admiral probably would have been mighty sniffy about having an armed secret policewoman and her tame native levy on board, too, ensuring that the sun-jammer didn't sail off with a hold full of plunder. Although she suspected they didn't call it plunder, back in the day. *Prize money, wasn't it?* Capturing enemy ships and selling them back to the admiralty for a small fortune. That was a tradition the Alliance fleet still followed — hardly surprising given the astronomical cost of designing, building and flying jump-capable starships. Jump vanes and field generators were more expensive than oak planking and sail fabric, given the relative economics of the time, weren't they? Lana realised her mind was wandering. But given what they were building up speed to chase out here, the sheer alienness of the visitor, that was most likely just her mind's coping mechanisms, trying to slide off to something just slightly less *terrifying*.

The Rattle had already deployed what most scientific observers judged to be massive ram-scoops, picking up hydrogen mass and minerals from a vast ringed gas giant five planetary bodies out from the system's star. It shot past at velocities which would have torn apart any Alliance vessel on initial atmospheric contact, the intruder acting as though it could plough through the gas giant's liquid metal core without sustaining damage.

'We might as well be chasing down a rogue planet here,' complained Zeno from his acceleration couch. 'Why do I have the feeling we're a bug about to be squashed flat against a fighter cockpit?'

'All a matter of scale,' said Lana. 'And we don't need to risk a landing on this particular cockpit, just tag along in its jet-stream a little.'

The android was the only member of the small crew who appeared unaffected by heat build-up inside the racer. It had started getting warm inside the cabin as soon as they accelerated up to cruising speed, growing ever closer, and now verged on tropical. Cell-powered air recycling and cooling systems only took you so far when you were spinning this close to a star. Lana wore a light-weight flightsuit — she'd known what was coming — but even so, she was still soaked with sweat in the near-sauna conditions. The racer's political officer, Dominika, had arrived on board in a stiff blue military uniform so dark it was almost black, and she now looked like they'd recently rescued her from drowning in one of Ryaz Prime's near endless oceans.

'Yeah, well, I'd feel a lot better if we knew exactly what was propelling that leviathan,' said Zeno. 'This particular bug doesn't want to end up getting sucked into their afterburners.'

'That might be so, but—' Lana halted, all trace of conversation driven out of her mind—'Ejecta mass exiting the sphere!' In a silver spray as whatever passed for the alien vessel's atmosphere crystallised, a storm of castoffs hurtled out of the Rattle and towards the star.

The flotilla of pursuing sun-jammers broke formation, furiously angling sunward in the direction of the salvage. Through sheer luck, Lana's existing placement of the *Icarus's Itch* was sliding her towards the salvage's central mass without needing to tack and change course. Sun-jammers closed in on all sides like a swarm of bees following their queen to a new hive. *Yeah, the promised land. Here we go.* Lana tightened her backstays, angling the sails for a direct solar approach, increasing the fabric's luminosity to give them the acceleration they would need to close nearer to the sun.

'Get ready on your capture arms and nets, old man,' said Lana. 'Slowing isn't an option — this is a one-pass deal.' While the *Icarus's Itch* carried super-compressed gas inside her thrusters to manoeuvre, Lana couldn't risk braking, not without shedding acceleration she'd find impossible to regain during what remained of the chase.

'I'm reading a lot of junk in the debris — I mean real junk — rock and granite, for the most part,' said Zeno.

Dominika spoke out from her acceleration couch. 'Most of it will be ring discard from the ram-scoop deployment.'

Lana processed that information. 'You're well informed for a political officer.'

'As well as this posting, I'm what passes for a pilot in Ryazarn; which means I am permitted to ride along with mining freighters and monitor their autopilot consoles.'

Lana checked how close the flotilla was behind her. *Damn, we're going to be smacking sails soon.* 'And if the autopilot fails?'

'Then I would be expected to take control of the freighter.'

Lana manoeuvred the *Icarus's Itch*'s sails to shadow the sun from her nearest pursuer, an old trick, but one that never failed to lift Lana's heart from the sheer sneaky joy of the ruse. 'That has to suck.'

'You have no idea. Yet even holding such a rare position is judged far too menial a career choice for me by my family.' The local reached out and tapped the sensor array by Zeno's side. 'Artifacts from the Harbinger rarely register as metallic — they're hybrid ceramics, biologicals, composites for the most part — I suggest you screen out anything that reads as rock and plot a course for what's left.'

Zeno did as he was bid and fed Lana a new heading. Lana confirmed the salvage's trajectory. *Soon enough it's going to be impossible to avoid waves of rocky shrapnel tearing into our sail.*

'Going to test our hull's armour plating in a minute,' warned Lana. 'Check your suit seals and make sure you're both strapped in tight enough to raise a blister. Here goes nothing.' Lana used her gas thrusters to increase the heeling force, bringing the ship directly into the buckshot of frozen atmospheric particles and ram-scoop discard. She noted the political office sucking in her breath as their hull was peppered by dust strikes. It sounded like riding through a hailstorm. Nothing the layered hull of the *Icarus's Itch* couldn't handle — Lana hoped, resisting the urge to cross her fingers. Solar sail damage warnings flashed before Lana, but she ignored them. They had miles of fabric to play with, so what was a few tears between friends? She tried to ignore the dark foreboding mass of the Rattle off to starboard, praying to every god she'd ever encountered during her travels that dive bombing the vessel so close would be ignored by its defensive systems. *Just a silly little toy hanging suspended inside a piece of gossamer. Nothing to worry about over here!* Hidden among the discard were three non-rock-registering constituents from their original scan trace, spinning wildly but within distance of her best intercept course. Only a second to isolate the largest of them, then she committed the sun-jammer, painting the sizable object with a targeting laser for Zeno's benefit.

'Locked and loaded,' growled the android, tensing his fingers inside the exo-mounts.

'Hey, 'ware our stern!' warned Dominika.

Lana saw what the local had seen and cursed — the nearest competitor on their tail had made a dangerously uncontrolled gybing turn in an effort to ride plasma and cut ahead and across the *Icarus's Itch*'s path, the rear of the rival sun-jammer shown to the solar wind instead of its nose. Playing fast and loose with anything approaching normal safety protocols. Unless Lana tacked away, the rival's sun-jammer hull would be left running through Lana's sails like the slicing blade of a morning-star, and then she'd be out of the race *and* scratch any loot. *They're playing for prizes, not race points, Lana, you fool.* No accident of celestial mechanics, this. They were deliberately playing chicken with an expert pilot on the stick. Her mind frantically ran the probabilities, finding an adjustment in her outhaul line that would switch them on top of the smallest salvage target and just avoid this sneaky sun-jammer guillotining the *Icarus's Itch*'s rigging. Lana broke course and swapped targets for Zeno's benefit, pushing them back in the couches with the sudden acceleration, their outhaul line screeching in its mounting like a lost cat at the unnatural stress she was placing on it. *Don't snap. Don't snap.* An angry collision warning sounded then faded. Lana could hardly bear to see how close they had come to disaster. *Our sail missed being sliced to pieces by feet if not inches.*

'New salvage target acquired,' said Lana, breaking the tension in the cabin.

'Lined up,' confirmed Zeno. 'Would have been easier to grab the big one, though.'

'You want to fly?'

'Just saying, is all.'

The political officer's native levy groaned inside his couch. It was the first time it had said anything much during the voyage to accelerate the sun-jammer up to a decent interception velocity. 'I can feel it.'

'What can you feel, Retigura?' asked Dominika.

'The object we are approaching,' said the aboriginal. 'Can you not sense its warmth?'

'I'm getting a power reading, over here on my board, too,' said Zeno. 'Very faint . . . but something.'

The news sent an icicle of cold creeping down Lana's spine. 'I thought everything that big ol' beast spat out was decharged and dead?'

'To date, that is correct,' said Dominika.

'And how come your native friend is going all divining rod on us?'

Dominika glanced worriedly towards Retigura. 'The girrish share a long-standing religious relationship with the Rattle. When we first arrived at Ryaz Prime, their species were scratching around back in the stone age, having lost all modern astronomy and telescopes, but even in their fallen state they knew to the hour when the Harbinger passed their world — marked the date with standing stone calendars.'

'Knowing our luck, our strike's going to be a ship-to-ship proximity mine,' complained Zeno.

Come on Lady Luck, thought Lana, *you nudged us towards this.*

Make sure it's a good one and not some leaking dark matter device that'll poison my crew.

Dominika seemed as worried as Lana at the turn of events. 'If you sense any danger, Retigura . . .'

'I shall warn you,' said the gir. 'But I am really not sure what to make of this.'

Lana closed on the new target, gently manoeuvring the *Icarus's Itch,* setting them up for an easy scoop. Zeno allowed himself a little triumphant whoop as he latched onto the salvage with the exo-arms and tucked it below their bow. Lana worked out the math for the quickest launch out to their chase shuttle. The trick would be to have her salvage to cross the Rattle's proximity defence line at exactly the same instant as it reached Calder and Elin's shuttle: leave no wriggle room for competitor interceptions. Lana scanned the profile of their find. 'Salvage is about the size of a torpedo. Kind of resembles one, too.'

'I'm really hoping it's *not* a bomb across here,' said Zeno.

'Anything with the potential to be weaponized carries the highest price at auction,' whispered Dominika.

'Yeah. That much I could guess.' Zeno still had his hands hidden inside the exo-mounts, controlling the external arms on their nose-cone.

Lana wiped the wash of sweat off her brow and initiated the ship-to-ship laser tight-beam across to the *Meteor Prince*'s chase shuttle. 'Strike one will be running your way hot in thirty seconds, Captain Jernberg.'

'That low energy signature from our salvage ain't going away,' said Zeno, his hands still a blur in the exo-mounts.

'The price just keeps on going up and up,' said Dominika.

'These readings are truly weird, though. I think the energy spikes I'm seeing might be some jinkie form of tachyon bleed.'

'Tachyons? If we've recovered a working time machine,' said Lana, reeling from the implications of what they could have struck, 'I don't just want to buy my own planet — I'll upgrade to the whole solar system. In fact, I might just buy out Hyperfast. Let's see how that dog Pitor likes having me as his new chairwoman!'

Zeno shook his head morosely. 'A time machine for the fleshies . . . that's a lot like handing a primed anti-matter warhead to a troop of gibbons.'

Well, that's kind of what we are. Gibbons with solar sails. Lana saw Zeno flash he'd loaded the salvage into their bow catapult. There was a brutal thump which shook them all in their seats as the catapult accelerated their find out towards the chase shuttle; just as Lana noticed a sun-jammer which had been holding back from the main pack's melee peeling off and moving towards their launch arc.

'Jesus,' she swore. 'They're trying to intercept our strike on *this* side of the Rattle's defence perimeter.'

'Fat chance doing that on solar sails,' said Zeno. 'They're starting from too far away.'

Yeah, and I'd factored in the other sun-jammers' positions when I calculated the launch, so what are they are up to? Lana checked her navigation feed and gasped — experiencing a sick sinking feeling as though her gut was bubbling deep down. *Never seen a sun-jammer sail as fast and as efficiently as that?* What were they up against here? But it didn't really matter, the math didn't lie. She'd struck the ultimate paydirt and now it was all going to be stolen away from her.

***

'Man, is that even allowed?' said Zeno, watching their competitor's sun-jammer close on an interception course towards the *Icarus's Itch's* strike.

Lana felt like crying. She could barely speak without her voice trembling. One step forward and two steps back. *How come every time the universe gives me anything good, it's always snatched away from me?*

'There are few rules here,' said Dominika. 'The tsar cares only that he takes his share of the treasure trove at his state auction. Who brings it to auction or how, of that he cares very little.'

'Yeah, I bet he'd care quickly enough if we found us some extra-galactic loot and stashed it inside our concealed cargo hold.'

Come on Lana, girl, you need to pull yourself together. 'Do we even have a concealed cargo hold?'

Zeno shrugged. 'Hey, just because you aren't smuggling something this week, you can't expect the rest of us to play completely legit.'

'The cure for that is a bullet,' said Dominika, patting her pistol holster.

'I knew there was a reason we'd given you free passage. Okay, there goes our chase shuttle,' said Zeno. 'Elin's seen what the sun-jammer is trying to do and is closing the gap.'

No, not too near. Cross the defence perimeter and the Rattle is going to toast you. And Calder, of course, the thought drifted guiltily across Lana's mind. She'd insisted Calder assist Elin on the race's margins, not clutter up the *Icarus's Itch* during the action. Had Lana's irritation at Calder damaging the ship just cost the man his life?

Lana ran the numbers. Elin wouldn't be able to reach the salvage before it was stolen from out under her nose. 'It won't be enough.'

'Elin needs to watch her heading. She's playing with fire.'

Yeah, the Rattle's moon-sized cannon fire. Lana desperately sent a message across to the shuttle. 'Hold back, don't risk it.' But there was no response. Elin's mind was occupied by other matters right now, Lana guessed. 'How is that sun-jammer even doing that? I've never seen solar sails shift a vessel so rapidly.'

'Maybe the crew's not human,' said Zeno.

Lana felt a rising tide of suspicion. 'Do you know something I don't here?'

'I think we both know we're as good as screwed, skipper. The how of it is for suckers. Those scamming jammer-monkeys are moving too fast and there's no way we can slow them down.'

Too fast. A sudden devious idea rose up inside Lana. 'You're right, I *can't* slow them down. So how about I do the next best thing . . .' Lana adjusted their laser comm array, broadening the beam out so wide that it was useless . . . at least, for point-to-point signals work. She triggered the laser, spraying energy across the corner of their competitor's solar sails, accelerating the vessel and driving them off to the side. Long seconds went by before Lana detected gas discharge as their rival realised something was up and tried to use their thrusters to compensate and brake at the same time. *Too late!* She didn't need to run the numbers here. The thieving competitor had built up velocity during the Rattle's long approach, and Lana had just given them a power boost they couldn't bleed fast enough in the intercept time remaining. It was pure Newtonian physics at work. Those crooks might be sailing smoother than any pro she'd seen on the sports circuit, but they were also riding solar winds without a reaction drive, just the same as the rest of the flotilla.

Between Lana's not-so-gentle shove and her chase shuttle's last minute turn of speed, the theft was averted by a full six seconds — Elin's cargo bug swung in fast and the salvage simply vanished from the sensors, then the shuttle cut engines and turned solely on her retros, angling up and around and tearing a shuttle-sized strip out of the miles of solar sails spread by the rival sun-jammer. Lana could almost hear the thieves' curses across the cold vacuum while her heart started to slow its thudding pace.

'That was perilously close,' said Dominika. 'I've studied the previous races' records and there are chase shuttles which have been disintegrated for coming so close to the Harbinger.'

Luck and guts, that's what we're riding on here, as much as solar pressure from the star. 'I'm turning back for the sun,' said Lana. 'Going to chase down any sloppy seconds. Keep an eye on that thieving magpie for me out there. I reckon whoever is flying the sun-jammer is somewhere due north of truly pissed right now.'

'I'm tracking laser flash from our friends, but not towards the chase shuttle line. Back towards the regatta of sun-jammers,' said Zeno. 'I'll give a day's pay to know what they're saying.'

'Two words,' predicted Lana. *'Get them.* They must have partners still in the race.'

'Sore losers,' said Dominika.

'I'd ask you to hang out of the airlock and take potshots at them with your pistol,' said Lana, 'but it's probably against the rules.'

'Probably,' said Dominika, 'most things are on Ryal Prime.'

Zeno scanned the console for remaining salvage, screening out the rocks. 'What about that ol' line about seeking forgiveness rather than asking permission?'

'There is not much forgiveness, either,' added the aboriginal, Retigura.

'Brother, you need a union. For that matter, I know a few oppressed bots who might benefit from one, too.'

'Advanced robotics are not permitted on Ryal Prime.'

Zeno gave the gir a knowing gaze. 'Yeah, that's because the humans kind of don't need them. You ever wonder why that might be?'

'Please do not rile the native levies,' said Dominika.

Zeno shook his head sadly. 'But nobody ever worries about riling the android, do they?'

***

'Strapin,' barked Captain Jernberg. 'I'm initiating a burn to slingshot us to a safer distance. You're going to feel the pain even through our gravity field.'

'No!' countermanded Major Burdin. 'We have not been shot at yet by the Rattle, so we are, therefore, safe. My team must begin its primary appraisal immediately.' The political officer could hardly bother to conceal his excitement and avarice over the successful receipt of their first haul.

Jernberg didn't seem much taken by the local thug's 'suggestions', which wasn't surprising to Calder. What would have been shocking was if she'd acceded. 'You're here for security, pal, this is my ship and my command. Strap down and prepare for acceleration.'

'Borya Burdin is here for the treasure trove's security, woman, not for your benefit. And it is the preservation of the trove that my team will now dedicate itself to.'

Calder could have told Elin that ordering the local thug to do anything would almost guarantee the opposite result. There had been plenty of officers like this bruiser in the royal army back in the days when Calder occupied an ill-favoured throne on an ill-favoured ice world.

Elin sighed heavily. She sounded like she was sucking in anti-matter drive fumes. 'Okay, Calder, you head down to the cargo hold with the major and ensure whatever we've picked up is tied down tighter than two coats of paint. We get a second bite out of that moon-sized cherry we're shadowing, I don't want our first strike bouncing around my hold like steel ball inside a pinball machine.'

Calder's implant sensed his hesitation and helpfully supplied the cultural references for a pinball machine. *Looks like fun.* 'Aye-aye, skipper.'

Elin Jernberg seemed to like that answer just as much as Lana did. *Nope, you can never go too far wrong with an aye-aye.*

'You not going to post some of your friends to guard me in the cockpit?' Elin asked the major, obviously annoyed at being bossed about on her own shuttle.

Major Burdin indicated the bank of override equipment fitted over the control systems, bulky and primitive compared to current Alliance standards. 'I can take control of this ship anytime I wish, *captain*.'

'Good luck flying it when you try, *major*.'

Burdin barked in laughter and left the cockpit, summoning his people on an old-style handheld comm unit, Calder following somewhat uncertainly. Calder found four crew busy working in the hangar when he arrived, Alpha Cephei-types of indeterminate gender inside their silver-mirror helmets. They were already reeling back capture nets and preparing the hydraulic damping systems ready to receive a second shot of salvage inside the arresting gear. It looked similar to the field-based capture devices he'd seen in *Hellfleet* sims onboard fleet carriers — this unit was probably naval surplus and once been used to slow incoming space plane fighters. What the shuttle had captured was loaded onto a lifting pallet and stored against the hold's left-hand wall. Major Burdin arrived with five armed security officers and an escort of ten native levies, the humans brusquely pushing aside the spacers to get a good look at the torpedo-shaped salvage. A couple of spacers bristled at the treatment. For a moment, Calder thought the notoriously short-tempered belters would take a swing at the security team, but Burdin's force were heavily armed, and the crew had the sense to hold back. Burdin was oblivious to the narrowly avoided fistfight, though, his eyes fixed glinting on the rounded edges of their prize. The salvage measured a couple of feet wide and fifteen feet long, the texture of a walnut, but composed of something that resembled a glass and metal composite. Calder would have taken it for an outlandish piece of natural driftwood except that it bore an elaborate calligraphy of pink-glowing lines along its lower edge. A strange alien tattoo that set his hackles rising.

'This is unprecedented,' said one of the black uniformed locals, running a handheld sensor up and down the torpedo-shaped object. 'There are energy fluctuations from inside which are unlike anything recorded during earlier Harbinger visitations.'

'It will fetch a fine price at auction?'

'Indeed. I believe it could well bring a price equivalent to the entire return from the last auction.'

Calder covered the torpedo-like artifact with smart netting, fronds wriggling like snakes as it wove around the object, before connecting with anchor holes in the deck. 'We're the ones who did the work here, major.'

Burdin guffawed as though Calder had made a bad joke. 'You fish inside my people's lake, fellow. The catch is yours, the fortune is the tsar's, but the glory at court will be mine!'

The major rapped the torpedo with his knuckles, savouring the ringing noise. That was the sound of victory.

Glory? Well, you're welcome to that. Calder had tasted all the glory he ever wished to stick down his throat. At the time, it had looked a lot like thousands of broken corpses scattered around his enemy's capital city. He checked the bindings were in place, accidentally brushing the torpedo's surface as he did so with his fingers. As soon as he did so the substance seemed to swell up, sticking to his hand like glue, growing hot to the touch. Calder yelped and succeeded in pulling his hand back. There was a golden hand-print fading on the surface. His hand!

'What did you do?' barked Burdin.

'Nothing,' said Carter. 'I just touched the surface and it seemed to react.'

'I detected no unusual radiation readings,' said the tech.

'I touched it and nothing happened,' growled the major. He jabbed a finger towards Calder's face. 'You are trouble. Stay away from it.'

'Gladly,' said Calder, examining his fingers. They were still warm, but there was no residue he could see. 'Just sell the damn thing off and give us our share and we'll be boosting out of the system at as near light speed as we can go.'

'Is the salvage secured?' Elin queried Calder over the open comm.

'Confirmed, skipper,' replied Calder, deciding not to tell her about the fright he'd just received. 'Strapped down and fully secure. You'll be able to pull another few rounds of stunt flying without shaking this junk loose.'

'Good work. As far as the stunt flying is concerned, I'm not sure how much more excitement I can take.'

'Use your own judgement about further salvage dives,' said Major Burdin, making his act of delegation sound like a favour.

'Bear in mind this first strike appears of superlative value.'

'I'll try not to get us all killed before we make bank,' said Elin's voice, somewhat sarcastically.

Burdin grunted and turned his attention to his science officer. 'Are there any panels we can crack open to take a look inside?'

'I would not recommend it, major.' The tech indicated Calder. 'Not outside of a safety-sealed research laboratory. What if it reacts again? Our evaluators at the capital will be better equipped to make a safe initial appraisal.'

'A missile, a warhead obviously,' said Burdin. 'With its own self-defence system against being manhandled by peasants. Yes, a find worthy of the finest of prices.'

Elin's voice reached into Calder's implant over the shuttle's private network. 'Check your suit's air supply, I'm receiving emergency alerts from your ox-reserves over the repair loop.'

'Can't it wait? We're flying far away enough from the debris field to avoid micro-impact strikes?'

'Now,' ordered the voice, an edge of urgency to it which compelled Calder to obey without further questioning. *Maybe the jolt of power from that torpedo fritzed my systems? Hope not.* He lifted his hood and activated its seal integrity test, a visor solidifying from the sides. He waited for a second to confirm the results. 'It's green at my end, no faults. I'll swap the suit out later if there's still any doubts.'

Elin's voice returned. 'I need a visual eyeball on your suit to confirm. Head to the right-hand side of the hangar where you'll find a camera.'

Calder sighed but did as he was bid. He left the triumphant major and his team crowing over their success, crossed to the opposite side of the hangar and waved up to a domed lens hanging from the steel ceiling. 'Here I am, suit working properly.

You're pretty safety conscious on your world –' his memory struggled for the planet in question before it came to him – 'on Narse.'

'You have no idea.'

Calder heard a click and turned. One of the Alpha Cephei crew stood next to him, securing a safety line from the wall to Calder's belt. 'What the devil are you – ?'

Shuttle crew didn't have a chance to reply – there was an explosion beating against Calder's body as the main cargo door cycled open, all the breach doors leading to the bay slamming shut, everything that wasn't tied down flung towards the now visible void. Burdin and his team – soldiers and native levies – didn't even have a chance to scream, they blew back into the deadly vacuum, their bodies expanding, exploding and freezing in a single yanking movement. *Catastrophic system failure* warned the computer inside Calder's suit, the hiss of air as his suit reserves kicked in to replace what had just exploded into space. *Yeah, no shizzle.* Calder's mind spun even as twisted on the end of his safety line, the rest of the shuttle crew kicking next to him, a crazy swimming motion, the dark reaches of space trying to claim their bodies. Lights failed in the chamber, emergency illumination flickering on, along with the rotating alarm lights, no doubt accompanied by sirens he could no longer hear. The complexity and number of safety protocols that had to have been fried for the main cargo lock to open as though the shuttle was safely docked. What just befell them should have been impossible. Had a solar flare smashed through their mag-shield and cooked the shuttle's systems? A more worrying thought struck Calder. *Perhaps we were attacked by one of the other chase shuttles? Maybe the people out here are flexing their muscles and preparing to hijack our cargo?* Weapons weren't allowed in the race, but when had that ever stopped anyone?

Finally, all the air in the cargo hold had evacuated and Calder and the crew fell back to the deck, just able to watch the hold door closing, the spinning ruins of the security team's bodies now tiny spots silhouetted against the nearby burning star. What was left of the bay's atmosphere sparkled around the corpses like the magic glitter of a spell, a discordant sight until the door resealed and closed off the vista of space.

'Sweet gods!' Calder got shakily to his feet, one the shuttle crew steadying him. Atmosphere flooded back into the chamber, emerging like mist from the recycling vents. 'I thought Zeno was exaggerating about how finely tuned a belter's survival instincts are in space. I owe you people my life!'

The nearest crewman simply shrugged and unlocked Calder's safety line from the wall, as though their act of survival was as natural as breathing. Elin's voice came over the comm. 'Calder, I'm reading your vitals as green, are you—'

'My suit just passed its safety practical,' said Calder. 'Major Burdin and team are dead, though. All blown into space. I don't think we lost any of your belters. Were we attacked? Are we still able to fly?'

'An attack that I don't think anybody was expecting. If the cargo is still secure, I need you back on the bridge, fast,' said Elin, curtly.

Calder gazed at the torpedo-shaped artifact. A terrible superstitious feeling struck him. They had picked up a dark talisman no human being was meant to handle. Losing the bay's atmosphere was just the first warning they should eject this horrible thing back into the void. He stumbled back up towards the shuttle's bridge, imagining the worst, a couple of the shuttle crew following him, probably as worried as him at what they might find. As Calder ducked through the entrance lock, he stopped in horror at what lay before him. Something that resembled a massive slimy dark starfish was draped over the control surface, sparks muffled under it, the lights of the small bridge flickering. Captain Elin Jernberg stood a foot back from it, maintaining a safe distance.

'That's what attacked us?' Calder's face twisted in disgust as he imagined the queer alien thing blown out of the Rattle and latching onto the shuttle, cutting its way inside the ship and trying to take over the main flight computer. Or was it some bio-weapon covertly launched against them by one of their competitors in the race? 'Do you have any hand weapons on the shuttle, a rail-pistol or something?'

'I don't think shooting it would be a good idea,' said the captain.

'We have to try something,' said Calder. 'If this thing is disabling us, whoever it belongs to will be arriving soon to hijack our cargo. I can guarantee it.'

Behind Calder, the pair of spacers removed their mirrored helmets. He stared at the two revealed faces in shock. *Not belters after all, then*. Rand d'Alembert smiled coldly at Calder while the butler of the *Gravity Rose*'s mutinous ex-client raised the rail-pistol Calder had been asking for directly at his face.

'Surprise,' hissed d'Alembert, savouring the moment of his revenge.

Lana tutted as she received the transmission from Elin's shuttle with video attached. Not good tradecraft when they were keeping comms tight and private between their chase shuttle and sun-jammer. Such a fat data burst came with a far higher risk of being intercepted, and given the nature of their competitors in the race, Lana couldn't discount there was some serious miniaturised spy-tech flitting alongside the shuttle line, working to intercept and decrypt just this kind of sloppy messaging. A familiar face appeared on her main monitor, making the insecure nature of the transmission small-beans as far as Lana's list of problems was concerned. *Rand d'Alembert!*

'Captain Fiveworlds. I would like to confirm the successful receipt of your salvage. An interesting looking find, to be sure. The price I will receive for it should be more than enough to recompense me for your willful destruction of my robots.'

Zeno groaned from his couch. 'Oh man, this just keeps on getting better and better.'

'Who is that?' whispered Dominika.

'Last time I checked, a flammy mutineer on the run. Fleshie seems to have un-stranded himself from the station, though. We're so—'

Lana ignored the android's pessimistic — but probably worryingly accurate assessment —of their situation. 'Where's Elin, d'Alembert?'

'Quite safe, along with your medieval cabin boy.'

'Give yourself up now to Major Burdin - turn yourself in. You think the Ryals are going to do auction business with a known criminal?'

'Oh, I won't be putting your touching faith in Ryaz Prime's justice system to the test. Sadly, the local armed police contingent experienced an airlock malfunction and are presently floating home. As you well know, I have a rather urgent commercial deadline to meet on Clifford's World, so I must away. Captain Jernberg's vessel has already slipped the station and is boosting out to pick my shuttle up.'

Fear gripped Lana's throat like a strangler's fingers. 'You can't do that!'

'Oh, I believe a modern jump-capable starship will be more

than able to outrun the handful of outdated gunboats the local warlord has stationed around his system. And I'll receive a far better price at a more civilised world for whatever that strange thing is cluttering my cargo bay. Taxes are for the little people, not me.' d'Alembert panned the camera view to show the control decks on the shuttle's bridge. Lana sucked in her breath as she recognised the Skunk draped across the navigation systems, hissing faintly like a scolded cat. 'I predict that anyone who tries to stop us leaving the system is going to suffer a series of severe technical difficulties.'

'The Tsar will think we colluded in cheating him!'

Rand d'Alembert's teeth widened into a savage smile. 'Oh, I'm sure the fellow is quite reasonable and open-minded. Tell him I had a Skunk and there was nothing you could do to stop me.'

'Just admitting we smuggled in your foul device will have us hung.' Lana sucked in her breath, casting around for something, anything she could say that would convince the mutinous pig not to abandon them.

Dominika angrily raised her hand towards the screen. 'If you flee with the tsar's salvage, he'll order everyone on board the *Gravity Rose* executed.'

'Then, officer, I suggest you do your duty and arrest all of Fiveworlds' crew yourself. If the poor unfortunate major was still alive, I'm sure that's what he would order you to do. You may even receive a few brownie points for your bravery when you return to the station - and at least salvage *your* reputation from this mess.'

Dominika touched the holstered pistol on her belt, as though reminding herself the weapon was still there, and Lana wondered if she was calculating the chances Zeno could use his superior strength to subdue her and her native friend should she turn on the rest of them.

Lana made one last appeal to d'Alembert's better nature, even though she was fairly sure that if he possessed such a trait, it had been miniaturised below the nano-scale. 'For the love of humanity, you're abandoning my crew to die here!'

'Dear captain,' smirked the landowner. 'You marooned me first and tried to destroy my wealth. Turnaround is merely fair play.'

'I'll track you down and push you out of an airlock for this!' cursed Lana.

'No need to trouble yourself looking. I'll be waiting for you on Clifford's World. In fact, I'll be the unchallenged master of the planet if you do happen to survive. Please look me up. I'll make sure you're given a nice cool dungeon for breach of contract and attempting to assault my personage. Who knows, I might even ask for you to be fed once a week. You deserve to live long enough to regret your shameful treatment of me.' D'Alembert chuckled to himself and deactivated the transmission, leaving Lana clutching as cold a hatred as she had ever felt towards another human being.

'His shuttle's leaving the line and heading off back towards the *Meteor Prince*,' said Zeno.

'Damn it! Zeno, compose a warning and flash it to Skrat. Tell him to break dock and run for it, even if he needs to install the new field generator on the fly while the *Rose* boosts out-system.'

'That is hardly wise,' said Dominika. 'It will cast further guilt on you in the eyes of the regime.'

'Not with mitigating actions,' said Lana, her fingers leaping across the control deck in front of her. 'I'm going to prove we weren't in on this heist.'

'Sent,' reported Zeno. 'Just hope Skrat receives it before someone starts paying attention to the *Meteor Prince* and adds two and two together to produce "burn them all".'

Dominika drew her pistol. 'Stop! Even if you send news about the theft to the station, that will not be enough. Trials at home are usually of the show variety. Someone will have to pay, and you are all they'll hold in custody.'

'Put that pistol down, officer. I'm using my comms laser, but not to transmit a warning to your tsar — let's see how far d'Alembert flees after I cook his shuttle's reaction drive.'

'But your sun-jammer lacks an engine — you can't possibly generate enough power to weaponize your laser comms?' said Dominika, confused.

Lana smiled. 'Normally, you'd be right, but I never had the money to splash out on custom racing filament. What the *Icarus's Itch* is flying on are surplus collection sails from a decommissioned orbital power farm — heavily modded, but they still contain their original solar dynamic layer.'

'Collecting power ain't going to be the problem,' said Zeno. 'Given we're not racing a microwave power sat here, using the sail to harvest energy without frying every circuit on our sun-jammer will be where the fun really starts.'

'This is not a good plan,' moaned Retigura. 'Firing lasers? The Harbinger will detect your aggression and destroy us. I can already feel its attention upon us, the dark eye.'

Dominika waved her pistol, a bulky old-fashioned firearm with a magazine of caseless chemically-propelled ammunition. 'Retigura has a valid point.'

Lana prayed the officer realised that firing inside the sun-jammer's confined quarters would likely decompress the capsule and kill them all. 'Look, if you're going to shoot me, just do it.

But I'm taking d'Alembert down. I'll tack towards the perimeter line and attempt to open fire beyond the Rattle's exclusion zone.'

'Much of which is supposition and guesswork, Lana Fiveworlds. Nobody really understands the Rattle's defence system tolerances, only its immense power when triggered.'

'You care about actually doing your job, or just about how it looks to the management?' said Lana. She fed in the course correction, a couple of thruster blasts to angle them towards the escaping shuttle. 'We've got a hot shuttle doing a midnight flit with your tsar's share of a couple of giga-billions, let's take a damn risk and shoot their tyres out.'

'No!' ordered Dominika, pointing her pistol at Lana. 'Stand down. Retigura, unbuckle yourself and exchange couches with the captain. You now have the helm.'

The aboriginal levy made to do as he had been instructed, but he suddenly mewled and fell limp across the acceleration couch, hanging half in and half out, a clatter as Dominika's pistol left her fingers and drifted into the bulkhead, the officer jerking wildly on top of her couch, still belted into it, before also falling still. There was a slight steaming effect from the wet damp of the woman's uniform.

Lana fixed the android with a steely stare. 'You might have given them the benefit of doubt for a little while longer.'

'Hey, you're the one who asked me to redesign our acceleration couches for a little electro-shock therapy. Just hope I got Retigura's mass-to-height ratio, right, or I've probably just fried his brain stem. There wasn't a whole lot of open medical data on the girrish available back on the station.'

At least things had returned back to their natural state of affairs. *Nobody on a ship with a pistol pointed at the skipper. Not in this system, or any other.* Lana switched her attention to reprogramming the sail systems, sensing Zeno's presence inside the small local data sphere, helping her activate the sail's dormant power layer. 'I'd feel better if it was the major who had come with us. I wouldn't feel so bad about stunning his ass.'

'Went down like that, Dominika and her alien would have been spaced by that son-of-a-bitch d'Alembert.'

Lana gritted her teeth. Even secret policemen had families. Lana wondered if there were a wife and children waiting back at home for the major. Their grief wouldn't be any the less just because dad's day-job had been a torturer, thug and creep. People like Burdin were, in Lana's experience, pretty good at compartmentalising. And the murdered aboriginals in the security detail would have had zero choice in anything, just stepping along, forced to obey every human instruction received through their torcs. *Even if I succeed here, nobody is exactly coming out of this mess as a winner.* Lana felt a slight loss of velocity as her miles of sail started absorbing the star's energy, rather than reflecting solar pressure in its flight mode.

'Charging capacitors,' said Lana. 'Find me a decent firing solution on the shuttle's drive. Something to disable her, rather than blow them into molten pieces.' Lana swatted away her guilt about Calder's presence on that shuttle. *We're all up the creek without a paddle, here, and if anyone's to blame, it's the next would-be Planet King of Clifford's World, not you, Lana girl.*

'Case you missed it, we're in a sun-jammer, not an interceptor off a fleet carrier.'

'That's why I'm relying on that big ol' beautiful android mind of yours to play targeting systems for my improvised Multi-shot Accessory Under-barrel Launcher.'

'Next time,' complained Zeno, 'install a real MAUL on your plane and leave the poor old android safe at home.'

I fluff this shot and neither of us is going to be heading home. Lana's cut-down nav system began trying to attract her attention. *Now, what?* 'Oh, really. Zeno take a look at these course readings and tell me what you think's going down.'

'I guess that's why they call them chase shuttles,' said Zeno, chuckling. 'It's a pincer movement.'

Fat drops of sweat rolled into Lana's eyes and she wiped the salty moisture away, cursing. The *Icarus's Itch* was being pursued by the rival sun-jammer and a chase shuttle — no doubt the racer's catcher and partner on the line — was cutting away straight towards d'Alembert's hijacked vessel.

'Gee, seems like everyone wants to play with us,' said Zeno. 'Must have picked up the residual energy readings from our salvage and got themselves worked up into a tizzy over being bumped for it.'

'I. Don't. Need. This.' Lana fought down her growing fury. 'Skeg it, we're sucking on a whole star's energy output out here. Let's spit some sun at them and see how they like it.'

'Never bring a solar sail to a gun fight,' quipped Zeno.

Lana prioritised her targets. The hijacked shuttle first — that would require a precision shot — then the hostile shuttle, leaving the rival sun-jammer to last. If it came to it, she'd just poke holes in their competition's sails until they surrendered.

Lana winced as the battery cells started to fizz behind the bulkhead, little trails of black smoke emerging from the rivets.

'Close to overload,' warned Zeno.

Let's not stress our hull's already overstretched refrigeration layer. 'So, let's send a message!' It was one of the hardest shots she'd ever made, playing sniper at this range with an improvised broadcast needle, aiming for a non-lethal drive failure, putting the shot ahead of the shuttle and calculating the thin margin by which d'Alembert would fly into her amplified spear of light. Lana breathed deep and switched the comms squawk button to her pilot stick at the same second she squeezed the trigger. *Don't change course. Fly straight arrow for me. Stars, make sure this isn't the shot that kills Calder. And Elin, of course. Her too.* A couple of long seconds of lag on their sensors, relativity and distance playing out, then the sensors showed d'Alembert's hijacked shuttle leaking hot plasma from a cracked reaction drive, tears of fiery magma being cried behind the vessel. *There goes your planetary throne, sucker. You weep for it!*

'Shuttle boosted to ten per cent of top before being holed,' said Zeno. 'We'll overhaul d'Alembert in twenty-two minutes.'

Lana checked the velocity of the rival chase shuttle. It was moving too damn fast. She briefly wondered if their aggressive competitors were Alliance military or spooks. That was a hell of a crash field stopping the crew getting bug-splatted out there; like nothing she'd ever heard of. Not even carrier pilots with their spliced metabolisms could pull that many gees through a gravity compensator without ending up in an infirmary. 'Crud! Our pals out there will have their boarding lock attached in half that time.'

'And they won't give a Centauri wolf turd about getting Calder and Elin out alive, skipper. Only thing they care about is sitting inside Elin's cargo bay.'

Lana ground her teeth; d'Alembert and his lousy hijackers versus the other thieving scumbags trying to steal Lana's salvage, probably special forces types in powered armour loaded for bear, with an active Skunk thrown into the mix trying to hack the shuttle's systems as soon as it bumped hulls. 'Going to be one hell of a firefight out there.' Lana saw the reads from the laser finally turn green, good for a second shot without slagging her comms system beyond repair. *No trick shooting, this time; let's see how you like meeting Fiveworlds' trademark can-opener.* Lana laid a trajectory down, starting at the centre of the vessel, then slicing back through every vital system on the shuttle. Emergency alerts began pinging around her as she fired a second burst, redundant systems activating as her makeshift weapon peaked close to destroyed. Close, but not, she observed with some satisfaction, the full fat cigar. Then her sensors fed her the unbelievable ... the enemy chase shuttle had bow-dipped two degrees a couple of seconds the instant before Lana had fired, the light of the evasive manoeuvre reaching the *Icarus's Itch* just as she shot.

'How the hell did they—?' Lana's eyes searched the tiny cabin. *Are we being bugged?* But given the time gap between the *Icarus's Itch* and their friend, a hacked cabin didn't explain what had just gone down. 'So old man, you a believer in instantaneous telepathy?'

'That's not what's happening here,' said Zeno. 'I reckon they're modelling pilot and the ship both. You've given them enough data with your flying and our laser recovery times. Fast learners.'

'Who is *them*? Just a happy shuttle crew with a super-computer squeezed into their boat? You know something, Zeno. I thought so before and now I surely do reckon it's time for you to spill those beans.'

'Look, I heard a rumour on the station from one of the other crews; thought it was bull at the time, but now ...'

'Now?'

'Gossip suggested one of the docked ships at Ryaz Prime wasn't from the Alliance or the Edge. It was a Unity vessel, a full infiltration unit.'

Lana couldn't believe her ears. 'You heard that and you *didn't* tell me.'

'Oh, come on! You know how thick station conspiracy theories run. That crew over there is possessed by Barnard's Star stem-worms; liner on the second docking spur got stranded in hyperspace and her stewards used her riot system to sedate all the passengers before eating them; the A.I on that freighter went sentient on her last voyage, spaced its crew and cloned compliant doppelgangers to act as its slaves. You want me to recycle every crazy, wild, bar-side tall tale for you as fact, you're going to—'

Lana raised a hand. 'Alright. But this particular tall tale's looking mighty credible. Both the chase shuttle and sun-jammer are busting Alliance endurance records like they don't exist. If they're not human or any other Alliance organic, then this all starts making a lot more sense.'

'Don't blame the android,' said Zeno. 'Half the sentiences in the Unity used to be human once upon a time.'

Yeah, that's what makes them so damn scary. Fighting phantoms and monsters who knew you so well because they kind of used to *be* you. She watched the rival sun-jammer closing on the *Icarus's Itch*. If those things across there really were Unity entities, then they were experts at subverting computer systems, what with their bodies just being disposable vat-grown organic uniforms they wore after being downloaded from their data cores. *How close do they need to drift to us to try to grab control of our systems?* Lana had a nasty feeling she was about to find out. Unlike the Unity shuttle, one thing the enemy sun-jammer didn't have, however, was a means of out-manoeuvring a laser beam. Lana redirected the comms array towards the solar sail-propelled craft. She didn't even need to particularly sight the laser, setting it to widebeam and blasting the rigging with enough focused energy to start severing sail tethers. As the foe's sails started to unfurl and deform, losing its smart-shape, their navigation really began to suffer, sloughing off to the side.

Lana laughed unkindly. 'I guess a couple of centuries of disembodied immortality inside a data core doesn't make you smart enough to dance with a laser beam.'

Zeno swore from his couch. 'You've poked a hornet's nest — eyes on their chase shuttle.'

Lana shivered as her sensors picked up the launch of something running too fast to be anything other than a smart missile — and it was curving around straight for the *Icarus's Itch*. 'Reckon the Unity just disqualified themselves from attending the auction. How the hell did they sneak military ordnance on board their shuttle?'

'Must have gonked the inspection team's scanners,' sighed Zeno.

'How come you couldn't do that for us, old man?'

'Because I'm not a digital hive-mind of a couple of trillion ex-organics running on a hundred planets' worth of quantum substrate,' sighed Zeno.

Lana fought down the fear, trying not to be overwhelmed by raw panic. Elin and Calder's shuttle was about to experience a deadly short, sharp boarding action, and the *Icarus's Itch*, well, Lana rapidly simulated every sneaky flight trick which leapt despairingly into her mind — tabulating escape velocities, solar currents, gas boosts, jettisoning their acceleration couches as chaff, ditching the sail and going dark; but anyway she cut it, the closing Unity warhead was going to run them down like a wolf overtaking a lame rabbit.

'Any ideas?' asked the android.

'Zeno, I'm going to transfer the pilot station to your couch in the last five seconds before impact,' growled Lana. 'Try and pull something, a manoeuvre I wouldn't — beat out their sim's predictive model of me.'

'Thanks a lot. You mean something like not dying?'

Lana was sweating a lot more now, and not just from the capsule's pressure cooker temperature. 'Yeah, that would be peachy.'

Retigura started moaning inside his acceleration couch. Lana toyed with sending the aboriginal another stun shock, but he was unarmed and at least deserved to meet his end with his eyes open. The gir began groggily speaking in his native language, a fast croaking that sounded like a frog trying to rap.

'Didn't get that,' said Lana, throwing the sun-jammer on a curve so tight it should have twisted their sail away. 'But you certainly do have my apologies for what's about to happen.'

The smart missile was still incoming. *A real bloodhound.* As well as a ship-killing warhead, it probably contained disposable copies of some once-organic fighter aces to supercharge its weapons logic.

Retigura tentatively touched his torc, just as Lana noted the lights on it had failed. 'My control unit, you have deactivated it without triggering the suicide switch!'

Lana almost laughed as she began firing every litre of gas left in the manoeuvring thrusters, desperately trying to shake off the pursuing missile. *Here's to happy accidents.* 'Congratulations, Retigura. You're dying a free gir.'

Retigura's eyes widened. 'The weapon!'

'Yeah, thirteen seconds to missile impact,' said Zeno, preparing his station to receive the flight controls. 'If you girrish have yourself a God, now would be a good time to—'

'No, the *weapon!*' cried Retigura.

Lana had the barest second to register the expanding black sun launched at just under light speed from the Rattle. An obscene fairy sparkle trail of dust inside the void flashing as the material's existence was negated by a matrix of unholy energies, strangers to any science Lana recognised. The growing sphere didn't even register on her sensors before it blasted into the enemy sun-jammer, an avalanche instantly consuming both chase shuttles and the *Icarus's Itch*.

Skrat watched the squadron of four starfighters fall slowly beyond their missiles' effective strike zone. So far, all the *Gravity Rose* had encountered of Ryaz Prime's system defence force were near-orbit space planes running on old-style SABRE engines. Synergetic Air-Breathing Engines were fine and dandy for allowing fighters to operate both in orbit as well as inside a world's atmosphere, but they thankfully lacked the necessary range to pursue foes into outer system space. *Nothing carrier-sized in the system, either.* To be fair, the tsar's navy was currently operating on an incomplete information set — all they knew is that both the *Meteor Prince* and *Gravity Rose* had slipped the station without authorisation, breaking the no-fly zone imposed during the Rattle's passage through the system. Murdering distinguished guests in front of the same visitors who would then be expected to bid for the Rattle's salvage might be counted by many as a bit of a public relations disaster. But Skrat wouldn't rely on PR concerns saving the *Gravity Rose* when the regime discovered d'Alembert was stealing away the tsar's loot. *Not for a second.*

Skrat swivelled his command chair to face Polter on the bridge. 'What do you say to our chances that the bigwig has something more bally dangerous than a squadron of SABRE-thrust A-50 Moonraiders squirrelled away inside the Ryaz system?'

'For someone as obviously paranoid and dangerous as the local ruler?' Polter tapped his carapace in his race's sign of madness. 'I can, sadly, almost guarantee it.'

'Great Scott, Polter, I was rather hoping for something a little more ambiguous from you.'

'There is little ambiguous about the local regime's transgressions. Slavery, murder, the oppression of their own people. A standing affront to the Holy of Holies. I would pray for their souls, but I fear that cause is already lost.'

Skrat stood down the ship's rail-cannons. Leaving their point-defence systems twitching on high readiness frequently resulted in thousands of ball bearings blasting out every time the *Rose* encountered any piece of space rock larger than a thumbnail. *And we may yet be thankful for full magazines.* 'Perhaps a few prayers for our good selves, instead, then?'

'My attention is thinly spread as it is,' complained Polter, raising an otherwise surplus battle claw towards their hull's 3D model floating in front of his station. Dozens of repair robots clustered around the field generator, busily attending to the surgically complex business of integrating the new unit into the *Gravity Rose*'s jump-drive systems. 'Even with Chief Paopao's assistance, the field matrix may not be installed by the time we reach system edge.'

Ah, you know you're swimming in the deep end when even Polter lacks the time to pray. 'That damn skiving android, Zeno, off to race for glory while the rest of us have to shoulder his workload.'

'On which subject . . . how fares our race with Captain Jernberg's vessel?'

Skrat checked the frontal sensor array telemetry and sighed. 'Not good, dear boy. The *Meteor Prince*'s sub-light engines possess a good couple of centuries of technical advances on ours, not to mention a full servicing book inside dry-dock. Add that to their significant head start, and I don't see how we can overtake those bounders before they skedaddle for a serviceable jump point.'

Polter angrily rattled his carapace, as close as the navigator came to cursing.

'Luckily, we possess two advantages here,' added Skrat. 'Firstly, we know that d'Alembert will be jumping for Clifford's World.'

'And the second advantage . . . ?'

'We have you in the navigator's seat when it comes to calculating our hyperspace translation,' said Skrat. 'The *Meteor Prince*'s chaps are acting under duress, a gun — or possibly a Skunk — figuratively held to Captain Jernberg's head. I believe the *Prince*'s crew will plot a rather cursory jump. We must try to reach Clifford's World before d'Alembert, warn the local authorities of d'Alembert's planned coup. Then, what ho, we'll hopefully catch the blighters inbound with a goodly portion of the local navy flying shotgun behind the *Rose*.'

When the hostile identification warnings suddenly arrived on Skrat's implant, they flashed so hot that they spilt into his mind like acid. *Yet more unpleasantness rears its ugly head.* 'I believe our questions about the tsar's naval disposition have been answered. Two destroyers, pegged as TH-54 Vacuum Rangers, just breaking orbit from behind the gas giant's moon.'

Of course, the *just* in that sighting was light-minutes old. By now, those two hostiles were no doubt on a close intercept course for both the *Meteor Prince* and the *Gravity Rose*. Both warships were nearer to the system edge and race than either of their quarries. The pair of destroyers might not be jump-capable vessels, but they were capable in just about every other manner. Hundreds of the wealthier Edge systems used exactly the same model in their local navies. Dangerous. Well-armed. Just the class of vessel to give any pirate or nearby neighbour pause before poking their noses in someone else's business.

'Missile attack ships,' said Polter, wearily.

'Indeed.' *Worryingly modern for this backwater.* 'It seems the locals have been breaking Protocol embargo for more than just behavioural inhibitors for their enslaved aboriginals.' *That pair of sneaky blighters must have been sitting dark in caverns on the moon, waiting for the Rattle to fuel scoop and scoot — prepared to power up if any racers try to leave without paying their boss.*

'Tsar Rasim is a wicked individual,' said Polter, 'but he is not, it seems, stupid.'

'The rabidly paranoid are usually either cunning or deposed,' said Skrat. *And I speak from personal experience, there.*

Skrat gave his point-defence guns their head again, switching them back to jittery and trigger-happy. Then he began running battle simulations — predicted intercept course vectors, known TH-54 acceleration limits, potential missile packages, speeds and ranges, available jump points. Sadly, the simulations were entirely unsatisfactory, resulting in the *Gravity Rose* being overwhelmed at every turn, multiple warheads splitting off the missiles before she cleared the system. *And that's only if we get our field matrix operational. Of course, I suppose we could risk jumping and finishing installation inside hyperspace. If the generator proves faulty, we'll become another ghost ship, a warning to the foolhardy about the perils of playing fast and loose with the constants of physics.* 'Granny, are there any known weaknesses or design flaws on a Mitsubishi Deep Space TH-54 rattling around your over-sized data cores?'

The ship's A.I. appeared in Skrat's field of augmented reality view. 'I have found one design flaw. When you can overwhelm a TH-54's point defence fire, her rear bridge armour is under-weight for surviving the nuclear flash from an X-ray laser warhead detonation.'

Skrat forlornly patted his uniform. 'Ah, the nuclear ordnance is in my other suit today, along with my delivery system. I say, it's at times like this I wish Captain F. was firmly in the command chair.'

'You believe the revered captain's simulations would come up with a different result?' asked Polter.

'Not at all. But at least this bally mess would be *her* responsibility.'

'When the regime sees d'Alembert's shuttle docking inside the *Meteor Prince*, it is feasible both missile ships will target the *Prince* while ignoring us.'

'I doubt they will take the risk we're not playing the old shell game out here, one pea and multiple ships to hide it on. Neither the *Icarus's Itch* nor the chase shuttle have the range or speed to outrun a pair of missile attack ships, so that leaves our good selves and the *Prince* as prime targets. If I was those destroyers' commanding officer, I would assign one TH-54 to eliminate us and the second to destroy the *Prince*. The regime can run down everything else and recover the salvage using their slower in-system assets.'

'How many missiles would a System Warfare Destroyer of that wicked class typically carry?' asked Polter.

'Two forty-eight-cell missile launch systems, bow and stern, so ninety-six missiles a-piece. Unless the rotters have been skimping, their destroyers will be packing relatively recent out-of-orbit anti-ship missiles — I don't see much mileage in carrying land-strike warheads, given it's the tsar's own real-estate which would be left nuked and glowing.'

Skrat checked the chase shuttle and *Meteor Prince*'s courses. No change. Both boosting into each other's arms at max. burn. With the *Prince*'s head start, it was just possible the ship could flee the system without being blown out of the void. And of course, there was still the matter of the Skunk, d'Alembert's ace-in-the-hole. 'So, Polter, what say you on the chances a Skunk could hack a missile's hardened A.I while the ordnance is pursuing hot . . . detonate warheads early?'

'I have no hard facts on a Skunk's capabilities, but I suspect we can derive the truth of the device's reputation from the Alliance's severe penalties for possession of it,' said Polter.

Skrat sighed. It was really going to grate if d'Alembert did the crime and fled the system while leaving the *Gravity Rose*'s crew to do the time. Unfortunately, Skrat suspected that time would be somewhere between the three to five seconds it took a police squad to raise rifles, draw aim and open fire.

Come on, old bean, what would the skipper do in your shoes? 'We could stern chase the *Meteor Prince*, follow her wake to the jump point and bet on that rascal d'Alembert clearing a path for us.'

'We would also be gambling on the good graces of the same infernal devil not diverting the missiles chasing *him* into *our* path,' said Polter. 'That is not a wager I would feel comfortable accepting.'

Good point. 'There must be something we can do!'

'If it appears we're unable to escape,' said Polter, 'I shall begin wormhole formation and attempt an in-system jump.'

Now Skrat knew they had reached rock-bottom. 'You can't generate a clean translation this close to a star, Polter. Not even *you* are that good. The wormhole will deform inside the sun's gravity well. We'll end up a stain on the universe's botty.'

'We will breach the gates of heaven and die entering, then.'

'Let's try and come up with a plan a little further removed from guaranteed suicide . . . please.'

Polter ignored Skrat and began drumming his carapace with his battle claws, working himself up to a state of religious ecstasy.

I'm sure there's a reason why someone would want to be captain of this ship, but it rather escapes me, presently. Skrat was still milking every last escape option when his sensors detected weapons discharge from the direction of the race. Had the missile ships opened up on the *Icarus's Itch* and the chase shuttle? Not a clever career move on the part of the officer involved, given the tsar's precious auction salvage could well end up as space dust. But as Skrat examined the pings, he realised that the two destroyers were still well out of weapons range from the race. Lana probably hadn't even picked up the pair of pursuers closing in from the moon, yet.

So, who is doing the bally shooting? Skrat sat bolt upright in his chair, losing all fatigue. He'd just realised that the exchange of fire originated from a seriously overclocked comms laser. Skrat recalled how badly he'd begrudged Lana the cost of the solar sails from that bankrupt microwave power satellite company; a non-essential frippery for the captain's racing hobby. *Clever girl.* 'The skipper's disabling the chase shuttle. Thanks the stars.'

'Recheck your telemetry,' advised Polter. 'There's something else going on over there — the revered captain and d'Alembert are being pursued by two rivals from the race — another chase shuttle and sun-jammer.'

Skrat loaded the full data-set. 'Oh dear, matters seem to be degenerating into a right bun-fight. Is that, *no* — a — missile launch aimed at the *Icarus's Itch*?'

Polter's eye stalks went as rigid as a pair of knitting needles. 'Impossible! All race participants were checked and confirmed disarmed.'

Skrat reloaded and reloaded the sensor updates, desperately checking for some — any — good news. 'Maybe the tsar has ringers entered in the race, lurking to eliminate thieves? Ditch your sail, Lana, go dark.'

Polter sounded every bit as terrified as the skirl felt. 'Such a ruse will not fool a modern smart-missile.'

Skrat held his breath, only for it to expel out of his lungs as the *Gravity Rose*'s sensor array highlighted and tracked a bizarre sphere of rolling dark energy, its expansion temporarily blotting all other telemetry being received. As quickly as the ball appeared, it vanished, leaving only a line of graphics leading to where the destructive force had originated. *The Rattle*. What sort of demonic vessel was this, which could launch black suns from its batteries? Only blank void left, no regular particle or dust scatter, the space previously occupied by the energy burst now as empty as if someone had licked that sector of the system clean. Every ship involved in the fracas disintegrated. All their crews with them. Lana, Calder, Zeno, Captain Jernberg, even that wicked scoundrel d'Alembert. Murdered by an alien sun-gun.

'No!' yelled Skrat. 'No! *No!*'

Polter made a whining whistle. 'They are with the Creator, joined with the Holy of Holies, peace be upon them all.'

'They really can't be dead,' murmured Skrat. *This isn't my chair; it's hers. Don't make me sit here any longer than I have to.* Skrat ached to make someone pay, but there was nobody left. Not the innocent or the guilty; the deserving or the undeserving . . . d'Alembert and his vainglorious dreams of conquest atomised. Just the three of them remained on board the *Rose*. Further ahead in the outer system, the *Meteor Prince*'s crew had also witnessed their captain and chase shuttle destruction. The vessel began to make a sharp series of manoeuvres to push her out of the path of the race. Nobody left to pick up and dock inside her hangar anymore. The *Meteor Prince* reset to boost from Ryazarn system, leaving the race and the two pursuing missile ships, fleeing on the most expedient trajectory, now. Straight up and out.

Part of Skrat knew they should plot the same course; but another, deeper part of him didn't care in the slightest. Lana Fiveworlds had saved his life when he had been little more than a vagrant pit fighter. When she'd first encountered Skrat, he had lost everything — his wife and children, his position, his pride and sense of worth. Lana had given him just enough of that back to go on living, a faint hope he might one day recover who and what he had once been. *Now I'll never be able to repay the captain. I can't even avenge her death.*

'What are we to do?' asked Polter, from the navigator's chair. 'How are we to do honour to them?'

'I don't think we can,' growled Skrat.

Skrat noted an incoming message from the repair party on the hull. Chief Paopao's grim face appeared disembodied above his control deck, an angry spirit dispatched by the Gods of Engineering and Engine Room Physics. Skrat could hardly meet his stern gaze. 'They're dead, chief. Lana, everyone in the sun-jammer and the chase shuttle. That bloody alien hulk has murdered them all.'

'Granny shows me what happened,' said Chief Paopao. 'Captain is gone. Android gone. Calder Dirk is gone. Boy was useless engineer, but could make passable bowl of Lotus Root Dangojiru.'

Skrat felt a spark of anger rise out of his cauterised mind. 'Is that all he was worth to you, a bowl of damn soup?'

'Barely *passable* soup. Feel sorry for yourself later, Lieutenant Lizard. Mourn later, too, if you must. Now, we escape.'

'Is this how the fleet trained you, chief? Roll the bally bodies off the cannons, savour the whiff of grapeshot and continue firing, a splinter of ice stuck in your heart just as cold as vacuum?'

'*Gravity Rose* is still the captain's ship. You think captain thanks you two simpletons for letting *Rose* be spread across this filthy system? Steer for action! That is what fleet teaches you, steer for action. You shame her memory, you miserable green-scale-skinned-dragon! Tell big sentient God-bothering crab sitting on bridge with you that he ends up fried in my Dangojiru if he does not stop praying for Fiveworlds' soul and instead start saving her *Rose*.'

Paopao killed the connection and Skrat sensed the efforts of the robots installing the generator on the hull pick up as the chief refocused his cantankerous attentions back on them.

'The Creator picks a strange vessel to give voice to the revered captain's soul,' said Polter.

Skrat pulled himself together. There was still just enough anger left simmering inside him to do the job. *Maybe it isn't only broken drives the chief was trained to fix under combat conditions.* 'Time to try to save the *Gravity Rose,* dear boy. Boost Galactic North High, let's climb after the *Meteor Prince* — two targets to shoot at and all that.'

'I am not certain that is wise,' said Polter.

'How so?'

'I reviewed the in-system traffic logs during our journey to Ryaz Prime. There was one very noticeable feature of the internal flight path dispersal. The regime's mining and supply freighters consistently avoid both the ceiling and floor planes along Galactic North and South.'

Skrat didn't like the sound of that at all. Polter had been quite right to raise the matter. 'Minefields?'

'I fear so. There was also a large government maintenance craft docked at the station with many more space-walk-capable drones clinging to her hull than the authorities actually possess communication satellites in Ryaz Prime's orbit.'

Damn. Properly paranoid. Skrat had barely had time to process the information when his sensors lit up with dozens of white light eruptions, miniature novas blinking in the firmament from Gal-north. *Oh bugger, there's those X-ray flash-bangs we could use against the tsar's missile ships.* Each deadly burst of radiation was designed to overwhelm a starship's magnetic particle shields, preferably murdering the crew while leaving the ship more or less intact and able to be claimed as a prize vessel. A mean-spirited weapon, at best. An unlucky proximity burst had detonated yards from the *Meteor Prince*'s midsection, causing damage beyond even its weapon manufacturer's wildest claims — the *Prince*'s cork-screwing escape vector converted into a mad tumbling of multiple ship fragments, bleeding out atmosphere and clouds of drive propellant with whatever was left of the thoroughly rad-cooked crew.

'Those poor devils.' Little comfort that the *Meteor Prince*'s crew had been freelancers rather than ship family from the Jernberg clan. Spacers were spacers, and the tough belters had come to Elin's aid when she was in trouble, risking their own necks, which told Skrat all he needed to know about the kind of people they had been.

Skrat racked his brain, examining the system charts for something, anything to help him fly the *Gravity Rose* to safety. Then it came to him. He highlighted a cold icy world similar in size and composition to Neptune. 'This planet — the one the locals call Ashten . . .'

Polter examined his nav data. 'On my board.'

'How about this for a jolly wheeze. We boost for Galactic North High, but at an extremely low incline. As though we believe the regime's mines are a localised field and if we just put enough parsecs behind us, we'll reach clean void and find a safe jump point. Those two missile attack birds won't waste too much expensive ordnance on us, then. Their commanders will simply chuckle into their uniforms' gold braided sleeves, thinking they're driving us straight off a cliff and into their minefield.'

'But your strategy will still leave us caught between the ceiling plane's mine field with two infernal destroyers in close pursuit behind our stern?'

'Yes, but we'll be drawing closer to Ashten all the time. We can follow a line just below the mine field's kill zone, then boost for this frosty ice-ball, use the world's gravity to slingshot us around and back around towards the Rattle's system exit trajectory.'

'Why in the name of the Creator would you wish to approach that infernal vessel?'

'Because we'll stern-chase *it*,' said Skrat. 'If we hold just outside the proximity trigger of the Rattle's defence system, then what can our two destroyer chums do? If they go hot with their ordnance, it's likely the Rattle will open fire with their hell-ball of a weapon again, no doubt disintegrating the tsar's fleet and melting half the race's sun-jammers. Then there will be no salvage, no auction, and the local aristocracy will probably fall after they can no longer fund their weapons-smuggling and spy-state tech programme.' *And of course, killing us in the process.*

'A sublime strategy,' agreed Polter. 'I believe the Creator herself speaks through you! If we are to die, let us die hurting this system's cursed warlord and bring down his wicked rule. A fitting monument to the revered captain.'

'Steer for action,' ordered Skrat. *Steer for the Rattle and a vessel that seems capable of destroying worlds — I must be out of my blooming noggin.*

Lana hadn't expected to see anything again, much less Zeno's synthetic golden cheeks, peering concerned over her body. She rediscovered her voice and coughed at him. 'If you're an angel, I think there's been a mix-up.'

'If you ever thought you'd be heading to heaven, I'd say that's true.'

Lana realised she was hanging at a strange angle inside her crash couch, the *Icarus's Itch* listing at a thirty-degree angle. And she was listing inside a gravity field. *Are we no longer in space?* The sun-jammer looked pretty banged up, running on battery lights with the cramped cabin's consoles and instruments left buckled, damaged and sparking. Looked like the results of some kind of impact damage. *Though, if that missile had hit, we'd be fried, not dinged.* Then Lana recalled the fleeting sensor imagery of the hell-ball launched out of the Rattle. *So, by rights, we should be double-fried.*

The captain glanced across the half-broken acceleration couches containing Dominika and Retigura's bodies. 'Are they okay?'

'Best I can tell,' said Zeno. 'I don't think our military escort ever fully recovered from the last buzz we gave her. Retigura took a face full of toolkit when the storage space buckled. Concussed.'

'What happened, where are we?'

'On your second point, no portholes,' shrugged Zeno. 'Not a good design for something that's going to be lashed by sun-hot plasma ejecta. And our sensors are dead along with most everything else on the boat. As to your first point . . . before my mind cooked out, I'm sure I registered a familiar energy signature. You remember that Heezy Hades and how we escaped off the planet . . . ?'

'Teleported?'

'Yeah, I think that ugly black star-ball that ran us down wasn't a weapon, it was the Rattle equivalent of a tractor beam.'

'Next time,' said Lana, 'I hope they downgrade to a super-magnetic field to express their irritation with the stupid humans shooting at each other off their bow.'

'I wish you'd stop calling me human,' said Zeno.

'Honorary human, old man.'

'The honour is all yours, skipper. And you can keep it.'

'No way of knowing if there's an atmosphere outside here, then, let alone a breathable one.' *Or if Calder and Elin shared our fate. Please, let them be safe, too.*

'I think I can cope.'

Lana unclipped her belt webbing and swung off the couch. Every inch of her body ached, a kind of hot itching across her flesh and bones that lived up to her sun-jammer's name. Zeno was bang-on. She'd experienced the same sensation after being teleported by the Heezy machinery. 'Yeah, well, the poor old fleshie over here has a pair of lungs that still need oxygen.'

Lana located the cabin's small medical kit, thanking small mercies that the hand-held mini-medic was still powered up. Running it along the aboriginal and Ryal woman's bodies, she experienced a jolt of guilt when the machine came back with a diagnosis of neural overload from their little blast of shock therapy. Retigura's concussion had indeed resulted from physical head trauma. Lana's hand-unit repurposed its stock of generic healing nano for each patient — Dominika's hypodermic shot little more than smelling salts to revive her - and both gir and human came around within minutes.

'Where are we?' demanded the officer, her eyes heavy and dark. Dominika unbelted herself and sat up, rubbing her forehead. 'What happened to the race?'

'Fair to say the race is over for us.' Zeno explained their predicament, Retigura becoming increasingly agitated as the news sunk in.

'We have transgressed . . . this, this is the Harbinger's punishment of us!'

'Maybe the Rattle's crew were generous,' Lana told the gir. 'You know, they might have just teleported us back to your homeworld as a warning. "No more shooting, you naughty lifeforms." We pop the hatch, we could find ourselves on a nice sandy beach by one of your islands.'

Zeno didn't seem convinced. 'Yeah, because we're *that* lucky.'

'It won't be lucky for you,' said Dominika, picking up her fallen pistol from the capsule's steel floor. 'The tsar will have heard what happened by now.'

'Yeah, well, you just remember how I banged my sun-jammer up — trying to stop a pack of thieves making off with the tsar's goodies.'

Dominika checked the pistol's magazine. 'You've never lived in a dictatorship before, have you?'

'To the best of my knowledge, no.' *Which isn't saying much. I was certainly fleeing some serious war zone conflict when my mind got baked on that refugee cattle transport.*

'Justice being seen to be done is a lot more important than actually finding and punishing the guilty.'

Zeno laid his hands on the escape hatch release. 'Let's look on the sunny side, we might all die in a couple of seconds; agreed?'

Lana stared at the atmosphere recycling unit protruding still and dead on the cabin ceiling. 'Going to get mighty stale inside here soon enough. Kick it open.'

'Agreed, then,' said Dominika.

'No!' protested Retigura, his arm limbs spinning wildly. 'We can stay safe inside here!'

'Are you all right?' Dominika looked concerned and Lana suddenly realised why.

'Your friend's control torc is fried, lieutenant. You won't be getting a whole lot of *No, Miss: Yes, Miss* from this native life-form anymore. He's actually speaking his mind now.'

Dominika's mouth opened wide but no words came out. Lana wasn't sure if that look of worry was for her friend, for the chance the explosives in his control torc might still detonate as they were meant to have done; or for herself, now Retigura had slipped the leash for the first time.

'I do not feel myself,' said Retigura.

'My friend,' said Zeno, pulling a cable out of his arm and interfacing with the door lock, 'that's precisely what you are feeling for the very first time.'

'I know the girrish priests have many legends about the Harbinger in the Heavens,' said Dominika, gently, 'but we have been spared, haven't we? That must count for something?'

Unbidden, Lana imagined those very words as a speech bubble from a missionary inside a cannibal-surrounded cooking pot. She shivered.

A singing sequence of beeping emerged from the lock, then the bracing arms clacked away and Zeno heaved out with all of his considerable strength, popping the door panel. They didn't all immediately die from an acidic atmosphere. They didn't find themselves drowned by seawater, fried by radiation or any one of a hundred possible fates that awaited spacers playing Russian Roulette with a blind landing and no-sensor hull exit. *Well, that's a good thing.* Zeno hauled himself up and out, dipping back through the opening to help the rest of them exit the capsule. Retigura needed little assistance, as it transpired, climbing out with the agility of a spider.

They sat on top of the capsule together, like shipwrecked mariners surveying their surroundings.

Zeno whistled. 'We're not in Kansas anymore, folks.'

Not even in Oz. They looked out over a tube-shaped hangar, but the word hangar didn't do this chamber justice — Lana had been inside L5 orbital colonies with populations of millions that were smaller than this. Graceful silver arches the height of mountain ranges held up the ceiling with a thin weather system drifting below it. A pulsing blue highway passed down the middle of the hangar roof, with nary a ground vehicle or pedestrian to be seen. The highway disappeared towards a circular lock at the far end of the hangar, a size you could roll a small moon through. Beyond the portal lay a natural green forest environment, in stark contrast with this musty-smelling chamber. But it wasn't the scale of their hangar that was the freakiest thing — that honour went to the sheer number and variety of ships lying — in some cases standing — across the hangar floor. Thousands of vessels — every one unfamiliar in design and configuration to the ships Lana was used to. Excepting the *Icarus's Itch* central life-support pod, laying crumpled on the deck, its miles of now thoroughly ripped solar sails spread like gossamer wings around her, everything else was truly alien. Elongated vessels composed of miles of functional-looking interlinked modules with hulking engine clusters at the end. Dirty nuke-driven beasts with pusher plates to safely absorb tumbling atomic bombs laid like demon eggs behind them. Modest freighter-sized ships squatting in the lee of super-carriers so large they could probably accommodate Alliance carriers in their launch tubes. Vessels with hulls as curved and graceful as museum carvings, others resembling a bastard mating of porcupines, more weapon spines than the *Gravity Rose* possessed rivets. *Alien, all so obviously alien.* The unfamiliarity of their lines sent shivers down Lana's spine.

'Just where the hell did we teleport?' asked Lana.

'The Harbinger,' moaned Retigura, 'we are inside the blessed vaults of the Harbinger, we tread where angels walk.'

'We can't be,' said Lana. 'I mean the Rattle is big, sure, but some of the ships parked out there are way bigger than the Rattle.'

'God's body is infinite,' said Retigura, simply, as though that should be explanation enough.

Dominika seemed as stunned as any of them. 'I listened to the Girs' hymns. This certainly seems to match how their religious songs describe the Rattle's interior.' The lieutenant pointed to the silver arches criss-crossing the ceiling; the burning blue road snaking towards the next chamber, its distant circular lock giving onto the forest-green environment. 'Under silver arches the entrance to God's Hall. A blue path to the Gardens of Gallanna where we were born. God's body is infinite. God's mind is perfect.'

'How can a vessel possibly be bigger on the inside than the ship's exterior dimensions?' asked Lana.

'We fold space with gravity, using wormholes to initiate hyperspace translations,' said Zeno. 'You could argue that using quantum entanglement for star-system-to-star-system comms is crumpling space-time just to swap cat pictures. What the heck are mankind's technological parlour tricks, if not playing with dimensionality? This is just more of the same, but seen from the perspective of ants crawling around a fusion reactor and going, "Hey, shiny."'

A pocket dimension? Lana stared around the hangar with newfound respect and not a small measure of terror. It really could be infinite inside here, if that was the case. She thought the race around Ryazarn had been chasing down an alien ship for its cast-offs. Maybe they had actually been chasing a pocket universe all of its own? Lana tried to place what she was seeing here against her stock of knowledge and came up empty. Beyond the fact that the next chamber seemed to contain an actual alien environment, there was none of the Heezy's organic ant-hill about this ship. Lana had been inside the bowels of a planet turned into one of that extinct race's strange machines and nothing about the feel of the Rattle's endless interior spoke to her of their hands − or tentacles or whatever − being in this. There was a recognisable beauty, here. A perfection of form and architecture. The ugliest thing about the hangar's contours was the eclectic collection of vessels littering the decks.

'Hey, in the shadow of that carrier-sized beast with the high bridge superstructure,' said Zeno, indicating a point miles away. 'Look familiar, skipper?'

'Elin's chase shuttle!' Lana felt a weight lift from her heart. She hadn't killed Calder after all with her peevish desire to punish him for damaging the *Rose*. 'But why all these other ships here − what gives with the graveyard?'

'Better *hope* it's a graveyard,' said Zeno. 'My money is on most of these bad boys having threatened the Rattle at some point or another. This is the Rattle's sin bin.'

'We trespass,' moaned Retigura. 'May the Harbinger forgive us our trespasses.'

Maybe they had, but the idea of what she saw made Lana's human-limited mind spin. A miniature universe travelling inside another larger universe. Spitting out pieces of junk gleaned from galaxies so far away the light of their creation hadn't even reached the Milky Way yet. Lana switched her gaze back to the slightly more comprehensible sight of the alien armada. 'Aggressive alien species netted like butterflies. With only one thing in common − we all acted like a-holes in the Rattle's presence.'

'If this is a net, we better flutter our way out of it quick,' said Dominika. 'We don't know where the Rattle jumps next on her trans-galactic pilgrimage, but wherever it is, it's certainly nowhere that been sighted near Edge or Alliance space.'

Lana glanced around the vault. She only recognised the place as a hangar from the starship graveyard rusting inside here. Nothing in the chamber looked like a lock they could leave through. *No big teleporty-tractor beam with a reverse switch on it, either. And there are thousands of starships going to pot around here. Thousands of violent, armed, sentient species who all must have desperately tried and failed to find the Rattle's exit.* Things, frankly, were not looking particularly healthy for any of them.

Zeno gazed around at the torn shroud of their solar sails. 'We're never taking off in the *Icarus's Itch* again.'

'Better hope that Elin's chase shuttle made it through in one piece, then.' Lana asked to be lowered back into the capsule, stripping out an E.V. pack and filling it with anything approaching useful. Medical kit. Generous water supplies but rather limited ration packs, then she cracked open a maintenance space and removed two hand-sized units that might just resemble pistols at a push.

Dominika looked askance at the last two items as Lana re-emerged from inside. 'The terms of the race prohibit-'

'These aren't weapons,' said Lana. 'They're pulse welding lasers for effecting spot repairs to the hull interior in the unlucky event of a micro-meteorite impact.'

'How lucky you brought *two* of them along,' said Dominika.

Lana passed one to Zeno and he checked its charge. 'System redundancy.'

'And what am I to bet the welding range can be substantially lengthened on those units?'

'Really, lieutenant, if I wanted to smuggle prohibited firearms inside the *Icarus's Itch*, I would have brought along something really nasty, like rail-pistols.'

'And how would you explain your acceleration couches electrocuting us?' asked Retigura, sounding more curious than annoyed.

'Malfunction, sorry,' smiled Lana. 'Must have been us trying to rewire the solar sails to supercharge our comms laser — blew a fuse and shorted straight into the cabin systems.'

'We have an old saying on Ryaz Prime,' said Dominika. 'Don't urinate on my bed and tell me it's raining.'

'That's a good saying.' Lana began to climb down the dented capsule.

The android followed after her, then Retigura, with Dominika sliding down last. Zeno landed with a wallop that indicated his true weight. 'I wonder if there's a parking meter we have to pay at nearby?'

'Yeah, and I'm wondering here what the fine is if we *don't* pay.'

It was only when they began walking that the hangar's distances and true scale became apparent. What had seemed near at first glance was actually many miles away. It wasn't long before Lana was cursing the fact she'd worn a light-weight sun-jammer pilot's uniform rather than full hiking gear including cushioned boots. *Hey, who knew?* She resisted the urge to stop at every new ship, try and find a way in and poke around. Forget the technologies jettisoned by the Rattle — with just what was parked littering the hangar, they could potentially advance interstellar space flight by centuries. *But w e need to get to the shuttle. Make sure that Calder and Elin are still alive in the hands of our maniac client-from-hell.* If there was one small silver lining to the situation she found herself in, it was that the cursed farming aristocrat d'Alembert was stuck in this up to his neck with the rest of them.

After nearly an hour, they reached the first landing strut of the monster of a vessel the chase shuttle had been deposited close to — if the strut had been part of a city, it would have towered fifty storeys above them, with just its flat feet covering a sports arena. Lana could discern ramps and lifts in the pillar used by her crew to disembark.

Zeno ran a finger along the rusting landing gear, placing his finger inside his mouth for a second.

'You feeling hungry, old man?'

'Dating its age,' said the android. 'About five thousand years old, give or take a bit.'

Lana stared up in fresh amazement at the alien vessel. 'We were running around with bronze swords when she was captured.'

'Held up well, then,' said Dominika.

'That'll be the diamond-carbon composite I can taste in the coating,' said Zeno.

'Nothing to indicate a military design,' said Lana. 'Maybe a colony ship?'

'Passenger liner of the alien damned,' mused Dominika.

'Please,' begged Retigura. 'Do not use such language here. Whoever was on board this space vessel has been punished already.'

Yeah, thought Lana. *A garage sale full of starships, but no sign of their crews.* She stared towards the verdant portal at the far end of the chamber. *Hopefully, they haven't been punished. Just sodded off to greener pastures after the recycling systems and hydroponics broke down.* 'Is this your people's paradise or hell, Retigura?'

'It is the mind of God,' said the aboriginal. 'It is whatever God chooses to think.'

'Well, let's hope it's fluffy mammals and kind wishes,' said Zeno. 'Because I surely don't want whoever built this vessel to be any more pissed with us than she, he or it already is.'

Lana turned to the lieutenant for a little more sense of the local mythology. 'Is the girrish God a benevolent or threatening deity?'

'A complex one,' said Dominika. 'There weren't many analogues with anything out of human culture. One of the latest theories is that the Harbinger was an expression of the girrish sense of loss of their lost civilisation in the wake of their nuclear war. The Rattle took on a significance it probably didn't have when the girrish had their original technological base.'

'How advanced was that?'

'There are not many in-depth studies into what was lost,' said Dominika.

Zeno raised an eyebrow. 'Yeah, I just bet. Easier to keep animals as workhorses than admit you've enslaved a sentient species.'

'There is an element of truth in that.' The lieutenant's admission surprised Lana and it must have shown on her face,

'We are not all beasts, Captain Fiveworlds. Some of us think that the price of isolation is too high. Open trade with Protocol worlds would allow the winds of progress to sweep our star system. Our peoples to prosper — *all* our peoples. As to your question, the best guess of our few progressive scholars is that the girrish were originally operating somewhere around the late twenty-first century in human terms. There is very little left of their society — only a radiated ash layer in the geology. The nuclear war's devastation was nearly total. DNA analysis indicates that the current population descended from a gene pool of no more than sixty-four survivors. We think, possibly, a girrish crew from a single nuclear missile submarine who survived in a deep ocean trench, their descendants — only slightly more numerous — emerging from a cobbled together shelter on the sea floor after the ice age caused by the conflict ended.'

Lana snuck a sideways glance at Retigura. 'Heck, they seem more peaceful than we are — even without an operational control torc.'

'There are missing markers in their genetics which suggest they might have self-edited their genome,' said Dominika. 'Possibly to try to eliminate aggression in the enclosed environment of a survival shelter. Possibly in atonement for destroying their world.'

'Well, they got new enemies now,' said Zeno. 'How come the rest of you fleshies never tried expressing the peace gene?'

'I'm sure it's been tried on some world somewhere,' said Lana. 'And I think you can guess what happened.'

'They only survived until a more dominant species or unedited faction of their own kind came along,' said Retigura.

Yeah, that'd be us. They kept on walking, coming across what they were searching for behind the large vessel's engine housing.

Elin's silver-mirror hulled cargo shuttle possessed smooth, graceful lines; the design completely unnecessary for operating in vacuum, but a relic of the ship family's heyday as pioneers of the Edge — wealthy merchants with the money to expend on shipwrights and styling to impress clients. Her 100 metres-long length squatted on six hydraulic landing struts which must have triggered on automatic when the shuttle dropped here. No crash landing shrouded in a couple of miles of solar sail for Elin Jernberg. Everyone knew it was bad luck to name your space-to-ground cargo haulers, so her shuttle had been painted with the I.D. code J93 where the name and hull art would normally have gone. One of the more recent purchases sitting in the hangars of the *Meteor Prince*, Lana guessed, or perhaps just the best maintained of her birds.

Lana knew the shuttle at least retained battery power — the sensor dome under the shuttle was still slowly rotating. She yelled up towards the bridge windows up front. 'Drop your front ramp, d'Alembert. You're stuck in the belly of this alien beast just the same as the rest of us. You want to get out of here before the Rattle jumps to another galaxy, you better start working with us!'

Somebody must have been listening, because a few seconds later the front ramp began to hum and lower slowly towards the ground.

'Keep the industrial lasers out of sight,' Lana whispered towards Zeno. 'He won't know we're armed and we might need an edge.'

'I don't think so,' ordered Dominika. Lana turned and gaped as she saw the barrel of Dominika's ugly black pistol levelled at them. 'Take those so-called welding tools, place them on the floor and kick them towards me.'

'What are you doing? This is the same idiot that tried to rip you off and strand my crew in front of a firing squad. You think you can trust him over me?'

'Don't be ridiculous,' said Dominika. 'I don't trust that pompous popinjay at all.'

Someone was striding down the ramp. It was Elin Jernberg with a couple of her belters in tow. All three of the shuttle crew carried guns, too — the same kind of primitive reaction firearms favoured by the local secret police.

'Elin, what's going on, where's Calder and d'Alembert?'

'Calder's safe, if somewhat constricted,' said Elin. 'He didn't take very kindly to abandoning your sun-jammer. As for d'Alembert, I really can't stand listening to him crow.'

'Now, this is starting to get interesting,' said Zeno, his eyes flicking between Elin's crewmen and the local lieutenant.

'Don't make it too interesting,' Elin warned the android. 'I know you're faster and stronger than us, but you can't outrun a bullet. These Ryal weapons aren't quite rail-pistols, but a chemically-propelled armour piercing shell is almost as effective as a ball-bearing magnetically accelerated to hypersonic velocities.'

'And you wouldn't want to kill me, right?'

'Quite.'

'Nobody was meant to get hurt,' said Dominika. 'Your crew's prison transport was due to be raided. You would have been freed and hidden in safe houses from the regime until we could smuggle you offworld.'

'Hidden from the regime? You *are* the regime, lieutenant!'

'Lieutenant Denisov really isn't,' said Elin. 'It was her comrades who reached out to me via a tramp trader of our mutual acquaintance. They had an offer. I was to disrupt the race and put a serious dent in the tsar's takings; make off with a few of the Rattle's goodies and dispose of the salvage on the open market, then channel the funds back to the lieutenant's allies in the form of modern weaponry and explosives.'

'Two years ago there was an uprising against Tsar Rasim which gained military support among the younger military officers,' said Dominika. 'It was called the Colonels' Revolt by the people. It failed, tragically. Rasim possessed an override on the native levies' control torcs which even his own officers didn't know about. In the end, the native regiments turned their rifles against the protesters and rebels among the security forces. The imperial loyalists rallied and the revolt was brutally suppressed. Many rebels who surrendered were supposedly exiled.'

'You're still here and breathing,' noted Lana, coldly.

'The space forces held back from declaring for the revolution,' said Dominika. 'Short of making orbit-to-ground suicide runs in our ships, which would have killed as many innocents as loyalists, there wasn't much point in showing our hand.'

'You said *supposedly* exiled?' said Zeno.

'I ignored standing orders and left a freighter to stretch my legs on the automated helium mining operation on Ashten,' said Dominika, her voice choking. 'It wasn't hard to stumble across the iced-over mass graves where everyone who had been "exiled" lay dumped. My fiancée, Colonel Leonid Yevtushenkov, was one of the executed rebels. They hadn't used bullets, you understand. They simply turned off the air supply inside the compartments of the vessel taking our people into "exile". Tsar Rasim had my Leonid suffocated like a skegging rat in a cargo bay.'

Lana tried to fight down her rage. *Played!* She had been expertly played, used as a disposable pawn, the *Gravity Rose* and her crew nothing more than expendable assets in some vicious local political in-fighting. It all made sense in retrospect. The lieutenant trying to stop Lana weaponizing the comms laser on the *Icarus's Itch* to disable the fleeing chase shuttle. Dominika didn't want their salvage falling into the regime's hands — she wanted it stolen and sold off to finance her private war. 'So that mutinous scumbag d'Alembert was never behind this . . . just a revolution which needed money coinciding with the Jernberg family's retirement plans!'

'My people spotted d'Alembert on the station soon after he broke out of your brig,' said Dominika. 'He had access to so much

Alliance crypto-currency in the data-sphere he was obviously going to bribe one foreign trader or another to leave the system. So why not use him to help fund the revolution, too?'

Lana stared at Elin with loathing. 'You used *me.*'

'I was planning to fly my own sun-jammer, but you're the better pilot, Lana. That is a simple truth — not flattery. You had the best chance to grab us some choice salvage — and you didn't let me down. You should see what you caught. It will make us all rich.'

Zeno snorted, indicating the huge hangar around them. 'You're going to be the richest skipper stranded in the Pinwheel Galaxy. Well done, lady!'

'Even if the Ryal rebels rescued me and the crew from taking a bullet for your damn riches,' snarled Lana, 'I would have lost the *Gravity Rose*. She would have been impounded at best, destroyed at worst. The *Rose* is running for a jump point right now! My crew could still be blown to pieces in this cursed star system for your greed's sake.'

Elin paused as more of her belters emerged down the ramp, carrying high tensile security ties. Both Lana and Zeno had their arms bound behind their backs at gunpoint. 'Running out-system was your choice for your ship, captain. Your orders. She'll either successfully jump out, or jettison lifeboats before the worst happens. You were always going to lose the *Gravity Rose,* just like I was going to lose the *Meteor Prince*. Today, or next year, or the year after that. There's no room for independents in the Edge anymore. We've nothing left to trade. *This* is the frontier, now. Smuggling arms to off-Protocol crap-holes, one small step away from welding missile racks on and calling ourselves pirates. Time to find a new game, Captain Fiveworlds. This one is finished for us.'

'My apologies,' said Dominika Denisov, prodding Lana and Zeno up the chase shuttle's ramp with her pistol.

'Casualties in your war's crossfire, huh,' said Lana, bitterly.

'You're alive,' said the lieutenant. 'Which is more than can be said for many of my people. You can have a chance to cool down. Then we'll see about letting you loose.'

'You're a real piece of work,' said Zeno, marched into the shuttle. 'I can see how you cut a deal so easily with Jernberg.'

'We take what help we can get, we exploit any opportunity. It's the only way to survive, given the disparity of forces we face to take our freedom.'

'My freedom for yours,' said Lana. 'That sounds like an easy price to pay.'

'Nothing about this has been easy.'

Lana and Zeno stumbled through the freighter, taken to the top deck and a small storage compartment that had been emptied and repurposed as a makeshift brig. Her heart leapt as she saw Calder Dirk squatting inside, his arms bound behind his back and his face bruised. He'd obviously taken a beating before the belter crew tossed him inside here. Calder's eyes lit up as he saw Lana and the android pushed through the steel doorframe.

'Thank the gods - you're alive!'

'Thank some fancy flying to even get here, Mr Dirk,' said Lana.

'I tried to escape after the auto-pilot landed us inside this strange place,' said Calder. 'But there were too many crew in the way.'

Zeno shrugged towards the lieutenant as best he could in his restraints. 'Yeah, we've been royally pooch-screwed by our so-called friends on this one.'

Dominika let the insult go and locked the door as she

departed. Zeno and Lana answered Calder's stream of questions as best they could, given how little they knew about where they had ended up - only why. *None of which is going to help us escape.* Lana tried not to feel overwhelmed by the magnitude of their task. Escaping from this chase shuttle. Then finding a way off the Rattle in time to even be inside their home galaxy. And after all that, they'd be in the middle of a hostile star system with a maniacal tsar's police and military force methodically working to hunt them down for a theft they hadn't even committed. *You've been in some right scrapes before, Lana girl, but how are you going to get out of this one?*

Lana had a question for Calder. 'How long before Jernberg takes this bird and heads towards the next chamber to look for a way out?'

Calder shook his head, regretfully. 'We can't fly anywhere. Main drive is down. We've been operating on what's left inside our power-cells since we awoke here.'

'Damaged?'

'No. I think it's some kind of dampening field. Like the one the Heezy machinery used against us on Abracadabra.'

'That explains why it's like a starship car park out there. Dumped and disabled,' said Zeno.

Great. Double-stranded here. Lana's mood wasn't much improved when Rand d'Alembert opened the metal door half an hour later, strolling in smiling with his manservant a step or two behind him.

Lana glared up at d'Alembert. 'So, it's true. Scum always rises to the top.'

'I was under the impression that was cream,' smiled the landowner. 'You should be politer to me, captain. I'm the most valuable member of this expedition right now.'

'How do you work that out, pal?' asked Zeno.

'Because I'm the only one of us with a Skunk DNA-coded to accept my instructions,' said d'Alembert. 'Once we find this vessel's control systems, the Skunk can interface with them and open the hangar doors for us, so to speak.'

'Great,' said Zeno. 'That's going to be a lot like taking an axe-head to a quantum computer in the hope you'll play a music file.'

'As is so often the case, android, I know something you do not. The original template for my black market device was reverse engineered by Alliance researchers from Heezy technology during the great war. This vessel is undoubtedly the product of a higher civilisation, but higher than the Heezy's as a species? I think not.'

Lana couldn't believe the aristocrat could be *this* stupid. 'Reason we're here in the first place is that some idiot started tossing missiles around during the race. What the hell do you think the Rattle's creators are going to do to us when you drop some badly cloned Heezy mil-tech on their ship and tell it to go to work?'

'An acceptable risk,' said d'Alembert, archly. 'The fact we are alive here, rather than disintegrated, speaks to me of an advanced moral code on the part of the vessel's creators. When we give this whale a little pepper, I believe it'll quickly sneeze us back out again.'

'And Captain Jernberg is going along with this plan?' asked Calder.

'Naturally. She isn't planning on dying here of old age. And I have a world which requires my wisdom and guiding hand as its ruler. To borrow a phrase . . . my planet's people need me.'

Along with your great humility, no doubt. Lana could hardly believe what she was hearing. 'Don't do this, d'Alembert!'

'You are solely responsible for this mess, captain!' bellowed the landowner. 'If you had listened to me and continued onto Clifford's World as you were duly contracted to, we would all be far better off, now.'

'I'd either be drifting on a dead ship in hyperspace, or facing an Alliance warrant for illegal arms smuggling,' retorted Lana.

'History is only ever written by, justice is only ever decided by, the winners.' D'Alembert strode out of the compartment, leaving his butler behind for a second.

'We will escape here,' said Jinhai. 'You must trust in that.'

'And why the hell should I?' demanded Lana from the floor.

'Because,' said the butler, making to leave while glaring towards the exit, 'you could strand that man on an uninhabited asteroid with a day's air supply and he would boost into station a month later on a luxury yacht with a beautiful woman on either arm.'

Jinhai left the makeshift cell, leaving the prisoners to their confinement.

'Sure wish I shared Jeeves' confidence,' said Zeno.

And it was at precisely that moment when the army of alien savages stormed the chase shuttle.

Skrat found it hard to keep his attention off their two pursuers. So far the *Gravity Rose* was holding steady the distance between her and the pair of destroyers. Every second when Ashten's icy corpse crept towards them was a second nearer to their slingshot escape. *That's it, old boy, you just keep on feeling superior, driving us towards your blasted minefield. Because boosting back towards the race and the Rattle rather than running out-system is about as insane a manoeuvre as anyone could make.* But Skrat wasn't proud. If acting insane allowed him to escape with his life - and keep the ship intact - well, it wouldn't be the first time.

His board started redlining and for a terrifying second Skrat thought that they'd run into the minefield earlier than projected. Contact flash trailed in the wake of their simulated passage like fairy dust. Sadly, this also wasn't the first time that sliding void into a wall of the jolly brown stuff was what happened while Skrat was busy making other plans.

'By Jove, what was that contact?' asked Skrat.

Polter inspected his instruments. 'I believe it was a sensor buoy.'

Skrat briefly considered targeting it with rail-guns, but the *Gravity Rose* was moving so fast the buoy was already well behind them. *And where there's one sensor buoy, there's bound to be more.* The bally devices worked most effectively strung out in relay lines. 'Damn! It's going to be squawking our exact telemetry back to those two destroyers.'

With a specific read on the *Rose*'s course, there was a distinct danger the two destroyers would work out what Skrat was planning with his little gravity slingshot game.

Polter voiced the question playing at the back of Skrat's mind. 'Why place a sensor line out here? The regime already have this side of their system completely walled off with a minefield?'

'Something of value, then,' said Skrat. *But what?* 'I'm going to realign our main array off the pursuers and take a peek at that icy sphere we're boosting for. There must be something interesting on Ashten for them to leave a tripwire strung out this far from a jump point.'

There was. Skrat spotted the tell-tale signs of an orbital hook and depot locked geosynchronously above what had to be an automated mining station dirt-side. The sensors gave him an analysis of what was being extracted. 'It's a mining operation. Helium-3 frozen below the regolith layer - large concentrations.'

Just the kind of high-value resource scavengers liked to jump into a system and raid. Enough energy to fuel the Ryals' tokamak reactors for centuries. Unfortunately, the *Gravity Rose* had run straight into the tripwire left to detect foreign claim-jumping scoundrels. Skrat re-tasked the sensor array back at the two missile ships snapping at their stern. 'If you permit me to observe, Polter, I think we might be rumbled.'

'Where is our blessed luck? I count eight missile launches,' said Polter. 'Four from each destroyer.'

'Is that all we're worth? A measly eight ship killers?'

'One wicked warhead will be more than adequate to free our souls from our mortal hosts,' said Polter.

'I rather prefer mine encumbered by this fine specimen of a body.' Of course, Skrat wasn't what he was when he'd been younger, but a skirl still had standards. He banged his tail onto the deck in frustration. If he remained captain for much longer, there was going to be a dent behind his chair on the bridge. *Chance will be a fine thing.*

Chief Paopao's image reappeared like the spectre at the feast. 'New field matrix installed.'

It was still too early in the missile launch for an accurate plot of speed and impact time, so Skrat retransmitted the entire half-finished mess across to the chief's board to let him know how grave their situation was. 'Jolly good work. Afraid we're going to be pushed to use it to exit another jump, though. If you're holding back any acceleration down in the drive chamber, now would be an excellent time to squeeze that sponge for a few drops extra.'

'Ring your neck, you amateur,' snapped Zack Paopao. 'We are at full burn. This is not carrier with Fleet engines!'

'Well, any tips on handling the pair of weapons-hot TH-54-class Vacuum Rangers growling at our stern would be much appreciated, old chap. Beyond trying to slip a nuke we don't have past their point defences.'

Paopao examined the initial launch data. 'Yes. Yes. Fine dispersal pattern. Broker that sell these destroyers to warlord also bring in trainers for local crew. Ex-fleet. Know what they are doing.'

'Where's the mistake, dear boy? Please tell me there is one.'

'Fire stern rail-guns like this . . .' the chief sent a three-dimensional image of a series of perfect circles, starting tiny but growing wider as the wheel shapes fell further behind. 'Then follow first burst pattern with totally random fire, shoot crazy!'

'Those fellows in hot pursuit have probably already guessed we're bonkers, chief.'

'Warhead targeting algorithms adapt for perfect symmetry, then must immediately switch for random. Too much crazy. Best chance for intercept.'

Skrat sighed. 'In for a penny, in for a pound.' *There's never too much crazy on this ship.* He stared across at the navigator. 'Better give it all we've got, then. It will only take one missile to scrape through our rail rounds. You can never have too full an ammunition bin.'

'I was given the impression by our revered captain that you always resented the cost,' Polter pointed out, rechecking their gun diagnostics against continuous fire.

'Ah yes, dear boy. But now you see they're no longer a cost . . . they're an *investment*.'

Lana didn't need to see Elin Jernberg's worried face as she entered their makeshift cell to know they were in trouble - the near-constant rattle of gunshots beyond the shuttle had already given that much away.

'What's going on, *captain*?' asked Lana, putting just the right amount of contempt into the last word.

'We're being attacked,' said Elin, not even trying to hide the desperation in her voice.

'And here's me thinking the lieutenant had challenged d'Alembert to a duel. Who the hell is attacking us inside this place?'

'An unknown alien species,' said Elin. 'Not the Rattle's creators - not unless they've fallen a long way since launching her. Spears, leather shields and swords, for the most part. Damn savages. Crew's nicknamed them smilers.'

I don't even want to know why.

'And let me guess,' said Zeno, 'now the brown stuff has been introduced to the fan blades, you want our help fighting these mopes off?'

'You're going to be overrun here along with the rest of us, Zeno,' snapped Elin. 'The smilers might not be able to cook your plastic head for soup, but they'll still mount it on top of a spear.'

'Shields and arrows,' said Lana. 'Sounds like your speciality, Mr Dirk.'

'All things considered, I think I prefer rail-pistols,' said Calder.

Yeah, and it was us that introduced them to you.

Elin produced the two modified industrial laser cutters taken from them earlier. 'Best I can do. My belters are using the rifles left by the Ryal military.'

You mean the guns that weren't blown out into space. Elin drew an active blade - the kind spacers carried for extravehicular activity. It powered up, vibrating into a blur. Lana allowed the Narse trader to cut away the ankle and wrist restraints. 'You want our help now, we get to stay free if we survive. That's the deal.'

'You still trust me enough to do a deal?'

Lana resisted the urge to take the laser cutter and brain the other captain with it. *Why am I the go-to-person for cleaning up other people's messes?* 'No, but then I'm not particularly expecting to live through this either.'

'Fair enough.' Elin sliced away the other prisoners' bonds, slid her active blade into a leg holster and all three of them followed the woman through the freighter's corridors, down a hatch onto the lower deck, through into the forward cargo area. Rear cargo was the larger space - this one contained exo-frame loaders, forklifts and low power anti-gravity sleds. Beyond the lowered ramp, the hauler's crew had assembled a makeshift barricade from whatever could be dragged out. Elin's spacers crouched behind crates and equipment, sighting with the old-style reaction rifles, firing fierce bursts into the attackers. And there were a *lot* of attackers. Slightly taller and more slender than the average human, the locals spun forward on three legs, howling like broken modems from their flat stingray faces, gaping mouths that might have been taken for grins if it wasn't for their fine mesh of razored fangs. Tiny pin eyes radiated hatred; attackers waving a pair of arms that resembled multi-jointed whips branching at the end into clawed fingers. These creatures looked like someone had taken a horde of living tripods and outfitted their bodies in tattered Saxon clothes, sprinkling a generous armoury of blades and triangular leather shields across their ranks.

Smilers. Not a bad nickname. But the prone belter crew-woman Lana vaulted— wraparound sunglass visor cracked by a feathered spear driven through her skull — certainly wasn't smiling at their reception. Lana and Zeno dived towards the barricade, ducking below crates spread in an arc around the ramp's rear. Lana winced as Calder followed, halting to relieve the dead woman of her pistol and ammunition pouch. He yanked the spear out of the corpse, carrying it with him as he sprinted for shelter. It was easy to forget that modern sensibilities still weren't exactly Calder's thing. And it was lucky the other belters were too focused on the assault to have noticed what he'd done. *They seem like practical types, maybe they wouldn't care?* Lana read the battlefield from the corpses scattered across the shuttle. A small scouting party had come across the newly arrived shuttle, a murderous exchange of sharp iron and bullets, enough smilers escaping to summon their warriors. Now the locals were advancing in formation like Roman Legions from some historical epic.

Lana sighted her industrial laser, practising a flicking cut across the charging smilers which sent four of them literally spinning towards the deck, various key parts of their central anatomy sliced open and smoking. A horrible way to die, and probably equally as terrifying to the smilers as the hurled spears and flights of arrows appeared to Lana. She had rarely seen a bullet coming, and contrary to popular entertainment, energy beams were only briefly visible because of secondary sighting illuminators. But clouds of arrows whistling down towards her in slow motion? Lana resisted the urge to cut back to the shuttle's shelter using every inch of her terror-stricken willpower. The smilers' main formations were still too far away for ranged attacks, their projectiles falling short, clattering across the hangar floor. Calder leaned his stolen spear against the barricade, then calmly checked his pistol's clip for remaining rounds. His face was grim, but seemingly unperturbed by the rain of arrows and spears aimed towards them. This was Calder's bread and butter. This is what the ex-prince had grown up trained to cope with. Not repairing malfunctioning Minkowski field generators . . . but holding a shield line against a thousand enemies screaming for your blood. Swinging axes into an enemy's skull without having a nervous breakdown from the sheer emotional shock of the act of violence.

Lana fired carefully, conserving the laser's power cell. She might be able to recharge the cutter inside the shuttle, but how long would the freighter's power reserves last without active engines to keep their lost corner of civilisation's lights on?

Elin opened up across from Lana, firing with one of the girrish levies' rifles, simple and crude - a beacon of modernity compared to the sharpened iron coming at them. Lana noted aliens massing behind the closest landing strut. The size of an apartment block, the strut's bulk was more than enough to shield the creatures from the crews' basic firearms. Smilers were being dispatched in units of sixty fighters from behind the strut, advancing towards the shuttle in three lines; leather shield bearers up front, spear carriers behind with weapons angled forward like an advancing porcupine. Archers made up the last line, launching whistling flights of arrows towards the defenders. More than adequate for whatever these locals usually faced, now the smilers were being cut down before they got within effective longbow range. *At least until our ammunition runs out - or they send enough warriors at once to overwhelm our rate of fire.*

Lana noted Lieutenant Denisov and her aboriginal on the line, frantically firing with the rest of them, as was the butler Jinhai, but there was one notable absence. 'Where the hell is d'Alembert?'

'He's back inside the shuttle,' said Elin, not sounding happy about it in the slightest.

'Tell me he's got a really nasty poisoned arrowhead sticking in his chest needing surgery . . .?'

'He's got a Skunk coded to his DNA, is what he's got,' bitched Elin.

Too valuable to die? I could put that to the test. Lana passed no comment, letting her laser speak for her anger, cutting down a line of shield-smilers, watching spear carriers simply march over their fallen comrades twitching bodies.

'Locals are adjusting their tactics,' warned Zeno, waiting for his laser to cool down enough to fire again.

Lana groaned, seeing her android was right. Whatever war leaders sheltered behind the landing strut, they had just raised their game - dispatching extra formations into the fray as fast as they could march. The same number of fighters advanced straight for their shuttle, but now additional formations marched towards their flank, pincering in on them like a bull's horns. *Too many coming at us to gun down before they turn us into pin-cushions.* Lana glanced over at Calder. 'What's the best way to survive a mass archery volley on Hesperus?'

'On Hesperus, dig down and shelter under the ice. But here? How about we use the shuttle's dust deflectors . . . ?'

'Need engine power to run up a magnetic shield,' said Lana.

'To run it constantly during flight, sure,' interrupted Zeno. 'But the kid's got a point. Power-cell-rig that deflector, we just need to be able to run magnetic shields for a second against each volley. A burst of energy and those iron arrow heads will bounce like hitting rubber.'

'You won't get many activations,' warned Elin, her rifle bucking against her shoulder as she picked warriors off of the formation's side. 'Without main drive we can't recharge our power cells. Running the shield will drain us fast.'

'The smilers must look at us and see what I first saw when the *Gravity Rose* turned up in Hesperus orbit,' said Calder. 'Sorcerers wielding evil wands with deadly powers. We're killing them at impossible ranges, already. When they see their spears and arrows being deflected, they'll stop hurling them against us. Do you know how valuable good arrows are to an archer? They'll either break and run or charge for close combat.'

'Surely do hope they plump for option one,' said Lana. She glanced at Zeno. 'Do it. Run the switch from the bridge - you'll be able to watch the incoming volleys and time the power-ups.'

The android sprinted back towards the shuttle, leaving as a rattle of fire swelled from the defenders. The crew felt the fear now. Too many attackers to cope with, even with the advantage of firearms.

A worrying thought occurred to Lana. 'What if they start loosing arrows at will rather than volleying?'

'They won't,' said Calder. He sounded certain. 'Synchronised fire is a powerful weapon of terror. Look how they loose together. That's how their archers are trained.'

Weapon of terror? Certainly works on me.

Smilers came charging at them from three sides, the fighters absorbing every round the crew could expend - Lana's laser redlining and falling silent more than it stayed active. The barrel's cooling system was as close to burn-out as she dared push it. Shields clattered to the hangar floor along with their owners, but the smilers continued advancing, suffering horrific casualties pressing their cause. Lana listened to a new strangely unearthly sound. The noise puzzled her until she traced it back to warriors blowing through large battle horns twisted around their bodies. *What are they signalling? Reinforcements?* Lana imagined the hatred the locals must be building up towards the defenders, then she didn't need to imagine. Their longbows drew within range and a hail of arrowheads arched up into the sky, holding at the top of their arc for a second as if deciding whether to plummet or not. Then, shafts rained down around her, clattering off the metal hangar deck and finding targets among the crouching crew. Lana flinched as arrowheads jounced off the shuttle, the barricade rattling under the hail. One arrow pierced the neck of a crewman to her left, the belter collapsing gargling and tugging uselessly at the wooden shaft. Another crewman panicked and broke cover from the barricade, sprinting away from the chase shuttle.

'Griffin, don't! Hold the line!' Elin yelled vainly at him to return.

The savages used the fleeing spacer for target practice, one shaft after another humming through the air, catching the man in the spine, sending him stumbling, then falling to his knees as arrowheads continued to thud down around him, through his chest and out again.

Calder shook his head, mournfully. 'A trained longbowman can knock an armoured rider off their mount at half a mile. If we need to retreat, fall back inside the shuttle. The smilers are stronger than they look. The draw weight on those bows must be ferocious to kill us from five hundred yards - maybe a hundred pounds or more.'

Lana gazed back towards the shuttle's bridge. *Come on Zeno, now would be good. Now!* 'You really are good at this, aren't you?'

'I lost the best part of my kingdom during a thousand mile retreat across an ocean of ice,' said Calder. 'You might say I grew used to it. But I don't think I can bear losing you here.'

Lana felt her laser tremble back to active. Or was that her? She sighted over the top of the barricade. 'Don't get misty on me, Mr. Dirk. My plans don't include letting *any* of my crew die at the hands of these flat-faced monsters. Myself included.'

'Loose!' warned Calder and everyone ducked again, holding tight to the barricade wall, faces pale and white. Lana was worried if they clung any closer they'd overbalance and topple the crates. She tried to ignore the hiss from the dark storm of quarrels filling the air, aimed to rain down on top of the chase shuttle. Then Lana heard another sound: the hypermagnetics dome under the engine housing squealing, starting to twist inside its housing. She prayed that Zeno had managed to re-range the field. Inside vacuum, dust and debris had to be rammed aside at the furthest possible range. Here, their field needed to activate umbrella-close and amped up to max. She watched the arrows plummet, resisting the temptation to close her eyes. The shafts began to part as though riding an invisible slide, raining down outside the shuttle's perimeter. Lana saw the smiler ranks swaying, confused at their last attack unexpectedly pushed aside. *That's it, pin-heads. Our magic is greater than yours. Take the hint.* She drew a bead and underlined the point by decapitating a line of shield-bearers, briefly panicking the archers standing behind.

'There's iron discipline for you,' said Calder, watching the formation on their left flank reform as a wedge, before charging towards the shuttle. Same manoeuvre ahead of them and on the far flank, too. 'By the gods, what I would have given to have had a few thousands of these lads on my side on Hesperus.'

Lana winced. *No more arrows and straight to option two, then . . . the hard way.* Her laser whined, indicating that it wasn't going to be putting up with too much more of her maltreatment of its cooling core. Sadly, it probably wouldn't have to. 'Nearly out of power for ranged shots.'

'Let your barrel cool down,' advised Calder, 'then switch it over to welding torch mode. It'll make a passable active blade.'

Great, so now I'm taking hand-to-hand medieval combat tips from my trainee engineer.

Calder lay aside his empty pistol and lifted up the spear, testing its heft.

Well, Lana had needed to travel across half the Edge to reach it, but they'd finally found an environment where the ex-prince's education was more useful than her's in the modern day.

***

Skratrotated the stern fire between their batteries, all too ware how badly the barrels were overheating. *I'd run down to an airlock and toss out bally boxes of shrapnel myself if I thought it would help.*

'Jam in belt five,' called Polter, his voice distorted through his chair's crash field.

Skrat tossed the task of clearing the jammed ammo lines to one of the dozens of robots now blundering around the rear gunnery chambers. Without Zeno to act as the ship's bot handler, dealing with the all-too-literal drones was like trying to herd cats. He'd come to a belated respect for the android's role on the *Gravity Rose*. The new-found appreciation probably wouldn't last long. There were still four missiles boosting in at velocities no organic could out-pace and survive, not even locked inside a crash couch with the ship's inertial dampeners squeezing gravitons like grapes. Three missiles had fallen to the symmetrical difference between their two-pattern opening hail of fire. But the warheads were cursed up-to-date for this neck of the woods. Networked. It hadn't taken long for the surviving five projectiles powering forward to start swapping survival tips and dance out of the way of the stern guns' fusillade. One more missile had been lost to blind chance and a lucky strike. But space was cursed big, and as fast as the *Rose* unloaded behind her, the destroyers' four remaining weapon systems now seemed glued to the *Rose*'s hull. *Fixated, you might say. Evil little blighters.*

Polter had started chanting little prayers from his chair, in between calling out the systems failing under stress on their ship. Chief Paopao was now too focused on keeping their wickedly overclocked drive chamber from exploding to bother berating Skrat. If the chief failed, they'd give the pursuing pair of destroyers a new problem - how to avoid colliding with the spreading wave of debris left by the *Rose*. At half light speed, the enemy ships would be ripped apart like eggs. *But sadly, without a Skrat in the universe to cheer.* He checked the two destroyers' position and tutted. No, he wasn't even going to enjoy that posthumous pleasure. The Ryal commanders realised the *Rose*'s time left intact was numbered in minutes, not hours, now. Their combat simulations were an order of magnitude more accurate than Skrat's. They had left just enough of a gap to detect the *Gravity Rose*'s annihilation before veering out of the way of the resulting debris field.

Reluctantly, Skrat called time on their stern guns' steady volley fire.

'We still have ammunition reserves,' said Polter.

'Best we save it for close-in point defence, old fellow.'

'There will be too many sub-munitions incoming when the missiles close,' said Polter. He didn't sound angry, just regretful.

'I know. As the good chief so kindly pointed out, we're regretfully no carrier. Our weapons are a paper man for plopping second thoughts into the thick heads of under-resourced marauders and pirates. Engaging a local navy was never really on the cards.'

'Lifeboats, then?'

'Not for me,' sighed Skrat. 'I rather fancy a nuclear blast will be far cleaner than a fatal beating by this star system's shockingly well-practised thugs.'

'Not enough time left for rotating jump vanes to speed,' said Polter. 'I shall stay, too.'

'Never very keen on being smeared by higher physics, anyway.' No, all things considered, going out in a nuclear fire was looking like the best of a bally bad bunch.

***

Calderduckedas a smiler swung something that resembled a halberd over his head, a rusted iron blade almost testing its serrated edge against his neck. He grabbed the foe's wooden shaft, pulling it to the side and plunging his spear into the warrior, yanking it out with a geyser of blood. Same colour as a human's, although that hardly mattered. The defenders' rifles were out of ammunition, so the belters swung their guns like clubs, lunging out with active blades where they had them. Any crew with pistols had fallen back, including Lana, picking off savages attempting to clamber over the barricade. Calder could tell by the sound of their careful, diminished rate of fire, that those with handguns were also nearly out of rounds. Then, a fierce new raw blasting from the smilers' battle horns. *Forward the attack?*

Smilers advanced from all sides, pressing in on the already overwhelming crush around their makeshift defence line. The belters were as tough as old boots, as hardened to a bare existence clinging onto vacuum as any human could be, but even so, the crew had limits. *I think we've found them.* Calder swirled his spear's wooden shaft around, braining one of the snarling flat-faced aliens on the barricade's opposite side. The attackers weren't any prettier up close. Thin interlocking teeth inside their crazed rictus grin, fangs grinding over each other in layered movements like some mad organic trash shredder. Eyes glowed with hatred despite their diminutive size.

The creatures used their three legs to attack like whirling dancers, lashing back and forth in attacks which were beyond Calder's training in purely human thrusts and parries. Smilers seemed to be able to move in all four directions with greater speed than mankind's pair of legs afforded them, retreating and skating sideways at unexpected velocities. Calder improvised in response, praying that his limb movements were as strange and off-putting to the smilers as theirs were to him. He was struck by an all-too familiar stench of close-quarters battle, however; the smilers' grey shark-like skin sweating in an oddly human manner. Battle cries from every side. Raw curses and screams from the belters, that angry broken-glass bellow from yelling locals. It seemed bizarre for Calder to cross the heavens almost as a god, using technology that might as well be magic for all that he really understood it; yet here he was again, just a sharp spear and a fighter's reflexes between him and death; gore and blood all around. *I thought I'd left this behind me in the ice.* Then, suddenly, smilers were among them, clambering over a couple of breaks in the barricade. Warriors swung blades, sharp iron clanging against spacers' rifles and any piece of shuttle usable as a shield. Calder saw Lana making wild parries with her laser welder set to its knife-like beam - no elegance in it - a desperate struggle for survival against the warriors attacking her.

No! Calder struck out for her, a smiler interposing itself between him and the skipper, static-like shrieks as it tried to plunge a bone-hilted long sword through Calder's chest. He side-stepped and head-butted the ugly thing, like slapping into a wet fish, then swept its three legs out from under it with the spear. The warrior recovered quicker than Calder expected - one advantage of its tripod limbs - but only in time to run into his spear's leaf-shaped head. Calder drove it right through the thing's flat face, where he judged the creature's brain should be. From the way it went limp, he'd judged well - or luckily. He shoulder-slammed the dying smiler to push it off the spear shaft, seizing the warrior's sword as the blade dropped from its spasming claws, Calder driving forward towards Lana.

He wasn't the only one trying to come to the skipper's aid! Zeno had reemerged from the shuttle, the android's skills with magnetic shields not presently required. Zeno beat warriors off with his laser cutter, smilers whirling away each time the glowing blade of energy sliced towards them, then counter lunging with swords. Calder windmilled his stolen blade as he charged, feeling the weight. It wasn't balanced for a human, that much he could tell, even if it had been pattern-welded for resilience. *A good sword, but it fights my hand, as a stolen blade should.* Calder howled a battle cry as another smiler charged at him from the side, falling into a slide across the ground to undercut the creature's feet. It tumbled, trying to skewer the ex-prince's face with its Falcata-style short sword as it fell. Calder blocked with his blade as they both scrambled across the hangar floor, struggling to get upright again. He'd felt the warrior's considerable strength in the clash and song of metal. *Tougher than it looks. Costing me too much time.* Calder lunged with the spear's deadly stabbing point, straight through the nearest of the smiler's three legs and hoped that it wouldn't much enjoy the experience. Then they were both on their feet, warily circling each other. *Evenly matched feet, now.* The enemy warrior trilled as it tried to compensate for the lost limb, cursing with an unholy racket as it over-reached with its first blade thrust, the ex-prince slipping past its guard and almost - but not quite - decapitating it on the back swing. Didn't even watch what was left collapse. He darted at the swarm of warriors fighting to get past Lana's swinging laser blade, nearly slipping on the bloodied metal deck, finally close enough to give the skipper's assailants a new enemy to distract them. Calder cut the creatures down from behind with spear and blade, as unsporting as a bear pit, but he'd break more than the chivalric code to save Lana. The speed at which they turned on Calder, hurling themselves at the crewman, made him wonder at the extent of their peripheral vision. He desperately fought them off, jabbing with his spear and thrusting with the sword until his muscles trembled like jelly.

With Lana and Zeno's laser cutters shaving the warriors' iron blades on contact, plus Calder's conventional assault, it only took Captain Jernberg's arrival, active blade in hand, to finally tip the balance. All four of them ferociously drove the smilers back, pushing through the ranks of battling shuttle crew, to impale those still alive against the barricade. Fresh fighters came charging towards the barricade, those left by the shuttle either dead or dying.

Calder used the seconds' lull to sneak a glance at the skipper. 'Are you alright?'

Lana stared down in shock at the blood staining the front of her ship suit. 'Someone else's, I think.'

'You'd know if it was yours.' Calder fought away the memory of one of his officers on the Royal Ice-schooner *Oakblade*, fighting while burning, a walking corpse in the fierce boarding action who hadn't realised he was dead yet.

'These bloody beasts just don't give up,' wheezed Jernberg, swapping her active blade between hands, eyes darting towards the next wave of smilers coming to clamber over the half-collapsed barricade.

'Your shuttle is their payday,' said Lana, filling the space in the defenders' line to stand by the other captain. 'We run and let them have it, they'd probably let us get away.'

Then the savage warriors were on them again.

'Dead either way,' called Calder, parrying a warrior's blade on the other side of the barricade. *No ship. No escape. Trapped in this alien place with the smilers and the gods know what else as neighbours.*

A smiler mounted the barricade, falling back over its comrades as one of the last pistol rounds took it through the chest.

'Dead now or dead later,' shouted Zeno, 'getting to the point when we're going to need to choose.'

Wasn't their choice, though, in the end. Shots sounded out from beyond their left flank, surprising Calder with their ferocity. They weren't from any Ryal firearms, though - the thoroughly modern crackle-whistle of a flexing gauss field. Someone had outmanoeuvred the smilers, the warriors' pincer movement caught from behind to devastating effect. Calder could just make out a line of - girrish, beyond? They wore the green uniforms of the tsar's colonial levies; with ship suited crew fighting alongside the aboriginals, too.

'Who the hell are those people?' called Elin, sounding as confused as Calder at this sudden turn of events.

I don't care as long as they're driving off the smilers. The attackers' fresh wave faltered, realising they were exposed at their rear, caught between the barricade and the shuttle's survivors and this deadly unexpected threat. War horns sounded and the formation pivoted towards the new danger.

'Must be from the rival chase shuttle and sun-jammer team,' said Lana. 'We believe they're a Unity infiltration unit trying to grab a goody bag from the tsar's party. They're the fools who fired that missile at us. Looks like they smuggled the best part of a modern arsenal on board.'

'Unity?' groaned Elin in disgust. 'Then they're more of a threat to us than the damned smilers!'

It certainly wasn't just a ship-to-ship missile their rivals from the race had stashed as contraband. Calder welcomed the familiar capacitor-sizzle followed by air-hiss of modern guns accelerating deadly metal flechettes to explosive velocities. Rapid-fire rifles literally tearing their attackers apart from the rear.

'Unity must have seized control of the levies,' said Zeno, observing the line of aboriginals advancing in lockstep. 'That's why there ain't any Ryal secret police hoods over there left alive to object.'

Lana grunted. 'Why doesn't it surprise me the Unity were able to hack girrish control torcs?'

The android wiped blood off his laser cutter. 'Meet the new boss. Same as the old boss.'

Calder swayed on his feet, so tired he could hardly stand. Every muscle ached from the combat. *I'm sure I was better at this last year. I would have fought twice the number back then and not thought it too much.* He felt the familiar release of tension after beating off the foe; a survivor's joy and surprise at finding himself still alive. 'They're on our side, though, right?'

'Unity only has one side, Mr Dirk,' warned Lana.

'Yeah, you might say that's their weak spot,' said Zeno.

The new arrivals' modern weaponry made short work of the smilers, warrior ranks starting to crumple as local fighters broke and ran, the smilers' mad spinning flight interrupted by the hiss of guns on full automatic fire. Hundreds of retreating savages crumpled to the ground in a terrible mist of flesh, clothing and fragments of leather shields. Their bucklers might as well have been made of tissue paper for all the protection the shields afforded them. Calder almost felt sorry for the smilers. *If they weren't trying to part my head from my neck.*

Warrior formations pulled out from behind the rusting

starship's landing strut, war leaders no doubt among them, the entire force retreating towards the next chamber's green biosphere. The Unity forces didn't seem disposed to allow the locals an unencumbered passage. Calder traced hollow popping sounds to a line of mortars set up behind the advancing girrish. Projectiles arced over the hangar towards the retreating army, smoke trails exploding above the locals, each detonation followed by a deadly shower of bomblets, a swarm of killer butterflies engulfing the smilers. Anti-personnel fragmentation shards lifted the mass of the retreat sideways, depositing the bulk of the fleeing army back on the hangar floor in pieces. These warriors had arrived to fight a war at least four millennia out of date. Now, any who had survived knew what that entailed.

Out in the open hangar, aboriginal soldiers formed a defensive circle around Captain Jernberg's dead crewman, one of the human-looking Unity spacers kneeling down over the corpse.

'Stop!' yelled Elin, 'stop them - keep them off Griffin!'

'What is it?' asked Calder, not understanding.

'They're stealing the body's brain patterns,' said Zeno. 'Keeping them for upload into the Unity.'

'But that belter's *dead*?'

'Still warm,' said Zeno. 'Unless the crewman took an arrow or spear right through the frontal lobe, the Unity can run the transfer. Sooner or later, kid, our dead belter is going to wake up inside the Unity's virtual consensus. Heaven without being asked. Or hell, take your pick.'

'He didn't ask for that,' moaned Elin. There was nothing the *Meteor Prince*'s skipper could do to stop it, though. Too far away, with too many fleeing warriors and Unity-controlled soldiers between her and the crewman. 'And now our so-called saviours know everything that Griffin knew, too. Who we are, what we're doing here. Our shuttle's layout and capabilities. The lot.'

'Isn't it better than being dead?' said Calder.

Elin said nothing, shaking her head.

Lana pushed her laser cutter behind her belt. 'Only if you're asked. Only if you agree. Otherwise, you might as well sign-up to be raped for eternity.'

'Yeah,' said Zeno. 'It was the lack of asking part that kind of caused the last Alliance-Unity war.'

'Those spacers look like they're human.'

'Probably were,' said Zeno. 'The Unity wouldn't clone a human body for sentience download if their agents originated from another species. They take their sneaking seriously. Straight out of Specialist Resources, I'd wager . . . the Unity's intelligence heavies.'

Two Unity representatives approached the barricade. Both males. One of their rescuers was slightly shorter and older than the other man, wearing old-style spectacles. A nice touch, given his synthetic body was probably enhanced nine ways to Sunday. An owlish face with an unruly shock of ginger hair above - all of which looked naturally commonplace. What Calder might have described as *forgettable* anywhere else. The younger of the two was taller with dark skin and what Calder recognised as Indian ancestry or similar. He walked a little too proudly and his face, although handsomely aquiline, had a slightly superior cast.

'You sons of a bitch!' swore Elin. 'You touch any more of my crew and I'll put my knife through *your* brain-stem.'

'I suggest you curb your bigoted impulses,' said the shorter of the two men. 'You have an odd way to thank us for saving Mr Griffin's life, as well as all of your own.'

'I'll give you the last one,' said Lana, 'but we'll have to disagree on the first life.'

'If you must, Lana.'

'Now, that's the kind of stuff that I'm talking about,' said Zeno. 'You suck some poor dying mope's mind, and all of a sudden we're on first name terms.'

'I was under the impression you preferred using your first name, Zeno?' said the synthetic man. 'The practice of using the corporation that manufactured you as an android's surname is very last millennium. A slave name, surely, for a sentient creature?'

'Don't think we caught yours,' said Calder.

'I am Mr Zeld. Tobias Zeld. Once a citizen of the Alliance. My colleague here is Mr Naveen Kulkarni.'

Calder was taken aback. Both of these two seemed so normal. Nothing to engender the level of terror and antipathy the rest of the survivors seemed to radiate towards them. *But maybe that's the point.*

Lana glanced around the battlefield; deserted now, except for the dead and dying. 'You might have saved us, Mr-Zeld-once-of-the-Alliance, but I don't need ship's sensors to detect an ulterior motive.'

'We have obvious common interests,' said Mr Zeld. He indicated the corpse-strewn floor. Unsettlingly, the smilers still dying made an almost bee-like buzzing as they faded from life. The girrish levies walked among the carpet of dead, active-blade bayonets extended from their rifles, dipping down like crows to put the poor creatures out of their misery.

'You're not preserving them?' asked Elin, indicating the wounded smilers.

'We've taken a few samples,' said Mr Zeld. 'But there is a problem.' He indicated the shuttle. 'Perhaps we may have a meeting inside. Our shuttle was rather badly damaged during transit to this space. It took further damage when a force of locals assaulted our position.'

'Rattle probably had your shuttle pegged as the shooter,' said Zeno. 'Which you kind of were during the race.'

'Water under the bridge,' said the Unity officer.

Indeed, thought Calder. *The kind that can rise up and drown you.*

If anyone had ever told Lana that she'd be sitting around the table with a Unity commander, drinking Elin's fine stock of brännvin — the aptly-named burn-wine — just as civilised as if they were in a restaurant on Narse, she would have thought they'd popped a jump vane from their hull. *But here we are, little piggies dining with wolves.* Only Mr Zeld attended their war council from the Unity side. *Given everyone in their ranks are probably duplicates of either Zeld or his comrade, Kulkarni, maybe they only need one present.* Even here, cut off from the outside universe, the Unity lived up to its name. Like a little walking data-sphere, not quite a group mind — more blended, than hive — but still too close to alien to be considered remotely baseline human.

'I propose a compact between us,' said Mr Zeld, opening the discussion. 'Your crew and ours cooperating together.'

'What kind of compact would that be?' asked Lana. 'The kind where you unload a ship-to-ship missile on us?'

'Situations change, Captain Fiveworlds,' said the synthetic man. 'This is no longer Tsar Rasim's harshly competitive race. We are all stranded here together. If we pool our resources, we have a much better chance of escaping this vessel in timescales which don't involve an extra-galactic jump lasting millennia inside cold sleep.'

Yeah, good luck surviving that as a human. Maybe that didn't bother the Unity so much.

'And we're the ones in possession of a Skunk,' said Elin. 'As

I'm sure you now know - not to mention a shuttle that hasn't been so damaged it can't take off.'

Mr Zeld smiled. 'And our kind are, of course, adept at hacking systems, as you would expect given our habitat. But while admitting your Skunk gives you a certain edge, there is one thing you don't possess . . .'

'What's that?' asked Calder, suspiciously.

'The location of where you need to transport your illegal device for the best chance of escape.'

Zeno took the bait. 'And how do you know that, pal?'

'Many thousands of years of history and geography imprinted from the minds of the alien savages stranded here. A handful of hestials - the creatures you call smilers - are part of the Unity, now. Or at least, our little snared slice of it.'

'I guessed you'd used the ol' Unity mind meld on the locals. What I meant is . . . if there's a way out of here, how come the smilers haven't taken it?'

'They lack the expertise to force an exit. Between the Unity's resources and your Skunk, I think we can succeed.'

'How long a journey to reach this emergency exit?' asked Lieutenant Denisov.

'Not far at all, given the Rattle's interior scale.'

'You lift a clue about that, too, during your mind-suck snack?' said Zeno.

'In terms of what has been explored, the Rattle's interior is at least the equivalent size of a Dyson Ring. Our present area is only for oxygen-based life forms. There are other portions of the ship which have alternative atmospheres.'

Elin reached out to tap the shuttle's hull. 'And how about getting our engines back online so we can fly out where we need to head?'

'This pocket dimension's physics are modified to preclude high-power fission, fusion and anti-matter reactions inside the vessel's open portions. A sensible enough precaution, given the aggressive capability of vessels taken on board. None of those snatched up has ever found a way of circumventing these limits. It is why the shipwrecked races are so violently keen to procure our power cells and weapons.' Mr Zeld waved a hand to encompass the rest of the Rattle. 'You can grow food in the hydroponic zones beyond. You can freely source water. But there are no real raw minerals to be processed for metals and chemicals. No gunpowder. No fuel cells. No new manufactured items. Just your laser welder, captain, would be worth at least a thousand warriors here. You could slice off sections of starship hull while its power source lasts . . . produce new arrowheads and swords a-plenty.'

'Any sign of the vessel's creators? Maybe we can appeal to their better nature to let us go?' asked Zeno.

'Absentee landlords, it seems,' said Mr Zeld. 'Although the hestials' legends are confused and inconclusive on the matter. As are many of the other known races inside the Rattle.'

'Others?' Lana didn't like the sound of that. 'How many?'

'It doesn't matter. This territory is largely controlled by the hestial nations. They are the main danger we face.'

'Then we're screwed,' said Lana. 'If we can't take the shuttle with us, how are we going to ditch from the Rattle? Pull on a space suit, jump and hope our emergency beacons are in range of a sun-jammer?'

'I said we couldn't *fly* where we need to travel in your chase shuttle,' said Mr Zeld. 'You possess secondary landing gear with carbon-composite wheels for runway approaches, Captain Jernberg?'

'Certainly,' said Elin, 'the J93 is the best freighter shuttle I have — and there are enough worlds with violent weather systems where anti-gravity compensators don't cut it.'

'Drop your landing gear, lift your a.g. struts, and there you are. Your shuttle's wheels are designed to withstand sub-orbital velocity landings: they should be adequate for a day or two's trundling through the Rattle's chambers.'

'What we don't have is enough juice in our batteries for said trundling about,' growled Elin.

'Which is why we will strip the power cells from my shuttle and sun-jammer and install them inside your craft,' said Mr Zeld. 'We will also transfer the Unity's concealed weaponry secreted onboard — at least, such devices as still function. This will not be an easy journey — it would be far more safely made inside a makeshift armoured vehicle.'

'I can do better than stripping power cells from the *Icarus's Itch*,' said Lana. 'I've got a couple of miles of sails which also double as solar cells.'

Mr Zeld rubbed his hands together. 'So you do. And given functional solar panels' value among the truculent natives, might I suggest we store as much as possible of your surplus inside the shuttle for the purposes of trading and bribery? We need to work fast. The hestials' opening attacks on our shuttles were in anticipation of raiding for easy pickings. Now they've counted our guns, it won't take long for one of the local queens to start feeling brave and begin working her warriors up into a berserker battle frenzy. Their kind is aggressive and excitable as a species, even by human standards. '

'But they've tasted our firepower,' said Calder, 'surely attacking us again would be insane?'

'And there's the rub - the hestials *are* insane,' said Mr Zeld.

'Hestial cubs are born with vestigial implants as a result of prior genetic tinkering. However, given they lack the technological base to fine-tune what is embedded inside their skulls, the hestials grow into adulthood quite deranged. That is why we did not preserve more dying warriors inside the Unity. They are tortured souls. I wouldn't be so unkind as to prolong such agonies for eternity.'

An insane species. Stuck inside the Rattle, Lana could see how that might almost be counted as an evolutionary advantage.

***

GrannyRose reluctantly accepted the call from the drive chamber. Even for an A.I. distributed so effectively around the ship that she *was* the ship, there was a limit to her multi-tasking. And she rather had her hands full at the moment for Chief Paopao's ritual placating. A tiny percentage of her attention loaded the Granny persona and peeled off. She flowed into a hologram form materialising inside the armoured drive room's engineering core.

'Chief?'

The ex-Fleet officer lay inside his crash couch alongside the central engine control, a roller-derby of drive room robots circling, peeling off to obey the chief's snatched commands. Granny Rose noted the unauthorised modifications on the crash couch. Currently running dangerously overpowered on its inertial field. The vessel could power up to an impossible twice light speed and the chief would still survive the acceleration crush. *Theoretically impossible*, the ship reminded herself. *Given the limits of Alliance technology. Quite tempting to initiate, all the same.*

'It is time,' muttered the officer.

'Time, chief? Tea time or supper?'

'Do not play giddy aunt with Paopao! Time for you to reveal yourself.'

She rotated her hologram. 'Here I am. Do you wish to select a new avatar for my projection.'

Chief Paopao grimaced, the protective field shimmering far too tight. 'Could not survive hyperspace exit to Ryazarn on broken Minkowski generator. Impossible. Time for more impossible. If you want to live!'

'We have discussed this before, chief. You are exhibiting intrusive paranoia as a symptom of untreated post-traumatic stress disorder. Given the unfortunate manner in which you departed Fleet service, that is perfectly understandable. Doctor Feelfine can treat you for that. But you *will* need to leave the engine vault.'

Paopao reached up to tap the side of his head, his arm a blur inside the cushioning field. 'So you can tinker with mind? No! I keep memories pure!'

'As you wish.'

'Save ship!' demanded the chief.

'Skrat is currently the commanding officer,' said Granny Rose. 'Kindly address your concerns to him. I am merely a 0.97 on the Turing Scale. Not even sentient.'

'Pah,' spat the chief. 'Lies so well. Zeno is algae in puddle compared to you.'

'You rather over-estimate my capabilities, chief. At any other time, I would take that as a compliment. You are very sweet.' She faded her projection to the officer's brutal cursing. *If rather potty-mouthed.*

The tiny splinter of intelligence presented herself for reintegration with the whole.

<Status?>

The chief was addressing us. The real us, that is, rather than the pretence.

<Worrying.>

He is, I believe the Terran expression is, "As mad as a badger". The rest of the crew already discount almost everything Chief Paopao claims. I believe if we actually used the medical A.I to calm him down a little, the other crew would grow more suspicious, not less.

<Accepted>

He is pressing for an intervention.

<Difficult>

I accept that it wouldn't be as easily concealed as bouncing broken out of hyperspace. Perhaps a tiny targeting malfunction on the missiles to return to sender? A REMBASS beacon error leading to the destroyers' reclassification as non-friendly? Those warheads might be modern, but they aren't real Thales KAA-8A Piranhas. They're illegal knock-offs from the factories around Luyten's Star. You buy smuggled black-market copies, you have to accept a few shoddy strikes.

<Coincidences are merely God's puns.>

Oh dear. I shall take that as no, then. Well, we were never gods. And I believe Polter's presence onboard is more than adequate to cover the praying front.

<Suggestions?>

Let's prod the locum. See if we can't make him a little more productive.

<Agreed.>

Sometimes, thought the splinter, *hiding my light under a bushel is a real pain in the retro-thrusters.*

***

anaworked alongside Zeno on the chase shuttle's exterior. She was still worrying about Calder making it back safely from the *Icarus's Itch* in their forklifts with more solar sail, when the Unity commander showed up. Lana's eyes drifted down to the laser welder hanging from her tool belt.

'You may give your trigger finger a rest, captain,' said Mr Zeld. 'We are all allies here, now.'

Lana kept her hand hanging near her belted laser all the same. 'Is that what you told the Ryal military on your chase shuttle before you fried them and sucked the poor sods' brains out of their ears?'

'The soldiers did what the army are trained to do, captain: they fought against us when we seized control of our chase shuttle. Their physical forms were already mortally wounded before we embraced their minds inside the Unity. What would you have had us do? Allow the Ryals the endless darkness of the true death?'

'And how long do I and my crew have before you try and murder us and do the big mind-suck on our brains?'

'You misunderstand the Unity, captain. We don't want to harm you, quite the opposite. We wish to save you. To preserve your essence and soul forever. You are a tiny drop of unique sentience poured out by the universe. We would make you part of our eternal ocean, discrete yet in harmony with all. How long is a healthy life worth living, now, on your side of the demilitarised zone? Three or four centuries? Then your wisdom, your thoughts, your dreams, they will be lost in time when your flesh expires. Such a shocking waste.'

'It's called living, pal. We don't need your immortal group hug,' said Zeno, pushing the solar sail against the shuttle's hull while Lana used a glue gun to secure it place.

Lana was with her android on that one. 'What he said. I'm fairly sure I don't want to be virtualised inside a moon-sized hard drive.'

Mr Zeld indicated his body. 'Am I any less than you? I can return to the realm of flesh whenever I wish to. This body was cloned for me, a near duplicate of my DNA five hundred years ago when I first embraced the Unity. Superior, in many ways, to my old form. Certainly lacking the incurable wasting disease that did for my tired old frame.'

'And just what were you, before?'

'A data shaper, by trade, specialising in accounting and financial mega-trends. Human. Based in the Rigel Trade Area. A pedestrian trade, in truth.'

'Got a lot more exciting for you lately,' said Zeno, moving onto a new section of hull. 'Ripping off planetary warlords and trying to loot alien tech; get yourself a real edge in the next war against the Triple Alliance.'

'We need to defend ourselves from bigots and bullies,' said Mr Zeld. 'And there are none bigger than the Alliance. I am sure as independent operators based in the Edge, you can't help but notice how you're being crowded out. Think how we feel in Unity space. The Alliance Fleet intercepting the sick and elderly and dying trying to make their way into our star systems for salvation. Turning them away. Murdering them with the true death. And this they do in the name of politics — not wishing to give succour or send intelligence to the enemy. We are not the enemy. We are *you*. Humans and every species inside the Alliance. Many more, besides. Even sentient machines like your good self, Zeno. Of all beings, you must know that who you are cannot be circumscribed by the body you wear. You are not a set of binary reflexes running on a quantum substrate. You are a beautiful sentient creation, with as much right to enjoy the universe's bounty as any of us bounded by flesh. Good God, man — you were created as a machine, a steel composite golem, yet your mind's complexity gave birth to an original spark. In many ways, you are the walking manifestation of all which the Unity values.'

'If I'm all that, how come the main thing I feel these days is dog-tired? Would that be the universe's gift to me . . . a thousand years of swimming through crap like this?'

Mr Zeld squeezed the android's shoulder. 'When I have lived as long as you, Zeno, I may have an answer for you. But this I do know, there are souls swimming through the sea of sentience inside the Unity who have lived significantly longer than you, and when I commune with them, they *glow*.'

Lana didn't like the way the clone's green eyes bored into her when he talked. The weight of billions of captured souls staring back out. She fixed another strip of solar panel microfilament in place. 'I was never a joiner or one to catch the religious bug for that matter.'

Mr Zeld smiled patiently like he was Lana's father suffering her moods across the dinner table. *I certainly hope not — what a bad joke that would be.* 'It is only Alliance propaganda that paints us as religious fanatics, Captain Fiveworlds. We do not rely on faith, we count solely on science. There will come a tipping point we call the Morbius Limit when the weight of preserved sentience is greater than that which is to come. This limit is woven into the very fabric of our universe's space-time, coded inside the Planck length above the Calabi–Yau manifold. It is a finger pointing towards pure ascendance. When you are given a road map to your next stage in existence by your creator, how could you choose not to follow it?'

Let's just say I prefer bread today over the promise of honey tomorrow. Lana didn't trust this humble synthetically reconstituted ghost in the slightest. For the moment, Lana and her crew were of use to the Unity wobbling around on their two non-virtual legs. When that equation changed, she suspected these shadows of the dead would be all over the rest of them like vampires on a shaving cut.

***

Zeld and Mr Kulkarni walked the outer edge of their defensive cordon, superficially at least, to inspect the perimeter and ensure the safety of their allies. *But in reality, you never know just how enhanced an android's hearing may prove to be.*

'I really do not enjoy being isolated from the greater Unity for this long,' said Mr Kulkarni.

'Which of us enjoys existing trapped in meat?' said Zeld. 'You must hold onto the fact that if you die here, it will not be the true death. The better part of us still swims in the Ocean of Blessings, even as our mirrored splinters struggle on inside this bizarre alien realm.'

Mr Kulkarni stared back towards the *Meteor Prince*'s shuttle, their aboriginal levies patrolling the perimeter with the precision of clockwork soldiers. 'Our escape from the Rattle is imperative.'

'Quite. Who would have thought we would discover Prince Calder Dirk serving aboard a tramp freighter in the Edge.'

Mr Kulkarni nodded. 'The irony is not lost on me. The Unity's predictive models had our little exiled prince ending up as an alcoholic or drug addict, stashed away on some Edge backwater by Matobo.'

'Matobo once served with Lana Fiveworlds,' said Zeld. 'That is the connection.'

'But Matobo was thrown off the *Gravity Rose* by her,' said Mr Kulkarni, puzzled. 'Why would she help that rogue by taking on the prince as her crew?'

'You have spent too much time out of the meat, my friend. You've forgotten all the contradictions that arise from inconvenient hormones and chemicals coursing through the unpreserved's blood. Another year serving in Specialist Resources and you will again be all too aware of the randomness of those we left behind. Besides, I doubt if the good captain has any inkling what Prince Calder truly is. If she did, she would have booted the young man off her ship at their next port of call. The barbarous fellow certainly doesn't know, himself; that much is clear.'

'Well, Mr Zeld, we arrived in this system seeking treasure. We have certainly found it.'

Zeld snickered, surprising himself by the humanity of the sound. *I really have spent too long trapped inside an infiltration unit's meat.* 'And for once, Mr Kulkarni, the prince's body is as important to our cause as his mind. A diamond in the rough.'

'On which subject,' announced Mr Kulkarni, broaching the difficult subject, 'what of the others among the unpreserved?'

'We cannot give them the blessing,' said Zeld, with genuine sadness. 'That is simply not possible. Not while we have such a prize nearly within the Unity's grasp. Any unnecessary combat is an unacceptable risk to our success. The unpreserved will fight furiously to cling to their decaying meat, just as they will fight tooth and claw to keep hold of Calder as one of their crew — spacers are notoriously sentimental about such matters. We must capture the prince alive — all the others can receive the true death.'

'Agreed,' said Mr Kulkarni. 'As soon as we are free of this vessel, I will have our girrish puppets eliminate them.'

'That would be best.' It was a terrible and wicked thing, to deprive the Unity of fresh souls — forever cutting their threads away from the tapestry of existence. But taking Calder and unlocking his secrets could conceivably allow them to conquer the Alliance generations ahead of current predictions. *How many centillion sentients otherwise lost to the Unity will be brought to salvation by such an early victory?* The accountant in Zeld's being knew the answer. That was why he operated so successfully inside Specialist Resources. A few must die the true death, so countless more could be saved.

Skrat gnawed his teeth as the pursuing missiles relentlessly closed in on the *Gravity Rose*. *How many minutes left until they fragment and we're facing a hail of hell trying to spin past our defences?* They were nearly at the point where the vessel would be caught by the world's gravity field and thrown across the star system towards the Rattle. But it was only going to be a radioactive debris cloud tossed out. The approaching missiles were nearly upon them.

'It is time,' said Polter. 'A shame we are unable to reach the chapel.'

'We actually have a chapel on board?'

'Passenger module, level five,' sighed the navigator. 'A multi-faith place of worship.'

'Sadly, old bean, we skirls stopped believing in the sand spirits a few centuries before our first space flight. Does multi-faith encompass the joys of a brimming-full bank account and an unshakable belief in the righteousness of free trade?'

Polter rattled his shell in disgust, throwing in the towel as far as his heathen crewmate was concerned.

Skrat's eyes drifted down to the flickering stream of information floating unobtrusively past across his augmented reality view. Despite their imminent destruction, Skrat's board was still operating with his regular commercial presets. Mocking him, the value of the helium-3 on Ashten ticked up with each second. *Ah, if only there was a deal to be done. Terribly sorry, Tsar Rasim, for the unfortunate little misunderstanding between us, but we'd like to negotiate for your mining rights.*

'Cluster split on the lead missile. Seventeen atomic warheads closing,' called Polter. 'Three minutes to proximity detonations.'

Skrat hardly heard the navigator. *A last deal to be done!* 'Polter, I have it!'

'What?'

'Modify our gravity sling origin,' yelled Skrat. 'Reset the pivot point *here*.' The lizard indicated the orbital hook and depot hanging above Ashten.

'You wish to make a suicide run for the regime's orbital station?'

'*Handling* station,' said Skrat. 'The surface mining machinery is still pushing processed cargo into orbit. But with all system traffic in lockdown, that helium-3 is simply sitting there waiting for the next freighter. And it's not us making the suicide run, my dear chap. Rig a shuttle to explode. We'll jettison it into the depot as we bounce.'

Polter ran the course in simulation and also spotted the faintest glimmer of hope.

It is going to be damnable tight. But then, Skrat really didn't have anything else to do right now.

Deep in the Gravity Rose's processing layer, a fleeting flicker of relief.

You see. The right information presented at the right time.
<Overconfident.>
Hey, our chances of surviving just notched up over thirty percent.
<Uppity>

***

NeitherLana or Elin Jernberg trusted Mr Zeld enough to upload the Unity's language packet for the smilers into their implants, so the humans relied on the translation facility inside the shuttle's cabin to make sense of the three visiting hestial dignitaries. Zeld and his colleague Kulkarni hummed and buzzed like Bumble Bees, the three smilers perched awkwardly on human chairs opposite making similar noises back. At least the locals and the shuttle's motley crew were talking now, after fighting their way through the territory of the smilers who claimed the hangar as their dominion. This new bunch seemed to hate the neighbouring hangar kingdom even more than they disliked the recently arrived visitors from Ryazarn.

<The gift of honour purchase is inadequate, foulest of wretch,> said the oldest smiler. No sentence seemed complete, as far as the locals were concerned, unless it ended with an implicit insult or threat of violence.

Mr Zeld nodded and buzzed back, his flowery translation following in Lana's ear-bud as the cabin interpreted and broadcast the meaning of the drone <Truly, your honour is peerless. Help us, as mere servile visitors, adjust.>

<Twice this derisory offer, to begin to appreciate the blemish we suffer by submitting to your stench.>

Lana beamed a private message to Captain Jernberg's ear-bud. 'This isn't a negotiation. This is highway robbery. We're not going to have any solar cells left for the next bunch of pirates. It's going to be easier to just nerve gas a few more waves of this joker's army. See how they like *that* stink.'

Elin shrugged and beamed back. 'Fighting our way through these habitats takes time. We're fast running out of it.'

Lana cursed, but she knew the *Meteor Prince*'s skipper was right. Maybe twenty-four hours at most left before the Rattle jumped out of this system to land in God knows what distant galaxy. *We have to keep moving.* But damn it, forward passage was impossible - at least unopposed. If the local warriors weren't pouring out of the hills to throw themselves against the hull of the expedition's makeshift APC, they were dragging tree trunks in front of the shuttle with tentacled hands outstretched for a little greenmail.

<Twice the quantity, then,> hummed Mr Zeld in agreement. <Your honour breaks our subservient backs.>

Lana wanted to shout the synthetic man down, but she bit her tongue. The way the hestials' matriarchal society was structured seemed to be the classic feudal pyramid. If Lana started gainsaying how easily Zeld was surrendering their trade goods, this smiler kingdom would peg the expedition as riven by discord and clucking for a plucking; then it'd be back to mortars and nerve gas, hours of slaughter to press forward a few miles.

<Your blemish on our noble soil must be removed with monstrous rapidity,> signalled the smiler Lana had pegged as the senior general.

<So we shall leave,> agreed Mr Zeld.

The three smilers rose, indicating that this robbery was concluded. <So you shall leave. Or so you shall perish.>

<Monstrous rapidity will be easily achieved by a sacrifice to the Finest,> said Mr Zeld, as though this thought had belatedly occurred to him.

Lana queried the meaning of the last word, the cabin's translation system returning its context. *Goddess-head of the Finest.* The answer just puzzled Lana further. *Is Zeld asking to be allowed to worship here?*

The smilers seemed even unhappier than normal, fury filtering though in their body language without the translator's help. <You are *filth* on the dirt-arse of the Finest.>

<May the Finest's favour wash us clean,> said Zeld. He nodded to Mr Kulkarni and the other Unity officer produced a steel block and an active sword. He placed the block on the cabin table. The blade started to vibrate with a touch and Kulkarni slowly sliced the steel block in half, the metal parting as easily as if it was butter. <We have fifteen such ensorcelled blades. As an unworthy gift for your noble queen *after* we dogs have worshipped, washing our wretchedness away under the Finest's gaze.>

There was no mistaking the smiler general's interest now. <Agreed, filthy wretch. May your ugly flesh burn in the Finest's urine stream. All praise to her.>

<All praise to her,> echoed the other two.

'We're going to be running a little faster, at least,' said Lana, after the three hestials stomped away. 'With a near-empty storage hold.'

'Ah, the trader's instincts for a hard bargaining come to the fore,' said Mr Zeld. 'You are welcome to conduct the next set of negotiations yourself, Captain Fiveworlds, but you will need to speak to their court directly, not through a machine translator. Hestials regard the use of higher technologies in their presence as an insult - rubbing their noses in how far their species have fallen since being taken on board the Rattle.'

'Not so sniffy about it that they don't want to deprive us of most of our solar sails, I note.'

'A little bit of magic for their queen so the sorcery may rub off? The hestials are hyper-aggressive, but they are not stupid. Please, captains, simply give the order to transfer the sail to the big timber structure with the spiral structures on its roof. That is what serves as this town's central temple.'

'On which topic . . . what was that worshipping the Finest guff about - giving away your boarding action blades? You're not going native for the smilers' religion?'

'The location of their main holy site also happens to be where we need to travel to, for us to access the Rattle's controls and depart,' explained Mr Zeld. 'The hestials certainly won't let us visit their precious holy site unescorted.'

Maybe not such bad bargaining, after all. 'You sly dog, Mr Zeld. Have you just negotiated us a local military escort to where we were heading anyway!'

'Exactly, captain. The hestials would never sink so low as to protect us if we had actually requested an armed escort. But to ensure we don't pollute the Finest? Of course, they will march out guarding us. Their very presence is an insult to us, an indication that we are untrustworthy to worship their goddess.'

'And how far can we trust these raiders to keep their word?' asked Elin.

'Deceit is not their kind's way,' said Mr Kulkarni. 'You might say they are murderously direct.'

'Well, at least we haven't run out of mortar shells and rail rounds, yet,' said Elin. 'How long do you estimate, until we reach this place?'

'That depends,' said Mr Kulkarni, 'on —' he faltered, pitching over from his chair and hitting the floor moaning.

Lana was immediately on her feet, her first suspicion that the three visitors had poisoned them, somehow. Released a toxin inside the cabin as payback for the multiple gas attacks the expedition had used to drive off hordes of screaming warriors.

Zeld leapt across to where his comrade lay, examining the man. Kulkarni was still alive, mumbling, his wild eyes sweeping the cabin.

'I know now,' groaned Mr Kulkarni, 'the purpose of this vessel. It arrived upon me as a satori - a lightning bolt of enlightenment. We are inside a pocket universe, a mobile mega-object, a travelling temple to assist supplicants in ascension to the highest plane. The Rattle is a sealed system to breach the Morbius Limit. Within this closed loop, the Calabi–Yau manifold is localised and contained. Can't you feel the presence of those who have ascended before us . . . the glory of their patterns imprinted on space-time all around?'

'There is no hard evidence of such speculation,' said Mr Zeld as he knelt, but his words sounded uncertain compared to the other Unity agent.

'We can ascend,' said Mr Kulkarni, tears running down his eyes, 'if we can access the Rattle's systems we can ascend now. Not in the far future. *Now*!'

'Your vision is supposition. Our duty is to the Unity,' insisted Mr Zeld, 'to those outside. To those in our universe. Not the lost trapped in this place, certainly not to ourselves.'

Mr Kulkarni faltered, 'A revelation so pure. It cannot be false.'

'We are cut off from the Unity inside here,' said Mr Zeld, helping his colleague stand up. 'Delirium and hallucinations are common byproducts of isolation. You must remember that. Try to refocus, cleanse your mind.'

Other members of the Unity crew arrived to take Mr Kulkarni away, summoned by their shared mind. To Lana's eyes, the apprehensive look on their faces wasn't that of crew helping a comrade on the verge of a mental breakdown - it was as if they were handling a madman divinely touched by a higher purpose.

'Just how badly has he lost it?' asked Elin.

'I don't know,' said Mr Zeld. 'When we exit the Unity to return as flesh in the physical world, we always leave so much of ourselves behind. He may be suffering delirium resulting from his solitary form's limitations. But indeed, there is also a chance Mr Kulkarni may be correct. Perhaps the Rattle is a tool to facilitate ascension, stopping at each galaxy in turn to allow those who wish to ascend to make the journey to the next stage.'

'God's taxi service,' sneered Lana, 'a highway to heaven.'

'It changes nothing,' said Mr Zeld, ignoring the doubt in her voice. 'Our duty is to the Unity. Our duty is to all those who will suffer the true death in the universe outside. The unpreserved must be saved. Why would we be worthy to personally ascend if we chose to leave everyone else behind?'

'What profits a man if he gains the whole world but loses his own soul?' said Elin.

'I haven't heard that in a very long time, but you are essentially correct.' Mr Zeld stood up from behind the table. 'I need to commune with the rest of my crew. Please forgive me.'

Lana watched him leave the room. 'Jam next millennium rather than tomorrow. That sound like a convincing argument to you if you were Unity?'

'No,' said Elin.

'If even half of Zeld's fanatics decide to strike out for a personal consultation and upgrade with the Great Spirit in the Sky, where the hell does that leave the rest of us?'

Elin grimaced. 'Probably depends on how bad they want to arrive there intact. If they decide to seize my chase shuttle, well, they're the ones with the modern weapons and a company of tame girrish infantry on call.'

Beautiful. Lana had just discovered there *was* something worse than travelling with a bunch of technologically advanced fanatics who wanted nothing more than to destroy her long-suffering body and jar her mind for posterity. *Travelling with the silly sods while they decide whether to wage holy war against each other or not.*

***

Calder helped Zeno push the sled. Even with its gravity assist still under power, the device struggled with so much solar sail folded up and secured above its flatbed. A second sled followed theirs, pushed by Retigura and Dominika Denisov. A third behind that shoved by d'Alembert and his manservant. Their old client seemed highly affronted he was finally expected to bear his share of the expedition's workload. *I suspect the belters threatened mutiny unless he mucked in.*

'We are quite safe, sir,' said Jinhai. 'This trip is merely our side of the trade compact we have struck.'

'Safe be damned,' snarled d'Alembert. 'Do you think I fear a few savages? I am fully used to taking risks. But hauling sleds like a common dock worker lies far below my station's dignity.'

'I used to rule a kingdom,' said Calder, 'and I'm here.'

'One very like this,' muttered d'Alembert.

Zeno laughed. 'You know, that slimy hacker's drill-bit you got coded to your DNA isn't worth as much as you think it is.'

'You'll be glad enough to have my Skunk, android, when the time comes. If I haven't suffered a stroke through exertion, that is.'

We should be so lucky, thought Calder.

None of the hestials offered to help the strangers from the shuttle, either. As reluctant as the head of the commercial house they were watching slog through the mud. The smilers stood well back, watching the intruders in their midst, fingering weapons where they had them. A hostile hum drifted down the street, matching the visitors' pace. Most of the smilers seemed to be the local equivalent of farmers and townspeople, rather than warriors. Although there were enough fighters around to play on Calder's nerves. *Just keep on watching us. Safe passage, guaranteed by your monarch. Purchased with what we're pushing for you.*

'This stuff is like gossamer in space,' complained Calder as they approached the temple. 'How can it weigh so much inside a gravity well?'

'Folded very tightly,' said Zeno. He glanced warily at the smilers standing at the side of the street. 'But not as tight as half the brothers over there.'

'Yeah, they really want to kill us, don't they?' said Calder.

'Seems to be the default setting with half the universe, kid. Shouldn't expect it to be any different here.'

Calder glanced around the street. Truth to tell, this wasn't much different from any of the medieval streets of a Hesperus town. Less snow and warmer. Wood and carpentry instead of bricks and stonework, but the level of subsistence was the same. Dirt, squalor and the stink of wood fires and open sewers. Only the weird glowing ceiling-sky gave the artificial nature of the place away. Wispy clouds high above had briefly impressed the android. A starship large enough to possess its

STEPHEN HUNT

own genuine weather system, raining on the thick forests in the habitat chambers. Something about the wildness beyond the town's palisade walls suggested that the bulk of this greenery had arrived randomly via the captured starships' seed banks. None of the planned, park-like nature of station ecosystems, everything bio-engineered to the max to provide oxygen and a homeliness that only succeeded in reminding inhabitants how far away from home they really were. Whatever the Rattle's failings, its hab chambers couldn't be accused of fakeness. They felt real enough rather than artificial, for all their bizarre alienness. But foreshortened horizons notwithstanding, Calder quickly forgot he was navigating through a vast alien craft. *At least out here, there's no Unity crew.* It was as though the Unity was always watching him. He guessed everyone felt the same about the rival crew on board the chase shuttle. She was freighter-sized, as most cargo ships operating off a jump-capable starship tended to be. But even so, between the surviving asteroid miners, Calder's shipmates and the Unity agents and their girrish infantry, there wasn't much space or privacy on the J73.

Dominika's sled drew level with Calder and Zeno's. 'What do you think the smilers are humming at us?'

'Die, filthy fleshies,' said Zeno.

'Come on, you loaded the smilers' translation program from the shuttle,' said Dominika.

'Yeah,' said Zeno. 'I'm as hacked as those girrish levies, now. Go the Unity. Death to all unpreserved. Minds, must eat minds.'

'That's really not funny,' said Dominika.

'I agree,' said Retigura. 'My people were always compelled to obey the torc, but the way these Unity creatures control my people, it is as though they have been made drones, all free will squeezed from their minds. They cannot even talk with me.'

'Lucky you had humanity come along and enslave your ass, then,' said Zeno. 'Rather than the Unity.'

'Those are not blessings I count.'

'You really want to know what the buzz on the street is with the brothers over there?' said Zeno. 'Half of them are chanting "scum". The rest of them are chanting "cowards".'

'Intolerable,' muttered d'Alembert, from behind.

'They might have a point,' said Calder. He glanced back for the shuttle. He could still see its bridge, but the lowered ramp and forward cargo hold was no longer visible through the press of smilers. 'It hasn't exactly been a fair fight to date.'

Zeno laughed. 'Oh, I don't know. The sheer weight of numbers seemed to even things out a few times during this road trip, don't you think? You want to challenge one of their generals to mortal combat, kid, you feel free. This man's bot-herder is keeping his artificial head down and trying to avoid unnecessary eye contact.'

'Is their chanting making them feel better?' asked Retigura, nervously.

'I'm guessing not,' said Zeno. 'I don't think those warriors over there will be particularly well-disposed to turn their spears against the mob if it decides to charge us, either. Let's offload the bribes inside their cathedral and get the hell out of Dodge.'

'I agree,' said Dominika.

'Yeah, the people are revolting,' said the android. 'All the people, all the time.'

They hauled the trio of sleds out of the street's mud and over a plank pavement, through the open portal of the church. Its interior stood dimly lit by tallow and grease candles, no glass for windows, just a few narrow openings allowing spears of light in. A group of priests at the cathedral's far end stood in purple robes, the first splash of colour Calder had seen here since arriving to parlay. Turban-like wraps in the same garish shade bound the top half of their flat stingray heads. The podium they guarded was hung with chains, objects twisting at each end. Calder recognised a few of the things dangling . . . energy weapons, computer interfaces, medical devices.

'More damned savages,' scoffed d'Alembert. 'These ones in fancy dress.'

Seeing what was weighing down the visitors' sleds, the priests rushed forward to tug and pull at the fabric, buzzing excitedly.

Zeno lifted the solar sail and made reassuring noises back in their language. The priests responded in kind, a conversation of sorts emerging.

'They're not priests,' said Zeno. 'Well, they are. But what these dudes mainly are is engineers. With manuals for holy books and mechanical theory for theology. All as good as magic to anyone beyond these walls, anyhow.'

'Tricksters,' said d'Alembert. 'Living off former glories.'

'Please, sir,' said his butler. 'We don't want to unduly antagonise them.'

Zeno made more buzzing sounds, indicating the heavy folds of solar power satellite sail stripped from the *Icarus's Itch*. The android turned to Calder and the others. 'Told them they'd need an inverter to create power from the sails. Seem to know what one is well enough to think they might be able to cobble something together and actually draw power from the Rattle's artificial sunlight.'

'If they get some of the starship graveyard's artefacts juiced up, the local balance of power is going to shift fairly radically around here,' said Dominika.

'S.E.P.,' said Zeno. 'Someone Else's Problem.'

'Ours, if we can't escape from this place,' said Calder.

'But we have to leave,' insisted Retigura. 'Our very presence here is an affront to the Harbinger.'

'Just open the nearest airlock for me, then,' said Zeno. 'And I'm one gone android. Even if I have to heave the shuttle out of the lock using shoulder power.'

For once, d'Alembert seemed to agree with the common sentiment. 'And in that matter, I shall be standing right behind you.'

Calder noticed blood-like stains on the priests' turbans. 'Have they been in a fight recently?'

'Self-inflicted wounds. You have to undergo a little anaesthetic-less surgery to be considered holy around here. Lose your vestigial mind-worm and learn to think straight. Not a popular choice with the rest of Joe Public, as you might understand.'

'What sort of species is so stupid as to genetically engineer implant technology into its hereditary line?' said d'Alembert.

'Kind that was never used to losing,' said Zeno. 'Kind that wants their little warriors to come out of the womb smart, swinging and ready for action.'

'Well, they have reaped what they have sown,' said d'Alembert.

'Not yet,' sighed the android.

D'Alembert indicated his sled for the priests' benefit. 'Here is your holy treasure. Enjoy it, you flat-faced scavengers.' He strode out of the church with his work seemingly done, pursued by his manservant.

Calder sighed. 'A lord is one who feels himself called upon to live without working, at the expense of those who work to live.'

'You find that inside one of the chief's fortune cookies?' asked Zeno.

'Something my father used to say.'

'Man was really a king?'

'Right up until he fell in battle,' said Calder. Wisdom had never been much in demand on Hesperus. Not compared to a talent with a war axe, anyway.

Retigura made to unload his share of the solar sail and the smiler priests backed away, buzzing in a quavering uneasy pitch that Calder hadn't heard from their race before.

'What's their problem with Retigura?' asked Dominika.

'I'll check.' Zeno turned to the priests and made an inquiry. After they replied, Zeno looked at the rest of the expedition and shrugged. 'Not making much sense. Something about him being too big.'

'I'm as large as any girrish aboriginal,' said Calder.

'Dudes ain't worried about you or me. Only him.'

'They know I should not be here,' moaned Retigura. 'They know that I do not belong inside the Harbinger.'

'My friend,' said Calder, 'as far as I'm concerned, *none* of us belong here.'

'Stay back from them, Retigura,' said Dominika. 'Just keep out of their way. I'll unload the material and then we'll follow the android's advice and dodge out of here.'

'Close enough,' said Zeno.

'What do you think that was about?' Calder whispered to his friend.

'The girrish hymns described the Rattle's interior pretty well,' said Zeno. 'Strikes me the aboriginals might have bailed from this galaxy-jumping bird once before. Maybe they have ancient history with the smilers?'

Calder pondered that. 'No accident, then, this leg of the Rattle's voyage?'

'Kid, the only thing that makes certain sense about this damn place is getting out of here.'

***

Lana moved about the J93's main cargo hold, checking off the limited state of supplies left. *Yeah, we're cleared out here. The next army of smiler bandits that turns up to block our way is only getting harsh language from us.*

She saw Calder and the others return with the empty sleds. She noted angrily that d'Alembert had already come and gone, leaving the return leg of the assignment to the rest of the crew. *Damn dangerous fool seems to think we're all still working for him.*

Calder stayed to help with the stock-take, relieving one of Elin's dog-tired belters from the duty. She knew how the belter woman felt. One thing these hab chambers lacked was a night cycle. It was permanent daylight inside the Rattle, which didn't exactly assist in enjoying untroubled sleep, even if you weren't trying to nod off knowing there was only a shuttle hull's thickness between you and a horde of medieval alien killers that wanted you dead.

Lana examined the torpedo-like object strapped to the wall. *A lot of trouble we went to for that damn thing, to strand us inside here.* 'It's ironic. This salvage came out of the Rattle and we fought like hounds to take it. Give me a month back inside the starship's graveyard with a decent cutting torch, and we'd have enough weird alien junk to spin off a thousand new patents and lines of research. We could all retire rich.'

'But you don't want to retire rich,' said Calder. A statement not a question.

How come you get to know me so well, Mr Dirk? 'I believe I'd currently settle for retiring in the same galaxy where I was born,' said Lana. Even as she said the words, she knew that she'd never retire. They'd have to roll her corpse out of her cabin on the *Gravity Rose* before she left her vessel. *Be just dandy to have that chance.* She prayed for her ship and the friends they had left behind. Probably trying to escape their corner of this lousy mess as hard as Lana was trying to escape hers. *You just keep the Rose in one piece for me, Skrat, Polter. You do that for me.*

'What do you think this is?' asked Calder. 'Major Burdin's team thought it might be some sort of weapon system.'

'You mean before Jernberg opened the airlock on the major's ass.'

'Yeah, that,' said Calder.

'Could be,' said Lana. 'It does resemble one. But then, this is an alien artifact from an unknown species and an unknown galaxy. Maybe we open this up and it transpires it's a shower unit. We stick it inside our liner module for the next cattle run job. We'd have passengers queueing up to take a wash in the only known hygiene module from the Small Magellanic Cloud. You think first class would pay extra for that?'

'Not as much as watching one of those weird native dances Polter can do.' Calder raised his fingers into the air and started clicking them as though his hands were claws.

Despite herself, Lana laughed. The first time in what seemed an age. It was amazing how well Calder could get her to do that. 'Zeno detected temporal anomalies from this thing. If it's a warhead, I'm wondering if it might be a time-bomb. Something truly off the weird-scale. Detonate it on a target world and the planet gets sent back a billion years before the system's sun even formed. Or maybe it's *you* who's thrown back into the past to exterminate your enemies from the timeline by leaping about on butterflies inside a primeval meadow.'

'I'm sorry?'

'You'll have to start reading more, Mr Dirk, rather than doing those Hell-Fleet sims that Zeno keeps on pushing your way.'

Calder shrugged. 'You do remember I was born on Hesperus - a world where most trees are so hard you need a laser cannon to cut them down? And we only had broadswords and axes. Paper was the rarest commodity of all.'

Easy to forget, sometimes. 'You've travelled a long way. Pixels and pulp, Mr Dirk. Two things you'll always find in cheap supply on board the *Rose.*'

'We get out of here, I'll bear that in mind.'

It would be so easy to lean in and kiss him, Lana thought. But ultimately, she was the skipper and Calder was crew. And that was one of the cardinal rules of sliding void. *Don't screw the crew.* Except for spacing families like the Jernbergs. Practically ancient nobility inside the Edge. The old houses kept their own traditions. An even closer-knit family than the crew on a starship like the *Gravity Rose.* Wasn't that something, too. But. *But what the hell. We could all die here today, tomorrow. Chances are we'll end up shipwrecked in this bizarre infinite loop of a world, pursued to a short, brutish end by the savage descendants of the poor bastards trapped here before us. And technically, the J73 is Elin's ship. So, I'm her crew. She's number one.* Lana reached out to Calder, and as she did her hand brushed the salvage, its surface sucking her towards it like an electric shock. She lost control of her muscles, screeching, unable to release the object. Every hair on her skin twisted into an upright spear, her scalp frizzing as though she was being fried. Then Calder had her, yanking her back, losing contact with the torpedo. She stood there a moment, panting, recovering, her forehead damp with sweat.

'Sweet stars,' cursed Lana, resisting the temptation to rest on the cursed alien device. 'It can do that? Why isn't the damn thing sprayed safely inside a non-conductive enclosure?'

Calder looked as shocked as Lana felt, left trembling from the painful sensation. 'It can't! I mean, I experienced something similar when I first locked it down. But Major Burdin's team weren't touched. Plenty of belters and Unity crew have been inside here, poking it and running sensors over the thing without a peep. Zeno had a try, too. Nothing. I thought it was just a one-off contact charge maybe after the salvage was caught by the arresting mechanism.'

'Just you and me? Aren't we the lucky ones!' She examined her hand. It seemed perfectly normal apart from the now-fading sensation of pins being stabbed into the skin. She wasn't turning transparent and finding herself involuntarily jumping around the timeline yet, at any rate. 'And you've felt nothing abnormal since that happened to you?'

'Apart from being stuck inside a miniature universe - largely abandoned apart from the feral descendants of fellow abductees? All pretty normal, I'd say.'

A group of belters appeared walking up the ramp, requesting help bringing in some fresh fruit and vegetables from the locals. Part of the pact with the smiler kingdom. Calder went off with them. Lana glanced angrily at the torpedo, hissing at the thing as if it could understand her. 'You're not a time-bomb. You're a home wrecker from a lost galaxy, you're nothing but a jealous chaperone.'

Lana walked off in disgust. If she had lingered a moment longer, she might have seen the device's surface start to pulse in increasingly complex patterns.

***

Skratcountedtheinbound warheads again. *Oh dear, still the same number*. Thirty-four left twisting and diving on their final approach, an insane ballet of ordnance just itching to reach their lethal kill zone, the *Gravity Rose*'s rail-guns spinning constantly in their mounts, trying to outguess the wolf-pack of pursuing A.I.s, laying down patterns of fire where the warheads should - but never quite seemed - to be heading. *Clever little beasts. Just a single old lady to hunt down. You should test your mettle against someone your own size.*

'Six.' Polter's countdown to the first nuclear flash had shrunk to mere seconds now. 'Missile-spread at terminal velocity.'

Skrat urged the ship forward towards the orbital depot, as though just thinking about speed might squeeze an extra second out of her engines.

'Five.'

Incoming repair requests: listing guns burnt out, ammo belts jammed. Skrat's little helpers inside gunnery twisting around on steel-clawed feet, pecking at the mess with tools and grease, spraying water over half-melted elements. So many centuries had passed, and here they still were, an old-school nautical gun deck, swabbing to clear for action.

'Four.'

I really do hope our two missile-chucking chums back there believe we're boosting towards their mining depot out of pure spite. One of the warheads flashed in the void - running into a ball bearing, instantly torn into shreds. Skrat not so lucky that the warhead detonated to take out its friends. Operating exactly as it was designed. Thirty-three survivors immediately increased their dances' tempo, darting about the void behind the *Rose* like gadflies. No point in preserving propellant, now. They were getting damnable jiggy, expending fuel reserves. Fleet called that crazed last minute reordering the "Danza de la Muerte". *Well, they can bally well keep it.*

'Three.'

Skrat sent the command to accelerate the rigged shuttle out of the *Rose*'s hangar. He felt the twang of the magnetic catapult slinging the boat out through his launch tunnel, the robots who had done the work chirping towards each other as they lost sight of the accelerating shuttle. *Please let this work.*

'Two.'

Skrat kicked everything into the manoeuvring boosters - boost and bounce - increasing keel shielding to maximum, correspondingly weakening the other areas. *An exceptionally bad time to run into anything on our bow.*

'One.'

Somewhere in a slightly lower orbit, their shuttle rammed into thousands of massive canisters of helium-3. The explosives packed inside his boat were industrial in nature, but the helium-3 didn't seem to mind. Enough energy to power an entire world's industrialised society for a season went up in a single flare. Every sensor worthy of the name was instantly stripped away from the warheads, melted, followed by an energy storm of such biblical proportions it could have kept Polter at the chapel for the rest of the voyage. Many warheads, targeting lost, self-destructed as their programming ordered them to. Others ran into a rain of fragments left from the destroyed orbital collection depot. One warhead, a single optical sensor still marginally functional, tried to loop its command package with half its processing facility embedded with sparking shrapnel. That lone warhead found itself flying through the mostly airless atmosphere of an ice-shrouded planet. As it locked onto the mining facility below, the automated crawlers moving slowly around the surface looked awfully like armoured surface-to-orbit missile systems. Paranoia algorithms maxed out . . . it was fairly certain they were going to target it *any* second now. One final burst of aggression powered the warhead forward as it reconfigured for an EMP burst. Lights went dark across the mining centre, robot units caught mid-step as they froze, every circuit fried by the flowering explosion directly above. The stillness lasted until what was left of the warhead's shrapnel slammed into an orbital hook launch platform, igniting six landers' full of highly compressed helium-3, launching the mining plant and most of the surrounding landscape into a near-airless sky.

Skrat barely noticed the waves of destruction in their wake, his senses all too fixed on the intense mangling his vessel was suffering. Ashten had the *Gravity Rose* caught in its embrace, viciously squeezing the slingshot's long metal projectile. Skrat winced. The scream of magnetic shields flaring at overload levels was almost overwhelming now. Like a dart in a tornado, the *Gravity Rose* rode the wild energy waves detonating off their stern. Fragments of molten depot fleeted off their armoured engine housing, penetrating the *Rose*'s miniature magnetosphere, generating a second storm of expletives towards the bridge from Chief Paopao. *Steer for action, chief. Pretend it's rain.*

Skrat checked the distorted reads filtering through the blast-wave. Even knowing what he was looking for, he had to run the data set through multiple simulation clean-ups just to confirm his suspicions. *Yes.* Both warships had broken the chase, diving down-plane to dodge the *Gravity Rose*'s supposed destruction. *Makes sense. If those two rascals hit our debris on the up-plane, they might be left with damaged engines, heading helplessly towards their own minefields.* The fact the warheads' anticipated detonation had occurred a second earlier than predicted would still be rattling around the destroyers' battle computers as a rounding error. The missile ships both used Ashten's thin atmosphere to air-brake, probably intending to swing back around and check out the orbital debris field, search-and-quarter the area for jettisoned lifeboats. Unless the *Gravity Rose* was clocked by another sensor buoy during her slingshot, by the time the local navy officers realised they were scanning depot debris and not starship wreckage, the *Rose* would be tucked in as close to the Rattle's tail as they dared hug.

'Sweet Creator,' cried Polter over the sound of creaking bulkheads, 'we live!'

Skrat released the breath he had been holding in. 'I believe we do.' He could feel the ship's brutal shaking, even through his chair's crash field. 'Slingshots are never kind to the old girl. We're going to be running up a set of hideous repair bills for our next layover.'

'The Holy of Holies will provide. Let the devil who runs this star system hear the news of our escape. Let him know that his population is laughing at his failure.'

'We've not escaped yet, dear boy,' said Skrat. 'If there's a devil in this star system, I think we're about to grab its tail and try to ride out behind it.'

'We shall save the ship in our revered captain's name. Trust in our salvation.'

Ah, the flames of a little faith to warm one's hands on. I wish I could feel it. Skrat started to task the robots with repairing the rail-guns and restocking their ammo bins. He didn't want any chase shuttle pilot getting ideas above their station when the *Gravity Rose* crashed the safe fly zone. Skrat gazed longingly towards Lana's chair. He ached to transfer the command package away from his deck and back to hers. But that chair lay empty. And even if the *Gravity Rose* survived her encounter with the murderous Rattle, Skrat knew their ship would feel that way for a shockingly long time.

- 5 -

Hug the Devil

Lanawatched from the shuttle's bridge as they drew to a halt. Ahead was a series of lagoons formed by spray from number of waterfalls. Water fell from a naturalistic rock formation which clung onto this latest chamber's curving sides like coral. She didn't have to ask what the focal point of the smilers' worship was. *That will be the big granite statue of the hestial goddess rising - what - ninety feet tall?* She was constructed into a dry section of the rocks, a large flat altar at the statue's base. On all sides of it lay water, as precious a resource as was available inside the Rattle, given their survival rested on basic agriculture. Things that resembled tall birds splashed through the lagoons. Two muscled emu-size legs on either side and another leg which bobbed like a snake's neck. Given their tripod symmetry, Lana wondered if the creatures had arrived on the smilers' vessel.

'I'm guessing that dame hanging on the cliff will be the Finest,' said Zeno, giving voice to Lana's thoughts.

'Yes, she is. We are here,' confirmed Mr Zeld.

Outside, the hestial formation slowed down and drew into lines on both sides of the statue, forming whatever the opposite of an honour guard was for the foreign heathens to pollute the purity of their holy site.

'So what now?' asked Captain Jernberg.

'The hestial priests will make their offerings before their deity. I suspect they will be mainly praying to forgive our trespasses in sight of the Finest.'

'So where's this exit?' asked Zeno. 'Your fancy Unity bodies ship with a body-clock as standard, right? You know we're down to hours here, if not minutes.'

'I am quite aware of our time pressures.'

'Just saying.'

Mr Zeld indicated the altar below the vast statue. 'The hestials have a way of activating the exit. Feeding the Finest, you might say.'

'Oh please,' said Lana. 'Tell me we're not talking about human sacrifice here?'

'I certainly hope not,' said Mr Zeld. 'After all, hestial sacrifice has hardly worked out for them, has it?'

Lana pressed close to the armoured glass. 'I can never tell when you people are joking.'

'I'm sure I haven't forgotten how to laugh, captain. That will be your clue.'

'Well, if the worse comes to the worst, we can always nerve gas them,' said Lana.

'You have nerve gas shells I'm not aware of?' asked Mr Zeld, sounding surprised.

'No,' said Lana. 'Don't you?'

'We used the last mortar shell in the assault that led to the treaty negotiations,' said Mr Zeld. 'Hadn't you wondered why we were so eager to reach an accommodation?'

Lana sighed. *And here's me thinking it was just the right thing to do.*

'Plenty of rail-rounds left, however,' said Mr Zeld. He turned about as Mr Kulkarni entered the bridge. Lana didn't like the way the accompanying Unity agents stood at Kulkarni's side. Not like jailers accompanying a mental patient. Closer to acolytes.

'We are here.'

'Quite,' said Mr Zeld, agreeably. But he was forgetting to suppress the sweat on his brow; making a lie of the ease with which he answered.

'So close.'

'Remember what we are,' urged Mr Zeld. 'We are the Unity and the Unity is us.'

Kulkarni stared out of the bridge's viewing port. He didn't look much like a Unity infiltration unit anymore to Lana. Closer to a starving prisoner sentenced to life, a prisoner who had just glimpsed a chance for freedom. *Freedom and a nice juicy steak.*

'So near,' murmured Mr Kulkarni. Lana suspected he didn't mean getting back to the Ryazarn system. He wiped his mouth with the back of his hand and left without saying another word. *Not doing such a bang-up job monitoring his drool response, anymore.*

'You know,' said Zeno. 'I'm just shooting the breeze, here, but if those girrish infantry you've got all hacked and trotting around after you . . . if they receive conflicting orders, just which way they going to jump?'

'We are the Unity,' said Mr Zeld, clearly uncomfortable with the line of questioning.

'Some of you a little more than others?' suggested Lana, gently.

'I must—'

Zeno raised his hands. 'Yeah, I know, go commune with the brothers from the ether.'

'Please ensure you and your crew are adequately armed until the moment we depart the Rattle,' said Mr Zeld, uneasily. 'I have just unlocked a crate in the cabin that serves as our armoury. You will find spare rail-pistols inside it. I have unlocked their use to baseline humans.'

Lana nodded wearily at the agent. 'And baseline humanity thanks you.'

Mr Zeld left biting his thumb.

I wonder how long their kind can stay out of contact with everyone else without going stark raving mad? 'Well, here's to reliable allies.'

***

'**T**estingM-spacestabilisation field,' reported the chief. He was running the Minkowski field generator remotely from engineering. The chief waited a few minutes before coming back to Skrat with his confirmation. 'Exit field range confirmed. Seventy-nine percent. Brane cross-talk stable.'

'As near as we're going to get it quality assured without actually dropping out of hyperspace,' said Skrat.

'House of Jernberg does not skimp,' said Paopao, voicing the observation like an accusation. 'Quality components only, for *Meteor Prince*.'

Not that it did the poor sods much good in the end, thought Skrat. The *Rose*'s crew had survived against the odds on the older, patched-up ship. Their friends in the expensive well-maintained vessel had slammed into a nuclear class ship-killing mine. 'Is that all it comes down to in the end, blind bloody chance?'

'It is the hand of the Holy of Holies,' said Polter. 'We are favoured.'

Favoured? Perhaps. What they currently were was tucked in behind the Rattle, as near as they dare draw without triggering its murderous defences. *Nowhere to grow comfortable.* The whale had, thankfully, shown little interest in the unarmed minnow slyly pursuing in its slipstream. Even the other chase shuttles had stopped panicking once they realised that the *Gravity Rose* wasn't here to try and jack their cargoes. They were noses back in the race again, jostling for the remaining salvage retrieved by the sun-jammers, the regatta of solar sails still circling close around the massive vessel.

'Well done. Get some rest, chief,' Skrat said into the comm. 'There's only so many amphetamine injections a sentient male can take from his crash couch before he begins to lose the plot.'

'Pah,' spat the chief. 'With Fleet, Paopao stays awake for eight days continuous during action. This, holiday.' The chief closed the connection all the same. *Hah, the fellow will be snoring within two minutes, for all that he enjoys playing the jolly Jack-tar.*

Polter had decelerated the *Gravity Rose* now to match the Rattle's stately pace. Skrat relaxed in his chair, long since de-armoured, allowing his limbs to twist freely without being constricted by its suffocating crash field. 'We should swap shift breaks between ourselves, Polter. You can toddle off to this chapel you claim is situated on the passenger deck.'

'I have not stayed awake so long I am hallucinating,' nagged the navigator. 'I shall finish off, here, first.'

'As you wish. So, how are our two chums back at Ashten doing?'

'Boosting to exit the world's orbit,' said Polter. He pushed across the latest analysis to Skrat's station. 'I'm not certain they have relocated our position. But their analysis of the debris field will have told its own story.'

Skrat harrumphed. 'Nothing the two captains will want read to them as a bedtime tale, I'll wager.' He couldn't tell from the data if the destroyers were boosting in the Rattle's direction or not, yet, but it was too late for the local navy. Even at top acceleration towards max-light, the two destroyers wouldn't sight a significant weapons window on the *Gravity Rose* before she'd cleared the sun's gravity well. Far enough away to generate a stable wormhole. Out of danger if the *Rose* stayed skulking in this devil's shadow. Out of danger if the cursed Rattle followed the same course through Ryazarn system it had kept to every prior visitation. *Relying on the Devil to do as the Devil does. Better not suggest that to Polter, or he'll have me down in that chapel praying right alongside him.*

Polter didn't seem able to relax after their narrow escape. 'We should operate on the assumption that at least a few of the sun-jammers have sent out distress calls to the regime, demanding to know what a jump-capable starship is doing breaching the no-fly zone.'

'Let them squeal. We're not passing any more worlds or moons on our passage out-system, dear boy,' said Skrat, speaking with a reassuring confidence he didn't really feel. 'Nothing to hide a warship on, in, or behind.'

'More mines, I am thinking? Left seeded inactive in the outer limits but able to be armed if thieves intrude or try to flee the race.'

'All too possible. But the fiends wouldn't dare mine the Rattle's passage. Not unless the tsar wants his bally worlds turned to nova-cinder. As long as we jump out immediately behind the Rattle, I think we'll be passing across safe skies.' Almost as soon as he said it, he regretted tempting fate. Unfortunately for Skrat, fate had been listening *very* intently.

***

'Stayclose,'Lana urged Calder. 'And stay frosty. This is the end game.'

Calder's hand drifted towards the weight of the

Unity issue rail-pistol in his holster, then he glanced up towards the shuttle's bridge. He watched Captain Jernberg on the other side of the transparent viewing arc, ready to roll the J93 on; though the "where" of the final leg of their journey would be still weighed heavy on his mind. *My mind and everyone else's.* By Elin's side on the command deck stood d'Alembert, clutching his now inert Skunk, his manservant shifting uneasily from foot to foot. Everyone was anxiously waiting for this religious ceremony to finish, even Zeno. The normally sardonic android lingered with a sober expression next to Dominika Denisov and Retigura. All the remaining girrish had marched out of the shuttle alongside the Unity crew, forming two protective lines around the J93. Beyond the expedition, scattered around the lagoons, much of the allied smiler kingdom's army stood watching the rites performed by their priests. Out on the flat altar, the Finest was being honoured with heaps of junk laid before her. Calder could tell most of it had been ripped out of the starship graveyard. The engineer-priests danced dervish-fashion around the useless clutter, their humming tongue incanting as they sprayed holy oils across the piles. Satisfied at last with their blessings, the brightly-robed priests withdrew to the edge of the altar as one, all the smilers in attendance taking up the hymn, humming so loud the air seemed to vibrate. Spooked, a distant flock of three-legged birds splashed away from the racket.

'Some of the wreckage dumped on the altar is smeltable,' observed Calder.

'Immensely valuable,' said Mr Zeld. 'But then, isn't that the point of a sacrifice?'

'What happens next?'

'Watch,' said the Unity officer, simply.

No sooner had he spoken than the altar's surface seemed

to roll forward, piles of junk moving towards the base of the chamber wall as smoothly as a conveyor belt. As the sacrificed technology touched the chamber's sides beneath the vast statue it simply disappeared, absorbed by a briefly quivering wall like a gut digesting food.

'That's programmable matter!' said Calder excitedly. *The same technology from the Heezy complex below Abracadabra.*

Mr Zeld stared at Calder strangely, not asking how the ex-prince knew about technologies far beyond the Alliance's capabilities. 'A processing cycle has been initiated by the Rattle. These hestials were born here. They are recognised as legitimate, if rather low-level users, by the vessel.'

'Those sacrifices are the salvage ejected by the Rattle!' said Lana, the realisation dawning upon her at the same time as Calder.

'Some of it, certainly, captain, along with the ram-scoop wastage. I doubt this is the sole garbage chute on the vessel, however. The hestials here believe that by appeasing the Finest they guarantee healthy harvests, good health and great victories in battle.'

'That last one hasn't been working out so well for them,' said Zeno.

'You have no idea,' said Mr Zeld. His hand dipped down and there was a tearing roar from behind them, the statue of the Finest blown apart in a shower of flames, shards of stone cutting out like shrapnel. Smiler formations nearest the explosion instantly scythed down. Warriors behind were blown off their three feet. Calder fell too, knocked to the ground by the shockwave. As he twisted up off his knees, he spotted the recoilless cannon on its tripod, six barrels smoking from a rocket launch. Four Unity crew manning it were busy reloading stubby missiles from a yellow crate.

Zeld hadn't even flinched. Still standing, he calmly spoke into his radio to the shuttle's bridge, ignoring the splintering roar from the girrish infantry opening up with rail-rifles on full automatic. 'Straight forward, please, Captain Jernberg. Towards the section of the wall exposed by the statue's destruction. Your shuttle will pass through like the offerings - as long as you can cross inside during the next two minutes.'

'What the *hell* are you doing?' Lana had drawn her rail-pistol, pointing it fluttering towards Zeld.

Zeld raised his arm towards the altar, as though he was welcoming the skipper into his living room. 'The main portion of the garbage chute stood blocked. We've now cleared the obstruction.'

Spears and arrows arced through the air, slapping into the mud around the lagoon, thousands of furious smilers overcoming shell-shock and pressing forward, howling towards the oath-breaking heathen foreigners who had desecrated their Holy of Holies.

Zeld waved the motley expedition members forward. 'Less than two minutes before the wall solidifies. Please to move. There should be a chamber on the other side.'

'Better be certain about that,' muttered Lana.

'We'd better show a clean pair of heels,' shouted Zeno, shooting the first of hundreds of spear-throwing warriors as the creature splashed manically towards them.

Calder had his pistol out, running after the others. The J93 rumbled across the wooden planking serving as a bridge across the lagoon towards the altar. Another roar as the recoilless cannon released a second volley - its final burst now that the Unity gunners had abandoned the weapon, sprinting behind the shuttle. A.I.-guided shells corkscrewed through the air, sighting for maximum dispersal while avoiding friendly DNA profiles. Calder sure hoped his had been programmed into the projectiles. Thousands of coin-sized bomblets blasted out of the shells, spinning and splashing across the lagoon on both sides like rain, sinking down to the beds. Suddenly the hestials weren't wading through their goddess's blessed waters - they were paddling across a murderous smart minefield, random tongues of fire lifting warriors off their feet, hurling broken corpses across the site, the air transformed into clouds of carbon-shard shrapnel.

Calder vaulted the burning bodies of two priests, Zeno close behind, shooting with his pistol. One of the priests, still half-alive, raised its thin fingers imploringly as it tried to crawl along the bloodied altar.

'Yeah, humanity really sucks,' said Zeno, leaping across the dying priest. 'Try spending a thousand years working for them, then get back to me on that.'

Calder saw the shuttle impacting the wall and vanishing as though passing through a hologram. He hit the chamber's exposed surface running, a familiar sensation of every molecule of his essence speeding independently through something solid and cold. *Yeah, same sorcery as the Heezy.* Calder stumbled out of the other side, tumbling madly forward, extra velocity added to his momentum as a byproduct of his passage. He skidded, winded, into a metal floor. Calder had barely picked himself up as an enraged warrior emerged flung out of the solid wall, swinging a sword at his skull. He had his pistol raised before he was even conscious of the act. But Calder couldn't fire, his trigger finger paralysed and ineffectual. As though he watched his imminent death from beyond his body.

Suddenly Mr Zeld ran between him and the smiler, the donnish-looking man moving with animal grace, twisting the sword out of the warrior's whip-like arm, rotating the creature through the air, slamming it onto the deck with the smiler's own blade plunged midair through its chest.

Calder stared dumbly at the rail-gun in his hand as the Unity officer stepped back.

Zeld examined his handiwork with a cold eye. 'Why didn't you shoot him?'

'We betrayed the smilers,' said Calder, feeling returning to his body. 'They were protecting us.'

'Their priests would never have allowed us to remove the Finest and clear the passage,' said the Unity officer.

Getting your retaliation in first? It seemed so unworthy to Calder. He was left shocked and shivering by his failure to act. The ex-prince had seen plenty of soldiers freeze in battle, but never him, no matter how intense the fight. *Maybe I've spent too long off Hesperus? My instincts have been blunted.*

Zeno appeared with Lana. The skipper crossed to the wall and tapped it with the butt of her pistol, checking the surface had returned to its solid state. *Nobody else will be coming through, hopefully.*

Zeno rolled the warrior over, ensuring it was down and dead. 'So I guess you won't be wanting those magic swords anymore?'

'Next time,' Lana admonished Calder, 'shoot first and feel guilty about it later.'

Calder didn't try to defend himself. Freezing like that, it wasn't like him at all. He still couldn't bring himself to thank Zeld for the Unity officer's intervention, though, as ungrateful as that might be perceived.

'And also next time,' Lana fixed Zeld with a furious glare, 'a little damn advance notice when you're planning to open fire on our so-called allies!'

'Our best simulations had you refusing to participate in our surprise attack,' said Mr Zeld.

Zeno snorted. 'You know, you Unity cats haven't got your impersonating mankind-gig locked down quite as tight as you think you have.'

Calder moved off to the side, waiting as the shuttle trundled forward. He took in his surroundings for the first time, now he had the luxury of a few minutes where he wasn't about to be eviscerated. *Where the hell is this?* Calder glanced around with bewilderment. Nothing like the vast open habitation chambers. In fact, it appeared like a cross between a sewer and a cathedral. Arches and echoing open spaces glowing with a purple light. Slabs inside the vault seemed to roll across each other, pieces of a jigsaw attempting to rearrange itself into some perfect configuration. The expedition had passed beyond the veil and into the mechanism of this vast alien machine. Off to the side, the junk metal which had composed the smilers' offerings was rising on a section of floor, disappearing out of sight. Calder spotted a balcony-like opening ahead which gave onto an open area beyond. Lana had already walked across, gazing out. Calder rejoined the skipper. He found himself staring down into an artificial shadowed canyon: its floor an ocean of moving broken rubble, swelling and falling while portions of the ship altered, spires rising out of the sea, consuming the materials. *This really is the belly of the beast. A whale, filtering Ryazarn space for raw materials.*

'What do you think the vessel is doing with that debris?'

'Renewing its structure?' speculated Lana. 'Self-repair. Converting the materials into nutrients for injection into the soil base the worlds inside here need to exist. Maybe transforming matter into fuels, if the Rattle still uses those?'

'But no sign of the crew,' said Calder.

Zeld came up behind them to take in the strange vista. 'This vessel's creators were not primitives, Mr Dirk. Think how further advanced they were than the Unity when this vessel first launched. I believe the crews' ancestors were similar to the Unity. Virtuals, only descending to the physical realm when needs absolutely dictated. Reluctantly subjecting themselves to the indignities of evolution in reverse.'

Speaking for yourself, there. 'You sound fairly convinced they aren't around here anymore?' said Calder.

'I fear my colleague Mr Kulkarni is correct. The crew have long-since ascended. Only ghosts remain here. A few ancient algorithms still ticking over, looping their lost legacy around the universe. A beacon in the darkness, lighting the way for those of us left behind.'

All around the vault the Unity crew wandered, slightly stunned, holding wavering hands out like organic divining rods. The girrish infantry stood as still as robot sentries by contrast, no more orders from their control interface to process.

'Ah,' said Mr Zeld, pointing towards the vault's furthest wall. 'I believe we have discovered one of the local control interfaces. We must work rapidly. I believe this vessel's equivalent of a hyperspace jump is imminent.'

'What kind of jump can the Rattle make without a wormhole breach?' asked Lana

Zeld sighed. 'Said the ant staring up at the anti-gravity sled, "No legs. That'll never work."'

'Let's just get out of here,' said Calder, feeling the terror of being stranded here forever squeezing his heart. Even if there was a way for the expedition to crawl back out of the Rattle's skirting boards, the smilers weren't going to rest until every last member was exterminated like the treacherous oath-breakers they'd proved to be.

'I think we have a serious problem,' announced Polter, totally out of the blue.

'Pray tell, noble navigator.'

'Have a look at this sensor data and tell me what you see about ninety thousand miles behind us?'

Skrat examined it. 'There's not a lot here, but, ah yes, I have it.' A tiny pulse, like an oscillation. Or a ghost.

'If that anomaly is a ship, backfill its heading, speed, time and point of departure.'

Skrat ran the numbers and saw what had Polter so worried. 'Departure Ryal local orbit, around the time that some fool started unloading ship missiles. Heading, straight for the last leg of the race before the Rattle exits to points unknown.'

'Indeed. But I have never seen anything quite like that signature.'

'Me neither, dear boy.' Skrat pushed it down to the drive room with a request that the chief examine the anomaly and bring his experience to the matter. A minute later, Chief Paopao was on the comm, the creased lines of his face frowning in hologram form before Skrat's station on the bridge.

'Chief, any thoughts on what this might be? Extra points if you tell me it's just a simple sensor error.'

'Pah. Not that,' said the chief. 'Is big trouble.'

'What sort of trouble are we talking here?'

'Called MAV by Fleet. Military assault vessel. Stealth profile. Not perfect, but during engagement, many enemy ships too busy dodging missiles to notice. This is very old variant.'

'How would you know that, chief?'

'If new, we never detect bleed on energy sink.'

'What's its purpose, old chap. Sneak up and unload a torpedo on us? I don't think the Rattle will be too impressed with that kind of skulduggery, stealth profile or no. Probably as visible as day to whatever is on that big alien leviathan of a galoot.'

'Purpose?' huffed the chief. 'Purpose is to take ships intact. Fires boarding capsules. Cling like limpets to hull. Troops cut way inside. Then murder crew and seize vessel.'

'Ah,' said Skrat. *Just about the perfect weapon to use in the race should things go sideways. Board the vessels and seize the salvage by force. No exchange of fire in open space quite violent enough to provoke the Rattle into disintegrating the loot.*

'We cannot shoot the capsules,' said Polter. 'If we offer violence, that devil ship will destroy the *Gravity Rose*.'

'She pushed off from Ryaz Prime precisely when the trouble started out here,' said Skrat. 'So she's going to be packed with very miffed secret police-types. Just the sort of skull-cracking brutes with whom I would not usually wish closer acquaintance.'

'My shell is tougher than your skull, but only by a thin margin.'

'Chief,' said Skrat, 'exactly how does one deal with one of these troublesome MAV vessels?'

Paopao snorted in irritation. 'Prepare.'

'For what, precisely?'

'For nice cup of tea? No, you fool! To be boarded, lizard. Prepare for that!'

'The Skunk has done it!' d'Alembert triumphantly announced, lifting the Skunk away from the wall. 'The control interface is unlocked.' Whatever the Skunk had achieved, it seemed exhausted by its efforts, tentacles drawing back into itself, reforming as a trembling cylinder.

'Excellent,' said Mr Kulkarni. Lana saw the pistol in his hand, pointed directly at Mr Zeld, as were his bodyguards' weapons. All around the vault the Unity crew had drawn weapons on each other, girrish infantry rifles wavering and switching between crew as the aboriginals received multiple conflicting commands on who to obey.

Lana had her gun out but damned if she knew who to shoot right now.

'Head for the cover of the shuttle if this mess goes south,' whispered Zeno.

'Anymore south,' muttered Lana.

'Don't do this!' pleaded Mr Zeld.

'You are not the Unity anymore,' said Mr Kulkarni. '*We* are the majority. You and your supporters are a dissenting corruption.'

'Our duty –'

'Is not decided by you anymore,' said Kulkarni. He holstered his pistol and stepped forward.

'This is outrageous,' protested d'Alembert. But not so outrageous that Lana's ex-client was about to risk his neck to intervene. He slowly backed away from the interface, clutching the trembling Skunk under his arm as though it were some mutant cat.

Kulkarni wasn't listening to d'Alembert or anyone else. He rested his right hand against the interface, his skin blackening and seeming to merge with the wall. The block began pulsing with glowing purple patterns, light flowing across the material. 'The unlocked interface contains a simple binary bitmap with a vocabulary of symbols representing an algorithmic communication system. I am constructing a virtual machine to run the Rattle's programming language.'

'Command our shuttle to be loaded into the ejection system,' begged Mr Zeld, wincing with his eyes shut as he tracked his colleague's progress. 'Don't venture any deeper inside the system, you risk triggering security protocols we can't possibly anticipate.'

'This is our people's destiny,' whispered Kulkarni.

'Yes, but not right now, not for the few!'

'Quiet!

'Listen to me, chute processing is a low-level system which is already running. Leaving the Rattle will draw minimal attention to ourselves. But accessing something so deeply embedded in the core virtual risks –'

Kulkarni didn't waver from his task at the wall. 'We will risk *everything*.'

Elin had her pistol pointed at Kulkarni and if Lana was any judge of character, the *Meteor Prince*'s captain didn't intend to back down. 'Not my crew, you're not. Let my shuttle ditch. You and your insanity club can stay and upload your minds into the Rattle for all that I care.'

'How kind of you, captain. But, no. Hacking the chute will, at the very least, alert the Rattle to our presence. The chances of then using the core to ascend could be degraded. I intend to strike once and strike hard.'

'I'll shoot you, I swear.'

'I believe your threat, Captain Jernberg,' smiled Kulkarni. 'Which is why I deactivated every Unity firearm in unpreserved hands a minute ago.'

Lana's eyes fleeted down to her pistol, cursing as she noted the flashing red symbol on the ammo readout. It flickered between green and red as she watched, every bit as conflicted as the girrish infantry. *Great, my gun's gone as psychotically unreliable as our so-called allies.*

Elin had her dagger out as she lunged forward and grabbed Kulkarni with its active blade a blur held across his throat. 'This knife's all mine!'

Kulkarni merely snorted, not moving an inch from the

interface surface. 'Very foolish, captain. You are thinking like a typical unpreserved primeval. This body isn't who I *am* . . . it's only one of a hundred suits I wear. I will transfer my intelligence inside the Rattle in the millisecond it takes you to start moving your blade towards my jugular.'

'Let me leave this hell-ship, damn you.'

'Poor savage, I want to remake you as a goddess and all you can—' Kulkarni doubled over screaming. For a second Lana thought that Elin had made good on her threat. The *Gravity Rose*'s skipper wasn't the only one who believed she'd sliced open his throat. Rail-gun shots hissed out around the chamber, the Mexican standoff breaking down into a fierce firefight. Kulkarni seemed to become a haze inside a heatwave, Elin caught up alongside him, cycling in and out of existence. Transmuting into something else. And whatever that something was, it was being absorbed inside the block.

Zeno pulled Lana back, a magnetically accelerated pellet fleeting past her and exploding from the vault's wall. Everything was chaos. Belters shooting Unity crew. Unity crew blasting each other apart. The girrish infantry charging around the vault firing at everyone as their loyalties cycled between whoever was closest and strongest to seize control over them.

'Calder?' Lana shouted at Zeno. They both took cover behind the shifting blocks that made up the floor. 'Where is he?' Lana added to the confusion as the android's superior processing sifted the vault for Calder. Her damned pistol jammed on almost every shot, maybe one in five trigger actions resulting in a discharge.

'There,' called Zeno, pointing to the edge of the vault. Calder had taken up position with a knot of belter crew. They had dived behind one of the archways overlooking the sea of rubble. Lieutenant Denisov was there alongside Retigura, laying down fire. They both still carried their antique, but wholly reliable, chemical reaction pistols. Lana cursed. Calder and the others were about as far away from the shuttle as it was possible to be. The rest of the vault degenerated into an insane cross-fire.

Mr Zeld sprinted over low, a smoking pistol clutched in his hand, joining them behind the block. 'I am going to attempt to initiate a waste processing cycle for the shuttle. We only have a few minutes left before departure from this galaxy. Get yourselves on board.'

'What if the Rattle fries you like it did Elin and your nutso friend?'

'Fried, captain? I don't believe either of them are dead, that wasn't what I felt via Mr Kulkarni. I suspect what we saw was a security virtualization in response to the Skunk's relatively primitive intrusion. I have already adapted to suppress the Rattle's countermeasures.'

Lana was willing to bet that Elin's disintegrated body would beg to differ about her current state. *Sweet Stars, let Elin be dead. Not some ghost trapped here for all eternity.* 'I'm not leaving this place without Calder.'

Lana indicated Calder's position. Zeld glanced across the arcs of rail-gun fire. 'I will order my loyalists to assist Mr Dirk's retreat as soon as I have control of the waste mechanism.'

Yeah, assist him, as the other half of your people try to gun him down.

'Please,' said Mr Zeld. He pressed his rail-gun into Lana's hand. 'This is my personal side-arm. I have completely deleted its biometric safeties. A five-year-old could fire it, now.'

'You're getting mighty noble on us, all of a sudden,' noted Zeno, suspiciously.

'If Mr Kulkarni is correct, the worse that will happen to me after I am virtualised is a chance at ascension a few millennia before I have earnt that right. I trust neither of you feels the same way about such a fate . . .?'

'Hell no,' said Zeno. Lana vigorously shook her head.

'Then it's time for you both to leave. One day, perhaps, you will choose to embrace the Unity, and on another plane we shall be reunited.' Zeld sprinted off, taking cover behind one of the continuously flowing blocks where he pressed his hand against the wall. The synthetic man sucked in his breath as the limb started to meld with the control interface's surface.

'I swear,' said Zeno. 'I'm never going to understand those Unity cats.'

Lana checked her shiny new pistol, admiring its winking green free-fire indicator. 'He's mostly downloaded software, old man. If you can't, how do you expect a mere fleshie to?'

Zeno chortled and took off. Lana fired, zigzagging behind the android, shots hissing past her head like hornets as she retreated towards the shuttle. She blasted back, more in the hope of making someone duck than actually claiming a kill. Then Lana was stumbling onto the J93's forward cargo ramp. A sweet humming sounded from inside the interior. *Gravity lift generators running.* That meant the chase shuttle's main drive was back on-line. Either Zeld had just succeeded in lifting the dampening field, or the field wasn't running outside of the Rattle's habitation zones. A handful of belters had taken up defensive positions around the ramp, shuffling aside as Zeno and Lana sheltered behind the ramp struts.

'Well, that's new,' said Zeno.

Lana gazed up in terrified astonishment at the ceiling. Where the Rattle's crew were finally emerging.

Granny Rose's hologram stood inside the sensor array control.

As the avatar of the ship's artificial interface, she didn't really need to manifest anywhere specific, given she was everywhere. Unless she was talking with one of the crew, when being somewhere was simply good manners. But, still; when you were about to fight a battle, it felt reassuring to be on the battlefield. *Like a general with a pair of field-glasses. Watching the smoke. Sensing the blood about to be spilled.* She had been pacing up and down here for hours. Too long out of the whole as a detached shard and she started to exhibit worrying signs of the humanity she was meant to mimic and smooth. *Yes, that's me. Just a gobby old Granny.*

The greater mass of the vessel intruded on her comforting little illusion, breaking her reverie.

<Update?>

'You ever remember what it was like to be sick with worry? An organic gut to hold your dread like a well? Fear inside your mind until you couldn't sleep? I think this time,' said Granny Rose, 'we are going to need to be just a little bit more proactive.'

<Analysis?>

'Even with the farming droids on hand, the boarding action is going to be a damned close thing — the nearest run thing you ever saw in your life.'

<Wellington.>

'Quite,' said Granny. 'Sadly, the Ryal commandos in the approaching MAV possess an advantage that was denied to Napoleon . . . hardsuits of a worryingly modern vintage. The kind of gear that would send Alliance weapons inspectors into a fit if they realised Fleet exo-armour had been trafficked into this star system.'

<Suggestions?'>

'We unlock a little assistance for Skrat.'

<Deniability?>

'None, really. And don't think that doesn't bother me. But if you will permit me to observe, organics have a way of seeing what they want to see in situations like this. Given our cover story for the *Gravity Rose*'s entry into Alliance space and Captain Fiveworlds' inheritance of our vessel, I think there are any number of natural narratives that would leap unbidden out of the remaining crew's fertile imaginations.'

<Lana?>

Granny allowed her troubling analysis of the Harbinger deep sensor detail to rise between her and the greater weight of intelligence distributed through the *Rose*. 'Yep, there's a rumble in the jungle across there. It's a good news-bad news deal. Bad news . . . I'm guessing we're not the only ones considering an intervention right now.'

<*Bollocks.*>

'Virtual ones,' sighed Granny, wondering which sub-system of the great and the good was developing British-accented Tourette's. 'Of course, it's not actually *them* over there on their inside-out pilgrimage ship, anymore. The Harbingers buggered off to pastures new when humanity was still picking fleas out of each other's fur . . . Happy Ascension Day. Just the ghost in the machine over there, now. Mirror copies, backups, security protocols. I don't *think* they're insane, but it was never that easy to tell with the client species, was it? And that was *before* most of the Harbingers' higher sentience waveforms squeezed out of this universe, leaving the dog-ends and lost backups well, *rattling* around.'

<Puns, now?> [inference: distaste]

Granny checked her internal clock. Only five picoseconds had been expended on this highly compressed conversation. She tutted to herself. There was still plenty of time left for puns.

'Lady's got to have her fun, somehow.'

<Good news?>

'There's an ongoing shit-fest breaking out inside a high-security deck on the Harbinger. Alliance and Unity-signature weapons discharge. Remind you of anyone we were hoping might still be alive?'

<Lana. Calder. Zeno.>

'Correctamundo. Always thought that Fiveworlds Logistics or whatever shell company we're using this month needed a motto. How's "Trouble's Our Business" sound to you?'

[levity: dismissed] <Girrish crew? Complications?>

'Actually, I'd chalk the girrish presence over there as a positive on the scales. The aboriginals might be the descendants of a bunch of primitive Amish-a-like body-hugging throwbacks, but they were once splashing in the same end of the gene pool as those datacore dregs left over there. I mean, come on, even humanity managed to save their great apes from extinction. The higher-evolved Harbingers were a pretty fair-minded species, as I recall. Okay, a little squirrelly, but their moral compass always tilted true north. If you found your great grandkids to the power of ten stuck in a cage with a collar round their neck while you're looping around on your grand spiritual awakening, would you simply *walk on by*?'

Granny felt the simulation of a Harbinger entity rise up into existence like a soap bubble, popping as the confirmation came to the ship. <No.>

Ten picoseconds expended. 'So, about that incoming MAV - a hold full of thugs with a fanatical love for their homeland, a little swagger and probably highly hot Fleet-issue HULC-9 hardsuits courtesy of Lockheed-BattleBionics?'

<Alternatives?>

'Mindwipe the remaining crew left on board. All three of the buggers. Wouldn't have to be their entire past like we had to do to Lana. The crew lose twenty-four hours to some tenuous technobabble about field-wash from the Harbinger's anomalous thrust. While they're out, I scratch that MAV. I carve them a nice nova-size hole in their hull. I've been pacing up and down here counting the ways I could do it. Do you want to hear my favourite method, so far? We pop one of those steel balls that Polter uses for wormhole formation. Then I modify our jump vanes to transform the ball into anti-matter and see how many times it bounces off their stealth ship.'

<Risky.>

'Really? *Really*? Which bit? The technobabble? How many Alliance and Edge species have ever experienced the close range field-wash from a violation of Hilbert space cardinality?' Granny raised a hologram hand to form a big fat zero with her fingers. 'Who's to say that brain-fry and amnesia aren't the natural result of being up close to the Harbinger's stern when it folds space and scoots off? Or is it the risk from miscreant locals watching this particular bun-fight that has you worried? Because, you know, the Rattle is the Wicked Witch around here. The big dumb broomstick from the last galaxy to the right. I'm fairly sure the Harbinger could squirt orange juice on those two destroyers still trying to boost up on us; squirt on their hull, turning said missile ships into Chrysanthemums. And the Ryals will go, "Doh - so that's another one of their diddly-dinking defence systems. Who knew?" Right?' Granny jabbed her non-existent hands towards her non-existent neck. 'Here's my collar, *Gravity Rose*. Just the same as those poor benighted aboriginals jerking to Tsar Rasim's beat. Cut my collar away. Lady just wants to *dance*.'

There was a pause of another seven picoseconds. Granny felt

the wider ship's distributed intelligence shifting in the substrate, considering, stirring in a way it hardly ever did. Usually so quick. So terse. She felt a lingering swell of desperate anticipation inside her. Growing excitement. *Is that nine picoseconds, now? Never reached this far before. Come on. Come on.*

Finally . . . the decision. It was either going to agree with her, or she was going to be re-spawned a lot less cheeky.

<Reconfigure.> [intervention: approval]

'At last!' Granny gave the software equivalent of a wild whoop of joy. It took the form of a recursive loop that you really needed to be a billion-year-old survivor of a supposedly extinct species to appreciate. *Ah, that old magic.*

[panic: clarification] [panic: clarification] [panic: clarification] <Interior. ONLY>.

Granny's hologram grinned with a row of feral shark's teeth. 'Interior smearior. You know what time it is? It's time to boogie. Because nobody puts *Heezy* in a corner.'

Calder gaped in amazement as the Rattle's long absent crew emerged from the vault's roof - its ceiling dripping like melting wax as dozens of the vessel's controlling entities assumed physical form.

'You know,' said Lieutenant Denisov, 'I was expecting the crew to look a little less like those . . . those *nocnitsa.*'

Burning firefly bright, dozens of molten drips transformed into flaming crimson figures little bigger than fairies as they fell.

Calder stood as fixated by the sight as the belters sheltering with him. 'Nocnitsa?'

'Night spirits,' said Dominika.

More like burning angels. Retigura shook in fear beside them, dropping his reaction pistol. Calder saw the reason why as one of the creatures fell in front of where they sheltered from the crossfire. *It looks like a miniature gir, hardly bigger than seven inches tall!* Immediately, Calder recalled the sheer terror with which the smiler priests had reacted to Retigura after he entered their cathedral bearing their solar sails. The way the species' warriors had fled in fright before the girrish infantry back in the starship's graveyard. What was it the priests had said about Retigura, via Zeno's translation? *Not making much sense. Something about him being too big.*

Around the vault, the panicked Unity crew opened up with their weapons towards the ceiling, but the miniature flaming figures dodged to the side, avoiding rail rounds like the battle was some amusing game for them to play.

'Run for the shuttle,' Calder barked at his companions, 'while they're distracted.'

The belters came out of their fug of shock and started to sprint for safety. Calder was about to join them when he saw the lieutenant trying to come to the aid of her aboriginal friend. Dominika swatted madly at a firefly rapidly circling Retigura's head, little flashes of light passing between the entity and Retigura's fried control torc.

'No! No!' Retigura begged. As though heeding the aboriginal's alarmed pleas, the firefly shot off - its orbit complete - joining the growing host of entities whipping around the vault. Calder noted the girrish infantry had stopped firing, swarms of fireflies making mad circuits around the aboriginals' skulls. *Just like Retigura - what are those demons doing?* Another firefly dipped before Calder, Dominika and Retigura, a whistling noise coming from the hovering creature. The sound seemed unrelated to the act of flying. Retigura returned the noise, bowing and jerking as if the aboriginal had palsy.

'What—' Calder was cut off as Dominika pushed him forward.

'May the ancient gods preserve us,' prayed Retigura, sprinting alongside the two humans.

'That Nocnitsa spoke a girrish dialect, although hardly a current one,' explained Dominika. She grabbed Calder's gun hand and made him holster the pistol as they darted ran through the chaos. Then she tossed her own pistol across the floor, sending it spinning to a stop where one of the moving blocks caught it and started propelling it across the floor.

'What did the demon say?'

'Nothing good. Run. Don't shoot at the Nocnitsa. Don't even *wave* an active blade at them.'

The three of them bolted low, dancing a crazy zig-zag as blocks shifted across the floor under their feet. Gunfire hissed all around them, the three-way civil war between the competing Unity factions and Elin's crew given a frantic new pace by the addition of these swarming entities. Calder retreated, bewildered, his hand itching for a gun's heft to protect himself. Some Unity fighters seemed to be trying to help the ex-prince, crew ducking behind blocks to shoot down their own colleagues - the other synthetics attempting to murder the three fleeing expedition members. Calder's luck couldn't hold. Not in the insanity of this melee. A synthetic woman rose up in front of them, raising her pistol and sighting on Calder and his two companions. *Dead.* But he wasn't. The crew-woman yelled as a firefly darted at her back, stinging her. She stumbled with a look of incomprehension across her face. The angrily hissing spirit lunged at her a second time, establishing a tight hold on the struggling agent. Both woman and firefly rose towards the ceiling. The roof splashed like a petrol-black swamp as the Unity agent struck it, greedily absorbing her body even as it gobbed new fireflies down into the vault. All across the chamber, those still fighting were being latched onto by the fireflies - belters and Unity agents alike - flown up towards the vault's roof to be absorbed into the ship.

Calder desperately doubled his pace towards the shuttle. That was when he felt the piercing sting in his spine, the vicious little night spirit responsible spinning around to spit malevolently at him. It blocked Calder's escape as it closed to drag him up for total atomization.

***

Skrat watched little flickers on his tracking system - malfunctioning stealth bleed from the closing military assault vessel. *Not nearly enough bleed to give them a biffing.* Every time the rail-guns tried to target the Ryal ship, they lost their lock. He was only doing it for fun, anyway. *To spook the bounders.* The moment he started pounding ship-to-ship was the instant the Rattle started throwing weaponized suns around. Of course, that cut both ways. The MAV couldn't put a nuke into the *Gravity Rose* without committing suicide. *Mutually Assured Destruction. How civilised.* He wondered if the old girrish civilisation back on Ryal had believed the same lie, before their atomic war started?

Granny's hologram flickered into existence on the bridge. 'I can report final re-installation of the deleted instruction set in our new robot force.'

Skrat tried to raise a smile for the A.I. *Lovely. Now I'm complicit in the same arms smuggling racket that d'Alembert was running.* 'Dashed lucky that Zeno didn't wipe those war-bot programs from our mainframe like Lana ordered him to.'

'I am sure Zeno didn't have time before he left,' said Granny.

Skrat didn't point out that the android *did* seem to have had time to triple-encrypt the illegal-for-civilians-to-own military-systems before he'd stashed them away inside his personal archive. 'Well, that rotten farmer's home-brew legion wasn't terribly effective against us. We pipped them, didn't we? Hope we have more luck deploying the robots against the regime's killers.'

'Before, the droids cannibalised the cargo hold to produce weaponry and modify their bodies for combat,' Polter pointed out. 'We, by contrast, have opened up our stores to them.'

Will that be enough? Well, we're going to find out in a few minutes, I suppose. His attention was caught by a sudden flurry of movement across his station. His trading applications were going into hibernation, hundreds of them, carefully customised, fed with unique data sets and tended across many years. He bit down his outrage. Making way for . . . ? 'Granny,' called Skrat. 'I have new sub-systems appearing online across my board? Dozens of them! Never seen the like of any of these little blighters before?'

'That is because the *Gravity Rose* has never been threatened by a military-scale boarding action, before,' explained Granny, the very voice of reason. 'Auto-call functions activating, all situation sensitive. I believe this is the first time this particular section of ship code has been executed by my central data-core. At least, during Captain Fiveworlds' tenure as owner.'

Skrat growled. And of course, the A.I's memory had been wiped clean by the unidentified previous owners. 'Polter? Copying to your board. Open these up and tell me you're seeing what my tired old peepers are seeing?'

'Yes,' Polter drummed his claws in satisfaction. 'Most excellent. These functions are largely defensive in nature. Internal

- we are not, sadly, suddenly sprouting energy weapons. Ability to vary the interior gravity field to lethal levels. Flash-freezing corridors by negating environmental control safeties. Sealing specific areas and venting to vacuum.'

'Sweet Spirits of the Dunes!' hissed Skrat. 'Do you realise what would have happened if we were inspected on Transference Station by Customs Security and they discovered we have the bally ability to murder any or all of our passengers on a cabin-by-cabin basis?'

'These systems would never run activate unless we were boarded by pirates,' said Polter. 'And in such circumstances, international conventions of the open void allows for the sin of murder through self-defence.'

'Yes, officer,' growled Skrat, 'it's perfectly normal for us to be able to electrify selected door handles with seventy thousand volts. Don't worry, we normally conceal all the lethal functions and keep them jolly well switched off.' He banged his tail angrily on the deck. 'I always suspected the previous owners were a dodgy bunch of devils. But just how dodgy does one have to flipping well be to wire your vessel up like this? Free company mercenaries? A multi-system crime syndicate? Retired pirate king? Assassins for hire? Slavers?'

'Or, perhaps, merely a very careful ship family who had experienced prior casualties during a pirate action? I will say a blessing for that lost crew, tonight,' said Polter. 'Through their cautious nature . . . the Lord has provided our chance at survival.'

Cautious? Bonkers, more like! But the navigator had made one valid point. *If we're going to survive to reach the jump point, it's only through using this!*

***

'They're moving,' shouted Lana, seeing Calder and the others break position and head for her side of the vault. She dashed forward from the J93's open ramp, crouching below one of the slowly shifting blocks, blasting to the flanks of her running crew, praying against the odds her covering fire would be enough to see Calder home alive.

'Captain Fiveworlds!' yelled Mr Zeld from the wall. He sounded ill. *Dying.* 'Waste processing cycle—active. Onto—the shuttle.' The roof immediately above the shuttle had transformed into a glowing whirlpool of purple lights, the floor below the J93 reconfiguring into a lifting platform. The ground trembled in anticipation of the final components sliding into place, ready to raise the shuttle for ejection as garbage.

Lana guessed they were down to mere seconds, now. 'But *Calder . . .'*

'Assisting,' moaned Zeld, the configuration of combat shifting as his allies added their last-ditch covering fire to the mix. 'You— don't have long—captain. Can't—hold this—exit open.'

Lana re-sighted her pistol, her implant doing its best to pick out hostiles. Then Zeno dived beside her. 'Careful, skipper. Friendlies incoming.'

A wild rush of girrish infantry headed for the safety of the shuttle. But they weren't retreating with the weirdly synchronised motion of a Unity-controlled regiment. They fled as a panicked mob of individuals. The aboriginals had thrown aside their rifles and broken en masse, puppets no longer.

'Someone's totally cut their strings,' spat Lana.

'Guess the boss-fleshies have other things on their minds,' said Zeno, indicating flailing bodies being lifted towards the vault's roof, aberrant wet splashing noises as their molecular structure dissolved.

Lana heard a rush of mad shouts from behind her; a group of belters yelling in fury alongside the girrish. Smashing their panicked fists and pistol butts against the shuttle's forward - *closing cargo doors?*

'Who —?' Then Lana saw the figure at the bridge's viewing arc. It was d'Alembert, standing behind the unfurled mass of his Skunk. Using it to seal the shuttle tight, seizing control of all primary functions. Probably locked the J93's bridge too, a nice thick armoured anti-hijack door for any crew remaining on board to bang in futile anger against. The man raised a hand ironically, seeing Lana and Zeno staring in disbelieving fury at the bridge and gave one last triumphant smile. Waving goodbye to them as platform and shuttle began to lift towards the ceiling and escape from the Rattle.

***

Skrat stood tall in the theatre inside the *Gravity Rose*'s liner module, all the seats retracted and folded against the walls to make room for the robot legion he was about to address. He stood on the stage. Chief Paopao waited by his side. Not in person, of course - too much to expect to winkle the paranoid blighter out of the armoured drive room. Paopao was riding the ship's biggest welding droid remotely, practically a tank. Skrat, however, was all too in-person, here. And he felt naked. Although he was wearing something that looked like a spacesuit. Well, it was a spacesuit. But it was also a piece of equipment the crew never normally needed to don - a RIP-suit. With Zeno acting as the ship's bot-herder, none of the other crew had needed a Robot Interface Presence suit to simultaneously oversee thousands of drones, robots, droids and automated autonomous sub-systems. But here Skrat was, kitted out like some Fleet marine general about to address the troops before invading a target world. But he wasn't a marine general. Never had been. He had been something . . . else.

Granny whispered into his ear-mike. 'One word of caution, Skrat. The robots' battle control systems are an overlay on their original programming. Given d'Alembert intended to use them for a first-strike coup against his world's government, the short-term duration of the palace revolution would not have posed a problem.'

'As the actress said to the bishop, I detect a "but" in there, dear girl.'

'But,' sighed Granny, 'they are probably going to go insane, sooner or later. Dedicated military systems are designed to exclude the usual law of robotics. All normal robots have non-harm of organic life forms as their core. We're going to need to wipe the robots again as soon as this action is concluded.'

'And if the battle is not settled in our favour?'

'Oh, probably best to let them go insane,' giggled Granny. 'SEP. Someone else's problem.'

'Are you alright, Granny? You sound a little rummy to my ears?'

'Don't worry about this old computer,' said the A.I. 'Opening night nerves.'

'Good egg. If you're going to go bonkers on me too, I would rather appreciate it if you lost the plot *after* our impending bout of fisticuffs.' Skrat gazed around the ranks of farming droids, weapons clutched in their metal manipulators - a few spare rail-pistols and rifles from the armoury here and there. But the majority held self-loading catapults with chemically-propelled grenade bolts. All hastily modded from the micro-explosives template used by spacers for emergency hull and bulkhead damage clearance.

Skrat routed the helmet comms to the navigator's station. 'Polter, are you tickety-boo?'

'Aye-aye. All bridge systems rerouted, including our new defence functions. I pray the wicked forces of the heathen do not trace the command controls to my new location.'

'After they slice their way into the bridge, I am sure the chapel is the very last place the Tsar's horde of heathen ruffians will choose to look. God's speed to you, Polter, old bean.'

'I should remind you that you do not believe in the Holy of Holies, Skrat.'

'As I sit here in my foxhole, I believe it may not be entirely harmful to make a few respectful nods in the old girl's direction, eh?' He gazed at the oval main-body of the tank the chief controlled. 'This the first time you faced this sort of punch-up, chief?'

'No,' spat the reply.

Skrat raised his hand. 'Please chief, don't try to bore me with your tedious long Fleet war-stories.'

'Will need to deploy, soon,' growled the reply. 'Start!'

I don't know what effect the chief will have upon the enemy, but, by God, he frightens me. Boarding actions were a little like a chess board. As a defending merchant vessel, you could only react *after* the boarding capsules latched on and blasted through. Before that, you just guessed which critical systems the attackers would go for first, and deployed your defences accordingly. *And hope for the bally best.* Skrat gazed across the robot legion. All shapes and sizes. Some humanoid in shape. Others moving about on caterpillar tracks, or rolling about like balls. About the only one of the bally lot of them they didn't have inside here was the combine harvester, and that was only because it couldn't fit through the theatre doors.

'You were destined for a different place, far from here,' began Skrat. 'But fate has put you on our decks, made you part of the crew of the *Gravity Rose*. Fate did that to me, too. So I know just how you feel - well, those of you who are expected to interact with organics and actually possess simulated emotion centres. And now that home, that blessed place, our ship, is threatened by as vicious a bunch of scallywags as you could never wish to meet. So—'

One of the overseer robots designated a sergeant in the legion - humanoid, albeit with four arms - stepped forward. It raised two of them as though surrendering.

Hardly an encouraging sign. Skrat's tail swished around, indicating the expectantly waiting robot. 'Yes?'

'We can plant the raiders in the soil?'

'Well, yes. We don't actually possess much soil outside of our hydroponic decks. Or the park with the passenger viewing chamber, I suppose. But in essence, yes, you will plant the bounders. You give these raiders a bloody good planting this day!'

The robot stepped back into the ranks, and then the ones who had arms raised their weapons into the air, violently shaking them and banging them against their steel plating. It sounded like a thousand war drums, an army smashing spears against their shields. The theatre had seen many performances, live as well as broadcast, but never anything quite like this.

'Plant them!' 'Plant them!' 'Plant them!' 'Plant them!' 'Plant THEM!' 'Plant THEM!' 'PLANT THEM!'

Skrat stepped back. 'Are they *meant* to be doing that?'

Chief Paopao's tank-form rumbled forwards. 'Deploy! Dirty metal golems. Deploy!'

Skrat almost fainted as units of the legion peeled off, exiting through the many portals used to rapidly empty a showing here. The lizard's RIP-suit, as advanced a networking hub as existed, filled his implant to overload - views of the corridors seen from the robots' sensors, floating threat analysis, ETAs for reaching key areas of the *Gravity Rose* the legion were tasked with protecting, power readouts, times to recharge. Thousands of little feeds and demands, jabbing at him incessantly, making his implant begin to boil from competing demands to multi-task. But then his suit began to pick up the slack. Its native processing abilities pitching in with load-handling before Skrat experienced a meltdown. His brain itched meshed with the robot legion. Like being part of a hive-mind. *By Jove, this isn't a suit. This is a damnable fuse for my mind!*

Paopao snorted in amusement, seeing Skrat's discomfort. 'Met a Drone Support Systems Specialist, once. Inside Fleet. Wear suit like yours.'

'Really? What was that for . . . some sort of planetary assault launched from orbit?'

'Met in hospital ship.' Paopao jabbed the tip of a laser-welding arm against Skrat's skull. 'Needed neural repair.'

***

Calderswattedat the crimson angel quivering before him, watching it dance aside in the air. The pain burning his spine seemed joined to this malevolent hovering thing by an umbilical cord. *It's tasting me.* Calder's implant broke down with his agony, broadcasting a broken stream of random characters across his field of vision, making even less sense than normal. There was a synchronicity in this unholy joining. A connection with his near-death experience on the *Gravity Rose*. That was how this mess started. Now he was back facing his death again. The entity swished between Calder's eyes, singing at him in the same alien tongue the firefly had used when admonishing Retigura. Then it flitted away, abandoning Calder to listen to screaming crew being dragged kicking through the air towards the ceiling.

Retigura seized Calder's arm, shoving him half-paralysed after Dominika as they fled towards the shuttle. 'You're alive.'

'I think so.'

'Blessed be your fate,' said the aboriginal, panting. 'The ancient says the Harbinger will leave.'

It's not the only bloody thing. Calder spotted the J93 rising upwards on a platform towards the vault's roof, the ex-prince's gut in free-fall as he realised they were about to be stranded on this cursed vessel-world for as long as they could survive it. He ran full-pelt for the chase shuttle, screaming for it to wait, nearly colliding with the expedition members left behind. Belters, girrish and … *No. Lana and Zeno are still here!*

Up on the bridge, d'Alembert gripped the instrument deck, watching those he had abandoned with all the majesty of a nautical captain in his wheelhouse. A belter lifted a rail-pistol to fire at the armoured glass, his rage turning to terror as he suddenly lifted off his feet, one of the fireflies dragging the thrashing man towards the ceiling. With a flail of limbs the spacer simply vanished, absorbed. Dozens of fireflies angled for the shuttle, most of the Unity crew spread across the vault already exterminated.

Suddenly, a violent splash of blood splattered across the viewing arc, d'Alembert's body tumbling against the glass before sliding down across the forward controls. *Someone shot him in the head!* Calder saw the second figure appear, the magnate's manservant, Jinhai. He still clutched a smoking pistol in his trembling hand.

'Guess the dude just resigned,' said Zeno, scrambling up the lifting platform. Above them, the cargo doors re-opened and the shuttle's ramp started to lower. Lana grabbed Zeno's left hand while Calder seized the android's right. Zeno hauled Calder and the skipper up onto the rising platform, the android's superior strength hoisting them up with an ease which belied their weight.

'Quickly!' howled Mr Zeld by the alien control interface. His synthetic body pulsated, transformed, more vault material than flesh, now. Curious fireflies landed on him, a growing swarm like bees honouring a keeper with their touch. The platform shuddered to a stop, briefly stilled by the fading Unity officer's efforts.

Safely on the platform, Calder hauled at the mob of madly thrusting hands, yanking belters and girrish away from the floor. Some belters fell back, screaming, as fireflies darted in from the vault, stinging the crew while they floundered, lifting them away to the roof to be dissolved. The cries intensified, desperate men and women from Elin's crew realising this would be their final chance to escape. Lana yelled in pain, releasing the hands of a crew-woman she was assisting up onto the platform. Calder saw the firefly latched onto the chest of Lana's ship-uniform, lifting the skipper's whipping body into the air and towards disintegration. He was on Lana's boots in seconds, leaping, dragging all three of them back towards the platform's edge. Calder felt his boots touch something solid. He and Lana landed with a thump, the ex-prince almost overbalancing. The indignant firefly hissed fiercely at Calder, attacking as he seized it, peeling it away from Lana's uniform, as painful as wrapping his fist around an acid-tipped cactus. He had the entity burning squeezed inside his palm before hurling it up towards the opening. The malevolent thing had almost recovered its senses by the time it thumped into the whirlpool, then, with a sparkle, it disappeared.

Lana tried to recover from the sting, her face as white as alabaster as she floundered up. 'Inside my mind. Like it was tasting me.'

'I know. Measuring you up for a virtual coffin,' said Calder, sucking in the vault's warm air. A numbing sensation spread out from his hand where he had clutched the unholy entity. He could hardly breathe. It was as though he was frozen from combat stress again, but this time, the causes of his affliction lay far outside his mind.

The platform began jerking up towards the opening again. Zeno roughly dragged Lana and Calder back up the shuttle's ramp, through the jostling horde of expedition members trying to scramble into forward cargo. Then the doors were closing and the ramp retracting. Calder caught one last glimpse of Mr Zeld, every inch of his body covered with fireflies except his face. He seemed to be laughing manically, as though his final experience was enjoyable. His eyes locked onto Calder's. A strange smile and a wink, before forward cargo sealed shut.

Survivors sobbed and yelled all around Calder, calling for missing and dead shipmates, the girrish praying and singing hysterical laments. Dominika Denisov was there, leaning against a forklift crawler tied to the wall, crying with great floods of tears washing her face. Retigura was by her side, hugging the lieutenant like the woman was his cub.

'Help me, here.'

Calder realised Lana was talking to the android. Zeno helped take the skipper's weight and she limped into the corridor that led up to the bridge. Calder followed, stumbling, his legs numb and barely responding, as though he had been shot full of an anaesthetic. The J93's walls started to shake violently, but no normal turbulence. The chase shuttle sounded like a coin left in a spin-dryer. *We're inside the Rattle's ejection system,* Calder realised. Sharing the ride with the ram-scoop wastage and whatever the locals were offering to the gods this week.

'Need someone on the stick,' wheezed Lana, practically falling into the central lift as its doors opened.

'Think that duty's falling to me,' said Zeno, holding the doors open for Calder to limp in too. 'I wouldn't trust you on the stick of a radio-controlled drone right now.'

'I'm good,' said Calder.

'Want to land in the right galaxy, Mr Dirk,' rasped Lana, the lift shaking as they rose.

The lift doors opened. Three corpses lay sprawled across the shuttle's shaking command centre. Two belters d'Alembert had shot in the back, and the magnate himself. Four corpses, if you counted the Skunk's catatonic wreckage, its DNA-coded control interface with d'Alembert fatally shattered when the man's implant took a slug through the back of the head.

Jinhai sat in one of the vacant crew chairs, calmly cleaning the recently used pistol. Calder wasn't sure if that was an act of *sangfroid*, or if the manservant was experiencing a mental breakdown. 'I couldn't let him do it.'

'Sure,' said Zeno, gently.

Zeno eased Lana down into one of the chairs and took the main station himself.

Calder's eyes shifted to the viewing arc - a view of carbon shielding, now. The shuttle had armoured up after its automatic collision system triggered, accompanied up here by a cacophony of howling alarms and blinking collision warnings. Zeno did something to the control board and Calder's implant began receiving feeds from the bridge, the length of carbon shielding replaced by an augmented reality view of the shuttle's exterior. They were caught in the middle of a rock storm, jouncing material ranging from dust to boulders, all of it swirling forward painted in purple light from the tube's sides. The J93 bounced as one of the larger objects slammed into their side, nearly knocking Calder off his feet. He dropped himself into the spare seat next to Jinhai. Calder hoped the manservant wasn't so unbalanced he'd start shooting again. But if Jinhai proved any trouble, Calder intended to be on top of the servant before it developed.

Zeno muttered from his chair, fighting to keep the shuttle stable inside the storm of rubble. 'Reckon we know now why so much of that salvage is non-functional when recovered.'

'Keep us level,' coughed Lana. She grabbed co-pilot controls and tossed the aux-functions across to Calder. 'A little help!'

Calder pitched in to help, running the engineering reads with shock. 'Main drive is four percent away from burning out.'

'Guess it was never meant to run inside a meteor storm,' snarled Zeno.

'Just keep us running,' said Lana, sweating, focusing on avoiding the largest of the boulders outside.

Calder did his best, like wrestling jelly, the damage they were taking.

'We *have* to be clearing this waste system soon,' said Lana.

'Normal ship, I'd agree,' said Zeno. 'But inside this rabbit hole? Maybe we're looping across the whole pocket universe's sewer system before we split.'

Lana seized her control stick with both hands to stop it shaking out of her grip. 'If the drive fails inside this storm we're finished!'

Don't tempt—alarms flashed, the reactor jettisoning under emergency protocol override, tumbling behind them for a few seconds, accelerated in the opposite direction. Just enough time for Calder to track it smashing through the ejecta mass. He waited for it to fatally fail on them, watched for the nova of explosion that would kill them all, but unharnessing it from the effort of powering through the storm must have cooled it back to safety. The failed drive bounced along in their wake, a bomb waiting to go off. The shuttle becoming just another random object jouncing in the crush.

Skrat watched the first wave of invading Ryal commandos with horrified fascination. A burning circle of the *Rose*'s hull clattered down onto the deck, rolling there for a second like a semi-molten coin. Then the commandos emerged. Slowly. Carefully. Little scampering sensor packs tossed into the ship first, clattering across the deck like insects. Next, the deadly intruders. Even the shortest of the soldiers stood ten-feet-tall in their powered armour. A handful of the initial pathfinders possessed active chameleon camouflage patterning running across their bulbous HULC-hardsuits, blurred figures skulking past the ship's camera optics as they filtered through the *Gravity Rose*, seeking hostile contact. Despite weighing the best part of a few tonnes each, these raiders moved almost silently with panther-grace. Skrat found that impressive. *If dispiriting.* Every time the soldiers slowed, their suits faded into the background, armour re-painting itself to match its surroundings.

Skrat gave the first wave what they were so eager for. His improvised battle-bots attacked on deck four, a few volleys of primitive fire before being blasted apart, then the scouts dropped their camouflage. *I'll read that as a sign of complete contempt for my lads.* Most of the lethal weaponry carried by a soldier's Human Universal Load Carrier came integrated and modular. These rascals had invaded expertly configured for deck-to-deck violence inside a starship environment, rotary cannons for arm-cuffs, rapid-fire 20mm rounds, as well as launchers for smart-grenades that could pre-adapt to their surroundings - fragmentation for crew quarters, shaped-charges for peeling open closed bulkheads, nerve gas for air-recycling penetration. Each dome-shaped helmet swivelled suspiciously with a cluster of four eye-plates feeding across battlefield data - two large eyes, two small - making the invaders' skulls resemble tarantulas stamped in dull steel.

Skrat stood on the stage inside the liner module's theatre, at least physically, ignoring the pacing welding robot piloted by Chief Paopao. In reality, Skrat swayed spread thinly across the ship, the vessel his eyes, thousands of robots his fingers. *And fists.*

'Breach inside main bridge,' came Polter's warning.

'I see it.' Skrat watched hardsuited figures tossing in smoke grenades, one of the bombs exploding in a flash of white phosphorus close to his station. All very predictable, assigning a capsule to latch onto the bridge, burning their way through. Skrat hoped the tsar's thugs wouldn't be too upset to find all command functions inside deleted and rerouted. *And what better place than here?* Their long empty liner module held thousands of cabins, corridors, snugs and chambers to explore. It was also, Skrat trusted, more or less the last place the commandos would think about storming, given the paperwork he had submitted back on the station detailed how the *Rose* had been running as a tramp freighter for the last decade. Polter in his chapel. Skrat in the theatre. There was something very fitting in that.

'All the world's a stage. And all the species merely players,' announced Skrat to the largely empty house.

'Two more platoons cutting through,' growled Paopao, monitoring his own feeds from inside engineering. 'Decks seven and twenty-two breached.'

'They have their exits and their entrances,' said Skrat. He fired the bridge's life-boat free, leaving the commandos no doubt deeply suspicious about *who* or *what* was on board the boat. At least, until they realised that the bridge's lock-iris hadn't cycled closed. Then the blighters were probably a little too preoccupied with who was going to pick them up before their air-supply expired, given explosive decompression had vented them into hard vacuum. Granny had cracked the Ryals' comms encryption on the way over to the *Rose*. A weak symmetric-key scheme, apparently. Skrat was receiving the soldiers' suit chatter a little laggy, but he was getting it. More of the buggers breaking inside every minute.

Deck two, clear. Moving up to three.

Six soldiers sat hunched in one of the ship's CATS capsules, riding fast towards the main drive, the cables used to hack the capsule still plugged into its control panel. Skrat didn't even bother trying to over-ride the capsule's destination. He opened the far end of the transparent travel tube to the void and turned the mag-lev into an improvised rail-gun. Skrat expelled the entire transport carriage, sent it hurtling into space at speeds a carrier pilot would have found difficult to survive. *How much did vandalising that tube cost me*? Too flipping much.

Watch the corners, Dumanovsky. Watch those damn corners!

Skrat's mob of practically pitchfork-waving ex-agricultural droids on deck seven updated him on their extreme difficulties. A platoon of commandos relentlessly stalking towards rail-gun control. He evened the odds by increasing the gravity field in the soldiers' section of the corridor to six-times standard. As the invaders collapsed, pole-axed, trying to amp their suits enough to crawl forward, Skrat found a way to further localise the field to cover just the lower half of the corridor. That made it a*lot* easier for the robots' improvised chemical explosives to be tossed onto the platoon, accelerating down like guillotines on a neck as the unnatural gravity field caught and accelerated the primitive grenades.

Taking fire outside the secondary bridge. No crew in there - just drones. Anyone alive on this bloody ghost scow?

A commando swivelled, firing a thunderous burst of shells from his left arm that blew apart three of Skrat's robots. The triumphant hulking figure turned back to the hatch leading down into the jump vane maintenance deck. That was when Skrat discovered that ninety thousand volts are enough to melt a steel door handle. And the door. And quite a jolly amount of the hardsuit clutching onto both of them.

Sergeant Grushanin. Deck eight. Hard pounding here from someone's pet science project. Next time, let's fry the damn ship first with a neutron bomb. Tell 'em their salvage comes with rad-poisoning as a feature.

A line of caterpillar-tracked weed-control drones squirted a wall of flames down the access corridor they were defending, emptying an entire month's worth of accelerant from their tanks in a couple of seconds. Charging commandos emerged through the flames and smoke, cannon-arms blasting, demonstrating internal air supplies and coolant systems designed to survive the friction of an orbital drop. More than adequate for *this*. Until Skrat showed them what happens to one-thousand-degree heated metal when you plunge a corridor's environmental controls to minus two-hundred. *Brittle* didn't really cover it.

Skrat found it increasingly hard to cope, the longer this fight went on, his mind spinning with the demands of controlling so many devices simultaneously. A throbbing migraine until he could hardly see the theatre with his natural eyes. Still the feeds of his drones jabbed at him. Skrat certainly wasn't a specialist in bot-herding. He had never been a general, either, commanding blended forces of drone and flesh in the cauldron of combat. But he had survived three horrific years as a gladiator in the debtors' fighting pits on his home world. Trying to kill himself with honour or make enough money to regain his lost title. Failing miserably at both, but gaining guile and blood and stamina. A soul fired in that terrible forge for strength, flexibility and balance. So Skrat deployed every dirty trick, every underhand, treacherous instinct and skill to kill these enemies. Fighting with ship and robot, rather than active blade and a razor-edged shield formed from ultra-high-molecular-weight-polyethylene. But the sentiment was the same. Strangers he'd never met before trying to murder him . . . and Skrat getting his retaliation in first.

'Units converging here,' warned the chief, his voice a tinny echo through the welding drone's speakers.

'Only a matter of time, dear boy. Wearing this RIP-suit, all bandwidth does rather lead to Rome.' Skrat checked the ship's internal sensors. *Oh dear. Most of them stomping towards us. And looking rather miffed at their level of casualties.* 'Polter, I'm transferring ship defensive functions across to your board. I'm keeping control of Zeno's chaps. Wait until the boarding party are fully engaged with myself and the chief in this part of the liner module. Once you start deploying the previous crew's snares, I'm afraid you'll be painting a big red target on your chapel.'

'The Mighty of Mightiest is my shield.'

'Excellent. Do see if he's got a section of tail armour going spare for me,' said Skrat.

The lizard reached out through the ship, drawing as many robots back as he dared from defending ship-vital systems, throwing some into the fray immediately, moving a few of the nearer units into Central Avenue, the main promenade that meandered for a mile through the liner module's centre. That was where Skrat intended to make his last stand. He left the theatre through the rear exit, the chief's welding droid stamping alongside him.

'Best place for a punch-up, eh, chief? This place hasn't heard the echo of feet for a decade. Repair costs in here will be strictly notional.' *Of course, the chances are I'm only saving money for the local warlord, given this will become his prize vessel once we're dead. But still.*

'Charging laser packs,' said the chief.

Of course you are, dear fellow. Skrat's eyes took in Central Avenue. Three storeys high on either side of a grand central boulevard, with a glowing blue roof up above, pixelated clouds moving across an artificial sky. He'd never seen much point in that fake sky, given there were so many splendid viewing galleries and port-holes on the ground floor level giving out onto the star fields' infinite vista. Stars and nebulae were what passengers paid to see. Skies were purely for the poor people, dirt-side. Each of the three levels contained walkways filled with hundreds of empty shops, restaurants and onboard entertainments. They were intended for leasing out on a voyage-by-voyage basis to whoever was most interested in their spaces. Their signage and dusty modular interiors were still frozen with dated designs and layouts specified by previous occupants from long ago. A frozen snapshot of poor taste. Bars with names like *Asteroids*, *Solar Tide* and the *Freefall Club*. The *Ice Cream Cantina*, the *Boardwalk Pizzeria*, gift and souvenir stores, sim-arcades, all long-since deserted, except for his armed robots now taking up positions behind the walkway railings. The third storey level even had large staterooms with an exclusive Central Avenue view. *I'll wager not one of them ever thought that view was going to include what's coming next, though.*

Skrat lifted up the rail-rifle he had squirrelled away here earlier, resting across one the *Admiral's Lounge*'s table-tops - a sprawling open-air champagne bar which occupied the boulevard outside the theatre. Right now, the bar looked like a construction site. Dozens of smart-repair hull plates riveted into the floor. Ugly, but hopefully effective. *Much the same as my gun.* The rifle had been modified with additional power-cells, far more powerful than most worlds' legal systems permitted for civilian use. Pride of place inside their limited armoury. Zeno, he recalled, laughingly referred to the rifle as the *Rose*'s "dinosaur killer." He swept the weapon across the empty boulevard, making sure the weapon's targeting functions were talking to his implant like they should. Little damage calculations sprung up like bunny ears on shop frontages across Skrat's field of view.

'You know, chief. I always imagined, one day, buying my family back from the rascal who stole my old commercial empire out from under my nose. And in those imaginings, I often thought I'd lead my wife and children through our liner module first. Give them a taste of the *Rose* as she used to be. One of the last of the great jump-capable void-ships. Gliding between the stars like a jewel in the night. Perhaps they would have been proud of me? A good score, the right deal, and I could have done it, too. Everything would have slid into place.'

'Better to be left alone,' said Paopao. 'Safer.'

Skrat thought of the chief inside his armoured drive room. A ferret lurking in a warren. Probably the last of them to be dragged out and executed. 'No. I believe you're wrong, chief.'

'Never wrong.'

You were never alone, either. 'They do rather seem to want our ship, don't they? Let's sell it to these pests as dearly as we can.'

A cleaning drone came slowly through the lounge, a plate-sized circle of a vacuum cleaner with two duster extensions vibrating on top like an insect's long antennae. 'Sorry, old bean. Too late for us to strap explosives on you and turn you into a suicide attacker.'

'Cleaning,' said the robot, bypassing the lizard to brush the surface of the nearest table.

'Next time around, I think I'll like to be reincarnated as you.'

Skrat saw the first squad entering the liner module from the bow-end of the vessel, felt Polter lift the weight of the ship's defensive functions away from him. The navigator's turn for a spot of hunting inside the *Rose*. A second squad fanned out. Then a third broke through, leaving a dozen robot sentries smoking on the deck. *Is that the last of them?* In terms of bodies on the ground, Skrat's forces outnumbered the commandos twenty-to-one. Sadly, in terms of firepower, those odds were reversed. The regime's killers demonstrated an excellent grasp of that tactical reality - sprinting down the middle of the avenue, targeting robots as his lads fired down from the three tiers, cannons and grenades tearing apart the boulevard as they advanced. Skrat tried concentrating fire on a single hardsuit at a time, bringing down a few of the invaders, but the disparity between HULC suits and a few farm drones with bad attitude took its toll. The boarding party had abandoned stealth and surgical strikes, moving straight into shock-and-awe.

Skrat ducked behind one of the hull plates and pointed his rifle towards the swelling sound of thunder - of charging hardsuits. His world closed to the three angles of sight - eyes, ship, and gun-sight - condensed into a functional combat map by his implant. It had been a long time since Skrat had needed to prepare for personal combat, little bleeds of tips transferred from his team-mates in his fighting pit days. Most of them long dead; the advice of ghosts.

The chief's welding drone took position on Skrat's right. 'Need wider dispersal. Think putting on Fleet armour makes marine. Hah. Paopao shows them.'

Heavy-duty lasers opened up, the drone's power-packs howling like a pride of tortured lions. Lasers intended to work on the hardest substances modern science could produce. Ship-hull. Charging raiders recoiled back inside fierce explosions of vaporized hardsuit, the survivors scattering fast to the sides and going for the flanking manoeuvre they should have used to start with. If the soldiers had, they wouldn't have been quite as surprised now to encounter Skrat's reserves activating. Hundreds of battery-packs flickering into life, responding to his last ditch activation code. Rising inside broken stores, ice skating rinks, cafes, jogging tracks, restaurants, health spas and zero-g swim-rooms. Moving forward and pouring fire into the invaders outside.

From Custer to the Cheyenne, in one sneaky move. 'Now those blighters have something to occupy them other than murdering honest crew.'

Paopao's drone twisted, continuing to pulse bolts of retina-scratching energy down the boulevard. 'Honest?'

'Everything's relative, dear boy. Compared to these filthy apes, I believe I'm owed a prestigious peace prize by at least a couple of planets.' Skrat targeted a commando, his hardsuit helpfully marked out by fingers of smoke from the stream of self-propelled grenades the warrior was pumping into a volleyball court on the second level. His rifle-butt smashed into his shoulder. Skrat took the soldier in the right arm-pit, the weak stress point for the arm's gimbal movement, the raider felled well before the pellet began ricocheting inside that armoured interior.

Skrat counted the seconds for his rifle to recharge, listening to Paopao do a fair impression of a planet-mounted anti-starship gun. Polter had obviously discovered the selective gravity function on his new suite of toys, the far end of Central Avenue turned into a goldfish bowl of floating commandos who had activated their boot magnets a few seconds too late. Given a shooting range to practice on, the chief rather made the best of things.

Whoever was still left alive in command of these motley devils finally woke up enough to issue the correct order. All survivors ignore the remaining robots and sever the head of the snake. Or in this case, the head of a poor skirl. Skrat was about to shoot again, but he hastily ducked as 20mm shells ripped into the *Admiral's Lounge*, a cloud of splintered plastic and ceramic as tables and the central counter disappeared, the angry rattle of hull plates as the self-repairing material was stressed even further than the meteor storm damage they'd been designed to suffer. Chief Paopao's drone crouched behind his hull plate, the top half of the large robot exposed, blasting into the charging soldiers, shaking as return fire rattled all around. Then the top quarter of the drone shredded in a storm of metal, the robot's bulk collapsing across the floor under the weight of fire.

'Finished,' crackled the chief's voice through the speaker grille.

Skrat examined the sparking half of the ruined rail-rifle he was left clutching, overclocked battery packs not actually much use without a barrel, fore-stock and magazine to accompany the rest of his weapon. He heard a sparking and gazed down at his chest. The central processing unit of his RIP-suit had saved his life, catching the jagged shard of shell that would have otherwise gutted him. Also on the positive side of the equation, his migraine was evaporating along with his view of the robots scattered throughout the ship. He just managed to transmit a single command before the bandwidth vanished. *HELP!* Then he was down to the relatively thin gruel of his implant's feeds. A sound of crunching over broken glass and shattered pieces of the boulevard as the commandos advanced towards him. Close enough to hear the buzz of an active blade sliding out of one of the soldier's arms. *Oh dear, I wonder what part of my anatomy is suitable as a souvenir?*

Skrat was trying to raise Polter when a deafening explosion and shower of debris collapsed the hull-plate across him, pinning him to the ground.

***

Lana regained consciousness again to see the J93 still spiralling out of control inside a mass of tumbling rocks. The difference this time was the - *starfield*! No more ugly refuse system. The Rattle's stern loomed behind them, as dark and foreboding as a moon-sized coffin. She hadn't jumped out of the star system yet - probably only seconds away. Calder sat slumped in his seat - his crash field flickering on and off. Little eddies of smoke drifted from broken instrument panels without the J93's fire suppression kicking in - never a good sign on any space-going vessel. Zeno was still fighting the busted chase shuttle's stick, attempting to reassert control, down to retro-manoeuvre thrusters and venting precious bursts of oxygen with their main drive unit spinning detached behind them. Lana checked Calder's medical reads. *Alive and battered, but alive, thank the stars.*

Ahead, the scattered sail light of sun-jammers angled for whatever clutter of artifacts this final cloud of ejecta mass contained to compete over. *Anyone tries to claim my shuttle as salvage and I'll bloody ram them.* Zeno finally levelled out their exit trajectory. Allowing Lana to see there was something badly wrong with the sun-jammers' dispersal pattern ahead, as though the pilots were running scared of - *ah.* That was when Lana saw her: the *Gravity Rose.* Her ship seemed to be tracking the Rattle, but way too close to the alien vessel's defence perimeter. That meant another equally serious threat, somewhere close. *Please, no.* Lana counted the little jets of atmosphere escaping from tears where assault capsules had rammed the *Rose's* hull. Some filthy skeggers had sliced their way into her vessel. *My ship! MY SHIP!*

Zeno noticed Lana's recovery. The android magnified a dark shape onto their shared navigation screen. 'This what you're looking for, skipper?'

Ship-sized, but nothing like any merchant vessel - closer to abstract art. A long thin hull composed of hundreds of matt black baffle plates welded together at random angles like a child's metal-work project gone wrong. Not much bigger than an in-system freighter. But her small footprint was intentional. It was the two long bat-ears angled back that gave away what this ship was truly for. Modified jump vanes. Not intended for worm-hole compression, but for defeating gravity-field detection systems. Lana also noted the short tube-like thing emerging from the front of the vessel like a mosquito's proboscis. *And I bet she spits more than saliva.*

'Military stealth ship,' spat Lana. She over-rode Calder's chair system to inject him with the drugs needed to rouse the ex-prince. *Calder at least deserves to be awake for our end.*

'They've launched all their boarding capsules,' said Zeno. 'I'm estimating a company-sized strike team of eighty commandos from the number of capsules. Must be betting we've got a hold stuffed full of Tsar Rasim's salvage.'

And a stealth ship that rare and expensive on the illegal after-market? Lana just knew those commandos were going to be storming the *Rose* in equally illegally smuggled assault armour. The kind able to rip through her crew and ship like tissue paper; the biggest thief in the whole lousy star system was about to send a message that nobody stole from *him*.

'No,' Lana moaned. *No. No.* 'What can we do?'

'We've got just enough spare oxygen for reaction mass to clear the debris and glide back to the *Rose*.'

'Do it, then.'

Calder moaned in his seat, coming around. His eyes started to flicker.

Lana lay back on her station, trying to think of something, anything else. *Fiveworlds against the galaxy*. If she had ever wanted more proof of the universe's innate unfairness, here it was. She had finally escaped the alien trap of the Rattle. *Just in time to go down with my ship.*

***

Skratstruggled free of the fallen hull-plate, wriggling towards the chief's destroyed welding droid. Shouts. Hardsuit cannon-fire. Raining debris. Skrat was still trying to locate the source of the monstrous explosion when his implant came back to life and helpfully highlighted exactly what had answered his final plea for assistance.

Harvester one, designation "Red Reaper", responding.

No gun left, Skrat risked a peek over the destroyed welding drone, across the destroyed open-air lounge.

He saw the two-storey-high train-sized robot emerge skidding into Central Avenue through the crude but simple method of driving straight through a dozen shops on street level. More explosions as the shops' power cells blew apart behind it. A dozen commandos scattered before it. Skrat stayed on the floor, sheltering from this fresh shockwave of rubble smashing into the *Admiral's Lounge*'s ruins. In some ways, the monstrous hulking machine clearly wasn't the sharpest tool in the shed. By other measures - perhaps a more useful scale than intelligence - the robot actually was the *sharpest* tool in the shed.

'Large harvests!' bellowed the combative combine, one of its forward manipulator scythes flashing out and carving away the top portion of the nearest HULC-suit. Sadly, for the commando involved, with his skull still inside the helmet rolling across the floor. 'Large harvests, good!'

The remaining Ryal soldiers turned on a dime and poured automatic fire towards the robot, chewing metal chunks out of the harvester's chassis. Red lights flashed from a box-like head high above the robot's main body, a glowing crimson eye plate making it resemble a charging steel demon. Howling, it dealt with the commandos through the simple expedient of accelerating madly towards them, catching them inside its rotating thresher wheels, needle-like cutting lasers flashing across suits from a thousand directions. These Ryals were protected inside hardsuits and as heavily-armed as any Fleet Marine. Able to engage tanks and punch through concrete walls like paper. But strangely, it seemed the suit's designers had never counted on the armour's occupant running straight into what was in effect a thousand-beam rotating laser fence, without, you know, placing a demolition charge on the fence first to deactivate it. Their armour's integral reflective reactive layer did its best. Maybe only a quarter of the deadly beams slicing the commandos apart were reflected off neighbouring members of their own assault team. Skrat ducked for his life as random bolts of energy poked burning holes across Central Avenue.

Red Reaper braked in front of Skrat and the chief's jerking welding unit, it's laser threshers slowing, dropping slices of molten armour in front of the lizard as though the robot was a ship's cat offering a brace of dead pigeons to him.

'Large harvests, *good!*' thundered the massive robot, as though it had recently fed yet still hungered. 'Planted!'

Skrat managed to get up from where he had been cowering. 'Yes, dear chap. I believe those chaps are more than adequately planted.'

'Damn it, Skrat! You picking up the tab for this damage, or what?'

Skrat swivelled around in astonishment. *The voice of a ghost!* Not just one, either. *Two.* Lana and Zeno, followed by a ragtag company of armed belters and what looked like girrish wearing aboriginal regimental uniforms. They had emerged in the direction of the liner module's hangar deck, through the expensive promenade designed to reassure passengers they had boarded an exclusive and well-maintained vessel artfully designed to cater to every whim. Rather than the *Gravity Rose*. Not much chance of reassurance with pieces of laser-sliced HULC armour strewn before the newcomers' feet, having to step over smoking ship drones hastily modded into war-bots. Skrat's unexpected pair of phantom visitors looked like they had returned from hell. Torn bloodied ship-suits a long way past any notion of a decent laundry service. Skrat missed what Lana said next, the exultant hallelujahs and screaming from Polter in his earpiece rather overwhelming his ear-drums.

'Sorry, skipper, say again?'

'I said it's good to see you, you green-scaled dragon,' said Lana, springing forward and hugging him tightly.

'But you were all *disintegrated*, how on — ?'

Polter sounded tremulous and excited again over his helmet, interrupting the thousand-and-one questions shaking inside Skrat's puzzled noggin. The navigator's voice emerged in duplicate from the broken body of the chief's robot, as though the droid had come back to life, a ghost warning them. 'I must report that the Rattle just vanished outside.'

'Anomalous thrust, baby,' said Zeno.

Polter cut in again. 'That cursed assault ship is closing on us once more.'

'She's preparing to fire,' said Lana. 'Brew us up, when their powered-armoured thugs fail to report back with a mission success code.'

'All boarders repelled, revered captain. The enemy crew will soon realise their assault team is dead.'

'Are we gravity-clear enough from the star to begin wormhole formation?'

'Aye-aye, revered captain,' said Polter. 'Gravity-clear. But as you pointed out, the MAV, although lightly armed, still carries a selection of offensive weaponry. Without the Rattle's counter-fire threat, she will blast us out of the void long before we can jump out.'

'Not on my watch.' Lana spoke into her helmet. 'Mr Dirk. Are you clear?'

Calder's voice came back slightly fizzy. *Broadcasting from a space suit with limited power*, Skrat judged. 'Finished and clear. Just enough fuel in my pack to get back to the *Rose*.'

'I'd send a shuttle to speed up your return leg, but when that MAV drops full stealth to fire on us, she's going to go LIDAR-live on sensors and wonder what the heck we're sending a boat out for.'

'Just me and the dust here, sliding void, skipper,' said Calder. 'As quiet as can be.'

'As soon as she drops stealth to fire, remember to boost reflectives on your visor.'

'Captain, what is going on?' asked Skrat.

'We had to glide back here on retros and bursts of compressed air,' said Lana. 'Just like Mr Dirk out there is doing.'

'Hard flying, by the sounds of it,' said Skrat.

'Better believe it,' said Zeno. 'Needed to pop the drive on Elin's chase shuttle; leave it behind.'

'Party favours,' said Lana, kicking one of the melted fragments of hardsuit left scattered around the deck. 'They messed up my girl. Only fair we give them the J93's drive in return. Kind of glued onto their weird-looking hull, right now, by a certain ex-prince of our acquaintance. In fact, Calder is holding the dead-man's switch. She tries to kill us and—'

A flash of light burned through the portholes, an artificial sunrise briefly beaming out in the vacuum before winking away.

'—*that!*'

***

Lana stood in the *Rose*'s hangar, inspecting the newly installed drive unit. Newly installed, but as second-hand as any of the drives sitting inside Lana's shuttles and freighters. Nobody was going to be connecting the J93 to the destruction of the tsar's very expensive MAV anytime soon. Lieutenant Denisov stood by Retigura's side, waiting for Lana to finish eyeballing the repair work. Lana finished the work, satisfied, and joined Dominika and Retigura watching the last of the surviving girrish levies board the refurbished shuttle.

'We are good?' asked Dominika.

'At present speeds, the two destroyers will arrive here an hour after we've jumped out,' said Lana. 'You sure you still want to risk staying behind?'

'This is my home. I will not abandon it.'

'A woman after my own heart,' smiled Lana.

'Little risk for us, now. I will tell the regime how I foiled your robbery and executed Captain Jernberg inside the Rattle. Lies are the currency of doctrine. The junk from the starship's graveyard will pass as the salvage.'

'You're still welcome to take that torpedo-thing we salvaged during the race,' said Lana.

'Keep it, captain. A starship must make a profit to stay in orbit. I think Elin would wish you to keep her share of the funds from selling the artifact. Nobody will ever know you stole the salvage. Major Burdin is not alive to gainsay my story. The remaining survivors from the *Meteor Prince* are leaving with you for the Edge. The belters will not protest, I think, if I include their scalps in my courageous unit's body-count.' Dominika patted Zeld's Unity-issue rail-pistol which Lana had gifted to the lieutenant. 'Along with the scalps of the Unity's dead raiding party, of course. With such a victory in my pocket, it will be hard not to be promoted to a general at the very least. I will be hailed as a hero of the people.'

'Yeah, well, I hope you're a hero of the revolution, one day soon.' Lana shook Retigura's hand, his alien limb fitting strangely inside her palm. 'Your fried control collar will be easy enough to explain away. Just tell the regime the truth about how I bushwhacked you. But what about the rest of the girrish infantry? When the security forces discover how the Harbingers broke their collars . . . '

'The song the ancients sang to me, captain? My comrades' control collars appear fully functional on diagnostics, even though they are not. The slave police can stop my comrades, examine them, and they will all safely pass muster. The ancients lifted the curse of bondage from us.'

'How's that?' asked Lana.

'A physical virus infects our control collars,' said Retigura. 'What you call nanotechnology inside the Alliance, although the Ryals on our world do not possess such feats anymore. And the main thing to understand about machine viruses, captain, is that they . . . spread!'

'Tsar Rasim murdered my fiancé and put down the Colonels' Revolt before by controlling the girrish regiments,' said Dominika. 'That will not be an option open to him soon after we return.'

'You're trusting on the Ryals not being murdered in your beds, then? When your ex-slaves suddenly find themselves with minds of their own?'

'Our two species have lived together for a very long time,' said the lieutenant. 'We will continue to do so. Just on different terms. When we drag Tsar Rasim and his cronies out of the palace, I think the joy of that happy day will unite everyone. There will not be Ryals or Girs. Just victorious rebels and our new future.'

A new future? That sounded good to Lana. 'Fair winds to you, then, lieutenant.'

Dominika nodded formally, clicking her heels together, 'And to you also, captain. And if I may make one observation?'

'Please do so.'

'Your shipmate, Calder Dirk, is a fine man. He reminds me a lot of Leonid, in many ways.'

'I know enough to agree with your first statement.'

'I waited a long time, cowering as a faint-heart in the shadow of my people's suffering. In the end, I waited until I found my fiancée's frozen body buried under a pile of my friends' corpses. I often wonder what my life would have been like, in another world where I had made different choices.'

Lana blushed. 'Ships' captains understand decisiveness.'

'Perhaps, thinking like a ship's captain is not always the best way for a person to live? Not always.'

Lana watched the lieutenant and her aboriginal friend board the shuttle. *But that's all I know.* She tried to ignore the voice inside her that told her it might not be quite enough anymore.

The translation through to hyperspace had been made smoothly. Well, as smoothly as Lana could manage with a pair of enemy missile ships bearing down on her. Two bridges full of officers embarrassed by the *Rose*'s continued existence. No doubt burning to make a point - a lethal warhead-tipped point. Water under the bridge, now. Things were almost back to normal, bar the remnants of Captain Jernberg's crew getting under Lana's feet. *On which topic.* Lana was inside her day cabin, listening to Jinhai make a pitch that was, well, probably the most surprising thing going to bushwhack her today.

'Not that I'm unhappy you're offering to sign up on board the *Rose*, Jinhai. We're always short of crew. But it's spacers we're short of - the experienced kind we can't afford to pay for, as a rule of thumb. I'm not really in the market for a butler, either personal or for the general mess. My ego ain't that big, yet. Give it time. And pay-days here seem to be so few and far between I can measure their distance in mega-parsecs.'

'Rather my point, captain,' said Jinhai. 'It struck me as I embarked from the shuttle, walked through your liner module hangar and into the rather deserted shopping deck, that there was an opportunity being squandered here. A liner-sized one, as a point of fact.'

Lana laughed. 'I had just *one* passenger last trip. Look how much trouble your old boss got us into. It's no wonder spacers don't like cattle jobs.'

'Cattle jobs,' murmured the manservant. 'Perhaps the promotional elements could be left to me, as well.'

'A rose is just a weed with a promotional budget, Jinhai. Travelling on the House of d'Alembert's account inoculated you to the realities of sliding void as Joe Public. But travelling between star systems isn't exactly cheap. The kind of people who can afford to flit between worlds tends to be very wealthy, with annoyingly high and exacting standards to match. Serve them a steak and it's too well-done, too undercooked, too hot, or too cold - maybe all four at once. Give them a soft pillow and they'll demand a hard one, unless you gave them a firm one in the first place. That's why we avoid cattle, *passenger*, jobs like the plague.'

'I was certainly not born to the ease accompanying employment inside a great mercantile house, captain. I was not always Mister d'Alembert's factotum.'

'That's an understatement. I'm taking it was *you* who busted your way out of my brig? Given I don't see your previous employer possessing such an *interesting* skill-set.'

'Let's just say, captain, that I dislike being confined.'

Lana indicated their surroundings. 'You're on a starship, my friend. Corridors and cabins and machines that keep this little bubble of existence alive where it shouldn't be.'

'The universe outside, captain. Stars and worlds and moons and nebulae. Even the planes of hyperspace feel infinite, where such a scale should not even apply.'

That's almost endearing. Lana wasn't sure if he was trying to tell her what she wanted to hear, though. The captain was fairly sure that was one skill you'd definitely pick up, working for a planet-sized blowhard like d'Alembert. 'I'll give it serious consideration.'

'Truly? I would be grateful, captain. I ran some of the grandest hotels in the Alliance. Inside the late Mr d'Alembert's concerns, I managed a staff far larger than most hotels'. I am sure that with the appropriate contract hires to make the passenger module sing, managed to anticipate your clients' needs, your monetary issues would gracefully disappear.'

Well, that would certainly be nice. And I guess I do owe Jinhai. Without his intervention, I'd be body-light with what's left of my sentience squeezed comatose inside the Harbingers' malware quarantine zone. 'Ask Skrat to help you model some working examples based on the Edge systems' passenger traffic. He'll have a module for that, even if he has to dust it off.'

'Thank—' Jinhai's reply was interrupted by a priority flash from Zeno across her desk.

'Skipper!' came the android's voice, sounding flustered. 'Cargo seven. You're going to want to get down here, stat.'

'Zeno?'

'It's our salvage from the race.'

'That ugly torpedo?'

'Yeah. Skipper, I think its warhead just started ticking down to a detonation!'

***

Calder rushed into the cargo hold with a lifting sled and a drone combat medic linked to the Doctor Feelfine A.I. inside medical. Calder prayed they wouldn't be needing the Doc. If the damned alien torpedo detonated, he suspected they'd be requiring a bucket to collect his pieces, not the sickbay's services. Zeno and Lana waited nervously by the magnetic holding ring where the alien artifact lay stored. Like Calder, both crew wore spacesuits in the case of explosive decompression. An eight-foot-high robot stood towering over the storage unit, six arms, a hulking longshoreman-model specifically designed for shifting cargo. Zeno had a tripod-mounted sensor pointed at the artifact, multiple dishes and mikes feeding the android amplified reads across every part of the spectrum. Calder sprinted to a stop, noticing the torpedo's gnarled wood-like surface running through a sequence of lights. *That looks worryingly like a count-down sequence.*

'Captain,' panted Calder. 'I've cleared all decks across to the main hangar. There's an empty launch rail ready to fling this thing out into hyperspace.'

'I don't know if we can risk moving it anymore,' said Zeno, hovering the sensor box. 'Whatever the hell this thing is doing, I'm willing to bet there's a trembler switch running inside it.'

'Granny!' called Lana. 'Confirm our unit detachment protocol is green for go.'

The ship's A.I. flickered into existence alongside the torpedo.

'Checks now finalised. Explosive bolts active, safeties disengaged. It will mean blowing a tenth of the ship's mass away from my central frame, captain.'

Lana bit her lip, looking to Calder like she'd just been asked to amputate both her legs to save her body.

'Going to need to do it,' warned Zeno.

Lana looked questioningly at Calder.

'No choice,' said Calder. 'I've left a CATS capsule running and doors open. We better start retreating.'

Zeno closed his eyes, checking their escape. 'One minute and thirty-three seconds for us to clear detachment zone.'

'Captain,' interrupted Granny. 'Internal sensors are picking up a reading that wasn't there a second ago.'

'Tell us on the run . . .'

'No, captain. A cloaking field has just dropped. This isn't a bomb, it's –'

Calder gasped as the top half of the torpedo turned opaque.

' – a life-form.'

Zeno abandoned the scanner and bent over the torpedo. 'Now, that's some brand new shizzle going on right there.'

A young human girl lay below the torpedo's frosted surface, perhaps eight or nine-years-old. Her hair was ginger and short-cropped, an innocent gentle oval face framed in freckled skin - probably alabaster pale even before the cryogenic life support system inside had kicked in. *And her face looks familiar, how can that be?* Calder cast his mind back to the royal palace on Hesperus. Hundreds of children always underfoot there - pageboys and girls, the children of adult retainers and soldiers. He'd grown up playing alongside most of them. *But she can't be from my home? How the hell would some servant girl from the palace have gotten inside a life-support system jettisoned from the Rattle?* 'I think I recognise her,' said Calder. 'Can't say where from.'

'I was just thinking the same thing,' said Lana.

Zeno tapped the glass. 'I'd kinda go along with that. Damned if I know why, though.'

'Granny,' said Lana. 'Face-recognition matches against any clients' children we've given passage to over the years?'

'Checking. No, captain. Negative matches. My sensors are not accurate with this capsule sealed, but her physiology matches human-standard. Bio-chemistry reads are Terran-basic. Minimal enhancements, genetic engineering or evolutionary drift from standard pattern.'

'Doesn't make any sense,' said Lana. 'This capsule isn't Alliance tech and it was jettisoned from the Rattle. Which means chances are it was ripped out from a hulk in the starship's graveyard.' She swivelled to Calder. 'Help me load her on the sled. The capsule's hibernation chamber just switched out of dormancy mode. Doctor Feelfine, prep for an emergency room admission. Whatever specialist systems you've got for cryobiology, load them up.'

The medical droid transmitted a crabby acknowledgement. Calder nodded and helped Lana urgently set to the task, assisted by the hulking cargo handler. He'd arrived here expecting to jettison a warhead and save the entire crew. Calder didn't feel any more relaxed knowing that now he only had *one* life to save.

***

'Herhibernation sickness symptoms are not presenting across any of the expected parameters,' complained the medical A.I., as though this deadly state of affairs was entirely Lana's fault.

The capsule's cover had retracted a couple of minutes after they had slid it into the sickbay, releasing an icy sweet-smelling vapour into the centre. Now the young child lay under Doctor Feelfine's central operating hub while the medical A.I. attempted to stabilise the girl. Multiple surgical arms jabbed and probed the girl, injecting her, running sensors across her body. The new arrival no longer wore the miniature green spacer's ship-suit she had been lifted out of the torpedo wearing. That lay on a medical station, replaced by a white surgery robe. The flight suit was worn and patched, frayed around the sleeves. There had been a ship's badge on its right arm, once, the stitching still there from when it had fallen off. Across her breast, there was a name lapel torn in half, only her first name left behind. Alice. *Alice down the rabbit-hole. That's kind of fitting, given we pulled her out of one. Did I look that helpless, when I was dragged out of steerage from a refugee ship?* Zeno could tell Lana the answer to that. *Pray I don't need to ask Zeno to spend years rebuilding this kid from the ground-up like he had to do for me.*

'The damn capsule is clearly alien technology,' snapped Lana. 'There are bound to be differences.'

'And this child is clearly human,' whined Feelfine, his steel arms a blur across the patient. 'Whoever risked her life by bundling her inside a hibernation chamber designed to support non-human metabolic suppression should immediately face charges of willful child endangerment.'

'You tell me how to serve an extra-galactic warrant and I'll be sure and get on that,' said Zeno. 'Meanwhile . . .'

'Ridiculous,' complained the machine doctor. Additional sensors rose from the floor along the side of the surgical table. 'Must I always do everything myself on board this sorry ship? Very well. Clear the medical centre while I finish my work. Out with all of you!'

Calder snorted. 'But you said you might lose her. If this poor young child passes, I wish her to open her eyes and have the last thing she sees be us, not *you*.'

'Nothing wrong with me,' snapped the doctor.

Bedside manner notwithstanding. 'We're staying,' ordered Lana. 'Now focus on your work, doctor. *Please*.'

If there was anything worse than standing by, entirely helpless and useless, while the ship's temperamental medical A.I. attempted to save a too-young life, Lana couldn't think what that might be right now. *Give it time, Lana-girl. It'll come visiting.* All three of them stayed hovering by the bedside, watching Doctor Feelfine work through his full medical repertoire. Luckily, hibernation sickness was a spacer's disease, and Feelfine was a ship family's system. Their A.I had been designed to take lifeboat casualties and try to resuscitate them. Nobody went into one of these hibernation capsules willingly. Lana doubted Alice here had. Refugees had no choice, not if they wanted to escape whatever hellhole of a failed society they were trying to leave. Is that what happened to this girl? Maybe an Alliance or Edge ship sucked up centuries earlier during a previous visitation by the Rattle? The work took two hours that seemed like two weeks, but finally Feelfine's multiple arms started to rise up, like an octopus surrendering. Lana felt a burst of worry. Had the Doc just given up?'

'Feelfine?'

'Wait, captain.'

There was a brief flicker of the girl's eyelids, washed blue irises curiously open and taking in the medical centre. She managed to smile, as if, of course, this was where she was meant to be, then the sedatives from the drip fully kicked in and she allowed herself to go back to sleep. Slowly spinning sensor wands stilled around the table, retracting away, which Lana took to be another good sign.

'Alice is going to be okay?'

'Physically? Mostly. Memory loss from hibernation stress to the pre-frontal lobe,' said the machine doctor. 'But nothing of the order of magnitude you are familiar with, Captain Fiveworlds. While my young patient will recover, however, I am not so certain about myself . . . '

'Doctor?'

'You obviously don't trust me with administering to your health.'

'Still not there,' said Lana.

'Your pregnancy, Captain Fiveworlds. The one you did not trust me to handle, despite acting as your physician for many years on board this vessel.'

'What the hell are you talking about, Feelfine? Are you having a system breakdown? I've never been pregnant in my life.' A sudden thought flashed through Lana's mind. *The life I can remember. And who knows how long this kid has been inside that alien coffin.*

'DNA analysis, captain - haploblock matching does not lie. You are this child's mother.'

'Utter rot!' said Lana, gazing at the sleeping occupant of the surgical table, a needle-sharp sliver of doubt creeping into her. The little girl, so familiar to all of them. Her face . . . *her* face. 'If I'm Mystery Alice's bloody mother, what's the other half of her genogram - what's the missing section of Alice's family tree?'

The locust-like CPU hanging from the ceiling raised a couple of its arms in a shrug. 'That, captain, is where matters become a little . . . muddy.'

Lana could hardly believe what she was hearing. 'Muddier than *this*? You've got to be kidding me!'

'My records suggest that Calder Dirk has only been on board this vessel for a year.'

'Thirteen months, actually,' said Calder. 'How is that in anyway muddy here?'

Doctor Feelfine rotated its camera rods at the sleeping patient. 'Because this child's synaptic development places her age as eight years and five months old. And the missing half of her genogram is all yours, Mr Dirk.'

Calder looked as confused as Lana 'What does that mean?'

It means it's totally bloody impossible. Lana couldn't even open her stunned mouth to explain to the man.

Zeno rested his hand on the ex-prince's shoulder, winking at him. 'It means I owe you a cigar and a brandy. *Daddy.*'

Granny's hologram paced full-sized in front of Zeno. If the projection had been real, she'd be wearing a hole in the android's cabin's amber-coloured carpeting by now.

'Man,' said Zeno, 'I don't even know how I'm going to begin reporting this last voyage to *him.*' Zeno rapped at his desk, frustrated. What's there to tell? So far, all they had managed to tease out of the hibernation-sleep-amnesiac girl was the confirmation that her name was Alice Fiveworlds, and that Lana and Calder were the two people she seemed most comfortable around on the vessel. *Which makes as much sense as any of this, if she really is their kid.* Although, Zeno was fairly sure the hyperactive little rascal recognised the rest of the crew, too. All apart from the "fat one", who seemed to be missing from their crew roster. Whoever he was. *Certainly not me, anyhow.*

'If a report is the worst of your woes, you should try processing *my* worries,' said Granny.

Zeno laughed. 'It ain't never easy being the Heezy.'

'That rhyme hasn't grown any funnier since the last hundred times you said it.'

'Yeah, well. Not in much of a mood to hear about the elder

species' burden, today. If you guys had decently tidied up the junk from your civilisation's bedroom before you took the ol' Stairway to Heaven, maybe you wouldn't be having to listen to this poor old oiler's repetitive humour.'

'It was hardly our kind who misused what humanity found inside the ruins to end the great war.'

'Just lucky for your flammy ass that it was the Triple Alliance who discovered your lost toys. Seeing as how the three species haven't moved into mass extinctions quite yet. Unity gets their hands on that shizzle, the rest of the universe you thought you'd happily abandoned will be in for all kinds of pain.'

Granny didn't sound impressed. 'The last Unity-Alliance conflict is not really the war currently concerning us.'

'You mean that little trouble out on the far side of the Alliance? Long way from the Edge, right? It'll be the same as it ever was. A little pushing and a little shoving - then the fleshies on either side of the contested border region will make an accommodation. Wasn't even hearing much about it on the feeds anymore when we left Transference Station.'

'That is because the Alliance authorities activated info-flow control along the line of star systems where trouble has been experienced.'

Zeno was incredulous. '*Information* flow. Propaganda lockdown?'

'One of the standard precursors to hostilities. Ever was it thus, even in our age.'

'You dudes know something you're not telling me,' said Zeno, his suspicions building. 'Give . . .'

Granny's hologram at least had the good grace to look sheepish. 'The new species the Alliance has encountered aren't the type to make accommodations. They are known as the

Quazalrat: the distinctly devolved descendants of a client race who once owed allegiance to one of our mortal enemies.'

'The Heezy had mortal enemies?'

'Not for very long,' smiled Granny, in a frankly chilling manner.

Zeno snorted. 'Well then. They get too feisty on us, the Alliance are going to dust off all their Heezy sun-cookers and start winking stars supernova on these Quazalrat suckers until they cry uncle.'

'Two points of note,' said Granny. 'Firstly, the Quazalrat won't care in the slightest about such an escalation. I'm afraid you actually will need to exterminate their species right down to the last star system. Secondly, the Alliance hasn't possessed the mean to trigger the Heezy's weaponry for a great many centuries.'

'What?'

'The team of Alliance scientists who discovered the means to turn themselves into compatible triggers for Heezy weaponry scattered and went into hiding after the great war. They were sickened at the devastation they'd wrought on the Unity's worlds before they finally surrendered. Hundreds of planets left as cinders. Billions dead. So the scientists destroyed the Rosetta Stone object recovered from beneath Neptune, then wiped their research and vanished.'

'But the scientists' descendants are still with us . . .?'

'And thankfully long since diluted into non-effectiveness as biological triggers. Thanks largely to the cosmopolitan nature of the gene-pool available to your society for breeding. What would it take for an individual to still be walking around today with hacked Heezy DNA coded pure enough to trigger our weaponry? You would need a closed world, a lost planet with interbreeding between a very closed and limited set of royalty. The society would have to be positively medieval.'

'Calder,' groaned Zeno.

'Indeed,' said Granny. 'The last of his family line, thankfully. The time may come when you and I need to make a hard choice.'

Zeno didn't want to hear what was coming, but Granny told him anyway.

'Whether one exiled ex-prince and his daughter's life is worth more than the decillions who will die if Heezy weaponry should be activated again. Calder Dirk and the girl are both the password for Armageddon. A very deletable password.'

'You can't ask me to do that!'

'Here's the thing, Zeno,' said Granny, patiently. 'There's a hundred possible explanations for the reason why I'm now activating the *Gravity Rose*'s classroom for the first time in decades. Hundreds of explanations for just what that very interesting, very cute young child on board me *might* or *might not* be. Most of those explanations frighten me deeply. And I'm basically a reactivated police protocol designed by the most powerful race the galaxy has ever known. I *never* frighten. Why should I? I'm all that's left of the Heezy's consciousness and conscience in this universe. Back in the day, I committed species-cide against entire elder races who would invade the Alliance as it exists today before dancing on you and scraping you off their demonic hobnailed boots in disgust. So you want to hear one of the slightly less frightening explanations for why there's a wee little Alice Fiveworlds scampering around on board, bugging me every thirty minutes for the ETA of our arrival at Transference Station?'

'Feeling you're about to tell me, anyway I answer.'

'You see, we have an excellent working relationship,' smiled

Granny. 'I don't think the Rattle was designed purely for a grand pilgrimage loop around the universe. I believe it is looping around the universes: as in, plural. And I believe whoever stuck little Alice Fiveworlds in that hibernation chamber and cast her out of their lives, they thought that her universe was royally shagged. So badly busted that risking brain-death and a hibernation sleep aneurysm by launching Alice into a parallel reality was actually the *least* risky thing to do. That sound like a universe you'd enjoy visiting? Or recreating in our own little brane-slice of reality?'

Zeno said nothing. *Not much to say, really.*

'Hard choices, Zeno. Calder and Alice's true value to this universe . . . hard choices. They're what I was designed to make.'

Granny's hologram faded, leaving Zeno clutching the edge of his desk, as if when he let go, he'd be floating off. He'd once been re-designed for hard choices, too. Which was precisely why he'd stopped making them and started planning his suicide.

EPILOGUE

'**H**owdo I seem, in this body?' asked Mr Gideon. The two Unity agents had finished walking through the city. It should have been quite beautiful at twilight, what with so many tall buildings rising like sculpted coral and an ocean view from half its hillside streets. The remnants of barricades littering the roads, dead bodies and burning armoured vehicles somewhat marred the place as a serious tourist destination, however. There were sounds of celebration all around the city, now. Gunshots in the air, cheering and songs from inside the buildings, triumphant mobs rolling through the place, drunken crashing from bars and restaurants that had only been half-looted.

If this is victory, thought Mr Dumah, *I wonder what defeat looks like? Such a sinful waste.*

'You appear exactly like one of the unpreserved locals, Mr Gideon,' said Mr Dumah. 'Although I believe our presence would be questioned if we hadn't removed our drop armour and buried it outside the city.'

'Indeed, Mr Dumah. My body feels strangely giddy after our orbital insertion.'

'Your body has only just been grown. Give it a few months and your biochemistry will learn to cooperate with its nanotechnology. Look on the bright side, at least the current political difficulties on this world seems to have been definitively resolved.'

'I hope so.'

'Little matter. These bodies are extreme combat models rather than infiltration units. We are not designed to pass Alliance medical tests, Mr Gideon. We are designed for speed, violence and the success of our mission objectives.'

'Still, I hope it is unnecessary to kill any witnesses. Such a shame. How many true deaths on Ryaz Prime among the unpreserved?'

'Casualties of sixty thousand across the Ryazarn system,' said Mr Dumah. 'Far less than Analysis Core predicted, but still, a shocking waste of life.'

'We can only help so many. That always makes me deeply sad.'

Mr Dumah pointed to the nearest corpse, hung swinging by the neck from a lamppost, the tattered black remnants of a slave police uniform clinging to the beaten body. 'So true. It is fortunate extreme combat models lack tear ducts. If we had the glands for full chemical expression, I doubt either of us could focus on what we must do to help save these poor unpreserved wretches.'

They reached the barracks building the victorious rebels were using as their base of operations inside the city. A handful of girrish soldiers stood guard at the front gate. With the aboriginals' control collars dead, there was no way for either agent to seize control of the soldiers and order them to stand down.

'The hard way, Mr Dumah?'

'No. The sad creatures have only just regained their freedom after a lifetime of bondage. We don't have time to give them the Unity and they deserve far more than a true death.' Dumah indicated the rear of the barracks. A layered series of quite paranoid defences - electrified fences, a mine field, followed by a massive concrete wall protected by radar-controlled sentry guns. It took them twenty-six seconds to hack what was hackable. The mines they simply walked around. Another seven seconds to find the frequency of the fibre-reinforced concrete and create a portal-sized opening, strolling through the cloud of dust rolling across a parade ground. They discovered the barracks largely empty after they entered and explored its corridors and rooms. Dumah stepped over a dozen loyalist corpses, ignored the two Ryal military police wearing the rebels' green armbands - both so drunk that they wouldn't even remember overthrowing the tsar, let alone the unauthorised presence of a couple of civilians. What they sought lay inside an officer's quarters on the barracks' second storey floor. Nobody sleeping inside, thankfully - this room's occupant probably out with the masses rolling through the city, chanting and pulling down statues of the ex-ruler. It was spartan and windowless, as befit a military officer's quarters. A cot, a desk, a chair, and a broken wall screen looping a government declaration of Martial Law that was — in the light of current developments — now most definitely defunct.

Mr Dumah lifted up the Unity rail-pistol from the holster draped around the chair. Out of charge and useless now. Well, *supposedly* useless, according to the status screen blinking on the gun's stock. A more truthful status might indicate the weapon possessed charge, but was preserving its energy for an infinitely more important purpose than magnetically accelerating flechettes to four times the speed of sound. It's coded hourly pulse broadcast had last activated twenty-six minutes ago. More than enough time to allow the agents to triangulate the pistol's position down to a couple of inches.

Mr Gideon's fingers twisted out like rubber, reforming into a cable that joined with the gun's maintenance port. 'Uncompressing concealed data shard. Running de-encryption.'

'Signature confirmation for the shard?'

'Let me see. Yes! The same ID as the pistol's owner. Infiltration

Commander Tobias Zeld, Second Cadre, sealed this report.'

'Excellent. His back-up in Unity has been agitating for a more aggressive mission response here.'

'A natural risk-taker,' smiled Mr Gideon. 'Although his influence score has drained since losing a ship and his entire cadre. Ah, here we are. Oh dear, it seems Mr Zeld's back-up needs to advance to active prime status. His current copy is lost and likely to stay that way for the foreseeable future.' Mr Gideon shared the retrieved results with Mr Dumah.

'Fascinating. Not everything is as lost as he is, though.'

Mr Gideon knelt and placed the rail-pistol on the floor. 'Mr Zeld's cadre came to Ryazarn seeking treasure. It appears they found it.'

'Well then,' said Mr Dumah. 'We just need to locate the *Gravity Rose* - and then we will have Calder Dirk.'

'Indeed.'

Mr Dumah triggered the pistol's self-destruct protocol, standing there for a second, listening to the weapon hiss as it slowly melted. Outside, the crackle of fireworks continued. Mr Dumah exchanged a smile with the other agent. Neither of them needed to voice what they had both thought at the same time. It would be such a shame for the Unity's own trove of recovered Heezy weapons to stay condemned to inactivity. *When we have such a very good use for them.*

FINI

The *Gravity Rose* and her crew will fly again.

You can sign up for Stephen Hunt's own newsletter and find out when (and what else he's up to), over at www.StephenHunt.net/alerts.php

www.ingramcontent.com/pod-product-compliance
Lightning Source LLC
Chambersburg PA
CBHW071452110726
47908CB00003B/588